Acclaim for Billy Coffey

"Billy Coffey is one of the most lyrical writers of our time. His latest work, *The Devil Walks in Mattingly*, is not a page-turner to be devoured in a one-night frenzy. Instead, it should be valued as a literary delicacy, with each savory syllable sipped slowly. By allowing ourselves to steep in this story, readers are treated to a delightful sensory escape one delicious word at a time. Even then, we leave his imaginary world hungry for more, eager for another serving of Coffey's tremendous talent."

—JULIE CANTRELL, *NEW YORK TIMES* AND *USA TODAY* BEST-SELLING AUTHOR OF *INTO THE FREE* AND *WHEN MOUNTAINS MOVE*

"[A]n inspirational and atmospheric tale."

—*LIBRARY JOURNAL* STARRED REVIEW OF *WHEN MOCKINGBIRDS SING*

"This intriguing read challenges mainstream religious ideas of how God might be revealed to both the devout and the doubtful."

—*PUBLISHERS WEEKLY* REVIEW OF *WHEN MOCKINGBIRDS SING*

"Readers will appreciate how slim the line is between belief and unbelief, faith and fiction, and love and hate as supplied through this telling story of the human heart always in need of rescue."

—*CBA RETAILERS + RESOURCES* REVIEW OF *WHEN MOCKINGBIRDS SING*

"Billy Coffey is a minstrel who writes with intense depth of feeling and vibrant rich description. The characters who live in this book face challenges that stretch the deepest fabric of their beings. You will remember *When Mockingbirds Sing* long after you finish it."

—ROBERT WHITLOW, BEST-SELLING AUTHOR OF *THE CHOICE*

"Some stories invite you in, but Billy Coffey's *When Mockingbirds Sing* grabs you by the collar and embraces you flat out. Beautifully written with characters made of flesh and bone, Coffey haunts you with truth, compelling you to turn the page. His best book yet."

—MARY DEMUTH, AUTHOR OF *THE MUIR HOUSE* AND *DAISY CHAIN*

"[*When Mockingbirds Sing* is] an engrossing novel on so many levels. A story of mystery, hope, opening our ears in a way we can truly hear, and the choice of belief. Coffey has penned a captivating tale that will linger with you long after the final page is turned."

—JAMES L. RUBART, BEST-SELLING AUTHOR OF *ROOMS* AND *SOUL'S GATE*

"*When Mockingbirds Sing* is a lovely, dark, fervent tale that grips and won't let go. At some point, I entered its pages so fully, the sky opened up and gale winds blew outside. It's that good."

—NICOLE SEITZ, AUTHOR OF *SAVING CICADAS* AND *THE INHERITANCE OF BEAUTY*

"*When Mockingbirds Sing* by Billy Coffey made me realize how often we think we know how God works, when in reality we don't have a clue. God's ways are so much more mysterious than we can imagine. Billy Coffey is an author we're going to be hearing more about. I'll be looking for his next book!"

—COLLEEN COBLE, BEST-SELLING AUTHOR OF *TIDEWATER INN* AND THE ROCK HARBOR SERIES

"*When Mockingbirds Sing* is a mesmerizing tale about believing in the unseen. From the vividly etched small town to the compelling characters—torn between fear and faith—there is much to savor in Coffey's story."

—BETH WEBB HART, AUTHOR OF *MOON OVER EDISTO*

"A modern-day parable featuring a cast of colorful characters, [*When Mockingbirds Sing*] begs us all to step into the Maybe and have the faith of a child."

—MARYBETH WHALEN, AUTHOR OF *THE MAILBOX*, *THE GUEST BOOK*, *THE WISHING TREE*, AND FOUNDER OF SHEREADS.ORG

"Billy Coffey's *When Mockingbirds Sing* will touch your heart and stir your soul."

—RICHARD L. MABRY, MD, AWARD-WINNING AUTHOR OF *STRESS TEST* AND THE PRESCRIPTION FOR TROUBLE SERIES

the devil walks
in mattingly

:::

BILLY COFFEY

Thomas Nelson
Since 1798

NASHVILLE   DALLAS   MEXICO CITY   RIO DE JANEIRO

Published in Nashville, Tennessee, by Thomas Nelson. Thomas Nelson is a registered trademark of HarperCollins Christian Publishing, Inc.

Published in association with the literary agency of WordServe Literary Group, Ltd., 10152 S. Knoll Circle, Highlands Ranch, Colorado 80130.

THE ENGLISH STANDARD VERSION. © 2001 by Crossway Bibles, a division of Good News Publishers.

Thomas Nelson titles may be purchased in bulk for educational, business, fund-raising, or sales promotional use. For information, please email SpecialMarkets@ ThomasNelson.com.

Publisher's Note: This novel is a work of fiction. Names, characters, places, and incidents are either products of the author's imagination or used fictitiously. All characters are fictional, and any similarity to people living or dead is purely coincidental.

Library of Congress Cataloging-in-Publication Data

Coffey, Billy.
  The Devil walks in Mattingly / Billy Coffey.
    pages cm.
  Summary: "For the three people tortured by their secret complicity in a young man's untimely death, redemption is what they most long for. and the last thing they expect to receive.It has been twenty years since Philip McBride's body was found along the riverbank in the dark woods known as Happy Hollow. His death was ruled a suicide. But three people have carried the truth ever since ; Philip didn't kill himself that day. He was murdered.Each of the three have wilted in the shadow of their sins. Jake Barnett is Mattingly's sheriff, where he spends his days polishing the fragile shell of the man he pretends to be. His wife, Kate, has convinced herself the good she does for ; the poor will someday was ; the blood from her hands. And high in the mountains, Taylor Hathcock lives in seclusion; and fear, fueled by madness and hatred.Yet what cannot be laid to rest is bound to rise. Taylor finds mysterious footprints leading from the Hollow, he believes his redemption has come. His actions will plunge the quiet town of Mattingly into darkness. These three will be drawn together for a final confrontation between life and death. between truth and lies"— Provided by publisher.
  ISBN 978-1-4016-8822-6 (pbk.)
  1. Secrets—Fiction. 2. Redemption—Fiction. I. Title.
  PS3603.O3165D48 2014
  813'.6—dc23   2013041041

Printed in the United States of America

14 15 16 17 18 19 RRD 6 5 4 3 2 1

For all who stumble forward by looking back.

Why is it thought incredible by any of
you that God raises the dead?

ACTS 26:8

The end of our exploring will be to arrive at where
we started, and know the place for the first time.

T. S. ELIOT

No live organism can continue for long to exist sanely
under conditions of absolute reality; even larks and
katydids are supposed, by some, to dream.

SHIRLEY JACKSON

Publisher's Note

Billy Coffey's novels are all set in Mattingly, Virginia, and can be read in any order. If you've already read *When Mockingbirds Sing*, you may be interested in knowing that the events in *The Devil Walks in Mattingly* occur four years before that.

Enjoy!

The End

None but my wife know of my trips beyond the rusty gate; none but my wife ever will. Kate understands why I must endure this long walk through the forest, miles of bearing up under a heavy feeling of being watched.

"Go, Jake," she will tell me. She will say, "Mind the woods" and "See if someone's come" and "Be home with Zach and me soon." And even though the fear in her eyes begs me stay, Kate never asks me to keep away from the Hollow. She knows I must come to this place. It is my duty both as sheriff and as a Barnett.

And yet even as I hold my name and station in the highest regard, that is not why I dare enter this wood and strike east and north for the grove. I come to this place of darkness because it is where the light of heaven once touched. I come here for the ones who were saved on a night long ago and for the ones lost.

I come because heaven is not without the past.

I walk here now just as I walked here on the night of my salvation—uniformed and holding Bessie at my side. The blood on my old tomahawk was wet then, and a color like deep crimson. Now it is no more than a thin line of dulled brown that glimmers in this struggling sun.

Aside from that—from me—I find all is as it has always been in this wild and mountainous place. Change may come beyond this wide span of gnarled trees and gray soil, but the Hollow clings to its past and will not yield to the passing of time. It endures. That is why I both loathe this land beyond the rusty gate and give thanks for it as well. It is an anchor to hold the world in place.

There is no sound here. Neither birds nor crickets sing, and what few animals remain in these thousands of acres are scattered and hidden. The forest is silent—tired. I make for the river and turn back to the forest when I reach the bend. I do not look to the cliffs. I must walk this wood and endure the eyes upon me, but I will never gaze at those cliffs again. It is a place of blood.

Beyond river and wood lies the field, and here among the stones and brittle grass I find the only track I've seen—an imprint of a front paw sunk in the dirt. I bend and place my arm to the ground. The paw measures nearly the length of my elbow to the tips of my fingers. More than the Hollow has survived unharmed. The bear, too, lives on. The print is fresh, no more than a day old. I look up and scan the trees. I feel eyes and hear whispers but see no movement. Though the bear and I have no quarrel, my grip on Bessie tightens.

The trail waits beyond the mass of thick oaks at the field's edge to my left. I step there, careful to keep between the two lines of stones that guard its sides, and follow it to the hidden grove beyond. Here, too, little has changed. Swollen vines still grow upon the limestone walls, covering what lies behind. The brittle bush in the back still withers in the dead soil and still offers its fruit.

And the Hole is still here.

I do not know that I expected otherwise. If the Hollow has lived on untouched and the bear still roams this cursed land, then the Hole would surely remain. I suppose it always will, and in that notion lie both Kate's hope and my purpose.

I stand at its mouth and move no closer, will not. To face

this blackness is to find yourself at once drawn and repulsed, and here more than anywhere else I understand that I am not alone. I ease toward the Hole and bend to my knee, mindful of the stiffening hairs on my arms and neck, mindful of what Kate said before I left.

See if someone's come.

There are no marks in the barren earth at the Hole's mouth. No one and nothing has come.

What remains now is the long walk back through a forest empty of what life a man's eyes can see but filled with what a man's eyes cannot. But I pause here nonetheless, as I always do, and stand facing the Hole. I do this so I may remember. So I remember true. The townsfolk do not know the truth of Happy Hollow and call it a place of evil. I know its truth and call it a place of memory.

I can still picture all of us here—me kneeling in this gray dirt beside Kate, Taylor Hathcock looking on in despair.

We were drawn to this place by a dead boy named Phillip McBride, who had haunted my dreams for a month. Even now the people of Mattingly will say Phillip died in the Hollow after throwing himself from the cliffs along the riverbank. Only Taylor, Kate, and I know the truth. There was no suicide. Phillip was murdered. Who killed him was and is an open question, I suppose. Kate would say she ended Phillip's life. Taylor would say it was me. I would say Taylor had it right.

Such is my burden still. The wounds I carry are not unlike the Hollow or the bear or even this Hole in front of me—they may lie hidden, but they are always there. My hurt remains with me. I came into this world pure and unblemished, but I will leave it bearing all of my scars. My comfort rests in a grace that will mold those scars into the jewels of my crown.

In many ways the story of what happened is mine. And yet

I can say it is Kate's and Taylor's as well. But at its heart lies Phillip. He made no distinction between those who blamed themselves for his death and the one who killed him. He came back for us all.

Part I

Wake, O Sleeper

· 1 ·

I sat on the edge of Zach's bed and stared at the small town of LEGOs and Matchbox cars that covered the floor. Took us a week of evenings to piece everything together—all the streets and buildings and shops that made up downtown Mattingly and the stretch beyond. Everything had to be just right (Zach would have it no other way), and as such we both still considered it a work in progress. But that night I wasn't thinking of how the courthouse could use an extra layer of bricks or that there needed to be another window on the Dairy Queen. I only pondered what a good father would say next. All I could manage was a weak, "You know you're in trouble, right?"

Zach lay there and tried to appear indifferent by holding his red blanket as close to his body as possible. The lower lid of his right eye had curdled to a dark and swollen purple. It looked as though an invisible hand was forcing him into an ugly wink. The cut scabbing the slit that bridged the tiny space between his nose and mouth looked no better. It was painful to be sure, though it wasn't a busted lip and a black eye that held my son's tongue. It was whatever punishment I would levy for his getting them.

Zach said, "He had it comin', Daddy."

"Danny Blackwell."

"Yessir. He was on the playground pullin' on Allie Granderson's pigtails. I tole him to stop, Daddy. *Twiced.* But he dint."

"So you figured you'd just wallop him?"

"Nosir, Allie figured *she'd* wallop'm. But Danny's got a hard head, and Allie started bawlin' after, 'cause her hand hurt so bad. An' then Danny understood he'd just gotten wailed on by a girl, so he started tuggin' on Allie's pigtails *harder.* An' that's when we tussled."

I put a hand on the covers above Zach's knee and felt my shoulders slump. For reasons I couldn't understand, lately the shoulders were the first to go. Zach saw that slouch. He said nothing and I pretended nothing was wrong, even if there was no hiding my sagging cheeks and the way the skin beneath my eyes looked like tiny potato sacks.

"Think what you did was right?" I asked.

I believe Zach thought yes. He was smart enough to say no.

"I don't ever want you to go looking for trouble, son. You go looking for trouble, trouble always finds you. Now I appreciate you standing up to a bully, but next time you go tell Miss Cole before you take your fists out. Okay?"

"Yessir." Then, "Is Momma mad?"

I said, "Your momma was once a girl like Allie," and left it at that. Sharing how I'd once caught a boy peeking up Kate's skirt while she was on the monkey bars would serve no purpose, especially since I'd walloped him a good one that day. "Now it being Friday and you being more in the right, the principal said you can come on to school Monday. But I expect you to make peace."

Zach pursed his lips. "It was real peaceful when Danny was holdin' his jaw."

I offered a smile filtered through a yawn I couldn't swallow. "That's not the peace I mean. Now say your prayers."

Zach closed his left eye to match his right and began with his customary, "Dear God, this's Zach . . ." His words were soft like a lullaby, and sitting there I felt my body grow heavier. I took a deep breath and pinched my arm.

"An' I'm sorry I whupped Danny Blackwell, God," Zach finished. "But I reckon I ain't a whole lot sorry, because he's plain ornery and IlikeAllieGrandersonjustfineamen."

I smiled again and said, "Amen."

Zach opened his eye and winced. He traced a finger parallel to the cut on his lip.

"Reckon I'll scar, Daddy?"

"I think by morning you'll give your momma a fright, but I doubt you'll scar."

He reached for the arm I was using to prop myself up and turned it to the lamplight. A thick ridge of pale skin no wider than Zach's fingernail stretched from just inside my elbow to near my wrist.

"I wish I could have a scar like yours," he said. "It's cool. Allie says scars make the man."

"I mean to make sure you never have a scar like this," I whispered. "That's why we had to have this little talk. Now you get on to sleep." I bent and kissed Zach's head, careful of the bad places. What came next were the words I said to my son every night, what every child should hear from his father and what I never heard from my own. "I love you, and I'm proud of you."

"Love you and proud too, Daddy."

I stepped over the quiet town lying in shadow on the floor and left Zach to sleep. Kate waited under the covers in the next room. The thick ringed binder that was her constant companion leaned open against her raised knees. Her almond eyes were bunched, and her finger twirled at the ends of hair as black and smooth as a raven's wing. She might as well have been back in high school, cramming for a test.

"Something preying on your mind, miss?" I asked.

She looked up from a worn page. "More than one thing. How'd it go?"

"As good as it could. He'll make peace Monday."

She closed the notebook and clicked off her bedside lamp as I eased into bed. "You tell him about coming to my rescue in the second grade when Bobby Barnes tried to get a look at my underwear?"

"Seeing as how that would defeat the purpose, I left that part out." I settled in and added, "Last thing I want is the sins of the father being visited on the son."

I sighed as smells of green grass and Easter breezes rose from the pillow. Frogs sang along a prattling creek beyond the open window. Far away a train whistled as it lumbered through the center of town. I was nearly gone, and I both welcomed and feared the going. Kate took my hand beneath the covers.

"Jake Barnett, you are the best man I've ever known." She paused before voicing what else had been preying on her mind: "Will you sleep?"

Part of me—the same wishful thinking that would reach for a ringing phone in the middle of the night believing it was just a wrong number—said, "Yes."

"Maybe they'd go away if you just talked to me."

Maybe, I thought. But there had been little talk of *they*

in the past weeks, at least on my part, just as there had been little talk of Kate's notebook over the years on hers. I guess that's how it is in most marriages. You learn what to talk about and what to leave alone, what to share and what to hold close. We were no different. Our lives both together and apart had taught us the same undeniable fact—secrets make people who they are.

I brought our joined hands up, turning mine to kiss hers. "Know what I love most about you?"

"Mmm?"

"Your hand fits perfect in mine."

With Zach asleep in the next room and Kate nearly there ("Wake me if you need me," she mumbled, to which I replied I wouldn't because there would be no need), I struggled for words to send heavenward that would keep Phillip away. Simple prayer hadn't worked from the beginning, nor the desperate pleas in the weeks that followed. Now it had been a month, and my tired mind was twisted such that I no longer believed grace would end my nightmares, but some magical arrangement of vowels and consonants.

I reached beneath the covers and touched Kate's thigh, hoping her nearness would keep my sleep quiet. Or, if not, that her nearness would shame me into keeping quiet. In many ways, that was the worst part of what I suffered—not the dreams themselves, but those frantic bellows upon waking that betrayed a fear I'd long kept locked inside. I kissed the top of Kate's head and closed my eyes. The last whisper on my lips was a petition for rest now, rest finally, that I would sleep, and then I wake *standing atop the pile of rocks along the riverbank and I know it's happening, it's happening again, and no prayer and no wishing can take me from this place—this grave. My home and bed and family are gone, left in some faraway place, and I know the distance between where I am and where I was is best measured in time rather than distance.*

The Hollow lies in late day around me. An orange-red sun licks the tips of an endless sea of gnarled trees rising from the spoiled earth like punished souls. And there are butterflies, butter-flies everywhere. White ones, covering the mound of rocks beneath me like fallen snow. They flap their wings opencloseopen in a hot, vapid wind that engulfs me. But even that sight does not frighten me as much as the sight of who lies at my feet.

Phillip. Always Phillip.

My eyes dip to his sprawled body. The hood of his sweatshirt is pulled tight, hiding his face. His arms and legs splay out at grotesque slants, his right hand reaching for the glasses that have fallen near the swirling river. I fight my thoughts, trying to push away the knowing that Phillip reached for his glasses because he wanted to see, and yet I think it nonetheless because that's what I thought that day.

Beside me, a sharp rock the size of a deflated basketball lies atop the pile. I pick the stone up and lay it on one of Phillip's broken arms. I turn, knowing another stone has taken the place of the one I just moved, another always does, because this is a nightmare and it's always this nightmare and please, God, wake me before Phillip speaks.

I heft the sharp rock I find at my feet, feeling the strain in my back. It goes over Phillip's head and face. The next conceals most of his bloody shorts, the stones after cover his legs and feet, on and on, stone after stone, just as I've done every night for the last thirty. And just as all those other nights, when I heft the final stone that will cover Phillip forever, I turn to see his body lying fresh upon the others I've just laid. And from beneath the sweat-shirt's hood comes a pained voice that is soft and far away:

You can't do it, Jake, *he says.*

I shrink back in horror. The butterflies twitch and flutter (opencloseopen)
and I shake my head NO, NO this cannot be, and I bend to where another stone has appeared. I place it over Phillip's arm, building the pile ever higher.

You can't, Jake. Do you know why?

I weep. I weep because I do know and because Phillip has told me before and he'll tell me again.

Because you're a dead man, Jake. You're a dead man and he's coming and you'll remember true, because I want an end.

I look over my shoulder and around the river's bend, all the way to where the tall cone of Indian Hill rises beyond. No one is coming.

He is, Jake. I'm coming too. I'm coming for you and you're a dead man. See? I have something for you.

*Phillip reaches out with the fist I've not yet covered. His fingers turn upward to the sky as the white butterflies around us leap. I scream. It is a howling wail swallowed by flapping wings that sound as thunder in the twilight around us. I tumble down the pile of rocks that cannot cover Phillip McBride and run toward the hill, toward home, and though I always say I will not stumble, I always do because I once did. My feet slip and spill me forward, and I feel the skin between the elbow and wrist of my left arm rip open against the rocks. There is no time to lie in shock of the blood that spills from that wound, no time to think of what I've done, because Phillip's heavy footfalls come behind me and I hear him say that he's coming, he's coming and I'm dead. His dead hand grabs hold of me, pulling, and I cr*ied out into the pillow beneath my face.

The hand on me was Kate's. It was her screams I heard. Not simply out of fear for me, but for the blood dripping from my scarred left arm.

· 2 ·

Kate Barnett let the phone ring three times that next morning, unsure why anyone would squander their Saturday by calling the sheriff's office on purpose. She eased her left hand to her mouth to stifle a yawn, spotted a dollop of Jake's dried blood on her fingertips, and wiped them on her jeans. The blood was still there when she brought her hand back and the phone chirped for the second time. By the third, Kate had already replayed the previous night in her thoughts: how she had bandaged her husband's arm and it had taken her an hour to calm him down, how it had then taken another for Jake to calm her, and how they had both finished the night as they had every night for the past month—her asleep in bed, Jake waiting for the sun from the porch rocker.

She picked up the phone before it could ring again and found herself in the middle of her usual "Sheriff's office, this is Kate." The voice that greeted her was Timmy Griffith's, Kate's brother and owner of the Texaco on the outskirts of town. Their conversation was brief, and Kate said she'd be right over. She tried calling Jake, wanting to ask how he was and where he was and how long he would be, but got only his voicemail. Doc March was at the office, having stopped by at Kate's request to check Zach's eye. The doc volunteered to help man phones that likely wouldn't ring. Zach leaped at the chance to be in charge and bid his mother to go, especially upon his discovery of why his momma was in such a rush.

Timmy had a name to give her.

Kate made the drive across town to the Texaco and gathered her notebook from the seat of her rusting Chevy truck. She found Timmy waiting behind the counter. He dried his giant paws on a red-and-white checkered apron three sizes too small. Kate stifled a grin at the bits of chicken breading dangling from the front. Timmy called himself an entrepreneur and the Texaco a modern convenience store. Kate had misgivings about the former (she knew few entrepreneurs who kept both a shotgun and a spit cup under the counter), but she harbored no doubts of the latter. Not that it counted for much, but the Texaco was the most technologically able business in Mattingly.

She tilted her chin up and kissed Timmy's cheek. "I see you're busy this morning."

"Hey, sis," Timmy said. "Thanks for coming by."

"Always a pleasure. So you got a name for me?"

"I do—Lucy Seekins."

Kate sat the binder atop the counter and flipped through the thick stack of papers. The earliest entries were all but faded and saved from disintegration only by the thick layer of Scotch tape that preserved them. The names on those first pages had been written in a young and idealistic script—*i*'s dotted with tiny hearts, smiley faces that marked successes—and corresponded to dates that began shortly after Phillip's death. She turned to a page with *211* scrawled in the upper right corner and wrote Lucy's name.

"Don't think I know her," she said. "I'll have to do some digging."

Timmy said, "No need," and pointed through the doors behind her. "Lives across the street."

Kate looked up but not around. "The Kingman house?"

"The very one. Moved in back before school started. Don't know much about her daddy, never seen her momma. Divorced, I guess. Lucy's in here quite a bit, though. Seen that black Beemer around town?"

"That's hers?"

He nodded. "Lucy's on her own mostly. Dad works. Chased her outta here a few days ago for trying to swipe smokes and drinks. Told her I'd call Jake if I caught her in here again. She's trouble if I've ever seen it. Always got a different boy with her too."

That last bit piqued Kate's interest. "Who are the boys?"

"Johnny Adkins, lately. I told him Lucy was trouble and that I might have to let his daddy know. The rest of 'em?" Timmy shrugged. "You'd know before I would. From what I've seen, it's anyone who'll give her the time of day. She's walking a fine line, Katie. Just go talk to her. You don't have to do any sneaking about."

Kate tapped her fingernails on the counter. She certainly felt sorry for the girl (which wasn't saying much, Kate generally felt sorry for everyone), but she knew there was little she could offer. Folk who drove fancy cars and lived in fancy houses were not the sort Kate tended to.

Still, it was a name.

"Okay," she said. "I'll go."

Timmy beamed. It was all white teeth and pink gums.

"Still coming tonight?" Kate asked.

"Might be late, but I'll be there."

"Good. Call me later."

Kate pecked her brother's cheek again and left, waving to the driver of an old John Deere as she pulled out and across the road. Her truck kicked up a cloud of dust against a clear morning sky as it pulled up Kingman Hill. She stopped at the mouth of a large driveway in the shadow of the towering maples and magnolias that circled the old stone manor. A cobbled walk led to a set of massive concrete steps. A ten-speed bicycle stood there, its tires worn and its handlebars duct taped. Kate climbed the steps to a wide porch and took in her surroundings. There were no rocking chairs or swings from which to enjoy the view, which covered not only the Texaco but most of Mattingly's downtown and the mountains beyond. The lawn was thick and lush and bore no signs of play. The old flower gardens lay barren. The bicycle below her seemed the only thing on the hill that had recently been used.

Kate was reaching for the brass knocker when the front door flung open, jarring both her and the half-naked boy about to step out. Their eyes met in a moment of panicked recognition.

"Johnny?" she asked.

The boy twisted away, fumbling with his jeans. Kate stepped back and turned away, but not before noticing the logo above the left front pocket and how new those jeans were. That it was Johnny Adkins was bad enough. That Johnny was nearly naked and trying to pull on a pair of Wranglers Kate herself had left on his front porch two weeks before was worse. She waved her notebook over her eyes like a shield.

"Hey, Mrs. B."

Kate heard him stumble for what she hoped was his shirt (and one she hoped she hadn't bought along with the jeans).

"Sorry. Didn't . . . didn't know that was you. Or anybody. Sorry."

A sweaty wind passed her, followed by the sound of bare feet padding down the steps and the click of a kickstand. Then came the sound of two worn rubber tires and a shaky, "Sorry, Mrs. B," as Johnny scampered away. Only then did Kate look— not back to him, but to the open door in front of her.

She took a deep breath to remind herself this was a name and it was page 211 (more, the *bottom* of page 211, which meant 212 was close), and called, "Hello? Lucy?"

No answer came. Kate stepped through the doorway into a grand foyer dominated by an antique grandfather clock. She heard singing from the room to her left, high-pitched and off key—the voice of someone trying too hard to sound too good. Kate looked into what she found was a living room. Several wing chairs and a love seat had been tastefully placed around a large leather sofa. Pillows covered the thick carpet. A stone hearth dominated almost the entire far wall, beside which was the biggest television Kate had ever seen. She passed her eyes over that briefly. What had her attention at the moment was the wooden mantel above the hearth. The collection of framed pictures there unsettled her in a way she could not define.

She turned toward the movement in the corner of her right eye and saw a young girl facing a mirror in the opposite corner, swaying to music piped through a pair of hot-pink earphones. Only one of her eyes and half of her nose and mouth were visible through the glass. She was short for her age, with a head of long and full auburn hair. Her legs were thick, almost stubby, and connected to hips Kate thought destined to grow east and west as the years went on. The left back pocket of her shorts hung inside out and limp. Her white polo shirt hitched up in the back, exposing bulging love handles and a back the color of chalk. To Kate, the girl looked like someone who longed to be pretty and knew she never would be.

She had yet to see Kate in the doorway, focusing instead on taming her hair with gentle, almost loving caresses of the brush in her hand. She turned the bristles down and brought the handle to her mouth (*This girl thinks she's Martina McBride,* Kate thought) when her eyes met Kate's through the mirror. The brush dropped. She spun around.

"Lucy Seekins?" Kate asked.

The girl retreated a step and thumped her heel against the wall's molding. Kate switched her notebook to her left hand and held her right up.

"I'm so sorry," she said. "Didn't mean to scare you. Are you Lucy Seekins?"

A nod. "What are you doing in my house?"

"I knocked," Kate said. "Guess you didn't hear me over your music. You've a lovely voice."

It was a small lie, one Kate hoped would smooth things over. Lucy didn't appear thankful.

"I'm sorry," Kate said again. "I'm just a little flustered, I guess. I saw Johnny Adkins leaving. He was all . . ." Kate shook her head. "*Bared* and . . . well, Johnny knows me."

Lucy winked. "Well, I'd say Johnny knows me a little better now. He's my boyfriend, you see. Miss . . ."

"Barnett," Kate said. "Kate Barnett."

Lucy backed away from the wall. She straightened herself as though remembering this was her house.

"Maybe you should tell me why you're here, Ms. Barnett. Otherwise I'm sure you can find your way out, seeing as how you found your way in."

Kate moved to the sofa and then thought better of it, considering the slanted cushions and tossed pillows she found there. She took one of the high-back chairs near the window instead. A stack of books sat upon the small end table beside her. Kate studied them.

"Your daddy a philosophy buff? Never could understand that stuff myself."

"They're mine," Lucy said, "and please don't touch them."

Kate didn't. "Pretty heavy reading for someone your age. They for school?"

"No, for me. We all need to get our answers from somewhere, Ms. Barnett." Lucy bent for her brush. "Where do you get yours?"

"Church, I suppose."

Lucy straightened and rolled her eyes. "You're not here to give me Jesus, are you? Because I'm afraid I'll just stick to my books. Church brings God down to man. I'm more interested in what lifts man to God."

Kate said nothing to this, though she thought that sort of thinking could do more damage to a young lady than any half-naked boy could manage. She also thought things could be going worse, but she didn't know how.

"I just wanted to introduce myself," Kate said, "tell you a little about what I do." Her eyes found the pictures on the mantel again. Mother, father, Lucy. Or at least a younger version of her. "I know you and your family are still new to town. I work out of the sheriff's office. Jake's my husband—"

"You mean the cowboy who thinks he's an Indian?"

Kate bristled at the way Lucy asked that, as though it were the punch line of some joke. Lucy crossed the room and sat on the sofa. She spread her arms along the cushions, massaging them like a memory.

"Yes," Kate said. "Jake. I work in an unofficial capacity. I guess you could say I tend to the needs of folk in and around town in sort of a . . . spiritual way."

"Isn't that like a violation of church and state or something?" Lucy asked.

"Well, I don't know, honey, politics doesn't count for much here. Mayor Wallis doesn't seem to mind, and I don't get paid for what I do."

"You work for free?" Lucy shook her head, but there was something in that quick turn that was more than disbelief. Kate thought it may have been admiration. "My father'd call you crazy."

"It isn't work," Kate said. "I see it more as fate. It's my destiny."

"What's that like?"

"Not working?"

"No," Lucy said. "Having a destiny."

The question caught Kate by surprise, and for a moment she thought Lucy had asked it in the same tone she'd asked Kate if her husband was the cowboy who pretended to be an Indian. But then Kate realized Lucy had stopped massaging the couch cushions and that wry smile she'd been sporting was gone. She truly wanted an answer, and the thought humbled Kate. No one had ever asked her what it felt like to do the things she did, not even Jake. And though she expected Lucy wanted to hear something else besides the truth, the truth was what Kate would give her.

"It's like being trapped in a room without windows and wondering if it's day or still night."

Lucy nodded as though she understood. "Well, I really don't get why you're here, Mrs. Barnett. As you can see, I'm not in need, spiritual or otherwise."

Kate almost told Lucy she was in need of both, that girls stuck alone in big houses who give themselves away to boys weren't just wanting, they were reaching. The problem was she knew Lucy didn't realize it yet, couldn't.

"My brother asked me to come. Timmy Griffith? He owns the Texaco down the hill."

Lucy sniggered. "That guy's your brother? Then I'm afraid you're just wasting your time. All that man wants to do is get me in trouble and take Johnny away. So now I'm thinking maybe you should just leave, if you don't mind. My dad will be home soon, and he won't be here long. I should get ready."

"I understand," Kate said. She rose from the chair, her mind divided between sadness over not being able to help Lucy after all and relief that her visit was over. "But Timmy doesn't want to get you in trouble, Lucy. If he did, he'd have called my husband instead of me." She tore a piece of paper from the back of her notebook and wrote Jake's cell number. "I don't have a phone myself, but the town thinks Jake should have one. Take this. Sometimes people need more than clothes and food. If you ever do, call me. Jake and I would love to have you and your parents over for supper. Welcome you to Mattingly proper, even if it's a little late."

Kate held the paper out. Lucy rose from the sofa and took it. She folded the page and put it in the front pocket of her shorts.

"When my father's here, I'd rather keep him to myself," she said. "And my mom died a long time ago. Now if you'll excuse me."

Kate didn't wait for Lucy Seekins to show her out. She said her good-bye and left, but not before casting a final look at the mantel. There were pictures of Lucy at various ages, pictures of the man Kate took to be Lucy's occasional father and the young woman who must have borne her, pictures of Lucy and her father and her father with his wife. But none of the fourteen photos on the mantelpiece was of Lucy and her mother.

That small observation told Kate much. No wonder the couch cushions were slanted.

· 3 ·

The idea of calling on Jenny had come to me late the night before, sometime after I'd awakened terrified and bleeding and before the first rays of the sun eased their way over the mountains. That idea should have been dismissed outright, but in the darkness of early morning even the worst notion can take on a sheen of good common sense. I left before Kate or Zach woke (wanting to avoid the lie of telling them I was going to do anything but break the very law I'd been sworn to uphold) and drove out to Hollis and Edith Devereaux's farm, just down from the hill country on Route 664. I parked behind their old barn and made the long slog up to where a plowed line marked the boundary of field and forest.

Standing there, I was confronted by the foolishness of my coming unannounced. A warning at least would have been prudent, maybe even necessary. Tromping through Hollis's woods was akin to taking your own life into your hands. After all, this wasn't the Devereauxs' front porch. This was Jenny's place.

I stood there trying to blink away the tired from my eyes and thought, *Tomorrow*. If I dreamed again tonight, I'd come back tomorrow. Then I thought of the white butterflies and the stones piled upon stones. I thought of Phillip's words and his dead hand upon me and looked at the bandage on my arm. What kind of dream opens an old scar? Makes you bleed again? I didn't know, but I knew it was the sort of dream I didn't want to endure again. I looked back toward the farmhouse to make sure Edith wasn't hanging clothes or feeding the chickens and slipped through the trees.

A worn path stood just inside. I followed it deeper into the thick woods and slowed myself, stepping only when a bird sang or a squirrel chirred and only to where the ground was hard and leafless, reaching out with my eyes and ears for anything that might be skulking about.

Not that it did any good. It didn't matter how hard I tried, every part of me had dulled by then. That's what happens when you get two, maybe three hours of sleep every night for a month. I didn't hear the movement to my right until it was almost on top of me. I crouched close to a dark boulder to my left and took off my hat, clutching it as Zach had his blanket the night before. Sweat poured from my face and arms. My heart jackhammered.

"Hollis?" I called. "That you in there?"

The answer was a shotgun round chambered. I dove behind the boulder as the woods exploded around me in a shower of limbs and leaves. Fear charged forward like a wild animal finally broken free of its cage. I sank into the earth and gritted my teeth, fighting to hold my bladder.

A voice boomed, "Get off'a my land," followed by another spray of buckshot that nearly grazed my ear. I reached to the small of my back, felt nothing. Now a deeper panic set in, one in which being shot at played only a small part. Of all the things I could have been thinking then, only one gripped me— I'd left Bessie in the truck, and wouldn't Daddy have given me an earful for that?

I screamed, "Hollis, you put that scatter-gun down."

The woods stilled. Cautious footsteps from among the trees, then fast, then a pause. And then came what may well have been the sweetest words I'd ever heard:

"Jake? That you?"

I raised my hands and then myself from behind the rock, pulling my fingers into my palms and squeezing them still. I much preferred the smell of gunpowder and the taste of earth than Hollis seeing me scared. I spoke deep and even: "I don't want no trouble, Hollis."

It was easy to see how the old man in front of me could have snuck up on me so easy. A morning's worth of farming had left Hollis's blue overalls a smudgy brown that blended his potbelly with the woods. A faded black Dale Earnhardt cap was pulled down over his ears. Even the nicotine-stained whiskers around his mouth were a kind of camouflage. The rest of his face turned three shades whiter when he saw me.

"Lord have mercy," he said.

Hollis lowered the shotgun and jogged to me in a herky-jerky old-man way. I dropped my arms and bent for my hat, aware that my legs were about to give way. Thankfully, Hollis picked it up for me. He handed it over as though it were his very life. I breathed easier. Not because of his show of respect, but because Hollis's own trembling body meant he was not aware of my own.

"You could've kilt me, Jake. Could've shorn my head clean off."

I spoke the truth: "Bessie's in the truck." Then the lie: "Didn't think I'd need her."

Hollis pulled a red bandana from the front pocket of his overalls and wiped his brow. He exhaled a laugh. "Ain't nobody supposed to be up here for 'nother hour. I thought you was the law."

"I am the law, Hollis."

"Oh, I know, I know y'are." Eager to make things right. "I mean the real law. You know"—he pointed a finger skyward and made three tight circles—"the ones with the hellycopters. Not like you, Jake. You unnerstand the way of things."

I smiled—smiling seemed best, as it was the furthest thing from how I felt—and said, "No harm. Just thought I'd come by and see what Jenny has."

Hollis flinched. It was small and quick but noticeable. He scratched at his beard. "How you know about Jenny, Jake?"

"Been in this town all my life, Hollis. Everybody but Edith knows about Jenny."

The old man's body went limp. The boulder caught him just before I did. Blood left his face despite the morning heat, leaving ashen patches of skin on his cheeks.

"You ain't fixing to take me in, are ya, Jake? I know keeping

Jenny ain't Christlike, but I lost near all our crop in the drought last year. An' beef prices . . ." Hollis shook his head, pleading. "Jenny gets us through."

"Ain't here to take you in, Hollis." My next words came out a syllable at a time in the hope that I could tell him what I needed without actually saying it. "I just wanted to see what Jenny . . . has."

The dimmer switch in Hollis's brain went from soft to bright. "You old dog." He smiled and poked me with an elbow. I tried smiling back but found I was fresh out. "Foller me. Jenny's right up yonder."

He led me on through the pines beyond, which opened to a small clearing where countless footsteps had mashed the fallen needles into wispy dust. Three large copper pots sat beneath a moldy gray tarp along the far edge. The first and third pots were large, the second smaller. Each was connected to the others by a series of copper piping. A fire burned beneath the first pot, fed by stacks of nearby oak. A filtered bucket sat beneath a tap on the last, ready for dispensing.

Hollis beamed like a proud papa. He led me to four wooden crates stacked beside a small pile of paisley dish towels.

"Best moonshine in the valley, Jake. Guaranteed to put you more at ease than anythin' you'll get down to the Texaco. Got some peach here. Good vintage too."

"What's the vintage?"

Hollis grinned. "Yest'day. How many you need?"

I started to ask how much moonshine it would take to chase away a dead boy and an army of white butterflies. I settled on, "One'll do."

Hollis fetched a jar from the top crate and wrapped it in one of the dish towels. He handed the bundle over and said, "That's ten bucks."

I dug into my pocket and fished out a small wad of folded bills, then promptly dropped it at my feet. I bent to pick it up and wobbled as I stood. Hollis watched, biting his bottom lip.

"What?" I asked.

"Don't mean to pry, Jake. It's just that you ain't looking so good. If you don't mind me saying. Seen your bandage there."

I followed his eyes to my left arm. "Just a scratch."

"Everything all right with Katie an' Zach?"

I handed over the money and said, "Yep."

"Cain't be work. Nothin' ever happens in Mattingly."

"Work's fine too."

"Must be your daddy, then," Hollis said, and then his eyes widened as he realized it couldn't be unsaid. For the past seven years there seemed to have been a silent agreement within the town that the subject of my father would never be discussed, at least in the presence of me or Kate, and especially with Zach. Hollis kicked a small rock by his feet. "Sorry for your loss, Jake. Don't think I ever tole you that. Your daddy near ran this town. His leavin' was hard on a lotta folk, but I reckon on you an' Kate especially. Weren't a better man. If you don't mind me saying."

I did mind. I said I didn't. Hollis was a good man, and I just wanted to go. Get some coffee somewhere. Try to wake up from another night's sleep that Phillip hadn't allowed.

I raised the jar and walked for the trees. "Thanks, Hollis. I'll see you."

"Hey, Jake? Always ask my customers if their jar's for rememberin' or forgettin'."

Phillip echoed in my head

(*You're a dead man and he's coming and you'll remember true, because I want an end*)

and I tried to push him away, tried clinging to the belief

those dreams were no different from any others, mere ramblings of an unsettled mind. I tried to tell myself there was no *he* coming, I was in no danger, and that the end Phillip spoke of was merely a deep-seated desire to lay down my own guilt.

I tried. And I may have even believed it. But I didn't believe it much.

What I did believe was that Phillip had been wrong about one thing. There was no need for me to "remember," because I'd never forgotten what I did to him along the riverbank that day and never would. I wore that memory like a heavy chain around my heart. I pressed on it as one would press on a bruise to see if it still hurt.

I turned and said, "Forgetting."

Hollis nodded as though mine was the usual answer.

· 4 ·

Few people knew of Charlie Givens. Those who did agreed that not only was he born to trouble, but the sole purpose of his head was to keep rain out of his neck. Yet even Charlie's leaden mind understood the dangers involved in his monthly trips to visit Taylor Hathcock in Happy Hollow.

It wasn't so much that most all of the Hollow was either lifeless or empty, or even that everyone in the county knew every inch of that dark wood was accursed. It was the eyes. Charlie could never step past the rusty gate without feeling those eyes on him. Watching. Waiting. He didn't know exactly what that steady gaze watched or waited for (nor did Charlie ever ponder what devilry lay behind it), but there was a certain comfort in those unanswerables. Ignorance may not have equaled bliss down in the world, but it certainly counted for protection in the Hollow as far as Charlie Givens was concerned.

And sometimes it was worse. Sometimes those eyes were accompanied by shadows that danced among the dead trees and whispers that sounded like tired groans in the stale wind. Charlie softened his fears in such circumstances by tipping into the beer he brought along. There had been occasions when two cans would be missing by the time he reached the cabin. That day Charlie was on his fourth. That's how bad the eyes were.

Nor was the going easy. Taylor once told him eight miles stretched between the gate that marked the Hollow's entrance and the ridgetop where he lived. Charlie believed that distance closer to twelve. Add the groceries he carried to the steep hills, thick patches of briar and thistle, and rocks that could either cut a man to the bone or snap him all together (not to mention the added burden of Charlie's own 230 pounds, most of which currently swung free and easy from the top of his camouflage shorts), and the result was nearly three hours of travel into hell itself.

But travel he would and always had, because Taylor was a friend. Even in Charlie Givens's world, that counted for something.

By the time he crested the final hill, Charlie was sure if the eyes didn't kill him, his overtaxed heart would. Brittle oaks withering in the dusty ground yielded to the camp, which amounted to little more than a one-room shack surrounded by an ever increasing pile of scavenged junk. Here in the Hollow's heights, the eyes fell away and turned their gaze elsewhere. A gentle breeze fell through a set of wind chimes fashioned from empty beer cans, filling the air with eerie clicks. Aside from those, the world was silent. It reminded Charlie of how death must be—not an end of something bad and certainly not the start of something better, just an *always* with the sound turned down.

He paused to drink from a barrel of water. A small path led from there to a high place along the ridge. Charlie followed it and found Taylor sitting on a large rotting log, scanning the valley below with a broken pair of binoculars. The spring sun had already bronzed his thick shoulders, turning them near the color of the ponytail hanging to the middle of his back. The edges of a wild-man's beard, full and frayed, poked out from the sides of his jaw. Beside him on the log lay the tattered book he always kept near.

He said without turning, "Knew you was close, Charlie Givens."

Charlie stopped. When he spoke, his words were colored with the slow drawl of the Virginia mountains. "Now, Taylor, that ain't true. I's quiet as a church mouse the whole way."

"That may be your mind, but I know better." Still with his back to Charlie, still scanning below. "You spooked a hawk when you crossed the gate. Hawk spooked a rabbit. Rabbit spooked a deer. Deer told the bear."

"How you know that?"

"Bear told me."

Charlie offered no response. Taylor spoke often of the monster that dwelled in the Hollow, which may nor may not have been a bear and may or may not have existed only in the dark labyrinth of Taylor Hathcock's muddled mind. Charlie didn't much care either way. He had more pressing issues.

"Well, I appreciate the lesson, Taylor, but I done bore your groceries all this way, an' if I don't go pay the water bill I'm gonna float."

"Time's drawn too short for that," Taylor said. "Set those rations down here and perch yourself. We need a word."

Charlie did as he was told, glad to unburden his arms if not his bladder. He placed the groceries (a box of Twinkies, a case of beer, two packs of pencils, three boxes of shotgun shells—always that, nothing more and nothing less) in the center of the log beside Taylor's book and sat at the opposite end.

He asked, "You find Her yet?"

Taylor kept the binoculars trained on the valley and said no, but Charlie knew She was down there, had to be. He squinted his eyes and peered the dozen or so miles below. Tiny cars crawled like ants along thin ribbons of roads, funneling in and out of the small downtown.

"Look at them," Taylor said. "Going everyplace and no place, all for naught. It pains me, Charlie. How you live down there in all that gaggle?"

Charlie watched the binoculars and wondered what Taylor saw. One of the lenses was cracked down the middle. Its opposite eyepiece was nothing more than an empty hole. By appearance alone, he thought the spyglasses would offer little more than a fuzzy image of whatever lay no more than five feet from Taylor's nose.

"Well, I live in Camden, Taylor. That there's Mattingly."

Taylor took the binoculars from his face. He reached for his book and the nub of pencil that marked his place, then scrawled overtop words that were already there. Charlie averted his eyes, wanting to see but not daring.

Taylor finished and said, "All's the same town and the same world, Charlie Givens. It's a poison to the soul, and I want no part of it. They don't come to my Holler. They say the devil walks here. You believe so?"

Charlie said he'd never even entertained such a thought and hoped Taylor wouldn't perceive that lie, because there had been many a time over the years when Charlie made the long walk back to the rusty gate believing the devil not only walked in Happy Hollow, he scarfed the beer and Twinkies Charlie bought him every month too. He crossed his legs (a difficult task for a man his size) and began a slow rocking back and forth.

"Found something last night," Taylor said. "Down to the grove."

Charlie stilled himself. "The grove? Somebody come up in the Holler?"

"No. Someone done come out."

"Done come . . . ?" Charlie paused, trying to let that sink in, but found it only floated at the surface of his thick head. "Taylor, how's that true?"

"Go tend your business," Taylor said. "Meet me inside after. But hurry up, we gotta go soon."

"Where we goin'?"

Taylor rose from the log and pointed to the sleepy town far below.

"Yonder."

· 5 ·

I found Hollis's first official customer of the morning on my way back from Jenny. I wasn't surprised at who it was. Bobby Barnes stood at the edge of the field and muttered a curse as he wiped a thick smear of manure from the bottom of his boot. I knew he'd panic, but I helloed anyway. Bobby flinched when he saw me and turned to run, then tripped when he forgot his foot was still in his hand.

"Now just hang on, Bobby," I said. The walk back from Hollis's clearing had helped repair my confidence. I was me again—the fake me, but the me everyone was used to. Of course, that Bobby wasn't carrying a shotgun also helped. "I don't want no trouble."

"I ain't doin' nothin'," Bobby said. "Hand t'God, Jake, I'm just out walkin' is all."

I kept my gait slow and stopped, reaching out my right hand to help him up. Bobby refused and managed it himself.

"And of all the hollers around here, you just so happen to pick Hollis's for your morning constitutional?"

Bobby's shoulders hitched twice when he shrugged. I looked away with a kind of embarrassment. Not even lunchtime, and he'd already come down with the shakes. I thought it awful, what people could become. Then I remembered the jar in my hand and thought of myself.

"This here's good a place as any," he told me. "You got nothin' on me, Sheriff. You know that."

"Easy," I said.

I held up the bulging dish towel in my left hand. Bobby's eyes burned a wide hole in my gut. Just like that, what swagger I'd found was lost again. The man in front of me stood a good six inches shorter and weighed all of 120 pounds, but I felt smaller. I often did. That's a way of looking at yourself that you never get used to.

"You been to see Jenny?" he asked.

I ignored his question and said, "Funny I should run into you, Bobby. Your name came up last night. Zach got in a tussle with a boy at school. You remember the one we had?"

"I remember you sucker punchin' me for lookin' at Kate's delicates, which I *weren't*," he said. "Now state your aim, Jake. I can run fast, and I see you dint come up here with that dadblamed tommyhawk neither."

I had him dead to rights, of course. I knew what Bobby

was doing there, and it was absolutely in my power to turn him around and send him back to town empty-handed. But I couldn't. I was just as much in the wrong as he was—more so, given the jar in my hand. I didn't want trouble. And to be honest, I pitied Bobby Barnes. Always had.

"Bessie's in the truck," I said. "Which is where I'm heading. I aim to keep moving and head to town."

Bobby shuffled his weight from left to right, like he was dancing on hot coals. I figured that was likely how his insides felt.

"So I can pass?" he asked. "You ain't gonna cleave my head and run me in?"

"Law only applies to what's been done, Bobby. Ain't gonna run you in for what you'll likely do. So I'm gonna go ahead and let you finish your walk, and you can thank me by not telling anyone I was here and by enjoying the fruits of your labor down at the shop instead of on the road. That sound like something we can agree on?"

Bobby took a step forward and extended his hand. I caught it between spasms. "You got that, Jake. You're a good man." He shuffled past and on into the woods, then turned just outside a slant of morning light. "Hey, Jake? You feelin' all right? You look some peaked."

"I'm fine."

He looked at his feet and stuffed his hands into the pockets of his frayed jeans. "I never saw nothin'. That day on the playground with Kate, I mean. I was lookin', but I didn't see. You tell her that for me?"

"I will. You be careful, Bobby. And mind what I told you."

Bobby nodded as that single regret slipped away. I'll say I was envious. Doesn't sound right, being jealous of the town drunk. And yet Bobby had just managed to lay down a small part of the heavy shame only Hollis's drink could help him shoulder. That was something I'd never managed myself.

I kept the jar out of sight as the farmhouse neared, then I veered right to the barn and my old Chevy Blazer. I placed the moonshine in the passenger seat next to Bessie and eased away. If Edith Devereaux saw me, she's never said.

The road turned from dirt to pavement a few miles ahead. An early warm spell had convinced me to remove the top over the back end of the truck. I settled into the seat and hoped the combination of sun and wind would keep me awake. Thoughts of Jenny and Bobby melted into a buzzing nothingness. The hum of the tires was steady, womb-like. My eyes fluttered. I opened them wide. They fluttered again. My body sank deeper into the seat. I knew what was happening, which was bad enough, and I knew there was nothing I could do about it, which was worse. People say it's the mind that rules the body. I'm here to say sometimes that's not true at all. My mind knew I was going asleep at forty miles an hour just as much as it knew something worse than running off the road would happen if I did. But my eyes didn't care, and closed they went. They would've stayed that way had the Blazer not fallen out of the mountain's shadow just then, signaling my return to the civilized world of cell towers and wireless calls. The phone lying on the console erupted into a fit of beeps and chirps that made me gasp and bolt forward. I righted the truck before it drifted off the road and stuck the phone to my ear.

"This is Jake."

"Hey, Daddy," Zach said. "Where you been?"

I swallowed hard and tried to find my breath. White pinpricks gathered into globs of gray in front of my eyes. I coughed into my hand.

"Had to run an errand," I said. "What's your momma doing?"

"She went out to the Texaco for a name. She tried callin' you, but you dint answer."

"She didn't leave you there alone, did she?" I asked.

"Nosir, Doc March's here. We're playin' checkers. Momma called him to come look at my eye. Doc says it's a beaut."

The road ahead curved to the right. Beyond that stood Andy Sommerville's BP. That's where I'd stop. Gather myself. Get some coffee. Andy was always good company, and if worst came to worst, he'd give me a ride back to the office. I'd just say the Blazer was acting up.

"You comin' in now, Daddy? Can I throw Bessie some when you get here?"

My words came out thick and drawn: "Gonna stop at the BP first. You and Doc been manning the phones for me?"

"Yessir," he said. "Ain't nobody called but Mr. Justus."

My heartbeat went from barely to thundering, making that spot hurt in my chest. I squeezed the steering wheel. "You know better than to talk to him, Zach."

"I dint know it was him until he talked, Daddy. It ain't my fault."

No, I thought. It wasn't his fault. Not at all. If it was anyone's, it was my wife's.

I asked, "What'd Mr. Justus want?"

"He ast if you were gonna arrest him today. You gonna haul'm in, Daddy?"

I forgot about sleep. Not even Phillip entered my thoughts. There was only room in my mind for Justus. Justus, and the fact he'd spoken to Zach instead of Kate.

"Don't think I will today," I said. "Phone rings again, you let Doc answer. I'll be there soon."

I hung up. Andy Sommerville was working a broom around the pumps when I passed. He waved. I didn't wave back. Such things happen, I guess. We get too caught up in our own lives and forget how to be good neighbors. But I'll say this: when the town came under siege and the world unraveled in the days that followed, I'd point to that moment as yet another failing in my life—I didn't wave to Andy.

· 6 ·

The table wasn't much, just an empty spool of electrical wire that served as Taylor's eating place, desk, and workbench. Charlie returned in short order carrying the groceries and a smile of relief. He sat and placed a beer and a Twinkie in front of himself, consuming both as though they made a fine meal.

"I dunno, Taylor," he said. "What we goin' ta town for?" Charlie reached for the can on the table. Taylor watched him grab the illusory second can in his mind before taking hold of the real one. Two yellow crumbs fell from his jowls. "You ain't been ta town since you was a young'un."

"Something, Charlie—'twas no mortal person—came up outta this Holler last night. Came up outta the *grove*, Charlie. Seen the marks myself, I did. Followed them all night on my hands and knees, leadin' straight out this Holler town-ward. Meaning me to follow."

"What was they? Hoofprints?"

Taylor shook his head. *"Sneakers."*

Both of them settled into an awed sort of silence that ended when Charlie asked, "Can I see the grove, Taylor?"

Taylor shook his head. "You know I can't do that, Charlie."

Charlie pursed his lips, leaving the half-finished Twinkie dangling in his hand. "It's cause I ain't awake, ain't it? Because I am, Taylor. Hand t'God."

"It is," Taylor said, "and you ain't."

"So what you wanna do, go down there lookin' for what came up outta here? Or are you lookin' for Her?"

"I'll find it first," Taylor said. "It'll show me Her."

"I could find Her," Charlie said. "You know that's right, Taylor. All's I need's Her name. Shoot, prolly look it up right in the dad-blamed phone book for you."

Taylor folded his hand atop the table and talked low and slow, the way a teacher would explain high things to a low pupil. "Charlie, you can't be privy to my unknowables. That expanse is just too big for you."

Charlie folded his hands, mimicking his friend. He stared at the four walls surrounding them. Taylor allowed this, hoping the distraction would help sway Charlie's mind. Besides, it wouldn't require much time to take in a cot, a busted mandolin, a fireplace, a shotgun, and a stack of wooden crates. Poking out from the crate on top was the bundle of ginseng Charlie would take with him when he left to sell back in Camden, payment for Taylor's groceries.

Taylor opened the book in front of him and covered it with his hand, lest Charlie see. He found a spot that wasn't really empty and wrote, *Charly gona help maybee.*

But Charlie said, "I cain't do it, Taylor. You go down there, you're apt to snap. We could get in trouble lookin' all round for somethin' you ain't sure what it is. I been run in five times over in Camden, an' I done got laid off. I gotta be still."

Taylor looked up and asked, "What'd you get laid off for?"

Charlie slouched. "Took somebody's microwave they put out. Boss man said it weren't mine for the havin', but dear Lord, all's it was goin' was on the truck." He shook his head as though mourning the stupidity of his world. "Who gets fired for takin' trash?"

"Reckon a trash man does," Taylor said. He wrote that down too. "Now look here, Charlie. Camden's not our end, we got business in Mattingly."

Charlie shook his head. "I cain't."

Taylor tried to keep his voice daddy-like and found it near impossible. This was why he'd never taken Charlie to the grove, why Charlie had never been told Her name. Because when you got right down to the center of Charlie Givens, what you found was weakness. Weakness so complete that one could respond with no less than pity.

"Charlie Givens," he said, "you ain't but a worthless nothing."

It was as if those words grew teeth when spoken and bit down on Charlie's ears when heard. His eyes watered. "Don't go sayin' that, Taylor."

"Now I know that pains." Taylor laid the pencil down and rested his hand atop Charlie's, squeezed it, telling him it would all be fine. "But it's gotta be said. This here's a place of Truth. And this here being that sort of place, I'm bound to say it. Why, Charlie, you're no more useful than that busted mandolin against the wall. Everything in this cabin was put here for me— put here for a purpose. All except that. It just sits there, broken with no use. Like you. I was once like that m'self. But no more. I ain't no nothing now, Charlie Givens. I'm a king." He spread his arms to moldy walls and lifted his head to the sagging ceiling. "This here's my castle. Free and beholden to none, Charlie, that's me. Now let me ask you this: You wanna be a king?"

"I do," Charlie said, and Taylor believed he meant it well enough. He also believed Charlie had a slanted view of what that truly meant. Taylor thought Charlie's idea of kingship might even mean living in a dead forest full of eyes and spending all his time watching through a pair of broken spyglasses at a town he hated for a Her he hated even more.

"Ain't much changed for you, though, has it?" Taylor asked. "Don't nobody pay you no mind, because you don't matter. You live in a little ol' trailer and spend your days on back of a trash truck. That's all the world reckons you're worth—picking up what nobody wants no more. And now you ain't even good enough for that."

Charlie's eyes settled on the table. He whispered, "Cain't even be no trash man."

"Well now, that just means you're meant for greater things," Taylor said. "You help me, Charlie. I don't know what's lingering for us down there, but I know it'll lead me to Her. All's I gotta do's find what's in those sneakers. But I can't do it singly. You're right, I forgot how to step in a town. I been in paradise too long." He slapped the table at that, making Charlie jump. "But see there? *I* need you. That's something. And you help me, I'll help you right back. Might as well get you some money while we're down there, seeing as how you're recently unwaged. Right? Lots of vendors down there. We can stop at the first place we see."

In the end Taylor knew that would be what swayed Charlie's mind. Not Truth, just simple greed. Taylor thought that tragic, as he thought all things were beyond the Hollow.

"Reckon it ain't hard to risk it all if you ain't got nothin'," Charlie said.

Taylor picked up his pencil—*Charly gona help!*—and smiled. He said, "Well, that's just fine, Charlie. Let's get on, then. It's a long walk to the gate. And don't you worry about those eyes on the going. I'll keep you."

Charlie rose and went to the door with a posture taller than Taylor had seen. That was good; Charlie needed some swagger to him. Taylor placed his book in the back pocket of his jeans. He paused at the door and looked at the shotgun resting against the crates, wanted to take it, then decided no. He rummaged through the topmost crate along the wall instead, pushing aside Charlie's ginseng. Mixed in with a length of rope, a hunting knife, two hammers, fishing line, and spare cloth was a folded burlap sack containing the flint blade he'd carved long ago. Taylor considered taking that, believing the extra protection would be necessary. Then he felt the power seeping out from the sack and opted for the hunting knife instead. Taylor walked outside feeling a bit taller himself. It was good, knowing one's purpose. Having a destiny. Especially if that destiny set you upon a path that led to only one end.

· 7 ·

The clean pair of jeans and denim shirt I'd left the house wearing that morning had turned to a stained canvas of leaves and dirt by the time I reached the sheriff's office. Kate had returned from the Texaco. She was at her desk scribbling in her notebook when I walked in. Zach and Doc March huddled over a game of checkers near the wide front window. I shook from exhaustion and what that exhaustion had almost done. The world looked like it had gone slanted. I smiled and straightened my shoulders as I walked into the foyer (*nothing to see here*, that smile said, *just a man going about his morning*), but then I stumbled over the gallon of gray paint I'd used to freshen up the front door the previous day. Kate went to me as Doc March rose.

Zach looked up from the board, the smile on his face fading. "What's wrong, Daddy?"

"Not a thing." (smile) "Just gotta sit a minute."

Kate took my arm, feigning a hug so Zach wouldn't be frightened, and guided me to the battered upholstered sofa in the middle of the foyer. I sat and winced. She reached behind my back and laid Bessie on the coffee table in front of us. Zach went to the small bathroom off my office as Doc March went for the leather bag on Kate's desk. His gaunt, wrinkled face fell into a look of worried determination.

"What's wrong?" Kate asked.

"Nothing. Almost fell asleep on the road. Shook me up a little. Fine now."

Zach returned with a Dixie cup filled with his panacea for everything from bad dreams to beestings.

"Here, Daddy," he said.

He lifted the cup to my mouth and turned it upward, spilling water down the front of my shirt. I coughed and thanked him.

Kate said, "Zach, why don't you take Bessie out back for a little while. Daddy's fine, just tired is all."

I nodded to him. My voice came out dull and cracking: "Just mind her like I showed you."

Zach hefted Bessie and made a slow walk from the sofa to the open back door, carrying the tomahawk like it was a live snake. He stopped at the gun rack by Kate's desk and offered a lingering look back. Kate nodded. Zach continued on.

Doc March strapped a blood pressure cuff and the business end of his stethoscope on my arm and told me to hush before I could tell him not to bother. He asked how I felt and where and if I hurt. All I could do was nod. I'd been dreaming of Phillip every night, sometimes as soon as I fell asleep, other times a few hours later. Always stacking those rocks, most times running from the butterflies. And even though a part of me knew those dreams weren't real, I still felt tired after I woke. Tired and scared. Not just because I didn't sleep either. My shoulders and back felt like tight knots. My arms hurt. It was as if I'd really been lifting those stones along the riverbank, one right after the other, trying to lay my memory to rest.

Doc said, "Jacob, your pulse and blood pressure are both high's the moon. I need you to take some deep breaths. Slow down."

I nodded again. Kate took my hat off and put her hand to my head. She kissed me there.

"You're still not sleeping?" Doc asked. "You should have called me, Kate. And, Jake, you should have let her. You and your fool pride. Runs in the family. Any other symptoms? Loss of appetite? Depression? What's that bandage on your arm?"

I mumbled, "Just a scratch."

"He had a bad dream last night," Kate said. She caught my stare, but I suppose by then she'd passed the point of tolerating such childishness. The doctor needed truth. If my foolishness couldn't part with it, Kate would do it for me. "It was worse than ever. When he woke up, his arm was bleeding."

"Just from thrashing about," I said. "Must've caught it on something."

For proof I pulled the tape on my arm and let the bandage fall. The scar was still there, but the cut was gone. Even the few drips of drying blood that had been there when Kate had wrapped it had disappeared. She looked at me, eyebrows scrunched.

"I can't make you better unless you're forthright with me, Jacob," Doc said.

"Just a dream," I told him.

The old man sighed and nodded his head. "Fine, then. But I'm going to up your medication nonetheless. Maybe we'll try something stronger. I'll pick up the prescription myself and bring it by."

I started to tell him no and thank you, but Kate interrupted and said, "We'd appreciate that very much."

Doc nodded and gave me a grandfatherly pat. "I'll be going, then. Pharmacy closes at noon on Saturdays. I'll drop your medicine by later and set it on your desk. Mind my advice to rest in the meantime, and you'll be fine. Zach too. Just make sure he covers up next time before throwing that right hook."

"Won't be a next time," Kate said.

The doctor laughed, thinking Kate should know better. "The boy's a Barnett, Kate."

He shuffled his aging frame away to the door and paused to remind me to take it easy. Kate smiled and promised I would. She waited for the faint click of the latch before her grin disappeared.

"Tell me what happened, Jake. What really happened. There's no one here but me now."

"Just what I said," is what I told her, but Kate wasn't convinced because I couldn't look her in the eyes.

"Then why are your clothes so dirty?"

I looked down and flicked a bit of dried mud from the leg of my jeans. Picked up my hat. Studied my boots. In the end I couldn't lie. I'd done that enough over the years, and in a way that had made me more tired than Phillip ever could.

"I went to see Jenny," I said.

"Jacob Barnett, are you serious? Is this so you can sleep?"

"Just supporting the local economy." I smiled. Kate didn't. "I don't know what else to do, Kate."

"Doc March is getting you more pills. Why don't you go talk to Preacher Goggins again?"

"Pills and praying don't work. I've tried both."

Kate reached down and took my hands. When she spoke, there was a pleading in her eyes. "Well, how about you talk to me about it, then? We've always shared everything, Jake. Good and bad. Why are you keeping this from me? What are you dreaming about?"

Butterflies. White ones.

"What about them?"

I looked at her, my eyes widening in one blink and narrowing in the next. I thought I'd spoken those words to myself, but Kate must have heard them. I shook my head and told myself that I was a good man for holding my silence. Because telling Kate of my dreams would only lead her to Phillip, and that was someone I wanted to keep as far from her as I could. Kate had spent too many years trying to get her distance.

I said the one thing I thought would steer our talk into a more favorable direction—"Zach called, said you went for a name"—but wasn't sure if it would work. For a moment it didn't. Kate didn't waver. Then, slowly, she did.

"Her name's Lucy Seekins. Her and her daddy bought the Kingman house."

"I remember hearing that someone bought that old place," I said. "Don't think I know them."

"I visited her. Not really what I normally do, I know, but then Lucy isn't the sort of person I normally help either. She's rich, Jake. Not much I can do for rich folk. But Timmy wanted me to go, and she's hurting, so I wrote her name down."

"Well, good then."

From the open back door came the soft thunking sound of Bessie against the wooden target I'd built long ago. It was regular, soothing.

"Dandelions," Kate said.

"Mmm?"

"Your butterflies. Maybe they scare you like dandelions scare me."

"Maybe so. Why is that?"

"I don't know," she said. "Just one of those silly things, I guess."

Kate said no more of Lucy Seekins, nor did I say anything of Zach answering the phone when Justus called. That still angered me, but I understood why Kate had to go down to the Texaco that morning and why she had to go alone. I understood that more than anyone.

She kissed the sweat from my lips. I squeezed her hand and smiled, *Nothing to see here.* Kate smiled back, *I know better,* and yet she asked no more. I loved her for it. We'd always shared everything, yes. But we both believed the real glue that held two people together was often the things that went unsaid.

· 8 ·

The great battle that often raged in Lucy Seekins's mind was whether it was worse to have a dead mother or a father who was never home. Most times that answer depended upon whoever happened to be closer at the time.

Her father had been in China for the last five weeks. On business, of course. Always that. A start-up or a shutdown, a merger or an acquisition. Lucy didn't know which because she cared for neither. All that mattered was that he was on the other side of the world and she was in backwater Virginia alone. In those times she missed her father most.

But when Lucy looked at herself in the mirror as she did now, she missed her mother more—longed for those small things they would never do together. Things like showing Lucy how to keep her hair nice and how to paint her nails.

What to say to a boy to make him love her. Lucy had been forced to learn these things on her own, and it had been a hard education.

That was Lucy's answer, then, at least for now—it hurt more to not have a mother at all than to have a father some.

The small digital clock by the sink gave notice that her father was already twenty minutes late, which meant it would only be an hour or so before he left again. He'd called from the airport to say the China thing had gone well but the Atlanta thing had not; someone there had jumbled something, flipped a switch instead of pushing a button maybe, and The Boys were sending him down there that evening. That's what Lucy's father called his bosses—The Boys. Lucy imagined them as pinstripe-suited old men who lit fat cigars with twenty-dollar bills and golfed at the country club when they were not moving her father around the world like a pawn on a chessboard. Yet he loved them, even if Lucy did not. To her that was one more shaky bridge over yet another yawning gulf between them.

Her brush moved in smooth, practiced strokes from the top of her head down to the right. The result was typical— good but not great, all Lucy could do. Her father would like it, though. He always did. *You have your mother's hair,* he'd always say, and then Lucy would grin and he would call her Smiles because that's what he'd called the woman he buried eighteen years before.

She ran a hand through her hair once more and caught a whiff of Johnny's cologne. The scent was not unlike anti-freeze—old and cloying, something no doubt swiped from his father's medicine cabinet—and yet the sensation gave Lucy a shiver of ecstasy. She closed her eyes and felt Johnny's close-ness once more, remembered the way he'd loved her. He had not said those words exactly. None of them ever did. But Lucy had discovered early on (and without her mother's help) that boys covered their hearts well. They liked to play their games, pretend they were men. But they always became animals when there was nothing but skin and breath, and that was when they said anything Lucy wanted. There was a great power in that, so much so that she often reveled more in the feeling of that power than in the act itself. It rekindled an ember long snuffed. Lucy supposed that was why the boys always said they loved her. Inhibition had never been a problem for her. She did not mind baring herself. Fate had brought her into the world stripped of what it gave other children; naked she'd remained.

Another glance at the clock—half an hour late now, and in this the constant pendulum inside her swayed once more, this time back to her father. Moved there by the sudden notion that being without someone hurt more when one knew the person who was missing. Her father was a hard man gone spoiled by the turns his life had taken. What goodness had remained in him since Lucy's mother died lay starved and shriveled, but he had provided.

Lucy curled the ends of her hair and winced at the split ends she found. She picked up a small pair of scissors next to the brush and trimmed carefully, not wanting to damage the one thing her mother had left behind. The blades worked open and closed in soft snips. She heard the front door open, followed by a long pause and her name being called.

"Coming," she said to the mirror, and there was a wide beam upon her face. She laid the scissors down and leaned in for one last look, hearing but not remembering the faint pop of the piece of paper in her pocket as it brushed against the sink.

She left the bathroom and bounded down the stairs two at a time. Her father stood in the middle of the living room, hands behind his ample back, looking as though the world had pressed down on him so long that the only choice he had was to grow out. Lucy hugged him as tight and long as she had all the times before. She kept him close, still believing in that little-girl way that her father couldn't leave again as long as she held on.

One arm came around her back and rested lightly there. The other remained clenched into a fist just inside Lucy's hands. Her nose filled with the stale scents of airline seats and rental cars woven into his suit. There, too, was a heavy reek of alcohol. He never drank on his trips away, so he said and so Lucy believed. Which meant the only time he needed to be drunk was when he was home. With her. Lucy's hug weakened only a little at that smell. His hand guided her away.

"Hi, Dad," she said. "It's about time you got here."

He looked at her, face covered with what looked like dark clouds, and said, "Hello, Lucy."

Only that. No *Hey, Smiles* or, *I'm so glad I'm home, Smiles.* He just stood there in the middle of the room, hand still behind his back, jowls quivering.

"I don't have long," he said. "Flight to Atlanta leaves in a couple hours. Thought you might need some money for groceries and gas, though."

Something was wrong. That much was plain. And Lucy could not escape the feeling that for whatever reason, that something was her.

"I think I might take some time off when I get back," he said. "That sound good to you, Lucy?"

Again—*Lucy.*

"Sure," she said. "That sounds great."

"Really? You don't think me being around will put a damper on your social life?"

Lucy smiled and said, "I don't have much of a social life, Dad. I have to keep the house, remember?"

"Oh. Right." He looked around the living room and nodded. "Looks fine. Clean up this morning?"

"Sure."

"Vacuum?"

"Yes."

"You missed this."

He brought the hand from behind his back. Lucy's eyes barely had time to register the small plastic square hurtling toward her. She flinched when one of its corners hit her in the cheek. She looked down at the carpet. Three shiny words written in bold blue stared up at her.

Safe and Effective!

Hot air filled the room, breaking Lucy into a sweat so complete that it made her toes curl. They were both silent—him waiting, Lucy trying to will the wrapper at her feet into the ether. A low crack shuddered through the walls. For not the first time, Lucy wished the house would fall down upon them both.

"Who is he?" her father asked.

Lucy shook her head and tried to speak, but all she could manage

(Safe and Effective! She thought, *Very effective, oh yes, but not safe)*

was a long string of syllables and half words.

The dark clouds on her father's face swirled, cutting her off. He roared, *"Tell me who he IS."*

"Johnny," she cried. "His name is Johnny." And then, as though it would make any difference at all, she added, "He loves me."

Her father moved forward in a rush. Lucy retreated until her back met the cold living room wall. The hands she had wrapped around him in love just moments before were now raised to fend off his anger.

"How could you do this, Lucy?" he boomed. "What would your mother say?"

She almost said, *I don't know, Dad, how could I, she never told me anything and you don't tell me anything and please call me Smiles because don't you understand I'm naked?* But then Lucy saw in a moment of perfect clarity that the man in front of her wouldn't understand at all. Not because he was never there or because he had no idea how to raise a girl on his own, but because he was just as bare. He was a man hollowed out by the sudden turns of his life, forever running away under the guise of his job so he could be spared from contemplating what he'd lost.

"You're drunk," Lucy told him. "I think that's what my mother would say."

The anger in his eyes flamed, then fell. He moved slowly and eased Lucy against the wall, embracing her in breath that was neither beer nor liquor but something other. He said it was his fault for not being there and her mother's for leaving so soon. Lucy waited for him to include her own guilt in the fracturing of what their family could have been, but no blame was given. She felt his large body pressing against her and thought at least there was that. And when Lucy's father said he couldn't quit drinking and didn't know why, Lucy knew for him. He had fallen into alcohol for the same reason she had fallen into boys—because such things hid the smallness inside them. And they both stank for it.

He loosened his hold and took in Lucy with sodden eyes. Ran his fingers through the strands of her dark hair. She met his gaze and saw in her father a sadness and a longing that tilted the pendulum back to her mother with such force that Lucy feared it would never sway back.

"Your mother had hair just like this," he said, the last words slurring into *juzzlitethizz*. "I loved her hair. Used to stroke it every night. I think I miss that the most." He held her again. "I miss her more now. Do you know why, Lucy?"

She shook her head.

"Because now I know you'll never be like her."

Her tears came in long sobs that stained the front of her father's shirt. He held Lucy as long as he could bear and then released her. He walked to the coffee table and laid down fifty dollars and whatever silver he carried in his pocket. On the way back, he stepped onto the wrapper. It made a crinkling sound that turned Lucy's stomach.

"I think it's time we talk about sending you away," he said. "Somewhere you'll have some supervision. I thought I could trust you, but I can't." He moved to the door and opened it, pausing with one foot on the porch and the other in the foyer, half in Lucy's life and half out. "I know there's only a couple months of school left, Lucy. And I know you're of age. But I'm still your father, and you will still obey me. If not?" He paused. "Well, I guess if you want to act like an adult, I'll have to treat you as one. That means you'll be responsible for your own home and your own money. College included. You will not see that boy again, Lucy. You make sure of it or I will."

Lucy huddled against the wall long after her father had gone. It was just her and the creaking walls.

· 9 ·

For the first time that day (for the first time in weeks), I felt relaxed. Evening air rushed through the truck, drowning me in the outside and drowning out Zach's warbling from the backseat.

Kate was on the phone with Timmy. Her notebook lay open across her lap, the pages pinned down by her right hand.

She'd been speaking of Lucy before Timmy called. I'd nodded in all the right places and said all the right things, more than happy to discuss Kate's newest name if it kept conversation well away from my dreams. That pretending didn't feel right. Felt, really, like another lie. I'd done that a lot to Kate in the years we'd known each other, which practically meant our entire lives. I told myself it wasn't so much a slew of falsehoods as it was the continuation of one—like legs extending out from the same hairy spider—but that notion offered little comfort.

"Jake's got a call," Kate said into the phone. "It's almost eight, Timmy. Nobody's gonna come in there this time of night on a Saturday. Close up and come on as soon as you can. Joey and Frankie will be there." She grinned, said, "Good, love you," then switched to the other line. "Hello?"

I took my eyes from the road long enough to see the color drain from her face. Kate's back stiffened against the seat, allowing the wind to tousle her hair. Zach kept to his singing in the backseat (something by Brad Paisley, I think, but maybe not), sweetly oblivious to the storm about to gather.

"Don't call," Kate said. That and nothing more. But it was the way she slapped the phone closed rather than those two words that turned my head again.

"Who was that?" I asked.

Her mouth moved and sputtered as though searching for what to say—a name, any name, would do. None came but the truth: "Justus."

My hand gripped the wheel. My shoulders tightened. Kate opened the phone again. She checked the number Justus had used and said she didn't recognize it. One of those prepaid cell phones, I guessed.

"How did he get hold of your cell number, Jake? He's always just called the office."

"He's got a lot of friends left in town, Kate. You know that." I considered leaving it at that, but didn't. I'm still not sure if that decision arose from the small bowl of wisdom inside me or the large reservoir of exhaustion. "He called the office this morning. Zach answered."

It was subtle (I thought perhaps a little too subtle), but I hoped Kate would hear the admonishment underneath—*If you'd been at the office watching our boy rather than out putting another name in your book, Zach wouldn't have had to do that.*

"What'd he want?" she asked.

"What's he ever want?"

Kate shook her head and ran a hand through her hair. The wind tousled it again. "How can you arrest him when you don't even know where he is? That man hasn't set foot in town for seven years."

"He's up in Crawford's Gap," I said. That was a truth my weariness made me forget to keep silent. That was another symptom since the nightmares began, one that Doc March had forgotten to mention alongside the loss of weight and the depression: all those things I'd kept unsaid trickled out through the cracks worn into me. "Don't know where exactly, but he knows I can find him if I want. That's why he calls."

The disappointment on Kate's face was plain even through the long shadows of the trees across her face. "How long've you known where he is?"

I shrugged. "While now."

"So you won't find him."

It wasn't a question, what Kate said. It was a statement. And though it pained me, I knew she was right.

"I won't," I said.

Zach squealed from the backseat. I looked through the mirror and saw him rubbing his arm, the victim of a wayward bug.

"I'm sorry he called," Kate said. "Really sorry, Jake. That's just one more thing you don't need right now."

"I'd really rather not talk about it, Kate."

But I knew we would, and I knew the reason why. Justus was a problem to fix, maybe one even bigger than what I'd been dreaming about, and Kate fancied herself a fixer of problems—out to right wobbly lives one name at a time in the hopes that it might right her own. I eased down on the gas. The sooner we got to Peter and Abigail's, the sooner Justus could be set aside.

From the back Zach said, "Hey, Daddy, lookit what flew in here."

Kate said, "Not talking about Justus won't make him go away. I know what a bad place he put you in, Jake. I begrudge him for that just as much as you do. But he did what he thought was right. You might not think so, I might not think so, but you'd be hard-pressed to find anyone in town who'd blame him. Other than Mayor Wallis, maybe."

"What kind of town do we live in if everybody takes up for a man who shot three innocents just out to do their job?" I asked. "He could've killed them, Kate."

"But he didn't."

"And that matters?"

Kate shook her head.

"See, Daddy?" Zach asked.

A truck approached around the next corner. It swerved a bit, first toward the center line and then to the white of the shoulder. Gray smoke billowed from the busted tailpipe. As our vehicles neared, I could see two men.

Zach tried once more to get my attention—"Daddy, *see?*"

"What, Zach?"

I looked into the mirror. Zach held up one small hand as my body went slack. Pinched between his thumb and forefinger was a dead white butterfly, its wings flapping

(openclosedopen)

in the dry current of air. I spun around in my seat—"*No, Zach!*"—and swiped at his fingers to get the horrible thing away. The Blazer drifted toward the middle of the road. Zach yelped when my hand hit his. He did not let go.

"Jake!" Kate screamed. Her voice was faraway, frantic. "Jake, what are you *doing?*"

I slapped Zach's hand again. He cried out. Words and emotions jumbled together in his mouth and came out in something that sounded like, "Maa, maa!"

I reached out

—"Jake, there's a *truck*"—

and closed my palm around the butterfly, feeling its dead wings buckle and break. I threw it

—"*JAKE*"—

out the window, then turned to see the truck in the opposite lane bearing down on us. I turned the wheel just as the driver blew the horn. Kate gripped me with both hands as the Blazer corrected itself. I threw up my left hand and offered an apologetic wave as the truck passed. It was not returned. Kate's eyes were black pools of fear and shock.

"I'm sorry," I told her. "Sorry. Zach?" I looked into the rearview mirror. Zach's face was ashen. Shiny paths of forded tears ran from his eyes. "Zach, I'm so sorry, buddy. I didn't mean to do that. I thought it was . . ."

(I have something for you, Jake)

". . . something else. Are you okay?"

Zach nodded in a way that said he wasn't right then but maybe later.

Kate's hands still gripped me. "Jake, what in the world were you doing?"

"Sorry," I said again.

I looked into the mirror as the battered pickup rounded the curve behind us. In the dwindling light I saw a man's face peering from the grimy rear window.

Had I seen that face clearly, I still wouldn't have recognized Taylor Hathcock. I'd never seen the man before, as far as I knew. But for those brief seconds, he and Kate and I were brought together again. And just as the first time, what followed was death.

· 10 ·

The first place they saw was the BP. The building was little more than a bricked white square with a few aging pumps out front. A sign at the edge of the road announced the price of regular gasoline. On the small marquee below that was a single word—PRAY. Taylor knew that to Charlie it was just another Mom & Pop in just another town, no different from the thousands of others that pockmarked rural America everywhere. But to Taylor that building marked the borderland of a world both foreign and evil. Yet it was too late to turn back, even if it had been in his heart to do so. To town was where the tracks from the grove led—to town and to Her—and Taylor would follow no matter his fear.

He'd allowed Charlie rest and all the beer needed to harden what softness remained in him. The result had left him stumbling and weak. The walk through the Hollow to the rusty gate had taken hours. By the time they reached Mattingly, night had fallen and Taylor longed for home. He reminded himself that great tasks made good men. That conviction alone bolstered him. For in all the things Taylor Hathcock had grown to want, none burned hotter in him than the desire to be a good man.

Charlie pulled in without direction and said, "This here's the place, Taylor, I can feel it." Taylor felt no such pull and closed his book. Charlie's eyes were two angry slits that still fumed from the way they'd almost been run off the road. Taylor believed that for Charlie Givens, any place would've been the right place just now.

They parked near the front doors and found the store empty. Charlie stopped just inside and locked his drunken eyes on the first shiny thing he saw—a display of bug repellant. Taylor left him there and roamed aisles of sealed bags and drinks trapped in plastic bottles.

"Yo," he called. "Anybody here?" When no one answered, he turned to Charlie and said, "See? This here promises to be as undemanding as I thought, Charlie Givens."

"Undemandin' as you thought," Charlie said. But there was a look of disappointment on his face, like he'd gotten all dressed up for the prom only to have his date not show. "I need me some beer, Taylor. I'm all antsy."

"Well, get you some and get paid out that register so we can go. I got a sneaker-wearin' something to locate."

The side door opened before Charlie could move. Two people walked through. At first Taylor thought the old man in front was the one whose trail had led them there, went so far as to see if there were sneakers on the man's feet, but was saddened to find an old pair of boots there instead. Yet there was a curious glint to him, a shine that Taylor found unsettling. Years of hard living in the Hollow had taught him to see what others could not, and what Taylor saw in that old man were secrets he could not decipher. His eyes met Taylor's. The old man smiled. Taylor couldn't understand why until he stepped aside. Then he knew.

The boy behind was still of schooling age, no older than Taylor when he had came to the Hollow to stay. His clothes were baggy and his hair unkempt. Wide eyes peeked out from behind pale skin that looked stretched too tight. Taylor saw a crushing sadness in the boy, some deep and unknown pain he took as proof that Charlie had been right after all. This was the place. And their arrival had been no mere twist of chance; it had been destiny.

"You work here?" Charlie asked.

It was a man who answered. "Sure do. How ya doing?"

"Here he is, Taylor," Charlie said. "I found'm."

Taylor kept his eyes on the boy. To the man, he said, "Yo, where's your beer, old-timer?"

"Don't sell any."

The old man kept his smile. Taylor saw what was written there—*I'm so glad you came, this boy hurts so.*

"You don't sell no beer? You hear that, Charlie? This man ain't got no beer to sell."

"Man don't sell no beer's a stupid man," Charlie said, and then something—either blood thirst or alcohol—made him bend over and laugh.

"There's a Texaco down the road a-ways," the man said. "Timmy'll sell you some beer."

He looked at Taylor and smiled again, as though that information was important.

Taylor nodded, understanding. "You tryin' to get rid of us?"

"Nope, just trying to help you out and trying to close up."

Just trying to help you out, Taylor thought. He asked, "You got a bathroom in here?"

"Back in the corner."

Taylor moved to the back of the store, his body pulsing with adrenaline. He found the door and flipped a switch inside that bathed the small room in a pale yellow and started a rickety fan in the ceiling. A toilet sat in the corner, a sink and mirror to the right. Taylor went to the mirror, drawn there by what he saw.

The river that cut through the Hollow flowed too fast and too gray to offer reflection, and Taylor had kept away from the still pools of rainwater and melted snow that settled in the deep places of the forest. He feared if he ever beheld himself, what he'd find staring back would be more monster than good man. Yet what looked back at him now was no demon, but a hoary face worn old before his time. The reflection did not frighten him, but it tired Taylor of what he'd been brought there to do. He remembered in his former life the farm next to his grandpappy's burning on one cold January night, and the firemen who had charged headlong into the flames. They had been normal men—town men—called to do extraordinary things. Not because it had been what they'd wanted to do, but because it was their duty. Taylor felt much like those men now.

He tightened the leather braid around his hair and jerked the door open to find Charlie pointing a lighter at the boy. The old man had put himself between them. He held a push broom at his side.

"What's goin' on here?" Taylor asked.

Charlie said, "Sissy boy over there's tryin' to preach t'me. Says I shouldn't have no beer."

"That right, sissy boy?" Taylor asked. He made a motion toward him, a slight waving of the hand that said, *Don't worry, son, I'll be strong even if you can't.* "You ain't got age enough to be shootin' off your mouth like that to us."

"But I do," the old man said. "Now I'm telling you boys for the last time—you get out of here. Now. Closing time."

Charlie watched them, fingering the lighter in his hand. The man turned to the boy and said, "Eric, you get along. Like I said, closing time. You two fellas get out of here too."

The boy—Eric—moved away and said, "I'll see you soon, Andy."

Taylor extended his left arm as the boy walked past, his mouth saying, "Come on, buddy, we ain't got no beef, right?" and his heart saying, *Do not think ill of me for what I do, but speak well of me in that sleepless land.* He wrapped his arm around the boy's back. There came a whisper—"This may sting," as Taylor pulled the knife. He thrust the blade toward the boy's neck and a voice from somewhere deep inside him screamed not to wake the boy there, wake him anywhere but *there,* and Taylor did not understand why but he obeyed that voice nonetheless, such was the power of its pleading. The knife veered away at the last moment and found the boy's chest and stomach instead.

The boy's eyes widened with sudden realization—Taylor saw it as the first stirrings after a long dream—and he went limp in Taylor's arms.

The old man screamed a shout that Taylor took as thanksgiving until he turned to see the broom handle arching downward. It connected with the top of Taylor's head, rending the world into swirls of blacks and reds, knocking him to the floor. Taylor rolled as the world spun, searching for his attacker, wanting an answer for why his assault had come. Charlie leaped forward. The old man caught him with the broken end of the broom, driving him back in a shout of agony. Charlie grabbed the can of bug spray and depressed the button directly over the lighter's exposed flame. The fireball seemed the wrath of God Himself, consuming the man's shoulders and head and dropping him beside the boy.

Charlie ran for the register and shouted, "C'mon, man."

Taylor rolled over and stared into the boy's eyes. "Wake," he said. "Wake, O Sleeper!"

Andy moved. Taylor stilled him with the broken end of the broom handle. Taylor considered waking him then thought no, one was enough.

One was plenty.

He looked at the boy again as Charlie stumbled for the door. Taylor bent low and whispered into the boy's ear, "Don't mourn me. You're free now, and you're welcome."

Charlie was already in the truck, roaring the engine. Taylor walked through the doors just as those firemen had come through the blackened hole of his grandpappy's neighbors' farmhouse years before, beaten and tired and smelling of fire. He climbed into the passenger's seat, reached over, and turned off the ignition.

"What you doin'?" Charlie asked. "We gotta roll outta here, Taylor." He reached for the keys.

Taylor slapped him away. "We'll do nothing but honor this moment, Charlie Givens. So why don't you shut that gas hole under your nose and do just that."

"What? Taylor, you're cra—"

"I said *shut up*."

Charlie did. He had that look about him again, like a child just after he'd been whupped. Taylor hated that look not for what it was but for how it made him feel. "Don't nobody know this town more'n me, Charlie." His voice was calmer now. "I say we're safe. So you just hush."

Charlie drummed his fingers on the steering wheel and divided his attention between the empty road, the gash on his head, and the tranquil bodies inside the store. When all three proved too stressful, he counted the money in his hand.

"You think I'm a good man, Charlie?" Taylor asked.

Charlie kept counting. He reached the end of the roll and counted again. He looked confused. "What'd you say?"

"I woke that boy," Taylor said.

"That what you call it?" Charlie asked. "'Cause I guarantee you he was more awake five minutes ago than he is right now. You dint say that was the plan, Taylor. We all in now. Robbin's one thing, but butchery's another. They catch us, we'll ride the lightning up'n Greenville for sure. I tole you you'd snap." He waved the cash drawer's haul in Taylor's eyes. "Fifteen dollars. You believe that? What kinda business that codger have when all's he got's *fifteen* lousy dollars in the kitty? That won't even pay for *gas*."

Taylor's bloody hands shook. His mind roiled in what sounded like a chorus of shouts. It was Andy's voice that rose to the top.

I'm so glad you came.

There's a Texaco down the road a-ways.

Just trying to help you out.

"Let's go get you some more money, Charlie," he said. "Fella said there's another fill-'em-up station down the way. But you let me play it. You screw this up, Charlie Givens, you'll bleed after."

Taylor thought the idea of getting more money was one Charlie Givens liked fine. He also thought that when it came to the slumbering, the only motivator greater than greed was fear. Charlie tore out of the parking lot and left a thick layer of rubber on the empty road.

Taylor leaned forward. He took the book from his back pocket and found the pencil he'd stashed inside. The blood on his fingers stained the pages. He was about to ask his question again—*You think I'm a good man, Charly?*—but then remembered Charlie had not answered the first time.

He decided not to ask again.

Part II

The Narrowing Trail

· 1 ·

I t would be so easy.

Lucy didn't know if she'd said those words or thought them. Some part of her believed it had been neither—that this was the one time her mother had spoken and Lucy had heard. Impossible, maybe, but Lucy was nearly convinced that impossible didn't matter because none of this was really happening. She was imagining it all, maybe, or maybe this was all a nightmare. Yes. She closed her eyes in front of the bathroom mirror, even eased her heels slowly together and apart three times, but there was only the steady hum of the fan in the ceiling and the feeling of tears drying on her cheeks and the absolute certainty that it really would be so easy.

She laid the scissors down, clunking them against the phone beside the sink. There was a kind of cosmic significance that Lucy's downward spiral had reached its end with a phone call to Johnny; Johnny, after all, was where that spiral had begun—right after he walked out and Kate Barnett walked in. Had Timmy Griffith's sister stayed away, Lucy was sure things would have been different. She would have taken her time cleaning up and surely picked up what her father had found. Everything would have been okay. Not great (Lucy thought things between herself and her father had never been great and likely never would be), but okay. It didn't seem fair that the course of one's life could be forever altered by the random actions of another.

There was no doubt her father would make good on his promise. That Lucy was eighteen and the school year was almost over didn't matter, he would send her away. He would hold his money over her head and use any trick, would maybe even talk it over with The Boys. It would be Glendale in Charlottesville or Lipscomb in Stanley, private schools just for girls like her that boasted locked doors and totalitarian rules with an aim not to educate the mind but break the will. He would do so, Lucy thought, because in the end all her father would be getting rid of was the daughter who reminded him of his dead wife.

Lucy raised the scissors and held them to the light. The florescent glow played along the blades. From downstairs came nine faint bongs of the grandfather clock.

She'd called Johnny that afternoon and told him everything, tempering it all by saying that she had a plan. They would run away. To where and for how long didn't matter so long as they were together—so long as he loved her. It would be like a storybook, Lucy said, everything they had always wanted, and her father would never have to lord his money over her again.

And Johnny said no.

Said he'd never had any idea Lucy loved him and she only had herself to blame for thinking he loved her back. And as for running away, Johnny said he'd never dream of leaving Mattingly. This was home, and he had to work his daddy's farm because one day that farm would be his own. Lucy begged even as she heard the door on Johnny's heart creak closed.

She cried and that door closed more. And then it shut with a driving thunder when he said Timmy Griffith had called the house not long before, warning Johnny's parents that their boy was in bad company with a girl from Away.

It was over, Johnny said. And then he said it wasn't like they were going to stay together forever anyway ("You're cute an' all, but Momma says all us Adkinses need is fields and Jesus."). But hey, Johnny said, if you ever want to invite me over when your daddy ain't home, that'd be really cool. He said maybe next time he could even bring some moonshine, make it a real party.

Staring into the mirror, Lucy's mind locked on that one word.

Moonshine.

She released one of the blue plastic handles on the scissors. The bottom blade fell, forming a flattened V. She placed her thumb and forefinger through the holes, took hold of her mother's hair, and began to cut. Lucy's breaths came in heaving gulps as curls and ringlets broke free—some falling onto the sink, others onto her shirt, most on the tiled bathroom floor. When the blades caught in her thick mane, Lucy pulled them out in clumps that left her weeping. Her fingers and scalp pulsed in agony, her cheeks wet and red, and when she was finished, what remained was nothing more than a disheveled mop. Lucy left everything there—the hair, the scissors, the phone—and took the stairs down to the kitchen. She poured through the cabinets and found a small pair of binoculars and one of the mason jars her father kept beneath the sink.

She passed the side table with its stack of books Kate had seen earlier (which happened to be only a small part of a collection neither Johnny nor any of the other boys ever took interest in) and went outside. She sat on the top step of the porch and tilted the canning jar to the stars, brought it down, and sniffed. The inside of the jar carried the same faint stink as her father's breath. Corn whiskey. Lucy hadn't thought of that possibility—moonshiners had been nonexistent back home in DC—but now it made perfect sense. It was moonshine that had spoiled the last bit of goodness in Lucy's father, moonshine that had poisoned him such that he was now going to send his daughter away. She vowed right there beneath the orange moon that if she ever found the man who had given her father that drink, that man would die.

Cool night air flowed over her, chilling the back of her bare neck. Lucy put the jar down and picked up the binoculars. Orion's stars rose just above distant blue mountains that loomed skyward like dark monoliths. Her father once said he didn't care much for the Blue Ridge. He'd grown up in the west, where the peaks were taller and sliced the sky. Lucy had always thought otherwise. Her father's mountains were but children upon the earth. Those she gazed upon now were primeval, smoothed by time and wind. They did not gouge the sky, but met it in amorous union. These mountains held secrets. They guarded magic. Lucy didn't know how she knew this, only that she did.

She panned the lenses down over the Texaco. Timmy was behind the counter, probably counting his money and patting himself on the back for the good deed he'd done in calling Johnny's father. A dirt-road colored pickup appeared out of the night and lumbered into the lot, stopping beyond the doors. Two bloodied men limped out. One of them was short and potbellied, the other taller, sinewy, with a ponytail and beard that swayed in the wind. A steady stream of crimson ran from the side of his head to his left shoulder.

The two men walked through the Texaco's doors and approached Timmy, who began a nod he didn't finish when he saw the condition of his last customers of the night. The three of them exchanged words. Timmy shook his head no and gave them a shooing motion.

It was the fat man who charged first.

He reached over the counter and connected a solid fist to Timmy's head, then grabbed for his collar. Timmy wrenched himself free and brought up the shotgun from beneath the counter. The bigger man leaped forward. Timmy was faster, catching him in the shoulder hard enough to back him away.

Far upon the hill where the old Kingman house stood, Lucy stopped breathing.

Fists flailed inside the Texaco. The tall man jerked the shotgun free and hit Timmy with the stock, sending him backward. Timmy recovered and landed another blow, knocking the gun free. The fat man charged just as Timmy's fingers closed around the hunk of ash. He leveled the stranger with it, sending him across on the floor. The tall man ran for the doors. Timmy followed but forgot about the body at his feet. He tripped and landed on his face.

The tall man stumbled to the truck and sat there. Lucy heard no roaring engine or squealing tires. Her heart lurched in her chest when she realized why. His friend had been driving. The keys must still be in his pocket.

He ran for the store and then stopped, no doubt thinking that if he went back inside he may well not come out. Lucy watched as he stood beneath the canopy lights, a feral beast caged and without options.

Lucy Seekins acted first and thought later. She ran inside for the keys to her BMW and took the lane as fast as she dared, not even slowing as she crossed the road. The man looked up as she swerved between the pumps and came to a stop mere feet from where he stood.

Lucy lowered the passenger window. She said, "Get in."
He did.

· 2 ·

Our Saturday nights with the Boyds had begun two years
prior, back when the recession first hit. Things had gotten so
bad that Trevor Morgan ran an op-ed in the *Gazette* weigh-
ing the likelihood of Mattingly disappearing outright. I took
that as just the sort of journalistic sensationalism Trevor often
used to sell his newspapers, which turned out exactly to be
the case. In the end the town held together just as Peter and
Abigail Boyd had—by equal measures of prayer and sweat.

Those weekend get-togethers kept going as the years went
on, mostly because Peter and Abigail were such good company. Their son, Josh, and daughter, Sara, were close friends
with Zach, even though they were a bit apart in age. Joey and
Frankie Munroe, Peter's cousins and volunteers down at the
rescue squad, had taken to joining us of late. Both had graduated high school with Kate and me.

We sat around the long picnic table under the porch light
in Peter's backyard that night. Kate said nothing about the
empty place she'd reserved for Timmy, and neither she nor
Zach had mentioned our near collision and the reasons behind
it. Given the ease with which kids surrender the before to the
now, I thought Zach had likely put the whole thing out of his
mind. But I knew Kate hadn't. She hung on to memories, the
bad ones especially.

Conversation was light and broad as the meal continued
on. The kids finished early, wanting to play more than gather.
Joey and Frankie joined them in a spirited game of dodge ball.

Both of the Munroe boys may have been a sandwich shy of three hundred pounds, but in many ways neither of them had ever grown up.

"You're not eating, Jake," Abigail said. "Something the matter with my cooking?"

I looked down at my plate and found only half my barbecued chicken and a bite of my slaw gone. I didn't even remember eating that. The only way I knew I had was the spicy-sweet taste in my mouth.

"Sorry," I said. "Good as always, Abby."

Peter squinted, cheeks bulging with food, and offered, "You ain't lookin' too good, Jake. What's up?"

Kate stole a look to make sure Zach and the kids were out of earshot. She whispered, "Justus's calling again."

Sad nods all around. Peter offered an understanding sigh. I suppose Kate had to offer some sort of explanation for my sullenness. I was just thankful that she'd kept my nightmares private. And the truth was that Justus calling had upset me more than I cared to admit.

Peter asked, "What's he want, Jake?"

"Just trying to pick a fight," is what I said. "You know how he is."

Abigail humphed. Peter smiled at her and looked at me. "My wife's too polite to say that man should count his lucky stars you haven't tracked him down and thrown him in jail."

I felt Kate's eyes on me.

"Nothin'd please our good Mayor Wallis more, I suppose," Peter said. "'Course, he'd have a revolt on his hands. More folk blame Big Jim for getting those men shot than blame Justus. Everybody knows he wanted Justus's land for his godforsaken strip mall, and he was tired of Justus holding the reins on what he could and couldn't do in this town. I expect Jim Wallis's the only one who thanked the good Lord for the drought that year. Justus wouldn't have had to take out a loan on the farm otherwise, and Big Jim wouldn't have gotten the idea to muscle the bank to call the loan in."

"Justus didn't have to shoot the men who came to collect," Kate said. "Sending them out there might have been Mayor Wallis's doing, but he didn't pull the trigger."

Peter shook his head. "No'm. And I suppose Justus has been paying for it since."

I said nothing, lost in my own thoughts. Kate said, "He called the office this morning. Zach answered."

Peter raised his eyebrows and nodded. "You two understand sooner or later that boy's gonna know? Can't keep it a secret, no matter how hard you try. It's a small town, Kate. Jake, people talk."

"Zach is six," Kate said. "He's too young to understand. We're trying to keep the world from him, let him be. And it's not just me and Jake who think it's best. Justus does too."

I looked out into the dark yard. Zach flitted in and out of the porch light's arc, chased by both Frankie and Joey. "Doesn't matter," I said. "Justus isn't coming back, and that's all Mayor Wallis ever wanted. Farm's still there and the strip mall still ain't. I made sure there was no trouble. It'll all be put away sooner or later."

Kate offered a sad grin and said, "Nothing's ever put away in this town, Jake."

I nodded, knowing just how true that was, and decided it was better to play with the kids than dwell on Justus. I left the porch just as my cell phone rang. I checked the name and called Zach over.

"Wanna talk to Uncle Timmy?"

"Sure."

Kate perked up when she heard her brother's name. "Tell him to hurry, Zach. He's already missed supper."

Zach flipped the phone open and said, "Hey, Uncle Timmy. Momma said to hurr—" He fell silent. I looked down. He handed the phone to me like it was a hot coal. "He wants to talk to you, Daddy."

"What's the matter?"

Zach didn't answer. He left me and walked to the porch, where he settled in Kate's lap. Conversation around the picnic table had moved on by then. Peter asked Zach about his black eye.

I held the phone up to my ear. "What's up, Timmy?"

There came a crash on the other end of the line, followed by a distant bonging sound. Then Timmy's voice—a panting, crackling mix of confusion and fear: "Jake? Two guys came in here all drunked up and turned on me."

I looked at Kate, who laughed at something Peter had said. Zach wrapped her arms around himself and stared at me.

"Jake?"

"I'm here." I turned away and found a private spot next to the woodshed. "You okay?"

"You gotta get here, Jake. I got one of them. Knocked him out and drug him into the cooler, but he's awake now. Other one's still outside. Their truck's still here. I think they killed Andy, Jake. Jesus help us, I think Andy's *dead*."

"What?"

It was my tone that caught everyone's attention. Kate's laugh shrank to an uneasy smile. Abigail stared at me. Peter rose from his place at the picnic table and left the porch. Joey and Frankie made their way over.

Another crash on the phone. Someone was trying to get out. Or in.

"I think they killed him," Timmy said again. "One of them—the one I got locked up—he said if I didn't hand over the money they were gonna kill me like they killed the man at the gas station down the road. That's gottta be Andy, right? They jumped me, Jake. I got one of them. Locked him in the cooler. But the other one's still *here*."

"I'm on the way," I said. "Lock the doors and wait for me."

"Jake?" Kate asked. "What's wrong?"

I shut the phone. To Joey and Frankie I said, "Y'all need to get down to the squad and take a truck to the BP. I think Andy's hurt."

The cousins had turned their backs and begun their walk to the driveway before I could finish. Neither ran—running would only imply panic—but their strides were long and quick.

"Jake," Kate said again.

I turned to Peter next. "Two guys came into the Texaco and jumped Timmy. One of them's cornered. Other's on the loose."

Peter said, "I'm coming with you," just as Kate said, "*Jake*."

I looked at her. Zach pulled Kate's arms tighter over himself like they were the harness on a carnival ride that wouldn't stop going down and down. We all turned as Frankie's big diesel rounded the corner and headed toward town. Moving fast.

I told Peter, "No. I'm gonna need you to get Kate over to the office. Zach'll have to stay here a bit until we get this straightened out."

Peter wavered. A trace of alarm crept over his face. In a strange way, I took comfort in knowing I wasn't the only one standing there afraid.

But I knew the anxiety Peter felt was not for himself, it was for me. I was a Barnett, oh yes, and may that name always be spoken in awed, hushed tones within Mattingly's boundaries.

But the particular Barnett in front of Peter had never grown to embrace his kin's storied past, even if I did cart Bessie around like a holy relic. To Peter, I was just Jake—good old Jake—the man who wanted a quiet life and never wanted trouble. But I was also a man who could get himself hurt down at the Texaco if I was worried about my family.

"Okay," he said. "I'll tend to Kate."

I moved to the porch and kept my voice as even as I could. "Something's going on at the Texaco. Don't know what, but I need to get over there. Kate, Peter's gonna take you over to the office. He'll explain things on the way." I bent a knee and lifted Zach's chin. "I'm gonna need you to stay here and watch over Abigail and the kids for a little while, okay? I gotta go be sheriff, so that means you gotta be my deputy. Think you can do that for me?"

Zach sniffled. There came a soft, "Yessir."

I kissed them both and did not turn back as I rounded the corner of Peter's house. I wanted to. You have no idea how I wanted to. But I couldn't bear to see the fear in my family's eyes. And more than that, I didn't want them to see the fear in my own.

The bubble light stashed beneath the Blazer's front seat was the only official means to signify whether I was on duty or not. It had been collecting dust there since the Christmas parade. Before that, I guess it was the Fourth of July. I slapped the light against the small bit of roof that enclosed the front of the Blazer and pulled out of Peter's driveway, shaking my head at that small but important revelation—the only time I ever acted like a sheriff was when Zach and I were inching down Main Street, sandwiched between Hollis's polished John Deere and a staggering column of old men from the VFW.

My mind was divided between the fear that something

terrible had happened and the hope that it was all a mis-understanding. As the road opened up, I decided it was likely a combination of both and neither. Not terrible, not good, just—

"A couple lying drunks," I said into the windshield. "Just a couple lying drunks and nothing more."

The single blue light spun. What few cars I met along the way slowed as I passed. Some drifted to the shoulder. Others stopped completely. Black shapes turned toward me, craning their necks, wondering what had happened.

I couldn't blame them for their confusion. Because Hollis was right—nothing ever happened in Mattingly. But I knew even then that something had. And as the lights of the Texaco loomed through the windshield, my only comfort was that for the first time in months, I was wide-awake.

· 3 ·

Taylor was too numb to be afraid, which was more than what he could say for the strange girl beside him. She gripped the steering wheel with fists that had gone a milky white as the driver's side tires jerked off the pavement. The car corrected just before smashing a wooden mailbox post and then corrected too much, sending them veering to the opposite side. The girl screamed a curse as the side mirror next to Taylor clipped a large green trash can parked at the end of a driveway. He turned to see refuse littering the street behind them. The sight of all that trash in need of picking up reminded Taylor of Charlie. Poor Charlie. He'd never even get to spend his fifteen dollars.

Hitting the trash can only strengthened the girl's grip on the wheel, which only made the car snake more. Taylor's head spun. He thought it could be the two beatings he'd taken that night, or maybe it was the thick smell of the fancy car's leather seats. Maybe it was that he'd left his only friend in the world knocked out and bleeding on a gas station floor. He rubbed the legs of his jeans and tried to put that thought away, found he could not. It had been a long while since Taylor Hathcock had felt shame.

"Take some air and ease off that gas pedal," he said. "Only place in this town more perilous than being in its stores is being on its pavement."

The engine's steady whine backed off, though only slightly. The girl failed to heed the stop sign on the next corner. Taylor shook his head in disbelief.

"What are we doing?" she asked.

"Fifty, near's I can tell. You hear me, lady? I said ease off. Take a right here."

They turned down a darkened street of brick ranch homes and Cape Cods adorned in various shades of yellows and tans. There were no streetlights—Taylor knew there wouldn't be, the only bright spots when he looked down at night from his log in the Hollow were in the center of town. A handful of glowing porch bulbs that welcomed and warned away. Most of the houses were dark hulls with small, lamplit eyes that stared out from behind otherwise empty windows. There were no late-night strollers, no teenagers sneaking home from some backwoods carousing. That was good. That was fine.

"Up ahead's a stop sign," Taylor said. "That's S-T-O-and-P, which means quit moving. Left there, then another right."

"Where are we going?"

"Away."

"What about your friend?"

Taylor couldn't think. His head was a throbbing mass of nerves and those houses kept staring at him, asking what he was doing there, telling him that he should have stayed in the

Hollow where he belonged. He reached for the book in his pocket and held it tight.

"Charlie's sung all his songs," he said. "There's no more for him. He was dull, not bright." Taylor rubbed the legs of his jeans again and saw Charlie sitting at the table in the cabin, heard Charlie saying, *I dunno, Taylor* and *You sure 'bout this?* and *You're apt to snap.* He remembered telling Charlie that he was meant for greater things. "I offered him the Truth, but he wanted the world instead. My heart pauses for him still."

She stopped at the sign, turned left and then right, taking them closer to downtown. The man at the fill-'em-up would have called someone by now, Taylor thought. That meant whatever law was in town would be on the way. He'd have to keep to the fringes. Get out of Mattingly. Get back to the Hollow.

"That Timmy Griffith deserved everything you gave him," the girl said. "I was going to get him myself. He ruined my life."

"The man back there?"

She nodded.

"You wanted to pain him?"

"Yes."

"You sound like Charlie," Taylor said. "Charlie hurt that man like he hurt that other man. 'Tis a sin, hurting folk."

She took her eyes off the road. A queer look passed over her face that was part fear and part amusement. "That so? How much of that blood you're getting all over my car is yours, and how much of it is someone else's? Now, where am I going?"

"Left."

He guided her around the downtown area rather than through it, opting for a labyrinth of side streets and alleyways Taylor had seen from afar but never up close. They passed no vehicles and saw no flashing lights. The town proper gave way to secondary roads that wound toward the hill country to the east and the mountains beyond.

"Why'd you come for me?" Taylor asked.

There came no answer at first. Taylor doubted she even knew. Yet he saw a hurt in the girl and a longing for freedom that reminded him of the boy he'd awakened in the BP—a hurt and longing that reminded Taylor of himself. He knew above all that every beating heart carried its own wound, that there was a thread coiled around that wound that looped around the pain in others, linking us all. Taylor thought maybe that was why the girl had come for him. He thought maybe that was her secret. And he knew all were defined by their secrets, and their choices as well.

"Maybe it's my destiny," she said.

Taylor's eyes shrunk and burned at the corners. He bent around the gearshift between them and looked down. Lucy tensed, sending the car toward the far edge of the road.

"What are you doing?" she yelled.

"What's on your feet?"

"What?"

"Your *feet*," Taylor said.

The girl lurched back as Taylor grabbed her leg. He smiled and fell back into the seat.

Sneakers. She wore sneakers.

He saw her as neither spirit nor demon. Still, "How come you got a girl's body and a boy's hair?"

"I don't know. How come you got a boy's body and a girl's hair?"

Taylor reached back and brought his ponytail forward, waving it in front of her eyes.

"This here ain't no girl's hair, lady," he said. "'Tis a king's mane."

Her lips flattened to a near smile. "Then where's your kingdom, Your Highness?"

Taylor pointed through the windshield to the dark mountains ahead. "Yonder."

Pavement gave way to gravel, which turned to a dark, packed clay. The forest closed in around them. Taylor guided her to the next left, which was little more than a broken place in a phalanx of oaks barely wide enough for the car to maneuver upon. Branches reached down and whipped against the roof. The sound was like fingernails on a chalkboard.

Taylor did not have to tell her when to stop; the rusted iron gate said that for him. He watched as whatever spunk left in the girl peeled away like a mask to reveal the child beneath.

"This is Happy Hollow," she whispered.

Taylor waited until there was nothing left for her to do but look at him. Then he said, "Hear me well, lady, and listen long. I have a question, and you'll be plainspoken in your answer. It's yay or nay, and all that rides on it is whether you're about to breathe your last in this sorry world."

She managed a small nod.

Taylor leaned in close. "Are you awake?"

· 4 ·

Timmy stood just inside the Texaco's closed doors as I pulled into the lot. He held the shotgun with the barrel high. It moved in small, sporadic circles, like a batter itching for a hanging curve. His starched shirt hung loose from khaki pants that had been torn above the knee. His cropped hair was tinged a bloody red.

I got out of the Blazer and tucked Bessie at the small of

my back. A '70s Ford pickup sat crooked at the far end of the building. It looked familiar in a strange way, though my mind was too muddled to place it. The canopy lights ended just beyond its front bumper. The moon took over from there, shining its passive glow over fields of shrubs and tall grass. I saw no movement there. High on the hill across the road, the Kingman house stood dark and silent.

The heavy clack of the doors unlocking made me jump. I managed to pull my arm behind myself, wanting to show Timmy that had been no jump at all, I'd just been reaching for Bessie. He cracked the right-side door just enough to speak.

"The one's in the cooler, Jake. Haven't heard'm in a while. Don't know where the other one is."

"That their truck?" I asked.

"Yeah. They were gonna kill me, Jake."

I took a long pull of air through my nose and let it gather before passing it over my lips in a thin stream. Doc March had suggested that little exercise to help me stay calm. I found it worked just as well in Timmy's parking lot as it had in my own bed.

I said, "Okay, Timmy. You did real good, but I don't want no trouble and I need to know what I'm dealing with. So why don't you just open that door and let me in."

"But he's out there, Jake."

"Maybe so," I said, "but not in this very spot. Come on, now. You can lock back up when I get inside."

Timmy opened the door just enough for me to squeeze through and clacked it shut again. His face was swollen, and his right eye would look like Zach's by morning. Timmy might have gotten them both, but they'd gotten plenty of Timmy too. I had to get him to the hospital, or at least to Doc March.

"You say he's in the cooler?" I asked.

"Cooler," he said. "Somebody done got their licks in on them both, Jake. Reckon that was Andy. Is Andy okay?"

"Squad's headed there now."

"The little guy, he wanted money. Said they killed Andy and the sissy he was with."

I blinked, trying to replay that last bit in my mind. "Somebody was with Andy?"

"That's what he told me," Timmy said. "Then the big guy, he asks me if I was awake. What's that mean, Jake?"

I didn't know. I took off my hat and ran a hand through my hair. My fingers came back soaked. There was no such thing as police procedure in Mattingly, other than staying ten feet behind Hollis's tractor during the parades. I had no deputies, nothing in the way of staff other than Kate, and even she was unofficial. I supposed I could call Alan Martin at the county police station in Stanley, but decided against it. Alan was forty minutes away, I was there now. Which meant I had to do this on my own.

"I'm gonna go in there and bring him out," I said. "You stand ready."

I moved past a tangled mass of overturned snack racks toward the cooler in back. There was nothing on the other side of the door but the steady hum of the fans. I pulled Bessie from my belt. Just as I was about to thump her against the door, my cell rang. I jumped—this time so fast and so completely that I couldn't disguise it as anything else—and pulled the phone from my pocket. Loud voices and a wailing siren greeted me.

"Jake? Joey. It's bad. Had to get everyone else up here too. Both trucks."

Both trucks. So the man in the cooler had told Timmy the truth.

"How's Andy?" I asked.

"Hanging on. He got burned up pretty bad. Banged his head too. Frankie says he's hallucinatin'."

"You said you needed both trucks?"

"You know that kid been stopping there in the mornings with his brother?" Joey asked. "Name's Eric?"

I did. I'd been in the BP more than a few times when the two boys from Away had stopped for their smokes and snacks. Kate had taken an interest in them (had even gone so far as to consider writing their names in her book), but it was Andy who'd taken to looking after the boys.

"I know him," I said. "He there?"

"Was. He's gone, Jake. Got stabbed. It's a mess down there at Andy's. You're gonna have to call in some help."

"I will."

Joey was still talking when I closed the phone. My heart felt like an anvil in my chest. I felt the world slip away. There was a killer on the other side of that steel door, and it was my job to bring him out. Mine, no one else's. That was a far cry from taking the Widow Cash to market every Monday morning and waving to parade-goers.

I said I'd been afraid of Phillip since the day he died. That's true in a way. Closer would be saying I'd been afraid of everything since that evening in the Hollow twenty years before. Terrified, not only at the thought of what I did to Phillip coming out, but that the truth of the man I was would come out with it. The only thing worse than sinning is living with it after, and in that regard you could say Phillip McBride had taken even more from me than I ever took from him.

Timmy stood watching me. His finger rested just over the trigger guard and his eyes held steady, waiting for me to do my job. A slow realization that I could not crept over me like rising water. In that moment I longed for my father. I hefted

Bessie, turned her head so the hammer pole faced the door, then banged three times.

"This here's Sheriff Jake Barnett. I'm gonna open up this door now. I don't want no trouble. You hear me?"

Silence.

Bessie shook in front of me. I slipped the pin from the handle and pulled hard on the door. The room inside was still but for the bobbing head in the back, behind a wall of frozen chicken containers. One of the men who'd beaten Timmy sat on the cold concrete floor, head rocking back and forth, whimpering into an arm so cold it had turned blue. Blood crusted into a serrated line from his right eye to his jaw. His shirt was torn at the chest.

I forced my feet inside. Cold air blew down from the vents above, pushing my hat down over my eyes. Gooseflesh sprouted on my arms. I rushed ahead, propelled more by adrenaline than purpose, and grabbed the man by his hair. He let out a cry that was all fear and no threat as I jerked him to his feet and spun him against the wall. I pinned him there with Bessie.

"What's your name?" I asked.

No answer.

"Where's the other guy?"

"He gone," was all he said.

I kept Bessie's blade to the back of his neck and searched his pockets. There were no weapons or identification, only fifteen dollars in cash.

"Where'd he go?" I asked.

"Don't matter. He gonna kill me. Said so. You won't even finish readin' me m'rights."

His rights. I shook my head, not having even thought of that. I holstered Bessie and said, "You are under arrest for . . . robbin', attempted robbin', almost killing Andy Sommerville, and killing Eric—" It occurred to me that I didn't even know Eric's last name. I left it at that. "You have the right to remain silent. If you don't be silent . . ."

I closed my eyes and cursed as the cold air blew down on us. The man turned his head as much as he could. The look on his face was a mix of amusement and shock.

"What kinda dumb hick cop are you?" he asked.

I barely heard him. I was still trying to think of the last half of the Miranda warning, something about getting a lawyer or a judge. I didn't know because I'd never had to speak it. I spun him around and led him out through the store.

Timmy raised the shotgun as we approached.

"Never mind that," I said. "Put that scatter-gun away, Timmy. Just get the door."

Timmy did. I led the man to the Blazer and put him in the back, then found an old pair of handcuffs at the bottom of the glove box beneath three of Zach's Matchbox cars, two tubes of Kate's lipstick, and a stack of Johnny Cash CDs. One of the man's hands went above the roll bar in the back, the other below it. I buckled the seat belt last. It wasn't the best way to secure a prisoner, but it was the only way I could figure.

I turned to Timmy and said, "I'm gonna drive you over to Doc March's. No objections."

He cast a wary eye to the backseat as I pulled the phone from my pocket to dial the office.

"Go on," I said. "All the fight's out of'm, Timmy."

The line rang in my ear as Timmy climbed into the passenger seat.

Kate answered and said, "Jake?"

"Yeah," I said. "It's me."

"Is Timmy okay?"

"Will be. Just a few bumps. I'd let you talk to him, but I

don't think he's up for it right now. I'm dropping him at Doc's. Andy's at the hospital. He's been burned."

Kate choked back tears. "What *happened*?"

"Two drunks looking for a quick dollar, near's I can tell. I got one, but the other one's in the wind. I need you to clean out the cell. Got a plate for you to run too. Can you do that?"

"I think so, yes."

"You'll have to call Alan Martin too, tell him to get people down here. And I need some crime scene people. To the BP first, then here."

"Alan, okay. What's the plate?"

I read the numbers off the truck along the curb.

"Anything else?" she asked.

There was. And while I took no pleasure in saying it, I knew it should only come from me. "You know those two boys been coming by the BP in the mornings? Brothers? Older one's Eric."

"Yes."

"Know their last names or where they're from?"

"Not offhand," Kate said. "Andy's caring for them. Why?"

"Eric's gone, Kate."

The silence that followed was a hurt that plumbed the deep places in Kate's heart where neither tears nor words could follow.

"I'm so sorry, Kate."

"I'll make some calls," she said.

I hung up and drove. No one spoke. I glanced into the rear-view mirror. The man in back had his hands manacled to the roll bar, freezing him into a gesture of surrender. He looked at me and smiled. I saw a malevolence in that grin, a warning that echoed not in anything he said but in what Phillip had told me the night before.

You're a dead man and he's coming and you'll remember true. Because I want an end.

I took my eyes away from the mirror and stared ahead. The nightmares alone were bad enough. But now I felt that Phillip had grown too large for my dreams, and I could not escape the feeling that he was watching me even then.

I was right.

· 5 ·

Kate dried her eyes for what she promised herself was the last time and pulled the warm pages from the printer tray. The low ink rendered the image atop the DMV report in clumps of gray and black dots, but the name and address were clear enough. Charles Earl Givens. That was who had done this.

She didn't need a clear picture to know he was a monster. Kate had seen enough of them over the years. They stalked the powerless and hid themselves well, never appearing as one would expect—with a goat's head or a spiked tail maybe, or razored teeth smiling behind bulging yellow eyes. No, the real monsters were disguised in flesh and bone—the Mr. Charles Earl Givenses of the world. They were the fathers who abused and the mothers who neglected. They were criminals who beat other people's brothers and burned kind old men and murdered innocent boys.

Bullies. That's what those monsters were, bullies all. Kate knew this and knew it well.

She stared at the smudged outline of that wide, unsmiling face, barely aware of the phone trilling on her desk. Likely someone else wanting to know what Jake was doing out with his parade light flashing. Kate knew it wouldn't be long before the fence post telegraph of nosy old women and nosier old men made its way to the hungry ears of Trevor Morgan, even to Mayor Wallis himself. Then again, she thought maybe that call was from Jake. Maybe he had more news of Timmy or Andy. Maybe he'd captured the man who had escaped. She lifted the receiver in mid-ring as Charles Earl's faint eyes mocked.

"Jake?" she asked.

"Katelyn?"

The pages fell from Kate's hand, fluttering in the air before fanning out like a blooming flower. Charles Earl's monster likeness landed facedown atop her open notebook. Kate swiped it away, believing the two touching one another a sacrilege, like spitting on a Bible.

"Katelyn?" she heard again, and the deep growl behind it.

"What are you doing calling here, Justus?"

"I call when the Spirit lays the need on me." The voice was the sort that straightened backs and buckled knees, with an inflection that always sounded just a hair away from rage. "What you doing at th'office, Katelyn?"

"Justus, I can't talk right now. Jake's coming in."

"What's wrong?"

"Nothing's wrong. Where are you calling from? And who gave you a phone and Jake's number?"

"Never you mind that," Justus said. "I still got friends, Katelyn, even if I can't count you an' Jake among'm. Tried callin' his pocket phone, but he won't answer. Figured I'd just call there and leave a message."

"A message saying what?"

"Wonderin' if Jake's gonna arrest me."

Kate shook her head and sighed. They came in spurts, Justus's calls. There had been years of silence after he'd shot the bank men and fled Mattingly—just enough time to let everyone think the whole mess was over. The phone calls had started only in the past year and followed no schedule. Sometimes Justus would call once a week, sometimes twice, and then he'd go silent again for a month. Until that night, those calls were restricted only to the office. Zach wasn't allowed to answer the phone during those times, which made him answering Justus's call that morning nothing more than a cruel stroke of fate. Kate wondered if she still would have gone to Timmy's chasing a name had she known that would happen. She knew the answer was yes. She would have gone for the same reason the Spirit led Justus to pick up his phone—because God had a way of shining His light at your back, casting yesterday as shadows that fell on today. The only difference was that for Kate, those shadows fell constant.

"Jake's not going to arrest you tonight," she said. "I doubt he'll arrest you tomorrow either. I have to go, Justus."

"Not afore you tell me what's that flutter in your voice."

A part of her wanted to say, "Nothing." A bigger part (one Kate would never share with anyone, and her husband especially) wanted to tell Justus everything. His voice intimidated Kate as much as it always had, but in a way it also gave her a kind of strength. It was good to know Justus was somewhere up in Crawford's Gap rather than in a jail cell, even if he did shoot those men and run from the consequences. Especially since there was only one prisoner coming in instead of two.

"A boy was murdered tonight," she said. "Over at the BP. Andy's in the hospital. They went to Timmy's next. He's banged up but okay."

Kate swore she could feel heat coming over the line—a bent but righteous rage.

"What happened?" Justus asked.

"I don't know. It was two men. Jake's bringing one of them in."

"*One* of them?" he boomed, and Kate suddenly felt like a little girl. "You mean one's a-loose?"

She was about to say yes when Jake came through the door. He held a bulging dish towel that Kate barely noticed in one hand. The other hand held Charles Givens's elbow.

"I have to go," she said.

"Katelyn? *Kate—*"

She hung up. Jake guided Charlie to the sofa and sat him there, dared him to move. Kate didn't think the monster would. It looked like all the will had gone out of him, likely spilt on the floors of Mattingly's two gas stations.

Jake crossed the room to her desk. His eyes were red and glassy, like he was caught in one of his dreams and couldn't find the way out.

He asked, "Where's Peter?"

"Sent him home. I wanted him to be there for Zach. Crime scene folks are on the way, and so is Alan. He'll take that thing on the sofa when they're done. How's Timmy?"

"Doc's got him," Jake said. "Says he'll be fine. You okay?"

"No, Jake, I am not okay," Kate said. She looked at the sofa. "Any sign of the other guy?"

He shook his head. "Most likely he's long gone."

"How could someone do such a thing? Not just hurt people, but leave them there to die?"

Jake said, "I don't know," but the way he cut his eyes to the floor made Kate wonder if that was true. The night had left her so fragile that for a moment she believed that look wasn't a simple glance away, it was an accusation—*You should know all about hurting people, Kate. Why don't you tell me how someone could do that?* "I need to get him fingerprinted. Can you fix him up?"

Kate stood there, hoping he'd meant something else. "What'd you say?"

"Can you get him, you know . . . clean?" he asked. "Can you clean him up?"

Kate's eyes grew wide and hot. She pushed her husband away. It was a hard ramming that sank her hands deep into his withering chest.

"You want me to clean him *up*?" she asked. "After what that man *did*?" Kate looked at the back of Charlie's head, and in a voice meant for him to hear, she said, "There's a special place in hell for someone like that, Jake."

She thrust her hands into him again, venting her rage against Charlie, against poor Eric and poor Andy and poor Timmy, against the asinine thing Jake had asked her to do. Her fists flew like pistons against his chest. Her shoulders caught fire and her lungs ran out of air, and Jake allowed that pounding, did not even move to protect himself. Kate stopped only when a part of her understood she was trying to punish him and he was wanting to be punished. Kate broke her promise and cried again. She fell into Jake's arms. He held her tight.

"I'm sorry," he said. "I don't know what's wrong with me. I should've thought of that. I'm so sorry, Kate. He's just scared."

Jake ran a hand down the back of Kate's hair and released her. However justified her outburst had been, Kate felt a pang of remorse watching Jake walk back to the sofa. He gathered up the small bundle he'd brought in and led Charles Givens to his office. Kate watched through the glass window as Jake brushed aside the plastic-wrapped uniform hanging from the bookcase behind his desk. He placed the wrapped dish towel on the shelf there and brought out a small first-aid kit, pausing to glance at the pills Doc March had left on his desk. The sight of her husband tending to Charlie's wounds sickened Kate. Guilt sickened her more.

She'd asked Jake how someone could do such a thing as hurt people and leave them to die, but Kate knew. She'd been a bully herself once, a monster to an innocent young boy, and because of that her life still smelled like fruit gone spoiled. The day she played her trick on Phillip behind the bleachers had never been far from Kate's thoughts. Sometimes she still heard the laughter, that mocking cackle from the boys and girls who'd been so eager to watch. Kate had told Jake there was a special place in hell for people like Charlie Givens, but that was wrong. No, there was a special place in hell for those who believed hell wasn't what they deserved. Because to hurt came easy to all, and that was why there was so much of it in the world.

She gathered the papers from her desk and crossed the foyer. The contents of the first-aid kit lay scattered atop Jake's desk. He fumbled with a bottle of peroxide and an unopened package of Q-tips.

"Use the cotton balls," she said. "Q-tips are for little stuff."

A small but grateful smile crossed his lips. "Got it. Thanks."

Charles Earl said nothing as Jake cleaned him, said nothing still when Jake stood him up and led him down the small hallway to Cell 1. There was no Cell 2. Stacks of aluminum softball bats, leather gloves, and buckets of softballs stored there for the church league lined the wall. Kate had left the lumpy cot and the broken rocking chair, though she thought those more than the monster deserved. She handed the papers over as Jake locked him inside.

Jake looked at the top page and asked, "Charles Givens?"

The monster sat in the rocker and smiled. "Charlie."

Jake nodded and studied the report. "You been a busy boy, Charlie. Disorderly conduct, drunk in public. Three counts of petty theft."

Charlie said nothing to that.

"Who's the guy with you tonight?"

"Same guy's gonna kill me 'cause I screwed up." Then, in the same voice one would use to offer a comment on the weather, he added, "Taylor gonna kill you too. All you."

Kate shuddered at that and moved closer to Jake, thankful for his quiet strength. And yet that strength seemed to leak away in the next quiet moments. She felt Jake's body give way—only slightly, but enough to cause a small moment of confusion and worry—and heard a sound like a stricken boy coming from his mouth.

"Says you live up on Brody's Lane in Camden," Jake said. "That near Happy Holler, is it?"

"It is."

The pages shook in Jake's hand. He crunched the report into a ball and tossed it into a bucket of softballs along the wall. "Taylor," he said. "That his first name or his last?"

"First," Charlie mumbled.

"He got a last name?"

Charlie shook his head. "I'm done talkin'."

Jake turned to Kate. "I gotta head down to Andy's. Think you can watch this guy?"

Charlie smiled and shook his head. "You crazy, Sheruff? There's danger about, an' you gonna leave her here with me? Sure she's safe?"

Kate didn't answer, only walked back down the hallway and into the foyer. She grabbed the first weapon she found from the shelf by the back door. Jake's eyes met hers as she walked back. He moved away as Kate racked a load into the shotgun in her hands. She drew the barrel through the bars. Charlie Givens's smile disappeared.

"You killed that boy and you hurt friend and family," she said. "You so much as scratch an itch, I'll send you to hell with a hole in your gut so big the devil'll spend eternity twirling you on his finger."

Jake started for the door. "Pretty sure she's safe," he told Charlie. "Not too sure about you, though."

· 6 ·

Lucy hummed. It was a song she didn't know and that didn't matter, because humming had always calmed her and that was all she could do. And then she couldn't even do that when she faltered and pitched forward against another rock at her feet.

She fought gravity until her hips tilted too far, then let herself go limp. All Lucy could manage was to turn her head and hope this time she would meet soft dirt rather than sharp rocks. That rapturous feeling of letting go—of surrender—was replaced by the sudden jerk of someone grabbing her. Lucy's feet steadied. The man nudged her on.

The last thing she remembered clearly were the names etched into the iron gate just beyond the hood of her car and thinking she had answered correctly. The man had asked if she was awake. Lucy had no idea what that meant, but the look on his face (it was the same jumble of anger, sadness, and long-ing she'd seen in her father only hours before) told her it was something important. She knew, too, that the man meant to have an answer. It was either yes or no, life or death. One flip of an existential coil that on some primitive level Lucy knew would be heads, he won, or tails, she lost.

So she'd answered, "Yes." And when the man's eyes widened and the sharp blades in his stare dulled, she'd added, "Of course I'm awake. You are too, aren't you?"

That seemed the most appropriate thing to ask. And Lucy found that despite her fear, she remained curious for an answer. Yet the man had only led her into the trees, where the Hollow swallowed them.

Lucy had no way of knowing how long ago that had been, though she was sure they were miles into the wilderness by now. The night appeared thick and black like tar. Towering trees with gray, reaching limbs hid the moon and stars, giving Lucy the illusion of walking through space rather than forest. Her captor said nothing. There had been times she was convinced he was no longer there at all, that he'd left her to wander until either the elements or exhaustion felled her. But then the man would reach out and push her forward (twice, those pushes were nearer a gentle guiding), and Lucy would realize she was not alone. Now she felt his presence near and could smell the blood and stink on him. She realized, too, that even if she could see nothing, something could see her. Watching her, with what felt like a thousand eyes.

She had been in Mattingly long enough to know of the Hollow. It was a usual topic of conversation during those weekend parties when the bonfires began to die and the boys wanted to get close. One Friday night right before George Hellickson rounded third and found Lucy waving him in, he'd told her how Happy Hollow was cursed even before the Indians arrived. Ricky Summers had said much the same on another Friday night by another bonfire, adding that you could see the soft spire of Indian Hill from the gate but nobody knew what lay on its other side, that it might even be the end of the world or hell itself. And it had been Johnny who'd told her

how every boy in town could trace his first steps into man-
hood back to daring a walk through the Hollow and scratching
his name into the gate. Johnny had laughed after, saying he
supposed that tradition would fade now that Lucy had come
to Mattingly. He said it was a whole lot more fun and a whole
lot less scary to call yourself a man after bedding Lucy Seekins
than walking through a cursed wood.

Lucy had taken no offense to that remark. She'd known
Johnny loved her even as he'd said those words. Now she wondered if he'd ever loved her at all.

She had always thought those stories to be the sort of
small-town superstition her friends in DC had warned her
about. Yet the feeling of heaviness that overtook her forced
Lucy to reconsider what she believed. The thick trees blinded
her eyes, but Lucy's ears worked just fine. That was what
bothered her. Because she heard nothing—no rustles from
the trees, no night birds, no wind. And there was that sense
of watchfulness crowding her, those thousand eyes, as if the
Hollow itself was *awake*.

She pushed that thought from her mind and concentrated
instead on the feel of the ground beneath her. Lucy felt the
man's hand on her once more. She didn't shrink from that
touch, was glad to feel it in all that emptiness. She leaned
against him as they made their way up a steep hill. Taylor
led the way down the other side and grabbed Lucy again, this
time with such force that it felt like the tips of his fingers had
reached bone.

"Hush," he whispered. "Tell me, lady, what walks here."

He pointed to a small clearing ahead. A hulking mass of
deep black edged its way out of the woods. Lucy swallowed a
scream as the man let go of her arm. He took two steps forward, putting himself between the thing and Lucy, and turned

to her. There, free from the pressing trees, moonlight filtered through the long hairs of his beard and sparkled his eyes. His chest was thick and wide, the skin on his arms taut. To Lucy, the man looked godlike.

He turned away again and cupped his hands around his mouth yelling, "I have no quarrel" into the night.

The shape still blocked their way. The man dared not move closer, nor would Lucy allow him. This time it was she who took his arm. They watched as the shape moved from its place and silently shrank back into the trees.

"What was that?" Lucy whispered.

"You'd know if you was awake."

He pushed her on, past the field where the thing had been. Lucy kept her hands to his arm as they passed. Rocks and brambles gave way to tall, brittle grass that clipped her bare legs. Then it was up again and more up, until Lucy heard the faint rumblings of white water far below.

The world along the ridgetop felt alien. Even the small cabin in front of Lucy looked to be little more than a mirage. Then the man pushed her through the open door, and Lucy knew this was no dream. She was alone with a madman deep in a haunted wood filled with a thousand eyes, and this was as real as anything she'd ever known.

· 7 ·

I slowed near the BP and caught a flutter from the living room curtain of a nearby house. Kate had said nothing about calls from townspeople wanting to know what was going on, but I knew there'd been plenty. People had seen me with my light running, and no doubt many more had heard the sirens from the squad trucks. But it was that small wave of a drape beneath a dwindling porch light that convinced me what had happened couldn't be kept quiet. News spreads like a virus in a small town, bad news like an epidemic. And as much as I knew Mattingly had faced its share of mindless tragedy over the years, I also knew there had been nothing like what had happened at Andy's.

The stone-faced trooper manning the lot's entrance nodded as I drove in. In many ways, the BP was everything the Texaco was not. Andy Sommerville's property was smaller, for one. As was the building—just enough room inside for a few booths, a drink cooler, and three rows of groceries that were always a few days short of expiration. A crime scene van and three county police cruisers were parked out front. Their roof lights (plural, mind you; I was glad not to have arrived with my puny single flashing atop a beat-up old truck) spun blue against the BP's white walls. Yellow police tape stretched across the perimeter. Two technicians picked through Eric's Jeep, parked near the side door. More techs busied themselves inside, measuring and dusting and snapping pictures. Two puddles of congealed blood lay in the middle of the store. Surrounding the stains was a series of tiny orange cones that looked like exclamation points. The air reeked of sweat and burnt flesh. Until I stepped through that door, I never knew loss had a smell.

Standing in the midst of all that violence and death was Alan Martin, a county investigator I'd known since our ball-playing days in high school. He motioned for the nearest tech, offered words I couldn't hear, and scrawled something in a small leather notebook. An unlit cigarette hung from the corner of his mouth. He made his way over and offered a strong hand that didn't seem real considering his thin frame. Somehow I managed a firm grip in return.

"Hey, Jake," he said. "You know them?"

"Small town, Alan, I know everybody. The boy was from Away, but Andy's a good friend."

"Then I'm sorry," he said. "Come on, let's get this over with."

He cautioned me to mind my steps, which I figured wouldn't be a problem since I couldn't move. My boots felt like they'd been planted in cement. Many, I suppose, wouldn't blame me. Many would say that anyone who hadn't slept the night before and the days and weeks before that, who in the last day had been shot at by a moonshiner, dreamed a dead boy and some mysterious "He" were coming to wreak havoc, seen his brother-in-law beaten, made his first ever arrest, and been hounded by a fugitive wanted for attempted murder, wouldn't be much expected to possess the full range of his faculties.

Maybe that's right. But I would accept no understanding because none of those things was going through my mind. I stood frozen in place by the sight of smeared death on a floor I'd walked on since I was a boy, and I was plain scared. It wasn't that same old fear either—the kind I'd always lived with and managed to hide well enough. This was something other.

I'd never felt called to sheriffing, never wanted to wear a badge. I'd taken the job six years before and a year after Justus ran, when Mattingly's then-sheriff, John David Houser, decided he was getting too old to do nothing and wanted to try his hand at farming instead. I'd tried my hand at a landscaping business, wanting to be an entrepreneur like my brother-in-law, and was barely keeping the family above water. The sheriff's job was mine for the having. I took it for the simple reason that I wanted no trouble. I needed a quiet life after Phillip. I needed a calm on my outside to balance the hell on my inside. Upholding a law no one ever broke had fit that bill just fine. But charging into Timmy's chicken cooler to fetch Charlie Givens had been too much. And standing there with my eyes full of what looked like two red snow angels on the floor and my nose full of what smelled like burnt copper, I knew my quiet life was done.

Alan stepped in front of the cones and spoke the obvious: "Happened right here." He filled me in on the rest, adding that one of the suspects likely had a good-sized lump on his head. He showed me the broken broom handle as proof. It was the same broom Andy had been using around the pumps when I drove by that morning.

"That'll be the one I brought in," I said, and then, to myself, *The one I tried to get Kate to clean up.*

Alan nodded. "We got everyone looking for the other one, along with the Camden and Stanley police. Got a good set of prints off the knife he left behind. We'll find out who he is."

"First name's Taylor," I managed. "Got that out of the other one. I'll try to get a last name when I get back."

I kept my eyes on the blood. All that blood.

"Hey," Alan said. He led me by the elbow toward the front doors, away from prying ears. "Jake, listen. I know you're not used to this sort of thing, but I don't want you to get all worked up. Chances are good this Taylor fella's gonna get as far from here as possible as quick as he can."

I'd said much the same to Kate. Still, it felt good to hear it echoed from someone who knew what he was doing. A single thought in my mind took root and sprouted: Maybe the worst was over now. Maybe all that was left was the hurting and the moving on. Maybe so. But in the meantime, there was the matter of not looking like a scared little boy to the real policeman in front of me.

"I'm not worked up," I said. "For Taylor's sake, I hope he

has moved on. He wouldn't like it if I was the one who ran him down."

Alan seemed satisfied at that. "Jeep out there the boy's?"

I nodded.

"No registration or insurance. Plates are expired. No ID on the body either. That how folks drive around here, Jake?"

I shrugged. "It's the country, Alan. Boy's name is Eric. Kate's working on the particulars." I paused, knowing I'd referred to Eric in the present tense. Then came an idea: "Andy's got a camera set up."

"We found it," Alan said. "Haven't had a chance to watch it yet. Your suspect say anything?"

"Other than Taylor's first name, no."

"We could take a look at the tape together. Might loosen his lips."

He had a point. I took off my hat and turned it over in my hands as pictures flashed through my mind of what had happened just a few feet away. The last thing I wanted was to give an air of fact to the things I imagined—to see that, no, Eric hadn't been standing *there* when he'd gotten stabbed, he'd actually been *over there*. Or that Andy had gotten only three shots in with his broom and not four before being pumped full of fire and bug spray. But like I said, I had to keep up appearances. I had to preserve that thin sheet of tough Barnett enamel.

We kept well wide of the blood and snaked our way to the cramped back room. A small black-and-white monitor sat atop three ancient milk crates by the breaker box. Alan brushed a thick layer of dust from the VCR and rewound the tape. I stared at my boots and offered a prayer that I could make it through what I was about to see.

"Any chance the Texaco has a setup like this?" he asked.

"Afraid not."

Alan grunted and studied the time stamp on the picture as the tape sped forward. "Okay, I figure this is about the time it happened."

The screen showed a panorama that extended from the counter to the side door and stopped at the second aisle. Andy was gathering the trash when Eric walked in. They left through the side door. Alan pressed the forward button again, turning minutes into seconds. He stopped when Charlie and Taylor pulled up. The rest was played out frame by frame in a silence that was louder than anything I'd ever heard.

When it was done, I could only say, "Sweet Jesus, help us all."

Alan switched off the monitor. For the next long moment, the only sound was the tape rewinding and ejecting.

"I expect that's all we'll need," he said. "Pretty cut and dried."

I thought it was too. The act, anyway. But what lay behind that act wasn't cut and dried at all. I'd never been one for intuition or a sixth sense. I'd never heard the voice of God (and after Phillip I didn't expect to, at least until my judgment). But I knew there was something wrong just the same. Something more.

I looked at the tape in Alan's hand. "Let me have that?"

"I'll need it when I pick up your prisoner. He's coming with us. Murder falls to the county, Jake. We'll handle the murder investigation, and I'll help you any other way I can. Keep some cruisers in the area, at least. Town won't take too well to outsiders patrolling their streets, but even if this Taylor fella's gone, I wouldn't take any chances just yet. Up to you, though."

I fell quiet and pretended to weigh options that didn't need to be weighed at all. Then I said, "Town's not so big, Alan, but the outlying hills are. I suppose some extra bodies would be best. Just for now, mind you."

And so it was agreed. Alan handed me the tape and said he'd be down later to collect Charlie. I gave the pools of blood an even wider berth on my way out.

God took that opportunity to at least say yes to one prayer. I managed to make it to the privacy of the Blazer before I vomited.

· 8 ·

Taylor pushed the girl through the open door and then stumbled through himself as the surge of adrenaline that had gotten him safely back to the Hollow puttered to vapor. What took its place was a deep throbbing in his head and the grim knowledge that he had at most four steps left before his legs gave out.

It had taken much longer than expected to reach the cabin, though it had nothing to do with Taylor's weakening condition. It had been the lady. She'd tripped and fallen and shaken and made more of a ruckus than Charlie ever could. It had been obvious to Taylor even before they'd left the gate's shadow that she'd never been in the wild. As such, he'd spent the majority of the walk trying to keep Lucy upright and trying to decide if she'd been truthful.

She had displayed both courage and wits, neither of which were attributes of the slumbering. And she still bore sneakers on her feet. Yet as the dying moonlight had shown down upon the edge of the field, Taylor noticed that not only were the tracks the girl left far smaller than those he'd found leading from the grove, her shoes carried a different tread as well. And she had not known of the bear. Wouldn't anyone who was Awake know of the bear?

He guided her through the cabin's dark interior and kicked

out one of the chairs from the table. Pain and exhaustion slurred his words. "Siddown."

She took her place and kept her arms tight at her sides, pushing them into the bulges of skin that blossomed over the top of her shorts. Taylor lit two candles and placed them on the table. Their wicks were nearly burned away. He wondered who would bring him groceries every month now that Charlie was gone. When he sat in the opposite chair, it was more a stumble.

The girl stared at him with dark eyes swirled with fear. Taylor saw she was comely but for her hair, but let that thought pass over and away. Pretty ladies were poison even if a blessing.

"You Awake?" he asked.

Her chin lowered.

"I speak it again because I have no confidence in your answer, lady. Everybody thinks they's Awake, yet they are not. Charlie believed he was. You saw his end. Let that be instruction"—Taylor leaned forward, careful to make sure his warning was properly received—"you best be sure what you give air to."

"I'm sure," she said.

He pulled out his book. There was much to write that night, much to ponder. He managed to scribble only *Lady says awa* before the shaking in his hands took over.

"What's your name?" he asked.

"Lucy," she said. "Lucy Seekins."

"Do you know where She is, Lucy—Lucy Seekins?"

Lucy's mouth closed even as her jaws loosened. They were like broken hinges. "Who's 'she'?"

Taylor reached across the table and grabbed Lucy's hand, pulling her to himself. She let out a cry that the Hollow swallowed full.

"I Woke that boy," he said. "I Woke him up because that's

where I was led. I done my part. Now if you're the one who come outta this Holler, you tell me where She *is*."

Lucy's eyes widened, an accusing gawk if Taylor had ever seen one. He knew this lady bore no truth in her. And if that was so, then it had all been for naught. The trip to town had yielded nothing. He'd woken that boy

(But did you? came a small, fractured voice. *Did you really, Taylor?)*

but he'd lost Charlie. He hadn't found who walked out of the Hollow, he'd found another comely girl. It shouldn't be like this. Taylor Hathcock was a good man. A good man shouldn't hurt this much. A good man shouldn't have to do what needed to be done. And yet Taylor understood that good men were often called to do bad things in a hard world.

He rose and walked to the door. The shotgun rested barrel up by the stacked crates along the wall. Taylor hefted the gun and felt the same twinge of sadness that had engulfed him in the bathroom at the BP. He didn't have a mind to see more blood that night. He'd seen too much already.

Lucy tottered in her chair. The caramel tan on her face and neck went white when Taylor racked the slide. He raised the barrel to her chest—

"I want to be awake."

—and held it there.

"What were those words?" he asked.

"I want to be awake," Lucy said again. "I want to be like you."

Taylor pointed the barrel to Lucy's face, searching her eyes for treachery, convinced plenty would be found if he looked long enough. But he felt as though a wet blanket had fallen over his shoulders and head, suffocating him. White and blue sparkles dotted his eyes and burst like tiny suns. Lucy's sobs—long wails that swept over him and through the open door—filled the cabin. It was a cry that brimmed with more than fear and poured forth with more than despair. It was a mourning not for what she was about to lose but for what she would never gain. That Taylor Hathcock knew this was not proof of his divinity, though he considered himself nearly as such. It was merely a lament he knew well, sung in the common language of hurt. He lowered the gun.

"I don't know if your heart is true, Lucy Lucy, but I know I can't set you a-loose," he said. "You cannot leave my Holler. You've born witness to too much."

He sat the shotgun back in its place and rummaged through the crates for a length of rope. Lucy did not protest as Taylor ran the line around her shoulders to her waist and legs. He secured her to the bottom of the chair, making the knots as taut as his shaky hands would allow. When he was satisfied, Taylor staggered to the cot on the other side of the room.

"You run, I'll know it," he said. "Nothing's hidden from me. I'm a king. You hear me, lady?"

The world fell away before Taylor heard her answer.

· 9 ·

Kate thought it could have been worse; she could have been talking to Justus again. Instead she was on the phone with Mayor Wallis, whose peaceful slumber had been interrupted by a slew of worried townspeople, and who was now worried himself because he'd reached Kate at the office instead of the Barnett house. Kate had never been a fan of Jim Wallis. The reasons were many, but what she settled on at the moment was how he'd done everything in his power to keep Jake from being elected sheriff. Kate managed to keep her voice calm and polite, promising the mayor things were being handled and that Jake would call as he was able.

She hung up just as Charlie yelled—a high, piercing scream that echoed down the hallway. Kate reached for the shotgun propped against her desk. Charlie yelled again. She drew the weapon up and pointed the barrel ahead, stepping soft and quick across the foyer.

"What's wrong with you?" she asked.

Charlie didn't answer. Kate's legs grew heavy as she reached the hall. The shotgun twitched in her hands. She hugged the wall beyond Jake's office and inched closer, peering inside the cell.

Charlie sat hunched in the far corner. His eyes were pale moons and his lips, once thick and almost slippery, had shrunk into two thin lines. Sweat gathered at the tips of his black mop of hair.

"What's wrong with you?" Kate asked again. She eased her hand farther up the gun's forend, steadying the muzzle.

"I heard somethin'," Charlie said. "He's a-*comin'*. I know it."

"Who?"

Charlie spoke the name the way Kate once whispered *Bloody Mary* into the bathroom mirror as a child—soft and shaky, wanting to think it would take more than a mention to summon him forth but not really believing it: "*Taylor.*"

"Jake says he's gone."

"He ain't *gone*, woman. Don't you see? He won't leave 'til he finds Her."

"Who?"

His eyes were wide, searching. Then, almost as if he would rather not shoulder the burden of fear alone, Charlie added, "He never tole me. Maybe it's you."

Kate said, "Let him come." The shotgun's barrel drooped. She brought it back up to Charlie's chest. Her muscles clenched under the weight, creating a wave of dull heat across her back and shoulders. "Settle down, now. I got work."

"Don't you leave me," Charlie said. His face bore the hopeless expression of the lonely and the damned. "Please just stay here. I won't try nothin'. Swear on a Bible."

"You ever seen a Bible, maybe you wouldn't be in this mess," Kate said. "I'd leave you here to rot, Charles Givens. That man you hurt at the Texaco was my brother."

Tears sprouted from the dull whites of Charlie's eyes. His chin quivered. "I dint know he's your kin, ma'am. I . . . I's tryin' t'get his money's all. I'm just a poor hurtin' man. Please stay. I don't feel so good. Your brother did most of the beatin', if that settles you. Show me kindness."

Kate winced. Of all the things Charlie could say, he'd chosen that. Kindness had been asked, and now she was bound to give it. But with that burden came a flicker of something else that chased thoughts of Eric and Andy and even her own brother away, and that was the open notebook on her desk. In that moment, Kate saw Charles Earl Givens as neither man nor monster, but as a name. One she could write just below Lucy Seekins's and take her to page 212. One more step along the road.

"Sit in the rocker," she said.

Charlie rose from the corner. He sat rubbing his left arm.

Kate kept her back to the wall. "What brought you here, Charlie Givens? How'd you grow up to get inside that cell?"

Charlie shook his head, freeing a tear. It struck the floor in front of him. When he spoke, Kate thought he'd used what time he'd spent not cowering in fear inside the softball equipment locker to ponder that very question.

"I dunno, ma'am. I reckon we all set upon a trail. Sometimes there's paths that're good or bad shootin' off it, an' you either take 'em or you go on your way. But there ain't no more paths after awhile, an' that trail narrows. The trail's all you got then, an' it's just a straight line to heaven or hell."

The front door opened and closed. Kate turned toward the sound. "You sit there," she told Charlie, and then left him weeping and hugging himself in the rocker.

She found Jake on the sofa facing the door, hatless and still. His hands covered his face, though whether he was trying to hide from something or wipe something away Kate did not know. A videotape sat on the cushion beside his hat. She put her hand aside Jake's face. He gripped it in his own.

"Are you okay?" she asked.

He wasn't, Kate saw that much was plain. But she also saw that Jake was trying, and she would let him.

"It was bad, Katie," he said, and with those words came a smell on Jake's breath that rocked her on her heels. "Worst thing I ever saw in my life. Had to show Alan I could handle it, though."

Kate said, "Of course you can handle it," but the look on Jake's face was much the same as what Kate had seen on Charlie's. For the first time, she thought maybe her husband couldn't handle it at all. Maybe this was just too much.

"I'm gonna have to sit here with Charlie Givens," Jake said. "Alan'll be covered up at Andy's for a while, then he's gotta get to Timmy's. Why don't you take the Blazer. Go get Zach and head home."

"What about the other guy?" she asked. "Taylor. Charlie's scared to death, Jake."

"Alan says Taylor's long gone."

"What do you say?"

"I expect he is. Town's surrounded by police. Road past Timmy's leads straight on to Camden. That's where Charlie hails from. I think Taylor too. You'll both be fine. Just call me when you get home."

"You sure?"

"If he was still in town, Alan'd—I'd—have him by now." He looked down the hallway. "Charles Earl been any trouble?"

"No. He's too drunk and too scared to be trouble. I think he's sick too."

"Maybe I'll get Doc up here to take a look at him."

Kate nodded. "Will you be okay, Jake?"

"Sure."

Kate saw his smile as valiant if not true and kissed him for it. She gathered her notebook from the desk and paused at the door, unsure if she should tell Jake of Justus. She decided no. There'd been enough trouble for one night.

"Taylor's looking for someone," she said. "A girl. Charlie says he doesn't know who she is, but I'm not sure about that."

"I'll get it from him." He lifted the videotape. "Caught them in the act at Andy's."

That must have been a horror, Kate thought. She realized how the stink on his breath had gotten there. "I love you, Jake Barnett."

"Love you too, missy. I'll meet you at church in the morning."

Kate left Jake to Charlie and prayed for his sleep. She thought of Timmy and Andy and poor Eric as she drove the downtown streets in the direction of the Boyds' house. She thought of the notebook beside her and of Charlie Givens, that monster who deserved a place at Lucifer's table no more and no less than she. Her mind stalled there until the road in front of her rose up in a wall of iron bars. Kate stomped on the brake and let out a cry. She sat there, arms straight against the steering wheel, as the headlights shone off the metal sign above the gate:

Oak Lawn Cemetery.

Kate didn't know how she'd gotten that far on the other side of town, other than by means of some internal compass. She thought that might be true enough. Sooner or later, Oak Lawn was where all of Kate's roads led.

The gates were closed each night at sundown, but they'd gone unlocked ever since the padlock had gotten lost three years earlier. Kate got out and swung the gates open. The Blazer eased its way through three centuries of Mattingly's dearly departed until it reached the top of a small knoll. Kate parked there and carried her notebook among the silent dead until she came to a simple headstone. The white candle by the marker was the latest in a long line of many she had burned through the years. She struck a match from a small container and caught the wick. Light flickered upward, revealing the single name etched into the stone face.

MCBRIDE.

She knelt by Phillip's grave as the hard night swallowed her sobs. Just as with Charlie, there was no going back for Kate. There was only a straight line to heaven or hell paved with guilt and remorse. And try as she had all those years, Kate supposed she'd known since Phillip died where her own narrowing trail led.

· 10 ·

I remained on the sofa and didn't answer when Charlie's voice called, wanting to know where Kate had gone. I kept my hands over my face, scolding myself for not thinking of Andy or

Timmy or that poor boy Eric. What consumed me instead was the way I'd acted when Zach found that white butterfly; the way I'd flinched—twice—in front of Timmy at the Texaco; the few bits of Abigail's barbecue and slaw that currently stained the BP's parking lot.

Those hands over my face weren't there to wipe tears but to hide myself. I'd always been so careful, keeping all that in. Being tough. What was I doing, acting like that? Letting people *see* me like that? And I knew it wasn't because of anything that had happened that night, it was Phillip. It was Phillip keeping me from sleep, stripping me down until I broke like a twig rotted from the inside out, which was crazy because Phillip was a *dream*, Phillip was the *past*, and the past is something that's gone and never rises up again.

I was embarrassed, and that embarrassment gave way to an anger against Taylor and Charlie (who was still in the back squealing through his tears for Kate). It was against a God who allowed old men to be burned and young boys to be gutted and the peace I'd worked so long to build to be shattered.

But most of all it was an anger against myself. The town would need a hard man in the coming days. It would need a sheriff worthy of the name Barnett. And I decided then and there that if I couldn't be that sheriff, I could at least pretend. I grabbed the videotape and my hat and went to my office, where I fished through my keys until I found the one that unlocked the top left drawer of my desk. Stale air filled my nose as I pulled out the handle.

The 9mm Glock inside stared up at me. Official issue, Mayor Wallis had said on my first day. I'd opted for Bessie instead. But she would be of little use now, especially with a man who'd already called me a dumb hick cop. I inserted the magazine and tucked the gun at my back. The small color television with a built-in VCR Zach sometimes watched stood on a table in the corner. I put the videotape in and forwarded it, then unplugged the TV and set it on the vinyl chair. I slid both that and the chair behind my desk down the hallway.

Charlie stood as I arranged the chairs in front of the cell and plugged the cord into an outlet along the wall. I pushed a button. The screen glowed a snowy white.

"What's this?" he asked.

"Got some questions for you, Charlie Givens. And you're gonna answer them."

I sat in the empty chair and pushed Play. Charlie leaned forward as the pixels took on the shape of him and Taylor walking into the BP.

Bent over heaving in Andy's parking lot, I swore I'd never look at that tape again. That was a promise I meant to keep. I watched Charlie instead as his mind sputtered and jerked to sort out what he saw. His head lolled to the side as though the people on the television were both familiar and not. Kate was right—the man didn't look well.

"Where'd you get this?" he asked. "I ain't watchin' this. You hear me, Sheruff? Turn that thing off."

"No," I said.

"Turn it *off.*"

I shook my head. When Charlie covered his eyes, I kicked the cell bars with a boot, making him jump.

"You look, Charlie Givens," I said. "You don't turn loose your hands, I'll come in there and tie them down. You under-stand me?"

Charlie's body shook. "I don't wanna see it."

I kicked the bars again. *"Look."*

He lowered his hands slow, fingers digging into his cheeks. Charlie watched himself finger the cans of bug spray and

Taylor roam the aisles, saw Andy and Eric enter through the side door. He watched as Taylor disappeared and Charlie's argument with Eric began and Taylor came back. He watched as they killed and tried to kill. And when it was over, Charlie said, "I want a lawyer."

I chuckled. "Only lawyer in this town lives four houses down from the man whose head you lit on fire. He sits beside that man in church every Sunday and buys that man's gas twice a week. Trust me, Charlie Givens, that man finds out what you did, he's gonna want you just as dead as everyone else will."

"I ain't sayin nothin'."

"Yes, you are," I said. "You're going to sit right there and answer every question I ask."

"You don't scare me," Charlie said. "You don't even act like no real sheruff."

I leaned forward and pulled the pistol from behind my back. Charlie's eyes bulged as the barrel fell level with the bridge of his nose.

"You're right there, Charlie Givens," I said. "I'm no real sheriff at all. I'm just a tired man fighting his own ghosts. Nothing more."

He was crying again. I'd never seen a man cry so much.

"You're from Camden, right?" I asked. "So you know of country folk? We're a law-abiding people, Charlie. 'Course, some say we're backward. Unenlightened. They say we cling too much to our guns and our God. I suppose that's all true. But you know, maybe that doesn't make us the backward ones. Maybe it's everybody else who's all turned around. Could be that's why we don't always accept justice as the law applies. Sometimes our own's better."

Charlie's voice shook. "Your badge says you cain't touch me."

"You see a badge on me?"

He shook his head like a dog just out of a bath.

"You and me, Charlie, we're gonna talk. Not sheriff to prisoner. Man to man. You'll answer me straight. You lie, you're done. Understand?"

Charlie nodded.

"Good." I pointed to the television screen, which had gone back to snow. "Why'd you two do that?"

"All's I wanted's that ol' man's money, 'cause I cain't be no trash man no more. Taylor woke that boy. Not me."

"What's that mean? 'Woke.'"

"I dunno."

I thumbed the trigger back.

"No," Charlie screamed. "I swear, Sheruff, I dunno what that means. That's just Taylor's word. He's always tellin' me I'm sleepin' an he's awake, but I dunno what that *means*."

"What's Taylor's last name?"

"Hathcock."

"Where's he from?"

"Camden."

"You got an address?"

Charlie laughed. "Ain't no mail deliv'ry where Taylor lives. Ain't no *nothin'*, 'cept eyes."

I didn't know what that meant and gave Charlie's nonsense over to either fear, alcohol, or whatever fever was running through his body.

"Why'd you two come here?" I asked.

"Taylor said he'd get me money. He's trackin' somebody."

"A girl?"

"No. Somebody Taylor thinks knows where the girl is."

"Who?"

"I dunno."

"Who's the girl?"

"I *dunno*," Charlie said. "Taylor never tole me. He's always lookin' for Her, ever since I knowed him."

"And how long's that been?"

Charlie scrunched his eyes and rubbed his arm. His breaths came in short pants. "Twenty years, near. Got lost in the woods one day. Taylor found me. I go see him every month as payment an' bring him groceries. He gives me ginseng t'sell in return."

"Where you take these groceries?"

He shook his head and pleaded, "He'll kill me."

"I'll beat him to it if you don't talk," I said. "Where's Taylor? You tell me now."

Charlie winced. His eyes were on the gun, but I know he was seeing Taylor. He felt trapped. Not because he was surrounded by concrete and iron bars, but because the sands in his hourglass were quickly spilling away and there was no way for him to turn it over and start again. I had no doubt Charlie was sure Taylor would kill him if he told. I also had no doubt he was equally sure I would kill him if he didn't. In the end, I supposed he based his next words on whose hand he'd suffer by more.

"I ain't," he said. "Kill me if you wanna, Sheruff, but I ain't tellin'. Taylor, he's the devil, plain an' true. Devil sees everything."

We stared at one another in what became little more than a playground dare to see who would blink first. Charlie's eyes never budged. I thumbed the trigger back and lowered the gun.

"Get some sleep," I said. "You'll be getting a ride to county soon. There's covers on the cot. I'll be down in my office."

Charlie said, "Don't leave me, Sheruff."

I got up and moved to the light switch.

"Leave that light on, Sheruff? Please?"

My hand lingered. Half of me wanted to leave Charlie Givens in the darkness he'd given himself over to. The other half begged to offer him a mercy I'd never offered myself.

I left the lights buzzing and pushed the desk chair back to my office. The anger in me had burned out, leaving only pity. The pistol went back where I found it. I ejected the magazine before closing the drawer, just in case Zach ever found the key and his boyish curiosity got the best of him on some rainy afternoon. Not that it would matter. Mayor Wallis has always been a skinflint. Admitted it himself my first day on the job. That was why the magazine was empty. The pistol might have been official issue, but the bullets were my responsibility.

· 11 ·

Lucy waited until the man's breathing took on the slow rhythm of sleep before freeing her shoulders. It was not a difficult job. His hands had been quivering such that the knots held about as well as a child's when first learning to tie his shoes. She shimmied her shoulders and lifted her hands free. The knots around Lucy's feet were tighter and more difficult to see in the fading candlelight, but they didn't take long to loosen. A thick runner of wax from the candle closest to her pooled onto the table. The flame flickered twice and then died, plunging the cabin into near darkness. The remaining candle hissed as though mourning the loss of its companion. Lucy knew she had to be gone before that last light went out. The thought of spending the night with nothing more than a sliver of moonlight through a filthy window was more than she could bear.

But she had to wait until it was safe.

The man lay curled up on the cot no more than a dozen

feet away, legs drawn to his chest, resembling nothing but a shadow of the person who had trekked her through a haunted wilderness. Now he appeared as a little boy, lost and alone.

His book lay on the table beside a worn stub of pencil. Lucy could see the faded glue marks where a cover had once been. The first pages were curled upward and torn. The page on top (Lucy believed it was the book's table of contents, though the paper was so stained with dirt and sweat she couldn't be sure) had been sheared halfway down the spine and repaired with a layer of peeling Scotch tape. She looked at the cot and slowly drew the book to herself, angling it to the fading light as she turned the pages. Chicken scratch covered them all. They had been written upon, erased, and written upon again so many times that tiny holes had been worn into the paper, obliterating the original words beneath. Twice she made out *Charly* and *hole*, but nothing more.

Yet deciphering what the man on the cot had written didn't matter to Lucy nearly as much as deciphering why he had written it. Page after page, scrawl after scrawl, with little regard for spelling or punctuation. Almost, she thought, like some sort of stream of consciousness. Lucy looked at the body on the bed and thought this was a man trying to make sense of his life. Trying to find his answers.

Only a single page near the back had been spared, but before Lucy could read it the man released a torrent of sleep-filled cries that sounded as if death itself had him. She shut the book and pushed it across the table, where it fell and crashed onto the floor with a sharp *bang*. Her muscles tensed into a ball. The candle flickered. The man fell back into slumber. Lucy decided she could wait no longer.

No more than an hour had passed since her captor had warned her not to run, but now Lucy decided it was time to do just that. She stretched out her legs and winced. Her muscles ached from the long walk and her knees burned from the deep scratches left by her stumbles. Lucy raised herself as quietly as she could and walked to the door.

The moon would help her, and her ears. She'd heard the river as they'd climbed the last big hill to the cabin. If Lucy could find that, she felt sure she could be saved. Rivers always led to civilization, and that particular waterway cut straight through town. She reached for the shotgun beside the crates. It was heavy and loaded and felt like death. Lucy eased the door open, careful not to squeak the hinges. The memory of the dark shadow they'd met in the field gave her pause, as did the Hollow's deep night. But there was no other choice. Leaving would be a risk, but out there was the only way of getting back to her life.

Lucy stood at the open door and paused at that last thought—*back to my life*. The black confronted her like a wall. One perhaps not there to keep her in, but to caution against her going.

Out there is my best chance.

Of getting back to my life.

Yes. But what was the life to which Lucy Seekins would return? The one waiting for her in the big empty house on the hill. The one of loneliness and searching. The days of playing party girl at school and nights poring over her books, playing philosopher in her own thoughts as she searched for answers she knew would never satisfy her pain. The life where classmates called her cool to her face and whore when she turned away. The mother who was gone

(*And that's because of you*, Lucy reminded herself, *don't forget that*)

and the father who smelled of corn mash and who was about to send her away forever.

That life.

Lucy's hand went to the crooked ends and patchy tufts of her hair. She swayed on her heels. Something inside her broke away as the great truth of what had caused her troubles came to bear. She had arrived in Happy Hollow not because of the man on the cot, but because of the very life she was about to run back to.

She looked at the man and thought, *I want to be awake. I want to be like you.*

At the time, Lucy hadn't known if that had been the right thing to say (or, for that matter, if there even was a right thing to say). And yet she knew she'd spent the better part of her life asleep. Her every day felt like a nightmare in which she flailed in quicksand, sinking ever deeper the more she struggled for freedom. And she wanted nothing more than to have those dreams end, even if it took a madman to do it.

Lucy Seekins rested the shotgun against the wall and eased the door closed. She returned to her spot at the table, where she watched the man sleep until the last candle died.

· 12 ·

I was in my office when Kate called to say they were home and Zach was asleep. She offered no reason why it had taken so long to call, and I didn't ask. I knew she was bound for the cemetery when she kissed me good-bye. It had been the weight of her lips and the sadness with which she'd pressed them against mine. There had been times over the years when those trips to Phillip's grave (which ran at least monthly and sometimes once a week, if the names to Kate's notebook came quick enough) became too much for me. I said nothing, though, neither that time nor all the others. Some pasts exist as a fog that rolls in and out of the present, formed not by air that condenses into mist but memories that condense into tiny doors that open to forgotten moments. Maybe you glance at a stranger on a crowded street who reminds you of a childhood friend or hear a song that was popular the first summer you fell in love, and in the space of that single beat of time you are flung backward to a who or a when long past. And yet it is only for that one beat. Those tiny doors never remain open for long for most of us. They ensure our former times are kept as relics, and the dust upon them is wiped clean only occasionally.

Yet the door to Kate's *when* was forever propped open. Her past existed as a light that shone upon her every day, blinding her to all else. Everyone else could see that past as well. All you had to do was drive through the gates of Oak Lawn and climb the knoll.

I told Kate I'd meet her and Zach at church and then called Alan Martin with Taylor's last name. Alan said he'd get in touch with the Camden sheriff and be down to collect Charlie. I hung up, leaned back in the chair, and put my feet atop the desk.

From the hallway came, "Sheruff, you still there?"

"I am," I yelled. "Go t'sleep, Charlie."

Charlie wept. The dark outside the windows and the faint hum of the office lights brought that familiar heaviness, and I felt my body draw away like a low tide. I stood before sleep could take hold, not wanting to be found dozing when Alan arrived, not wanting to see Phillip more. Doc March's pills sat next to the phone. I couldn't remember if they were to keep me awake or put me so far under I wouldn't dream of anything, so I let them be. I moved to the bookcase instead and brushed aside the uniform Mayor Wallis had presented to me along with the pistol. The thick plastic bag with *Kimball's Dry Cleaning—Stanley, VA* stenciled across the front had never been unzipped. I watched the office lights flicker at the edges of the silver name tag above the pocket—it read BARNETT, nothing else—and remembered what I'd said to Kate and the mayor that day:

"I don't need a uniform. Everyone knows who I am."

Of course what I'd meant was, I'll store the softball equipment in the cell and take the Widow Cash to market every Monday and I'll ride in the parades, but don't expect anything else from me because the only reason I took this job was so I'd never find trouble again.

The uniform made a soft swooshing sound when I brushed it aside. I reached onto the shelf behind and brought Hollis's jar to my desk. The tide in me retreated further, building, making me sit. I couldn't remember if Hollis had said Jenny was good for remembering or forgetting. I didn't care as long as she kept me awake. The lid hissed and popped as I wedged it open. The scent of peach filled the air.

I toasted dead boys and living burdens and turned the jar upward. Cold fire washed over my teeth and gums. My throat clenched and let go, forming a vacuum that sucked most of the moonshine down. Every nerve in my body protested. I bent over, gagging as tears wet my eyes.

From down the hall: "Sheruff? I need you, Sheruff. Something's goin' on."

"What's wrong?" I asked, but my voice was clipped and hoarse and barely carried beyond the door.

"Sheruff, help me, Sheruff."

The tide rushed in. It was a roaring wall of sleep that turned my bones to liquid. I fell back into the chair and tried to push myself up—

"Sher . . . huff . . ."

—but couldn't. The tiredness held. So tired. Of that weight, of that everything. My eyes fell on Bessie. I'd need Bessie, Charlie needed help and he was scared. I moved my hand and *stretch for another heavy stone to place upon the ever-growing mound of rocks beneath my feet. The cliffs tower over me, framing a dying sun. White butterflies fill the trees around us. I look down, but Phillip isn't there. He stands along the riverbank now, peering out from beneath the drawn hood of his sweatshirt. I place the rock atop the mound anyway, trying to cover the place where he doesn't lie, hoping I can still hide him, that I can still make him go away.*

It won't work, Jake, *he says.* Do you know why?

"I need to go back," I scream.

No, Jake, *he says.* There's no more back. Back is dead. You're all dead.

I lift another rock, place it down. The mound grows high against the drawing sky. My own Tower of Babel.

"Charlie's in trouble."

He's no paths left, Jake. Just as the boy Eric. I was there, Jake. Do you know that? I stood with him as the angels bore him away. Do not mourn him. Mourn Charlie. He's come to the end of his choosing. He's met his end.

Phillip raises his fist the same as before, the same as always. His bloody fingernails gleam in the evening.

Do you remember, Jake? I'm coming. I'm coming to give you this.

"No," I scream. "I don't want it I just WANT YOU TO LEAVE ME ALONE."

I'm coming, Jake. I'm coming for you all.

*Phillip inches his fist closer, lifting it to me. The Hollow seems to lengthen and widen around us, as though taking a deep breath. Phillip's fingers begin to loosen, and I scre*amed and jumped from

the chair, toppling it into the wall. Silence filled the office.
There were no calls for Sheruff. I reached for Bessie (knocking over both Doc's and Hollis's medicines in the process) and
raced down the hall.

The figure inside the cell was still, mouth open to his chest
in an expression of frozen surprise. Vacant eyes stared out at
nothing.

Charlie Givens was dead.

Standing there staring at him, not knowing what to do
and wanting nothing more than to wake up, I believed Phillip
McBride had come for him.

And I believed I was next.

· 13 ·

The Sunday edition of the *Mattingly Gazette* was the week's
largest and most important. As such, it took the longest to
compile. That night it had taken even longer than usual,
because Trevor Morgan kept having to answer the phone.

At first he counted the calls as the very sort of breathless
speculation that had sold many a Sunday edition over the years.
And yet the calls had kept coming, and from all over. Saying
that *something*—that was what they always said, people never
used the precise nouns and detailed verbs Trevor Morgan had
built his life upon—had happened down at the BP, and that
something else had happened up at the Texaco, and Jake Barnett
had been seen driving with his flasher on. None of this was
enough to take Trevor away from his assigned duties, however.
He'd chased late-night phone calls before, only to find the
vague *something* nothing more than a wayward cow or swamp
gas or someone dipping into Hollis Devereaux's moonshine.

But then the mayor had called, and what Trevor Morgan's uncle said was fuzzy enough to excite and terse enough to frighten—"Get down to the sheriff's office, and hurry up. Something's happened."

The foyer stood empty when Trevor arrived. He thought that odd, considering he'd parked behind Jake's beat-up Blazer, the mayor's Caddy, Doc March's pickup, and two county police vehicles. He looked through the window into Jake's office. Empty too.

"Hello?" he called. "Anybody here?"

A noise from down the hallway. Mayor Wallis walked around the corner. An unlit half of a cigar poked from the wrinkles around his mouth. Gone were the ramrod posture and unflappable confidence Big Jim had cultivated over the years. In their place were slumped shoulders that squeezed his swollen paunch into a rectangle between a pair of red suspenders and the top of his blue dress pants. He rubbed his sparse head, turning his comb-over into a push-down.

"Hey, Uncle Jimmy," Trevor said. "What's going on?"

"We're on the clock, Trevor. It's Mayor Wallis." He fingered the gray stubble on his chin and winced. "Come on, boy. It's all back here."

Big Jim turned and disappeared back down the hallway. Trevor followed, mindful that the bottom half of his stomach had firmly pressed against his spine. He turned the corner to find the mayor settled next to a suited county man he did not know. Jake stood to the man's left. His face held a milky pallor and his hair was slick with sweat, making what looked like dark commas plunge down over his ears.

Trevor said, "Hey, Jake."

The sheriff nodded and made his way over. "Trevor, what're you doing here?"

"Big Jim called me."

Jake nodded and leaned in close. When he whispered, the small patch of space between them filled with the scent of peaches.

"Can I ask you something, Trevor?"

"Sure, Jake."

"Am I awake?"

"What?" Trevor turned from Jake to Mayor Wallis, asked, "What's going—" and then stopped as he followed Big Jim's gaze into the cell, where a county coroner stood watching Doc March flash a small penlight into a dead man's eyes. "—on?" he finished. "Holy cow, Jake, who is that? What happened?"

"That's a good question," Big Jim asked. "Evidently the whole town went to pot a few hours ago, and the sheriff never bothered to let me know."

"Jake's been a little busy tonight, Mayor," the man in the suit said.

Trevor turned to him. "I don't believe we've met, Mr. . . . ."

"Martin. Alan Martin. County."

"You shoulda called me, Jake," the mayor said. "Dang it all, you shoulda called me as soon as you heard about Andy."

"Andy?" Trevor asked, remembering the calls. "Andy Sommerville? What happened to Andy?" He reached into his back pocket for his notebook.

Big Jim slapped it away. "Leave that stupid thing alone, Trevor. We're still trying to figure out what happened here."

From inside the cell, Doc March turned and said, "Excuse me, gentlemen, but could you continue this discussion elsewhere? There is grave work to do, if you'll pardon the pun."

"Sure, Doc," Jake said.

Mayor Wallis led the way to the foyer and sat on the sofa. Trevor and Jake followed. Alan remained behind to survey the scene. Trevor supposed the county man smart enough to leave small-town business to small-town folk.

If the mayor looked older that night, Jake appeared almost ancient. Trevor knew the town had been whispering that something (that word, again) was wrong with their constable, though no conclusions had been reached. Some speculated Jake had taken to visiting Hollis's backwoods, others that it was trouble with Kate. Nothing would please Trevor more than the latter. Most every red-blooded Mattingly male between twenty and fifty had crushed on the former Kate Griffith at one time or another. To Trevor's generation, it was as much a part of crossing the bridge from boy to man as carving one's name into the rusty gate, even after that nasty thing she did to the McBride boy became public knowledge those years ago.

Yet Trevor had never defined what he felt for Kate as mere infatuation, nor was it a boyhood crush. Some people were for the fairy tale. Trevor always thought Kate was his destiny, but he never got that chance. The thin gold ring on her finger had been put there by Jake instead, and the only thing that grated on Trevor Morgan more was that the man who'd stolen his love had slid into the job of sheriff simply because of his last name. That Trevor's own uncle had handed over the keys to the *Gazette* just after being elected never entered into the equation. The difference was that Trevor did his job well, and Jake never could.

"Who's that man in there, Jake?" Big Jim asked.

Trevor reached into his pocket again. This time the mayor didn't slap the notebook away. Jake began with the call from Timmy and ended with finding Charlie dead. Trevor scribbled with passion, not believing his luck. Murder. Mystery. Mayhem. It was perfect, the story of a lifetime.

Big Jim shook his head. "This is gonna be hard on the town, Jake. Hard on all'us."

"It will," Jake admitted. "But the storm's passed, Jim. We just have to try and clean up so we can all get back to normal."

Trevor thought that made a good quote and wrote it down, then reconsidered. Even a rookie journalist knew the difference between a source who said what he knew to be true and what he wanted to be true. Trevor thought the good sheriff was engaging more in the latter. He also thought Jake had left a good bit out of his story. If so, then maybe the storm hadn't passed at all. Maybe this was simply the first head winds.

Doc March, Alan, and the coroner made their way up the hallway.

"What's the verdict, Doc?" the mayor asked.

The doctor looked at Jake, who offered a weak nod.

"The preliminary examination is that the poor man died of natural causes," Doc said. "I'd say a heart attack."

"C'mon, Doc," Jake said. "That guy was my age."

"Can happen to anyone, Jacob, not just old fogies like Jim and me. Tell me, what was his emotional state?"

Trevor poised his pen above a fresh sheet of paper.

"He was drunk," Jake said. "Mad. Scared. I don't know, Doc. Mostly scared."

"Of what?"

Jake said nothing, only looked at them. It was enough time for Trevor to set aside his bias and believe on the facts alone that Jake Barnett had gotten into something he couldn't get out of and was trying to cover himself.

"I don't know," he said. "Charlie thought Taylor Hathcock was coming after him. Said he was the devil. He was pretty worked up."

"Well then, there you are." Doc folded his wrinkled hands behind his back as though waiting for applause. "It's fight-or-flight, of course. The body's natural way of protecting itself.

If one is faced with a life-threatening situation—and from what you say, Jake, Charlie Givens certainly believed he was in one—the body responds by supercharging itself with adrenaline. That chemical is extremely dangerous in large amounts, especially in unhealthy people. Most deaths are due to damage to the heart. My opinion, and this good man beside me concurs, is that's what happened here. Charlie was in a cell, so he couldn't flee. Fear was all he had, and that was his end."

"Wait," Trevor said. He'd written all of that down, but he needed Doc to say the right words. "You're saying the man in there was . . . scared to death?"

"In a manner of speaking."

Jackpot.

Alan spoke up: "Your doc's findings line up with the coroner's prelims. I'm gonna get this guy outta here for you, Jake. I'll need that tape too." He turned to Big Jim. "We have roadblocks set up all through the area, Mayor. We'll find Taylor Hathcock. Just a matter of time."

Trevor excused himself. He had to get back to the office, make some calls. Vicki Chambers, the *Gazette*'s receptionist, then Steve Ramsey, the cub reporter. The Sunday paper would be late, but it would be worth it.

Jake met him at the door and held it closed by pressing his hand against the fresh paint.

"Listen, Trevor. This all might make you giddy inside, but it's gonna put a scare in people come morning. I know you have to write something, and I won't stop you. But you do it right, you hear me? Just the facts."

"Sure, Jake. Wouldn't have it any other way."

Trevor smiled on the outside, hoping Jake couldn't see the cackle oozing up from behind his teeth. Unlike most everyone else in town, Trevor Morgan knew the sheriff was not his father's son, at least when it came to temperament. That almighty Barnett name only carried so far. This was the story he'd always prayed to catch, and it was one he could milk for weeks.

But first he'd have to write it.

Huge letters for the headline. An editorial for the op-ed page too, the title of which came to him on the way back to the newspaper. And it was so perfect, so utterly wonderful, that he thought it'd been sent via heavenly messenger.

Part III

The Devil Walks in Mattingly

· 1 ·

Kate slept alone that night, though this time it wasn't because of her husband's dreams. Jake had stayed at the office. Too tired to drive home, he'd said over the phone. Kate suspected it was something else when Jake told her of Charlie's death and what Doc March had said was the cause. He also told her that Trevor Morgan had made an appearance. She knew what that meant. There would be one doozy of a story in the *Gazette* come morning.

The newspaper box was empty when Kate and Zach left the house, confirming her fears. It was early, though—just after six o'clock, and Kate soothed herself by saying the paper never came before six thirty. She had little time to worry, though. Church would start in three hours, and she had to make it across town and back before the church bells rang. She ran her errand (which turned out to be quite a nice bit of police work, if she said so herself) and pulled into First Church lot just in time.

The First Church of the Risen Christ—the marquee out front of which continually announced OUR DOORS ARE

WIDE OPEN AND OUR MINDS ARE MADE UP—had stood for over a century on a stately plot of tree-lined earth three blocks from the town center. Though the Lord had His pick of spots to reside in Mattingly (there were eight churches within the town limits alone; "One for every color of the rainbow," Kate liked to say), most were of a common accord that He dwelled in First Church most often. Reverend Reggie Goggins had both the largest congregation and the mayor's ear, a powerful combination. The lot was expansive, but on that morning the crowd was such that Kate had to park in the grass between two blooming magnolias. That was her first clue that word had already spread; even the backsliders packed the pews when the world bared its claws.

Kate wiped a streak of strawberry Pop-Tart from the corner of Zach's mouth and tried not to look at his black eye. A crowd had gathered at the steps leading into the sanctuary. A dozen people or so, all attired in their Sunday best. When Kate saw all those people, she wished she'd driven slower. Or stopped at the sheriff's office to pick up Jake first. But there hadn't been time for that, not with the quick trip to Andy's house and the talk Kate had with a murdered boy's brother.

"When's Daddy comin'?" Zach asked.

"Soon, baby."

They moved in the grassy places among old cars and dirty trucks, where the ground was peppered with blooming dandelions. Kate stepped through these as though navigating a minefield, careful not to let a single yellow flower brush against her. She knew she looked like a fool even as tremors of nausea built in her stomach. It was a running joke between Kate and Jake, the way she hated those weeds. It would remain funny until the moment near the rusty gate when she remembered true. Zach willed his body forward, trying to keep up. Kate's blue dress ruffled in the breeze. A county police car drove by. The crowd followed it with their eyes.

The crowd hushed when they saw Kate and broke away from the stairs toward her. Reggie Goggins led the charge. Kate reached down and lifted Zach up, holding him close. He yawned and settled his face into the crook of his momma's neck. The preacher extended both hands as he neared and took the free one Kate offered.

"Hello, Kate," he said.

"Reverend."

The people pressed in, friends with worried eyes and harried faces. Kate took their questions one by one, wanting to get inside but not wanting to deepen their fears by turning them away.

Yes, Andy was hurt and his friend Eric had been murdered.

Yes, Timmy was hurt too, but he was going to be fine.

Yes, Jake had gotten one of the men and the other was still loose, but he was likely far away by now.

Yes, the man Jake arrested died overnight.

Kate said all of these things, pausing for the Sweet-Jesuses and Lord-have-mercies the crowd offered, all the while knowing she wasn't really comforting anyone and Zach was hearing it all. She cupped her boy's head too late for him to un-hear, but it was soon enough to block the words Hollis Devereaux then spoke.

"Ol' Jake'd never let anyone get away with somthin' like that," he said. "Bet he took care'a that fella afore the courts could. Prolly used Bessie to do it."

There were nods and more than one amen to that notion, which offended the preacher at least partway and Kate completely.

"Jake did no such thing, Hollis Devereaux," she said, "and how dare you say otherwise."

The old man tilted his head downward, pushing his beard into his wide chest. Edith Devereaux, who was so deaf that her ears served only to hold up her thick glasses, patted her husband on the arm and asked what was wrong.

"Jake is a good man," Kate said.

"That's what I'm sayin'," Hollis told her. "He's a Barnett, Kate. That's all."

The bell tolled, summoning them all inside. Hollis apologized for whatever slight he'd offered. Kate took the hand that Preacher Goggins released and put it on Hollis's back. She told him it was fine and she was sorry, that they'd all had a long night.

She and Zach sat in the Barnetts' accustomed pew, midway along the left side of the sanctuary. Word spread from those who'd been outside with Kate to those who hadn't. The soft sound of organ music mixed with even softer smells—the oil on the pews, the musty pages of the hymnals, the perfumes and colognes of the congregants.

The buzzing ceased when Jake stepped inside the sanctuary and removed his hat. He kept his head low and walked the outer aisle to where Kate waited. His clothes had gone unchanged since the morning before, and his hair was a tangled bird's nest that somehow complemented the look on his face. He smiled. To Kate, it was the same nothing-to-see-here grin that had greeted her and Doc March at the office the day before. She reached up and took hold of him.

Jake settled between her and Zach, who hugged his father and said, "Didja get the bad man, Daddy?"

"I did."

Reverend Goggins rose as the organ finished and began his welcome. Kate leaned over and asked, "Are you okay?"

"Been better."

Heads bowed for the opening prayer. The preacher thanked

the Lord for the blessing of a new day, however hard that day was, and asked for protection over the town and a healing for the broken. After that came a moment of silent reflection. Kate, having prayed herself out sometime between Jake calling about Charlie's death and her idea of how to get in touch with Eric's family, looked at her husband instead.

Jake's eyes were clenched shut, lips pursed into a look of pain. He lifted his head only partway when the reverend said his amen, keeping his eyes angled down to the hymnals in the rack. Such was the way Jake Barnett always conducted himself in the presence of God. Kate believed it was her husband's deep piety that rendered him such when in the presence of the Lord, though that particular day she gave it more to his deep exhaustion.

She leaned over and said, "I got hold of Eric's brother."

He turned to her. "How?"

"Came to me last night. I figured he knew Eric was with Andy, them being so close. And I figured that if Eric never came home, his brother'd call Andy's house. I went over there with Zach this morning. Door was unlocked. There were four messages on Andy's phone, all from him. Their last name's Thayer."

"You talked to him?"

Kate nodded as the preacher spoke of the week's events—the Tuesday night softball game against Mattingly Methodist, the Bible study Wednesday night, the cookout next Saturday afternoon. All important things that now seemed unimportant to everyone, Preacher Goggins included.

"Hardest thing I've ever had to do, Jake. We didn't talk long. I couldn't, what with Zach there. Eric's brother—Jabber's what he calls himself—said he needed to get to the hospital. He wanted to know if you could meet him at the BP. Said there was something he needed to get."

"What is it?" Jake asked.

"He wouldn't say, but I told him you'd meet him down there after dinner. I'm sure it's nothing Alan Martin can't part with."

"Okay. I'll get down there."

Kate said nothing for the rest of the service and moved only to scratch a spot on her left foot, where she feared a dandelion had brushed. It was enough to have Jake there, even if it felt to her like a part of him had fallen missing. They sang old hymns and passed a plate full of ones and fives, the bounty of common folk. Preacher Goggins announced that given the events of the previous night, his sermon would not be the one he'd prepared. He spoke of the pain of this world and the darkness that shrouds its every corner, even a place so peaceful and good as Mattingly. He talked of the burdens of living and the faith needed to overcome them, and Kate found her heart opened and raw. It was like cool water poured into a fresh wound.

When the final blessing was given and the congregation was sent back out into the world, two sights greeted the congregation. One was another county police car making its rounds in search of a murderer. The other was Trevor Morgan happily stuffing a thick stack of Sunday papers into the box across the street.

· 2 ·

Taylor woke believing it had been a nightmare, that was all. Nothing more than the ones that had come all those times before. What told him otherwise was the lady staring at him from the table.

Memories like butterflies fluttered from his reach the more he grabbed for them, then settled as Taylor's mind stilled. He saw the boy he'd Woke and the old man who'd tried to stop him. He remembered Charlie and the Texaco. And he remembered her—the girl with the hair of a woebegone boy. She had saved him, had sworn she was Awake and then confessed she was not but wanted to be. Taylor remembered tying her in the chair before his weariness took hold. Now the rope lay in a coiled pile upon the dusty floor.

A wan smile crossed her face. Delicate branches of smooth skin wound their way down her sullied cheeks, marking paths where tears had fallen. She wiped her nose with a hand that had sprouted a crop of brown and black bruises.

"Your knots weren't tight enough," she said.

Taylor eased his weight onto an elbow and winced. His lower back felt stuffed with gravel and his pulse thumped through the wound on his head. He worked his jaws loose and said, "You didn't go."

"No." She turned her head toward the shotgun against the wall. "Could have. Could have killed you the same way you were going to kill me."

"I don't kill," Taylor said. He rose and managed to take three wobbling steps toward her. "Killin's a sin." He took his book and looked through the lone window. The sun was already over the mountains. By now everyone down in town would know what had happened. As would She. "Reckon you're hungry, Miss . . ."

"Lucy," she said, and Taylor had a vague notion she'd told him that the night before. "Lucy Seekins. And I think I should know the name of the man who kept me last night."

"Taylor Hathcock. Pleasure."

He went to the stacked crates along the wall and removed the burlap sack, then unrolled it on the table in front of Lucy. Her eyes widened at the flint knife. Taylor felt the deer sinew that fastened the blade to the stag handle. All those years, and it still held true.

"Are you going to hurt me, Taylor?" Lucy asked.

He wasn't. Taylor remembered pointing the shotgun at her, not wanting to hurt but willing to just the same. But she'd stayed. The girl had saved him and then she'd *stayed*.

He tucked the blade into his belt. "Left my other knife in town. Meant to keep this hidden away forever. It has power. But a man needs blade and barrel if he's to live out here. Why didn't you flee from this place, lady? Did fear hold you when my own binds couldn't?"

Taylor looked into her eyes, searching. The night had changed her. Night in the Hollow often did that. It forced one's eyes inward. Where Taylor had seen falsehoods the night before, he only saw truth now. The lady no longer cared what would be safe to say and what would be dangerous. It was truth Lucy Seekins would speak now, and Taylor saw she would follow that road where it led.

She said, "I didn't have anywhere else to go."

The morning stood bright, the sunlight glinting off what few leaves the dark forest allowed to grow. A soft breeze carried the perfume of wildflowers and earth. The day was as perfect as one could be in the Hollow. And yet Taylor closed his eyes to all that beauty upon hearing those words. He knew the hurt of having neither hope nor home.

"I won't harm you," he said. But knowing what he wouldn't do to Lucy wasn't the same as knowing what he would, and on that Taylor had no notion. He reached into the top crate for the binoculars. "We need a word. Some Twinkies somewhere in these crates, I imagine. Charlie liked to squirrel them away. Water's in the barrel out front."

Taylor left her and limped across the small clearing to the

edge of his ridgetop. He sat on the rotten log and wrote first, spelling out as best he could what he remembered from the night before, then pointed the lenses to town. Lucy followed shortly after and sat on the far end of the log. Charlie's spot, Taylor thought, and he thought he would always refer to it as such. He passed the binoculars over the BP first, then the Texaco. Both had been roped off by the police, the parking lots empty. Downtown looked strangely quiet as well. Tiny blobs of people moved about on their way to worship. There was no sign of Charlie. Taylor wrote that down.

"What are you looking at?" Lucy asked.

"Pain and despair, lady." Taylor looked at her, saw the way Lucy's eyes drooped and her mouth tilted down at the corners. Her hair stuck out like blunt spikes in some places and lay matted in others. "Seems to me you may know of such things."

Lucy ignored that. Said, "You can't see much through those. One of the lenses is missing."

Taylor handed the binoculars over. "See for yourself."

She took hold of them by the brass casing and brought the eyepieces up. Taylor watched Lucy's bottom lip give way. She brought the binoculars down and turned them over in her hands like they were a piece of alien technology. Which, he figured, maybe wasn't far from the truth.

"How's that possible?" Lucy brought the lenses up again and smiled. "I can see almost *everything.*"

Taylor felt a sharp pang of jealousy at the way they looked stuck to her eyes. No one had ever looked through his spy-glasses. Charlie had never even asked. They were Taylor's alone, and yet he'd handed them over to this girl like something had taken his brain hostage, like

I was supposed to.

Yes, like that. Like that exactly. As though a divine hand

was gaming things, arranging them and assigning meaning. Just like the cabin and the binoculars themselves. Like the rotten log upon which he sat, there at the perfect spot to gaze down over the valley and the town. Lucy looked at him, her pale smile brighter now, and Taylor gave himself over to the belief that this was perhaps the way things were supposed to unfold all along— something had to come up from the grove so Taylor would take Charlie to town so the boy could be woke so they could go to the Texaco so Charlie could be lost so Lucy Seekins could come.

"You said last night you was Awake," he said. "Then you said no. Then you said you wanted to be. Which of them was fiction? I'd have your answer, lady, and I'd have it true."

Lucy's smile disappeared. She handed the binoculars back to Taylor.

"I was scared." She looked away, down into the valley. The wind played with her hair. "I didn't understand. The rope came off right after you fell asleep. I thought about running away."

"Holler would've taken you. There's things here that're hungry, lady, and for more than meat."

"Maybe," she said. "I was going to try anyway, though. But then I thought about what you said. I want to know what you meant."

"I'll speak to it as much as I'm able," Taylor said. "It's nothing I've spoken to afore. I believe I must, as we've been drawn together." Taylor rubbed his beard, not sure where to start or how much to say. "I come to this wood as a young'un. You'll find that hard to believe. No one comes to Happy Holler, you'd say, but I did. Ma an' Pa's gone then. He's a drunk and cared not for me. She cared for any man but not the seeds they'd plant in her. I was with my aunt then, but I come here for good when I was of age. I imagine she was glad to see me go.

"I was running, you see. We all run from something, Lucy

Seekins, and I remember it was a terrible thing before it turned beautiful. Sometimes I still dream of it, but in that dream all I hear's voices in shadow. That's when I found this place. Found that cabin. There was a fresh stack of wood in the hearth, but no ashes. Cot was made but not slept in, and there was the busted mandolin agin' the wall. Fresh water in the barrel outside, like it'd been just poured. And these here spyglasses sitting in the middle of the floor. It was like someone put all this here just for me. Don't know who built it all. Maybe it's always here, waitin'. So I stayed on. I stayed and I found the truth."

"What truth?" Lucy asked.

And so here it was.

Taylor rose from the log. When he bent down in front of Lucy, she did not flinch.

"The truth, lady, is that all you see through those spyglasses, all you know and think and feel, all you *believe*, is. Not. Real."

He paused and held out his arms to catch her, lest the power of that revelation fling Lucy forward. She stared at him, trying to understand, and Taylor offered a slow nod that was both hopeful and sad. Lucy's swollen belly jiggled beneath her shirt. A guttural sound worked its way from her lips. Then she exploded into a cackle that slid her backward rather than forward.

"What'd you say?" she asked.

"This whole world, lady. Ain't none of it real. All's a dream."

Lucy bent forward and fell into the kind of laughter so intense and all-encompassing that it's rendered soundless. Taylor slowly drew his outstretched arms back to himself, vaguely aware that his hands had curled into fists.

"Are you kidding me?" Lucy asked. "You're loopin' *crazy*."

"Why's that?"

"Why?" She was upright now (her body, anyway, Taylor

thought on her insides Lucy Seekins was stuck in a perpetual slouch), and her laughter had gone to calm. *"Because."*

"No," Taylor said. "Not good enough, lady. You think I'm wrong, prove it."

"You think you're right, prove it."

She was having fun. Taylor couldn't understand why that was so, but she was. And that she was in such a shiny mood in the midst of the spookiest wood in ten counties made him even more certain their meeting was no accident. It was meant to be.

"Do you know you're in a dream when you're dreaming?" he asked.

"No," Lucy said, "but I know I'm awake now."

Taylor snapped his fingers, making her at once flinch and giggle. "So you say. So everybody says. But how do you *know?*"

Lucy chortled again. "Because I'm sitting here talking to you."

"But how do you *know?* You don't. You only think you're awake because you never supposed you ain't."

Lucy shook her head, but it wasn't a hard shake. She smiled, but that grin was not solid. She ran a hand over her head and down the back, stopping when she felt no more hair.

"You're wrong," she said, and yet Taylor heard those words tinged with a weary sadness. It was as if Lucy had said that not because he was wrong but because no amount of wishing would make him right.

"Tell me what's wrong about it," he said. "Go on, because you cain't. I know you cain't, just as I know we were brung together. You tell me you've never once said you're sure of what's true and what's false. Tell me you never felt a pain so deep and been in trouble so bad you swore it weren't real. Confess that you never been deceived by what you feel and what you believe." Taylor leaned in closer. "Tell me, lady, you never searched your heart and knowed there was something beyond, some other place that's not here you know is home."

Lucy sat staring at him as the Hollow's weak puffs of breeze played with the remnants of her hair. Taylor, seeing her silence but not her thoughts, only took all of that as more doubt. He looked away toward Mattingly, this time with only his eyes. The town looked smaller that way, less dangerous, though he knew that was a lie. If he would ever find who had walked out of the Hollow—if he would ever find Her—he would need Lucy's help. The only way she would help was if she believed. And the only way she would believe was if she saw. He did not begrudge Lucy for that. Sight always came first, faith trailed after. It had been true for him, and Taylor supposed it was true for all.

"I'll show you, Lucy Seekins," he said. "I'll prove you I'm right. I know a special place. Charlie, he always wants to see it. Tells me all the time. But I tell'm nosir, Charlie, that place is holy and not for you. But I'll show you, lady, just so you'll know. Then you'll see. Then you'll believe."

· 3 ·

THE DEVIL WALKS IN MATTINGLY
A special editorial by Trevor Morgan,
Editor and Publisher

For nearly three hundred years, the town of Mattingly has epitomized the ideal of Rockwellian charm. Our needs are basic, our wants few. Our children roam free in unspoiled wilderness and play upon streets both safe and clean. Danger and crime are nonexistent. Society as it exists on the evening news is a peculiar and foreign place. Those among us who must venture into that world for work or travel do so as outsiders whose hearts are continually bent toward home.

Perhaps it was arrogance that convinced us it would always be this way. Perhaps it was ignorance with which we believed we could venture into that bizarre otherness without that otherness venturing into us. Regardless, our fair town has now taken the full brunt of what it means to live in a violent age. Mattingly could not hide forever. The world has found us.

The coming days will no doubt bring much reflection regarding the crimes of Taylor Hathcock and Charles Givens. For now our fair hamlet must weather the numbing shock associated with their heinous acts.

And yet that these two men killed and maimed with evil in their hearts is not the issue. What burden we must now bear is the intent behind those acts. The town of Mattingly should fear less what happened on its quiet streets only last night than the motive that could drive two men to rob a town of its innocence.

Dare it be asked if that motive was the result of deeper ills that reside not only in the hearts of Taylor Hathcock and Charles Givens but in us all? Can it be said that even in the midst of such wickedness, there is a divine hand?

Such were the questions this writer considered while gazing upon the lifeless body of Charles Earl Givens. Such was the feeling of dread when our sheriff stated that Charles Earl believed his accomplice to be none other than Lucifer himself. Such was the notion of judgment when our own imminently respected doctor pronounced that death as the result of fear—fear of the very man who may still lurk within Mattingly's boundaries.

The citizens will make their own determination. And yet in the mind of one who has kept a hand to the faint pulse of our town for over a decade, there can be no doubt that not all is as it appears. For are not all offenders alike, each burdened with debts we cannot repay? Are there any who could stand in front of that great Judge without the downcast eyes and crestfallen face of the guilty?

Dare it be asked if Taylor Hathcock's and Charlie Givens's actions are the punishment for our own collective failures? Did our own evils invite this end upon us, knowingly or otherwise?

Perhaps. If that is the case, then we must fear the coming days. One can only hope our elected sheriff can rise to the occasion. For now we may all say the worst period in Mattingly's history began on a Saturday night at a beloved citizen's place of business, but we have yet to know where it will end.

It was the same all over town. Everyone clamored for their own copy of the *Gazette*, drawn by the blaring front page headline (TWO DEAD, ONE SOUGHT IN GAS STATION ROBBERY) and an article that took up most of the first two pages. But it was Trevor's editorial that stirred them all, and in places many had gone to great lengths to leave quiet.

Some read for answers, wanting to understand the in-comprehensible. Others sought to reinforce rumors that had already spread. A few simply wanted copies to tuck away as keepsakes, hoping they would be able to take them out again on some far-off day as a reminder that, even in this, people found a way to move on.

Trevor Morgan spent that Sunday afternoon cleaning his tiny apartment above the *Gazette* and trying to decide the best place to display the Pulitzer that would surely come.

Hollis Devereaux shouted both the front page story and the editorial to Edith from the quiet of their front porch. He was tired from the long trip they'd taken to the hill country after church. He was more tired once the reading was done. Edith wondered aloud what sin could bring such evil to their town. Hollis kept silent. He thought long of Jenny.

Mayor Jim Wallis remained inside his spacious house on Maple Street the entire afternoon. He meant to throw his nephew's article away as soon as he read it—Trevor had gone overboard before, but Big Jim thought this was a whole new level of blather—but found he couldn't. The newspaper remained open on his lap a long while. Big Jim had long comforted himself in the belief that one had to wallow in the muck from time to time in order to be a good politician—for the good of the town, he'd always told himself. Those words rang hollow now. There were so many things to be ashamed of, not the least of which was that sorry business with the strip mall seven years before.

And high in the hills of a forgotten corner of wilderness known as Crawford's Gap, a fugitive wanted for three counts of attempted murder returned from his morning walk to find manna for his wandering soul. Waiting on the steps of the abandoned one-room cabin he'd claimed for himself were two jars of Jenny's finest peach moonshine, courtesy of Hollis Devereaux. He reached for the copy of the *Gazette* wedged between the jars first.

Justus sat upon those steps and read long. By the time he was finished with half a jar and all the newspaper, he was sure of two things. One was that his days of hiding had come to a merciful end. The other was that Jake Barnett was no man to save his town.

· 4 ·

Taylor said, "Hush now, this holler's no place for noisemakers," but Lucy didn't want to hush. She wanted to keep asking questions, lining them up in neat rows one right after the other, if only to hear the sound of her own voice. Skulking through the Hollow was something she didn't care to do in silence, even if it was the middle of the day and even if she was with Taylor. Because Lucy saw nothing move from among the trees and heard nothing scurry from the brambles and dead grass, but she still felt eyes on her. She thought Taylor felt them too. It was the way he kept the shotgun balanced in one hand and his flint knife ready in the other.

"So if this isn't real, then we're really not talking, right?" she asked. "What about when I dream? Does that mean I'm dreaming that I'm dreaming? If I'm dreaming, why am I hungry? People don't dream that they're hungry. Or thirsty. Or tired. And why do I have to be quiet? Is there something out here you're trying to hide from? Is it that thing that was in the field last night?"

Just noise at first, a barrier to keep that sense of a Watchful Someone (or—and this notion felt both truer and worse—a

Watchful Something) away. And yet Lucy found the more she asked, the more she really did want to know. Taylor's answers might provide some levity to an otherwise frightening situation. It was like asking a child why the sky was blue just so you could hear an answer that was sweet and innocent in an almost sad way.

But Taylor hushed her and said the time for prattling was over, that Lucy would just have to see for herself. He spoke this with an air of confidence that still did not sway her, though it wasn't for lack of wanting.

"Tell me you never felt a pain so deep and been in trouble so bad you swore it weren't real," he'd said.

"Confess that you never been deceived by what you feel and what you believe.

"Tell me, lady, you never searched your heart and knowed there was something beyond, some other place that's not here you know is home."

LucyLucLu had not been able to answer any of those while sitting on that rotten old log and staring out over the valley. She had been too busy remembering. Remembering how she'd faced herself in her bathroom mirror after her father had gone and how she could have sworn it all hadn't happened, of how she'd been convinced of Johnny Adkins's love until he'd said that had all been in her mind. She thought of where her mother was.

And yet as Taylor led her on through that dark and lonely wood, Lucy knew the proof he had for his dream was likely no more mysterious than an ordinary thing he'd twisted into something magical. Some ancient pictogram carved into a rock, she thought. Or a tree trunk shaped like a gnome.

She hummed a tune (Taylor said nothing to this, though Lucy believed he listened along just fine) as he led her through miles of trees. He stopped at a field where large gray boulders lay scattered like headstones of giants. Beyond stood a stand of oaks so thick that Lucy doubted she and Taylor could even squeeze through. Taylor stepped among them nonetheless with a grace she thought unnatural, his body bobbing and bending without effort, his graying ponytail free. He paused just inside the tree line and offered a hand. Lucy stepped over the exposed roots and under low-hanging limbs, relishing the strength in Taylor's calloused fingers. At his touch she felt her heaviness leave and the eyes upon her gaze elsewhere. The woods opened ahead. Shafts of light, filtered into a pale orange by the gray trees, fell upon the forest floor.

Taylor stopped here and looked at her. "I've brought none to this place. Until now, I've only come alone. Do you understand?"

Lucy nodded, hearing what Taylor had said but also what he'd meant. Perhaps it was the way the sunlight played at the edges of his dark eyes, or maybe it was simply the strain of the long walk bearing down on her legs and lungs. Whatever it was, in that moment Lucy saw a tenderness to this man that surprised her. And she decided that whether Taylor was about to show her primeval doodles or funny-shaped trees, she would show him tenderness in return.

They walked over a slow rise and found a path bordered on both sides by lines of laid stones. Taylor reached for Lucy's hand and led her down its middle, cautioning her not to step beyond the rocks. She was about to ask why when the trail ended at the crest of a small grove. Thick layers of decaying vines grew from the limestone walls surrounding it. In the back of the grove stood a lone withering bush, naked but for the tiny red berries that grew upon it.

Taylor looked to the right and let go of Lucy's hand. All feeling left her when she followed his eyes.

At the far edge of the grove stood a hole as wide as a car was long. Its opening was a seamless circle, blacker than any starless night, with a circumference so crisp it gave the illusion of sharpness at it edges. That impossibility registered in Lucy's mind just before the other, more obvious one.

The hole was not in the ground, it was in the air.

Hovering not six inches above the dead forest floor upon some unseen axis, as though the hole had not been made out of the Hollow, but the Hollow had been made around the hole. It was a wonder or an abomination, Lucy couldn't decide which and wouldn't contemplate either for long, as a part of her knew to do so was to court madness.

She left Taylor's side and slowly made her way forward and around, easing aside the void. The circle shrank to a thin vertical line, then to nothing at all. She moved on behind it, putting the hole between herself and Taylor. The hole was gone. So, too, was he. Lucy continued left and Taylor reappeared, smiling as though he'd just said the sky was blue because God had paint left over from coloring the mountains, and that answer, however sweet and innocent it was, had been right. She stepped around the circle again, and Lucy was almost not surprised to see the reverse of what she'd seen before—the nothing first, followed by the thin vertical line, and then the hole's wide, black maw.

Her mouth felt as dry as winter leaves. "What is this?"

"My testimony," Taylor said. "Proof that all I say is so. Now you tell me this, Lucy Seekins, you being so smart and sure: How could this be in a world that's real?"

The Hole called to Lucy in words she felt more than heard. It stood regal, almost aloof, as if the world around it were something less than itself. She took three steps and reached for its tarry surface, as clear and still as glass. Taylor ran forward and took hold of her.

"No," he said. "Never do that, lady. It's holy, you ain't. There's animals in this wood, but they keep clear. Birds too. No beating heart dares go near, because it's all unclean. But hazard a look here, and let your eyes see."

Taylor bent Lucy low at the Hole's mouth. Her body felt charged, like being consumed by a small yet steady shock, and the matted bits of her hair pulled toward the opening. Yet there was no buzzing sound of electricity from there, nor a husky wind as would come from a cave. There was only silence.

Silence and possibility.

"Here, lady." Taylor pointed to where a plain impression of a shoe bottom had been made in the dirt. He pointed to another. Then another. They rose and followed the tracks through the grove and to the path, where they had mixed with their own. "Found them yesterday. Tracked them too. All the way to the rusty gate."

Lucy stared at Taylor first, then back to the Hole. "You mean someone came out of there?"

Taylor nodded. "I don't know who it was, or what. But I know it's here to show me where She is."

"She who?"

"Not yet," Taylor said. "I brought you here so you may believe, lady. I aim to know your answer."

She looked to the Hole again. Felt its tug. And though Lucy Seekins had never believed in anything, in that moment she found faith enough.

"Yes," she said.

"You'll swear your aid?"

She kept her eyes to the mouth

(so black)

and nodded.

"Then I need you to get back to town," Taylor said. "I cain't go there. Won't. You got to find Charlie. Now look here at these prints." He traced the lines in the dirt with his fingers. "You see how the treads are wavy-like, like a wide *W*? You look for one wearin' sneakers that match these tracks. You find him and meet me back at the gate. If you can't find'm or Charlie, you gotta look for Her yourself. She'll not be hard to find, I expect. Ask folk, they'll know her. Ask them where Kate Griffith is."

Lucy's eyes flashed. "Who?"

"Kate Griffith. But be wary, lady. She's a trickster. Trust her words and be charmed by her acts at your own peril, or you'll find your own end."

"What do you mean?" Lucy asked.

"I mean she has murder in her heart. I know that well. Because she once killed a boy, and she near killed me."

· 5 ·

Our own copy of the *Gazette* waited when we arrived home. I wanted to leave it in the box (wanted to let it rot there, actually), but I pulled over at the end of the lane nonetheless. There would be no avoiding whatever Trevor wrote. It would be echoed and ruminated upon by the whole town in the coming days and in my presence especially, as the people of Mattingly considered me a voice of calm reason to balance Trevor's hyper assertions. But more than that, I pulled over because I didn't want Kate to know how much I feared doing so. The way she reached her hand through the window and into the box—like the rolled-up paper inside was a bleeding animal—made me think she felt much the same.

I showered for the first time since Friday night and thought of the blood and stink the hot water could wash off and the memories it could not. I dressed and found Kate alone at the kitchen table. The room smelled of simmering beans and baking cornbread. The coffee maker gurgled on the counter. The newspaper lay open on the kitchen table, propped at an angle by something I could not see. Kate's eyes were puffy and red, as though she'd caught a nasty case of pinkeye.

"Where's Zach?" I asked.

"Sent him out to play." She turned the newspaper to the front page and slid it to me. "Don't think you'll want to read what that skinny little nut job wrote, but I guess you should anyway."

I pulled out a chair and smiled. "That's no way to talk about a man who's pined for you since kindergarten."

Kate smirked. I read through the front page article, pleased that Trevor had stuck to the facts. Even the subtitle—SHOCK-ING ACT LEAVES OWNER HOSPITALIZED—seemed appropriate. But then I turned to the op-ed in back, and for a terrifying moment I thought Trevor had come to the sheriff's office the night before looking for a story and instead found everything I'd tried for years to hide away.

"Can you believe that man?" Kate asked. She sniffed and reached into the pocket of her faded Wranglers for a tissue. "Stooping so low as to say Taylor Hathcock's the *devil*? That we're the ones responsible for what's happened? How can he say such things?"

"I don't know." I stared at the article again,

(One can only hope our elected sheriff will rise to the occasion *because he's coming, Jake, and I'm coming too*)

our newspaperman's words mixing with Phillip's own, until my tired mind couldn't tell if I was reading or hearing. I took Kate's hand and said, "You know this has nothing to do with you. Tell me you know that's right."

But Kate's swollen eyes and the creases in her face told me she knew no such thing. And there was the fact that from my seat I could see the newspaper had been supported by Kate's notebook. If I'd been a few minutes later out of the shower, I would have no doubt found her thumbing through those worn pages of names, trying to prove Trevor (and herself) wrong. I folded the newspaper and slid it across the table as far away from us as I could.

"I told Trevor to keep it to the who, what, when, and where," I said. "Guess he couldn't help going to the why. Thought I could . . . I don't know."

"What?" Kate asked. "Threaten him?"

I shrugged.

Kate patted my hand and smiled as she dried her cheeks. "Wrong Barnett, honey. You're not what your father was, and that's why I love you."

We were quiet. From outside came the sharp report of Zach's cap gun, followed by a yell to "Stop!" and "Freeze!" as he battled some invisible evil.

"Did you sleep last night?" she asked.

"Hard to get comfortable knowing a man died in the next room."

Kate said, "I can imagine." And then she raised the same question that had welcomed me to the past thirty-odd mornings, one she'd offered with a tone of hopefulness in the beginning, but lately tinged with dread. "Did you dream?" she asked, and I knew what would come next was her asking what those dreams were and what was haunting me. "White butterflies," I would say, and Kate would sigh and smile and say, "Yes, it's like my dandelions, isn't it?" but it wasn't. It was not like that at all. Already the start to that conversation was upon my lips, but whether it was the sight of Kate's breaking heart or the feeling of Trevor's stinging words, what I uttered was, "I dreamed I was in the Holler."

Kate bunched her eyebrows. "Happy Holler? Why are you dreaming of that?"

My shoulders slumped as the smell of dinner wafted over me. How long had it been since I'd eaten? I wiped the sleep from my eyes and couldn't remember.

"I went there once," I told her. "Back in high school."

Kate looked at me, her mind temporarily drawn away from Trevor's accusation (which I knew she believed had been aimed right at her; memories were long in a small town, and Phillip's death was something no one would forget). Her sad eyes brightened. She slapped my hand and chuckled.

"You took the walk, didn't you? You really took the walk? I thought that was all a bunch of bull."

"It is mostly," I said. "Every man I've ever known's gone to the gate as a boy. Trevor. Bobby Barnes. Joey and Frankie went together because they were too afraid to go alone. Even Hollis, Big Jim, and Justus went back in the day." I paused, trying to decide how much I could say. What came next was more whisper than talk: "But you know what? None of them actually do it. It's bad enough to stand there and take the time to carve your name. But to walk in?" I shook my head. "A lot of that place might be campfire talk, but you can't go there without thinking something's watching you. Something dark and big. They all say they take the walk, but all they really do is run, and in the other direction. Except for me. I walked the Holler. All the way past Indian Hill."

Kate sat silent and studied my eyes. Her smile was still there, but it had melted a bit into a look of worry. "You've never told me any of that."

I shrugged. "We all spend our lives trying to prove

something. Back then I wanted to prove to Daddy that I was a man. Figured if I could show that to him, I could show it to myself. I wanted to find out who I was."

"So your name's on the gate?"

"No."

Kate leaned forward and placed her chin in the hollow of her hand. What she asked were two words—"What happened?" Nothing so different from what she asked every day when I returned from my rounds or from lunch at the diner. Yet sitting there in the quiet of the kitchen, a part of my resolve crumbled. Had I not read Trevor's article, I would've given Kate the same sort of vague answer I'd offered about my dreams—*I don't remember,* maybe, or *Nothing happened at all.* But that was a lie and another leg on that big hairy spider, and I felt the truth I'd locked inside forcing its way upward from my heart to my tongue, where it gathered in a bitter taste. It was as if Kate had cracked a frozen spigot inside me and it was all about to rush forth with no concern for the life we'd built or the son we had. It was only those last two things, the twin pillars that supported my sad world, that gave me the will to hold the truth silent yet again.

"What happened in the Holler that day, Jake?" she asked again.

I said all that was needed—"I found out who I was."

· 6 ·

Everything was different, everything was the same. That's what Lucy thought as she parked at the end of the drive and plodded up the walk. The house, the empty front porch, the view of the town—just as it had always been. And yet everything had also been altered in a way she could not define. She stood there on the sidewalk, touching the spikes and cowlicks of her hair, wanting to understand. Then Lucy lit upon the answer as though she'd found a lost treasure in a dark room.

The change hadn't been in the world. It had been in her.

She walked upstairs and found the knapsack she carried to school, emptied it of books and tardy slips, and filled it with as many clothes as she could find. Whether the shirts she chose matched the shorts and jeans she packed didn't matter, nor did Lucy make room for the array of lipsticks and eye shadows and hairspray stacked upon the large vanity by her bed. Taylor didn't seem the sort of man who cared about appearances. That was good as far as Lucy was concerned. Maybe now she could finally stop trying to be pretty.

She paused at the bathroom on her way back down the stairs. Chunks of hair still covered the tiled floor. Lucy left this as well. On the coffee table downstairs was the fifty dollars and change her father had left. Lucy shoved the money into her pocket and heard the crinkle of the paper Kate Barnett had given her.

The open door beckoned. Lucy paused there and turned for a final look at her old life as the knowledge of what was happening dawned over her. This was good-bye, nothing less. A farewell to all she knew in glad exchange for what Taylor had shown her. She had scoffed at the notion that nothing around her was real, had even clung to those doubts when confronted by Taylor's hole in the world. But standing there in the foyer of her home, Lucy believed that not only was such a notion possible, it explained so much.

People had always been powerless in their dreams. They were victims of monsters and decaying teeth and high floors that gave way. But it had not been Lucy's nights that always haunted her, it had been her days. It was the monster of her father and his drink and the decaying teeth of her slippery hold on someone—anyone—who would stay and not leave. It was the swaying floor of all her questions of what was true and what was false and why she'd always felt such hurt and lonliness. Now, finally, Lucy perhaps had found that answer.

Because she was sleeping. She'd been sleeping all this while.

She dropped her bag and stepped into the living room. Johnny's shiny wrapper stared up from the floor. Lucy paid this no mind. What she focused on instead were the pictures on the mantle, pictures of Lucy smiling and her father smiling. Her mother smiling. All those teeth flashing for the camera, all of them so happy and so peaceful until one took the time to notice the empty eyes behind those grins. Only her mother seemed truly delighted. In many ways, that hurt Lucy the most.

She reached for the lamp by the sofa and tore away the shade, yanking away the brown cord connecting it to the wall. She gripped the top just below the bulb and swung, crashing the heavy base against moments remembered and moments never known, splintering them into jagged pieces of glass that flew against the walls and into the shag of the carpet. Lucy plunged the lamp into the flat-screen television, shattering its face into a wavy scowl. She sent the coffee table flying. Cushions and chairs were torn and tossed. The books were next—Lucy's precious pages of answers that only begged more questions and big words that offered little truths. She rent the pages and ripped the spines, the wisdom of man falling like hay against the truth that lay in a hidden Hollow grove.

The kitchen was next. Lucy flung open the cabinets beneath the kitchen sink and pulled out every mason jar she could find.

She stacked them into a shiny, smelly pyramid and smashed these as well, vowing vengeance upon the evil soul who had filled them and emptied her father. Only then did Lucy leave. To her it was a proper good-bye. She charged back down the lane, windows wide and music blaring, and drove for town.

She didn't know whether to look for Charlie or Kate first, then decided they would likely be in the same place. Two county police cars passed her on the way into downtown, driven by angry-looking men glowering from behind mirrored Ray-Bans. Aside from them, the streets were barren. Houses looked abandoned, their shades pulled tight and their front porches unoccupied. Downtown was no different. Cobbled streets gleamed empty in the afternoon sun. Storefronts lay shuttered and closed. Even the park, normally alive with activity in this weather, slumbered.

Lucy drove Main Street and tried to make sense of the nothing she saw. She passed the church on one side and the newspaper box on the other, then pushed down on the brake and reversed when she saw the headline.

TWO DEAD, ONE SOUGHT IN
GAS STATION ROBBERY

She knew who the one sought was. She did not know the two dead. For a fleeting moment, Lucy considered the possibility that Taylor had killed someone

("I woke that boy, I woke him up because that's where I was led")

and wondered what it meant if that was true. She parked along the curb and found four quarters in the money her father had left. The paper in the box's window was the only copy left. Lucy pulled it free and read the front page, her mind not bothering to speak up and say she had left her car behind and was now drifting toward downtown on foot. She followed the note at the end of the article to Trevor's op-ed.

Dead. Charlie Givens was dead. And so was a boy named Eric.

The bliss that had coursed through Lucy as she'd driven from her house upon the hill was replaced by a weight that settled over her lungs. Her legs kept a slow, staggering gait toward the town's center as her mind tottered between one thought and its opposite.

Taylor was a madman, he was a prophet.

The boy was dead, the boy was awake.

Kate was a murderer, Kate was not.

This was all real, this was all a dream.

Lucy felt the world go wobbly and off center, as though she were moving through a fun house of mirrors rather than downtown. She closed her eyes and searched for a center that could hold her steady and found the memory of Taylor's hole—not her own center (*Or is it?* came the thought), but maybe the center of the world. The center of everything. That calmed her when nothing else could, so much so that even if Lucy Seekins was unsure of so many things, she was certain of one: she would stand in front of that Hole again. She would do that if she did nothing else.

She heard a thumping sound, a soft *plonk!* that was there and then not and then there again. Lucy looked up, confused to find that she'd traveled nearly three blocks and somehow found the only person on Mattingly's streets that day. The small boy pitched a grimy tennis ball against the steps of the sheriff's office. It caught the lip and—*plonk!*—shot skyward in a long arc that ended in his hands.

He stopped when he saw her, his arm drawn back. "Hey."

"Hey," Lucy said.

"What's your name?"

"Lucy."

"My name's Zach."

There was no one nearby; the town square was barren, the only sound the grinding of the clock tower. The nothingness was surreal. Like a dream. The door above the steps opened and Lucy thought *yes, a dream.*

And then she felt the floor beneath her life give way when Kate asked, "Lucy?"

· 7 ·

Kate didn't know who it was at first, didn't even know if the person standing by the steps with Zach was a boy or a girl. It was only when she opened the door that she recognized Lucy, and only then because of the shorts. It was the same pair Lucy had worn the day before, only now they were covered with splotches of dried mud and what looked like ash. The back pocket was still turned out. Bruises and dried cuts ringed her knees. But it was Lucy's hair that took Kate's breath. It was like some evil prankster had shorn her head and left behind just enough to shock and pity.

"Hi," Lucy said.

She gave Kate an apprehensive look and took a small step away from Zach, who stood watching them both.

"What happened?" Kate asked. She moved from the doorway and took the first step down.

Lucy matched it with a step away. Her eyes blinked and blinked again. She licked her lips as though thirsty.

"Is everything okay?"

"Everything's fine." Lucy nodded so hard and with a speed that convinced Kate that everything wasn't. She held the newspaper up in one hand. The other ran through what was left of her hair and stopped at a bald patch just above her left ear. "I just read this. It can't be true."

Kate took another step down. Lucy watched but didn't move.

"That's what we're all thinking, but I guess all the thinking in the world can't change things. You didn't know?"

Lucy shook her head. "Where is everyone?"

"Hiding, mostly. Scared out of their minds by what the paper says. Don't let that bother you, Lucy. You can't take what Trevor Morgan writes as anything near truth. Why don't you come in?"

Kate took the rest of the steps, meaning to guide Lucy into the office, but her closeness sent Lucy backward off the sidewalk and into the street. Zach took a step toward his mother, unsure of the situation. His arm cocked back, ready. Kate looked at him. That he held only an old tennis ball rather than Bessie didn't seem to matter.

"I don't understand what's going on," Lucy said. "I really don't know you, Mrs. Barnett. First you come in my house, now you're trying to get me inside. I'm just gonna go." She took another step back. "I don't think I like you very much."

"Hey," Zach said. He wound his arm and stretched it out behind him. "*Everybody* likes my momma."

"Zach," Kate said, hushing him. She looked at Lucy and said, "Wait. Okay? Just wait." She didn't move, thinking that even a step away would be enough to send Lucy running. At that moment, all Kate wanted to do was keep her there. She didn't know what had happened to this little girl, but something had. Something horrible. "You don't have to come

inside. I'm just gonna go over and sit on the steps, okay?
You can stay right there if you want. I won't move an inch.
You just look like you could use someone to talk to, Lucy.
That's all."

Lucy said nothing. Kate turned her head and stepped slow
and easy, the way a person would walk so as not to spook
an animal. Zach eyed her and moved closer, putting himself
between them.

Kate touched his shoulders and said, "Why don't you go
throw your ball against the wall for a bit, Zach. Me and Lucy
need a word."

Zach didn't nod but he stepped away, keeping the strange
girl square in his sights. He walked the ten feet or so to the long
blank wall on the other side of the steps. His tosses were slow
and deliberate. Each time the ball bounced back, he caught it
and glanced at Lucy.

"You didn't see anything from your house last night?"
Kate asked.

Lucy said no. Her expression was flat and still, like frozen water. Kate remembered the smile Lucy had offered the
day before from the Seekins's living room sofa and how it
had unsettled her. Now Kate wished she could see that grin
once more.

"I should have checked on you last night, after everything," Kate said. "It was all just so sudden. Timmy got hurt
and Jake had to leave. I had to get here and call the state
police. I should have thought of you up there all alone in that
big old house, right there where those two men were. I'm
sorry, Lucy."

A sound escaped Lucy's mouth that was midway between
gasp and snort. She shook her head. "Your brother got beat
up, and you're apologizing to me?"

"No one likes being alone," Kate said. "You were alone."

Lucy took a step closer to the curb. Zach caught the tennis ball and took a step closer to them both.

"I wasn't," Lucy said. "Alone, I mean. How's your brother?"

"A little banged up, but otherwise okay. Gas station will be closed for a couple days. Andy's too."

"You said I can't believe everything in the paper. Did a boy really get killed?"

Kate stole a quick look at Zach. Zach was quicker and had already turned away. "Unfortunately that's one thing Trevor got right. His name was Eric Thayer."

Lucy took another step. Both feet on the sidewalk now, though Kate noticed Lucy's toes were pointed away toward the street. Everything about this scene upset Kate, but nothing bothered her more than seeing those feet turned to run. It made her feel like a bully. Like a monster.

"Which one killed him?" Lucy asked.

Kate cocked her head to the side, not understanding. "Does that matter?"

"I don't know. I guess it would make me feel better knowing the one who killed him was the one who died here last night and not the one who got away."

"Well, in my mind they both killed Eric. They both put Andy in the hospital. They both hurt my brother. I'd say the rest of the town believes the same. One of them's not our problem anymore. It's the other who's got everybody scared." Kate pointed to the newspaper. "Also the one's got Trevor talking like a revival preacher."

Lucy held the paper up. "Charlie Givens died of fright. Is that true?"

"Charlie Givens died of a heart attack, nothing more," Kate said. "Don't let that nonsense scare you, Lucy. Jake's got the county police all over this town. They'll get Taylor Hathcock. Just a matter of time."

That didn't seem to bring as much relief to Lucy's face as Kate expected. Zach eased a bit more to his right and tossed his ball against the bricks.

"Taylor Hathcock," Lucy said. "Is he from around here?"

"No. Jake thinks he's from Camden. Charlie Givens was from there."

"So you never saw them before?"

"Me?" Kate pointed to her chest. "No, honey. Camden folk and Mattingly folk generally agree the mountain between us is there for a reason. We don't mix well."

"You're sure?" Lucy asked. "You told me you help people. Maybe you helped Taylor and forgot."

"I don't forget the people I help," Kate said, and she thought, *If you doubt that, I have a notebook full of names to prove it.* "They're criminals. Why in the world would I know someone like that?"

Lucy seemed to consider that. "I don't know," she said. "I just don't understand."

"I think we're supposed to be disgusted and mad and hurt, but I don't think we're supposed to understand. I think if we did, we'd be less human than we are."

Lucy stepped forward. She was so close that Kate could reach out and touch her, but she didn't dare. Zach moved back to the steps.

Kate said, "Tell me what happened to you last night, Lucy."

Lucy looked down to her shorts and legs. Felt her hair. "I got in a fight with my father. Guess I cut my hair to get even. He left again. He always leaves, it's his job. I went to a party after that. Guess things got a little out of hand. I wasn't home when everything . . . happened."

"When's your daddy coming home?"

"Wednesday."

"Well, until then, if you'd feel safer staying somewhere else—"

"No," Lucy said. "I'll be fine."

"Mayor Wallis is calling a town meeting tomorrow night, just to get the facts out and calm people down. It'd do you some good to come. Might put your fears to rest."

Lucy nodded. "Maybe."

Kate thought they were done then, at least for now. Lucy stepped off the curb and back into the street, then turned around with the newspaper in her hand. "Have you ever thought there was another world out there?" she asked. "A better one?"

"You mean like heaven?" Zach asked.

"No. Maybe." Lucy looked at Kate. "I mean, have you ever gotten the feeling that everything's . . . broken? Like the more you try to put the pieces back, the more you realize they won't fit together again?"

Kate offered her a tired smile. "You have no idea, Lucy. No idea at all."

She closed her arms around Zach and thought of the night before. She thought of the tears she spilled at Phillip's grave and how the dark had closed in around her. She thought of her notebook. They were pieces, both. Fragments Kate had spent twenty years trying to fasten together in the hope those two broken halves could make a whole. For a moment as brief and silent as heat lightning, she thought back to that day behind the high school bleachers. She remembered Phillip's face and how his eyes had sparkled as she'd taken his hand. And there on a quiet street with Lucy and Zach, Kate felt the veil between worlds begin to thin.

It was only for a moment, nothing more. Just long enough to feel breath upon her shoulder and hear the soft whisper of her name uttered by a voice she'd never forgotten.

· 8 ·

Taylor had remained near the rusty gate all this time, hiding in a thick copse of pine and writing in his book. He didn't want to remain there, so close to the world. Yet he'd been reluctant to go back to the cabin too, afraid for Lucy to make the long walk back alone.

The sun had been high when he watched her pull away and head to town. Now the moon took its place. Taylor's body had not run free in those long hours between, but his mind had. As the day wore on, his thoughts followed a meandering trail that dipped and turned through the thorny places inside him, casting doubt where a slim hope had been until Taylor became convinced that Lucy Seekins would not return. She'd been caught, maybe. Or she was lost. Either seemed likely. The one remaining explanation (and try as he might, Taylor could not help but consider this the most likely of all) was that she had simply fled. Dwelling on that thought was like toppling the first in a long line of carefully laid dominoes and being unable to prevent the consequences—Lucy had run, which fell into Lucy finding the sheriff, which fell into her telling the town of the dream and the Hole, on down the line, one after the other, until the last domino had been struck and Taylor was left with only the certainty that the whole town of Mattingly was on its way to usurp his kingdom. A panic as black as the night flooded him. That feeling only increased when the wind carried the steady whine of Lucy's engine. Taylor saw headlights like demon eyes coming down the narrow way. The car stopped at the gate. The headlights stayed on. A door opened. Shut.

Then, "Taylor?"

Lucy stared into the dark. Taylor crept close, easing himself from the pines near the gate.

"Who's with you, lady?" he asked. "You mean to betray me?"

"No. Nobody's with me. Where are you?"

"Where I am don't matter. Where you been does. Sent you away hours ago."

"I went by my house," Lucy said. She stood on her tiptoes, trying to pinpoint his whispers. "Then I went to town like you asked. Come out, Taylor. You're scaring me."

Taylor did, though only after a long pause that was meant to show the lady who was in charge. He rose just outside the gate, scaring her in the process, and peered at the car's empty seats.

"You're alone," he said. "You found no one bearing shoes?"

"Everybody wears shoes, Taylor, and none of them leave footprints in concrete. Whatever you're looking for, I doubt we'll find it. Maybe that's the point. Maybe you're not supposed to find whatever it is. Maybe it's supposed to find you."

Taylor hadn't thought of that, though he'd never admit it. This lady was a smart one. "Charlie?"

"He got arrested," Lucy said. Her eyes caught the moonlight and flickered. She looked at her feet. "I don't know what happened after that, but he's dead."

"What say?"

She couldn't look at him. Instead, Lucy reached out and laced her fingers through Taylor's own. "I'm so sorry, Taylor."

"Charlie's dead?"

She nodded and flinched as though bracing herself for the sadness that would come. But it was more bewilderment that crossed Taylor's aged and cracked face. Because Charlie couldn't die. No one died in the dream. They either woke up or they kept right on dreaming, and Charlie couldn't be awake at all because Taylor was the only one who could do that and he hadn't and so what happened and why was everything suddenly so hard to figure?

"Taylor?" Lucy asked. She squeezed his hand and leaned in, laying her head on his chest. Taylor's long beard rubbed against her cheek. "What are you going to do? They're after you. There's county police everywhere. They know your name."

"Let them look all they want," Taylor said. "Won't nobody come to this Holler. You sure Charlie's gone?"

"Yes."

"But you saw no proof?"

"No. I guess they'd already taken him away."

Taylor smiled. No proof.

"What about Kate Griffith? Did you find her?"

Lucy buried her head deeper into him. She said nothing. Taylor was about to ask her again when she finally spoke.

"I didn't find her. I haven't been in Mattingly long, Taylor. I don't know a lot of people, and nobody was out for me to ask. Everybody's scared. It's all in the paper. I know what happened last night. A boy got killed. Did you do that?"

"You assume it was me?" Taylor asked. "Charlie was there too. Don't go thinking you know a story because you've been told a chapter."

He had not lied with that answer, but nor did Taylor believe he had told the truth. And he understood Lucy felt much the same when she pulled herself away from him.

"I don't know if you did it or Charlie," she said, "but I want you to know I didn't come back because of you. I came back for what you showed me in the woods."

Those words should have riled him, but Taylor accepted

what Lucy said without a word. Charlie was gone. Taylor didn't care why Lucy came back, only that she had.

He kept her close and said, "'Twas me that Woke that boy."

Lucy stepped away. Taylor tried to hold on to her but couldn't. She shook her hand from his.

"It was you?" she asked. "You killed him?"

"I *Woke* him."

"By killing him."

"By *Waking* him."

"Fine, then," Lucy said. "You woke him by *stabbing* him."

Taylor took a step toward her. "How you get out of a dream, lady? You wake up. You wake up, and you ain't *there* no more. That boy, he's gone now. I saw his heart and couldn't stomach it. That old man wanted to keep him right on suffering, but I couldn't abide by it. You see?"

Lucy looked as though she didn't see at all. "Everybody's saying you're the devil."

"Devil ain't a man," Taylor said, "the devil's *in* a man. Like he's in you right now, tempting you to doubt despite the wonder I showed you. He was in that old man. In Charlie too. Charlie just wanted that money, and I had to back his play. That's what friends do for friends. As I'd do for you."

Lucy blinked. Her eyes softened. Taylor thought he'd just said something magical, but he didn't know what.

"You'd do for me?" she asked.

"I would. You take that as you like. I won't make you stay if leaving's in your mind, and I cain't make you believe. It takes time for a mind to sway to the unthinkable. But if you doubt me, you think on that Hole. That Hole's all you need to know I speak the truth. Get back in that car if you want, lady. Go home to what life you lived. But know you will not cross this gate again if you do. The few who tried found themselves wishing they hadn't, and on that I'll swear. Or you can come with me and help me find what came up outta this Holler. He'll tell us where Kate Griffith is. Then you'll see fine."

Taylor stepped aside, clearing the way to Lucy's car. He swept his arm out, almost shooing her way, and waited for her decision.

"She's not a Griffith anymore," Lucy said. "I know that much. She's married."

Taylor lowered his arm. "Who'd she wed?"

"The sheriff. His name's Jake Barnett."

Taylor's flesh came alive in a series of quivering goose-flesh. He could almost feel his arteries widening, the blood rushing through his body in violent pumps, swooning him. Jake Barnett, he thought. Jake had wed Kate. And now the meaning behind everything that had happened in the last day came so pure and bright that Taylor attached a kind of beauty to it. He saw it as the hand of God, the very hand that had built Taylor's cabin and breathed magic into Taylor's binoculars and felled the tree that became the perch from which Taylor looked down on the town that had robbed him of all.

"I know why I had to wake that boy." His voice was quiet, a whispered awe that barely reached Lucy's ears. "It's because of Jake. Jake and Kate both. To . . . *draw* them."

"I don't know what you mean," Lucy said.

"There's things you know and things you don't, lady, but those things will come. I'll see to it. But you have to help me. You have to go back to town and find me Jake's phone number. Charlie had a little phone he put in his pocket. I'll need one of those too. But you have to do it right now."

"Why?"

"Because whoever came up outta this Holler means to put an end to something, and he needs me to do it."

"Are you going to hurt them?" Lucy asked.

Taylor said no. Lucy believed him. Much like Taylor had believed her when she'd said she couldn't find Kate.

"Then I don't have to go to town." Lucy dug into her front pockets. A cell phone appeared from one, a slip of paper from the other. "I have Jake's number right here."

· 9 ·

Despite everything that had happened—or maybe because of it—I was determined to make that night as peaceful and predictable as all the nights once were. I tucked Zach into bed as always, still said, "I love you, and I'm proud of you," still smiled when Zach answered the same.

Yet it seemed even as I did and said those things that nothing had continued on as it once was. Zach may have peered back at me through the same eyes (one bright and healthy, the other black and swollen) as he had Friday night, but now there was a fear behind them. And he may have laid his head upon the same pillow as he had all those nights before, but this time I spied the orange tip of his cap gun poking out from the edge. Put there, I knew, in case the bad man came. Even the toy town on his bedroom floor had been altered with a handful of yellow twist ties wrapped around the Lego BP and Texaco. That sight broke my heart in a way nothing else did. I understood then that I couldn't keep the world from my boy forever. There were dark things he'd have to encounter, secrets he would have to know. I could try to hide those things from him, could build up thick doors around him and lock them tight, but still the truth of the world he lived in and the blood coursing through him would seep through the cracks like a heavy rain.

I supposed much the same had happened to Eric Thayer's brother. Jabber, he called himself. He'd been waiting at the BP when I arrived. It was a short meeting punctuated by long silences, an "I'm sorry" from me and a "Thank you" from him, there being little else that seemed proper to say. He'd wanted a box from under the counter inside, something he said would make Andy feel better. It was beyond me how a person could lose someone so close and still have room enough to mourn someone else, but I asked no questions. I simply went inside and fetched an old wooden box I'd never seen before, stepping around the red snow angels on the floor that had been scrubbed a dull pink by the county's cleanup crew. I didn't know if getting that box was the right thing to do. I didn't much care.

I waited until bedtime to tell Kate all of this, hoping talk would keep me awake. But that well of exhaustion bubbled up in me again when I left Zach's room, and Kate was already asleep. I crawled into bed and shook her, gently at first and then harder. Wanting Kate to wake up, wanting to tell her of Jabber and Andy's box, willing even to speak of Justus. She mumbled and stretched out her hand. *I reach down for another stone and turn, meaning to place it on the pile. On Phillip's shattered leg, perhaps, or to hide his bloody chest. But he isn't lying at my feet, nor is he looking up to me from the riverbank. He sits instead atop the rockpile, a king surveying his realm. His sneakers rest upon the rocks, his hands on his bloody knees. The hood of Phillip's sweatshirt is pulled tight. Only his broken glasses peer out.*

You need to stop, Jake.

The sweat on my face glistens in the setting sun. My back cracks and pops as I straighten. Even here in the dream, I'm tired.

"Because I'm dead," I tell him.

Yes.

"*Because you're coming back.*"

Yes.

"I can't," I tell him. *I bend again and lay the stone over Phillip's shoes.* "I can't stop," *and I think—I'll have to bury Charlie next, because I killed him too.*

You didn't kill Charlie, *Phillip says.* And neither did I. Charlie killed Charlie. Can't live like he did and expect to go on forever, can you?

I bend for the next stone and realize it's the one I just laid. I look at Phillip's shoes. He wriggles his toes and smiles. The worn canvas ripples with the movement.

See? *he says.* Do you know what hell is, Jake?

I don't answer. I raise the stone in front of myself and hold it there as though covering my nakedness.

Repetition, Jake. Hell is repetition. It's doing the same thing over and over and never changing anything. You cover me with rocks, I'm still here. You scream, no help comes. You run, but only back to this place. Do you see what your sins have wrought?

Phillip stands and steps down. I shudder when his shadow falls over me and drop the stone. There is a crunching sound as the rock topples down—twenty feet, as I judge it—and lands at the river's edge. I feel Phillip's icy hand slip into my own and the primal scream that touch kindles inside me.

But I do not scream because I know no help will come. And I do not run because this is hell and sin is a circle, and the faster you run away, the sooner you return to it again.

Phillip squeezes my hand. I'd free you, Jake. He's come and so have I, and you are a dead man just as Kate is a dead woman.

"No," I beg. "Leave Kate alone. We were just kids—"

So was I. Do you remember, Jake. Do you remember true?

Before I can answer, the Hollow's dead calm is torn by a deep thrum that shakes the trees. The river churns below us. The earth shudders and gives way. I'm thrown forward as the scream I've held tight is loosed. Phillip grips my hand and pulls me back.

Time to go, Jake. He's coming. The only way out is through, but there's power in believing. Do you hear me? There is power in believing.

The sun grows dim above us—orange to brown to blackish-gray, like an open sore staining the clouds. The thrum pulses in my ears. I feel it in my teeth. Trees uproot and fly skyward. Phillip releases me and I am sucked up. I reach for him, frantic, but Phillip steps back and lifts his fist to me. He says he'll see me soon, because I'm a dead man and Kate is dead too, and I will remember. We all will remember. I hurtle toward the hole in the world and close my eyes opened to the dark. My hand stretched up toward the ceiling, still reaching for Phillip. I lowered it to wake Kate and stopped when I heard that thrumming sound again. It was my cell phone vibrating. The word *Private* glowed on the screen.

I pushed the covers back—still not sure if I was asleep or not—and carried the phone down the hallway. Dreaming. *I'm dreaming*, I thought, because I couldn't feel myself moving at all. I floated instead. Or was being pulled. Yes, now that I think about it, that's what I felt. I was being pulled, and Phillip was doing the pulling. Right through the screen door and onto the porch.

I opened the phone and said, "This is Jake."

"'Lo, Jake."

The voice was gravelly and deep and wholly unfamiliar. I looked at the screen again. PRIVATE still shone.

"Who I got here?" I asked.

There came a sigh and, "Guess remembering was asking too much, Jake. Didn't think you'd be one to forget so easy."

The cool breeze against my skin helped wake me. I rubbed my eyes and gripped the wooden bannister on the porch, telling myself this was real, I was real.

"I'm sorry," I said, "I'm still half asleep. Tell me who this is?"

"I'm the man what's waking your town, Jake."

A thought forced its way through my tangled mind. My voice trembled when it spoke. No amount of bravery could keep it from doing so. "Taylor?"

"Winner winner chicken dinner," came the reply. "Give that man a prize."

"Where are you?"

"Now, Jake, you think I'm dense? No. An' don't bother trying to find me over this fancy deviltry I'm talking into, because that's been fixed. I hear all it takes is touching a few buttons and you're called *Private*. That means you cain't trace me and we can talk proper. We got a lot to ruminate on, Jake. Our time's come. Do you understand?"

"No," I said. My voice was little more than a series of rattles in my throat. I took a deep breath to calm it. It didn't work. "Tell me where you are, Taylor. I'll send some boys to bring you down to the sheriff's office. We can talk there."

"Apologies, but no. I'm without Charlie now. You squirreled him away, that it? To befuddle me? That trick almost worked, Jake. As sure as the day, it almost did. But I got tricks too. Charlie weren't the only one helping me. Got me a smart one."

I closed my eyes and gritted my teeth. Hearing Taylor's voice was bad enough. Knowing he was still free and had another accomplice was worse.

"Charlie's dead, Taylor, and I put his dying square on you.

Eric Thayer's too, plus the two men you hurt. You'll ride the lightning straight to hell if this is your course. Your only chance at living's to surrender and plead mercy."

Taylor laughed. It was a shrill sound, like a crow cawing. "Living? I'm the *only* one living, Jake. Not like you. But I know that pain. I remember it well. We've had our troubles. I ain't forgotten that even if you did. You saved me, Jake, so I'll only warn. Just this once, mind you. Call off those county men. You do that tomorrow first thing, or your sins will find you out."

"What sins?" I asked.

Silence. I had no idea what Taylor would say, but to me that pause was something intentional, like he was savoring the telling the way you savor a bite of food and roll it around in your mouth before you bite down.

"I know what you did that day in the Holler, Jake. To that boy."

Waves of heat and tightness spread across my chest. The world folded over and engulfed me. There in the quiet darkness of my front porch, I dropped to my haunches.

"Now don't get all worked up, Jake," Taylor said. "It's okay. I know it must pain. But I fancy the pain of ever'body in that town knowing what you did'd be worse. That right? You ain't told your own boy, have you? You tell him what you did, Jake? You tell Kate?"

"How do you know of my family?" I asked. My grip on the phone was tight, my voice still shaking, but now it was anger rather than fear that colored my words.

"I see far, Jake. You call them mounties off. You do that, I'll hold my tongue. I'll let your secrets be your own. They'll fester on your insides, but you'll live on the outside. Ain't that what matters to you in the end?"

I said nothing at first. My mind was too busy, my thoughts buzzing like a swarm of flies over something rotten. Because Taylor was right. God help me, he was.

"Where are you, Taylor?"

"Close, Jake. I always been close."

I heard a click as the line went dead. I closed the phone and looked out over the blank night. The stars were out, tiny pricks of faraway white that shone over the mountains. I followed the bends and dips of the Blue Ridge until my eyes rested where Happy Hollow lay. Far away, the clock tower tolled.

I opened the phone. My trembling hands betrayed me twice, but I managed to punch in *69 on the third try. There was no number for me to dial. Just a few buttons, he'd said. That's all it took to tame the deviltry. Because Taylor knew tricks too and he had a smart one to help him now.

I wanted to pray then. I wanted to beg for help and rescue. But I knew buried in that petition would be a subtle request to roll that snowball of lies a little farther down the steep hill my life had become, even if it would someday grow so big it destroyed everything.

I walked inside and eased the screen door closed, stared at all those fragile holes in the mesh, then closed the front door as well. My fingers touched the small switch on the knob. I clicked it, then fingered it again to make sure it'd been fully turned. I had never once locked that door. Not before bed, not leaving for work. There had been no need for such a thing. This was Mattingly, after all.

That night Zach tossed and turned and kept his cap gun close. I did the same with Bessie. Sleep didn't come, but I doubted Phillip would have visited me again anyway. I figured he'd already said his piece.

· 10 ·

It was not the buzz of an alarm or thundering music from the radio that woke Lucy the next morning, but a sharp perfume that licked at her nose and flooded her mouth with saliva. She kept her eyes closed and rolled her head, content to smell rather than see. There was breakfast—she smelled meat and something that could be potatoes—along with the faint sweetness of burning wood and the soft sulfur of smoke. Above it all was Taylor's musky scent. She turned her nose into the soft bed of pine boughs beneath her one last time, breathing in earth and sky.

She opened her eyes and saw Taylor watching her from his place at the table. Lucy quickly lowered her gaze to the faded plastic bowl in front of him. Steam rose from its contents in tendrils that curled and disappeared. A metal cup sat beside the bowl. Another bowl and cup, these larger and more full, waited at the empty place across from him.

"I gathered breakfast," he said. "Figured you'd be peckish."

Lucy rose and crossed the room in four small steps. She plucked three pine needles that had stuck to her chin and shook her hair out as she sat. The bowl in front of her held some sort of stew, the broth thick and near the brim. Taylor spooned a hunk of meat into his mouth. He smiled as he chewed. Lucy picked up the tarnished spoon beside her and stirred the bowl. Clumps of meat rose to the surface, surrounded by white masses she took as some sort of vegetable.

"What is this?" she asked.

"Rabbit and cattail shoots."

Lucy winced and sat the spoon down.

"Case you forgot," Taylor said, "this here's no downtown.

This is free land, lady, and living such means providing for your own needs. Now go on. It smells good. If it smells good, it'll eat good."

It did smell good. Lucy inhaled and the scent traveled well south of her nose and settled into the roomy part of her stomach, where it came to life in a series of hungry rumbles. She eased the spoon into the bowl and fished out a small bit of meat and shoots. Taylor watched as she raised the bite to her mouth.

Flavor exploded over Lucy's tongue. The meat was lean and juicy, with just a hint of wildness that balanced the salty, cucumber-like taste of the cattail. She swallowed and plunged her spoon in for more, taking two bites and then three before swallowing again, feeling Taylor's smile but not seeing it. Though she had tried once that morning and twice the night before, she could not look at him. She had not known Eric Thayer and had never seen his likeness, but still it was a dead boy's face she saw where Taylor's should have been.

"Got some pine needle tea there in your cup," he said. "Good for your insides. But take care not to drink it if you're in the family way. It'll slay your darling inside."

Lucy thought of Johnny and what still lay on the living room carpet in the place she once called home. She said, "I'm not pregnant," and drained the cup in one gulp. It was not as good as the food but pleasant enough. Her torpor sloughed off like an old skin.

"You'll be late for your studies," Taylor said. His tone was a cautious probing, if not dispassionate. "Reckon your ma and da will be missing you too."

"I don't care to see anyone at school right now." Lucy pointed to her head without looking up, without looking at him. "I'd rather not play twenty questions with this. And I'd rather not talk about my parents."

Taylor seemed as though he understood that sentiment well enough. "That what got you acting so standoffish this morning?"

Lucy took another bite and asked, "Why am I hungry if I'm only dreaming? And why am I getting full if what I'm eating isn't real?"

"Because you're not really hungry, and you're not really eating."

"But I *am*."

"Are you certain?" Taylor asked. "Truly so?"

"As sure as the world is round," Lucy said.

Taylor smiled and raised a finger skyward. Lucy had a strange feeling she'd hit upon the very point he wanted her to. He said, "Well now, folk once said the world's flat, did they not? Now they say it's round. And they were firm that the stars drifted around us too, but now they say we go round the stars. They know so much, but they always change their mind of what they're sure of. How much of what they know is so and how much is what they only wish is so?" Taylor put his spoon down. "Let me inquire of this, Lucy Seekins—we found this world's plump, not fat, and winged, not still. You ever wonder what folk know of today that'll be torn asunder tomorrow?"

Lucy fell quiet. There had been just enough fact mixed in with what he'd said to silence her. To make her listen.

"But that ain't what's got you riled, is it?" Taylor asked. "I sent you from this Holler a friend, but you came back a stranger. Why's that, lady? And no secrets. This's a place of truth, and I'd have you speak as such."

Secrets, yes. Lucy did have secrets now, and that muddied what truth there was to be found. Taylor had asked her if she'd found Kate in town, and Lucy had said no. Why had she said no?

She thought of all Taylor had said of Kate and all Kate

had said of the boy. Eric had been his name. Eric Thayer. And though Lucy had hoped (as if the heart could hope such a thing) it had been Charlie who'd killed that poor boy, a part of her had known even while Kate spoke that it had instead been the man at whose table she sat and whose food she ate.

And what did that mean? Who could Lucy trust?

Kate Barnett certainly acted like no killer. Taylor Hathcock certainly did. But there was something other to him, a woundedness that in some ways made Lucy forgive him for the sins he'd confessed. She thought of the way she'd faced Kate the day before on the sidewalk in front of the sheriff's office—legs pointed one way, feet the other. It was the same way she'd faced Taylor at the gate later that night. It seemed to Lucy at that moment an outward expression of her inward condition. When it came right down to it, Lucy Seekins simply didn't know where to go. She never had.

"The boy you . . . *woke*," Lucy said. "I can't look at you without seeing him. I wonder what kind of man could do that to someone else, and I wonder if that's the kind of man whose floor I want to sleep on and whose food I want to eat. I heard you talking to the sheriff. You said he took Charlie, but they didn't. Charlie's dead, Taylor. I know you don't want to believe that, but you have to. And I want to know what all that talk about Jake being in the Hollow was and what boy he did something to, because you said no one comes here. I want to know how you can know people but they don't know you at all."

Taylor set his spoon down and leaned back in his chair. "I Woke that boy out of love. You've a mind to call it sin, well then, fine. But iniquity comes to us all, lady, so the Lord can be who He is. He wishes grace and mercy upon us. Sinnin's the only way He can give it. As for Jake Barnett, I will not speak on what he did in my Holler. I'll say only that our paths crossed once and will cross again. Of Charlie, I do not know. But I expect I'm not done seeing him."

"Why?" Lucy asked.

"Because I did not wake him, and so he still slumbers." Taylor nodded. "Yes, I will see Charlie again. Only those who get roused are never seen again, as you can imagine. No one dreams once they're awake, lady. Why would you? You're in the real world then. That's why no one comes back. I reckon if someone did, it'd mean this world weren't a dream a'tall."

There was more Lucy could have said—wanted to say—but it was all caught up in her like a knot, and to speak would only bind that lump more. Could she blame Taylor for what he'd done to Eric Thayer? Oh yes. But could she blame Taylor for believing his friend Charlie was not dead? When Lucy herself still believed in her secret heart that one morning she would be roused by the feeling of fingers through her hair and open her eyes to her own dead mother? No. And in that way Lucy believed the man across from her hurt just as she herself hurt. She supposed that was why she raised her chin to Taylor and no longer saw the image of a dead boy, but the countenance of one wearied by a long passage. A man whose burden lay unseen but heavy upon him, and whose only hope of continuing on lay in someone who would share his yoke.

Lucy did not see Eric Thayer in Taylor's face, she saw herself. And in that moment Taylor Hathcock became not the horrid thing he'd done, but the lonely man he was.

"Will you take me to the grove?" she asked. "I want to see it again."

"I'm bound to watch the town," Taylor said. "You can go. Mind the way, though, and don't let this wood enchant you. God's in this Holler, lady, but so's the devil. If you come upon either, let 'em know you have no quarrel, just as you heard me say the night I brung you here. And watch the sun. I need you at that meeting tonight, if you're still of a mind to help me. Kate may be there, and Jake for certain."

"I'll go," Lucy said. Of that she had no doubt. It was what she would tell Taylor of Kate and Jake that she still doubted very much.

Lucy rose to leave. She paused at the door to see Taylor smile and to feel herself smiling back. To see them yoked together, as only the hurt could be.

· 11 ·

The first thing I heard that morning was the wearied voice of Mayor Wallis decreeing both the elementary and high schools would be closed that Monday. So the town could mourn, he said, and if the county school board had a problem with that, they'd goshdarn better bring it on. That was Big Jim—always speaking to the voter instead of the person, always acting tough. I didn't buy it. Big Jim might publicly say he was keeping everyone home so they could honor the dead and the hurt, but I had a feeling the real reason was that he figured no parents in their right minds would send their children anywhere that day. Not with the devil on the loose.

It was all fine with Zach, of course. No school meant he'd be spared the hassle of making peace with Danny Blackwell, for one. And for another, he'd get to spend a quiet day at the sheriff's office with Kate and me. We rode from home with him singing from the backseat and Kate holding my hand. She asked if I'd dreamed. I told her no.

Traffic along the way was a steady stream of tractors and trucks and family cars. Their occupants raised a hand as we passed. Kate and I waved back, comforted that at least a portion of the town was endeavoring a return to normal. Then two county police cruisers passed us, reminding us that normal would be awhile yet.

That sentiment only grew when we reached town and found a crowd of bowed heads and shifting eyes waiting in front of the sheriff's office. Hollis Devereaux stood with one foot on the first step, playing with his beard. Bobby Barnes waited beside him, along with maybe thirty other townspeople I can't remember. I only glanced at them long enough to know their faces were familiar. It was the unfamiliar face I was looking for. It was Taylor. On the top step, away from the gathering but definitely part of it, stood the Widow Cash. Mayor Wallis marched down the courthouse steps just up Main Street, coming toward us.

Zach asked, "What's goin' on, Daddy?"

"Not too sure."

We parked along the walk. Kate opened the passenger door and stepped out, meaning to ask the people Zach's question. "What's—" was all she managed. Those waiting pressed in and spoke at once. She looked at me through the open window and mouthed, *Help*.

I got out of the Blazer and flipped up the seat. Zach scooted into my arms just as those who couldn't get to Kate got to us. There were shouts and outstretched hands grabbing for my shirt and hat. Zach's thin arms closed tight around my neck. I wormed my way through the people, trying to get to Kate, and demanded quiet in a deep voice that surprised me.

"What in the world's goin' on here?" I asked.

The crowd started up again, each person with his or her own answer, none of which was clear. Bodies jiggled to the right and left as someone cleaved a path through the crowd. A polite but firm voice said, "Excuse me" and "Pardon me" and, once, "Move it *now*," until Big Jim stood at the forefront of them all.

"Jake," he said, "I need a word."

"Well, you gonna hafta get in line, Mayor," Hollis told him. "We's here first."

A chorus of support rose that pulled Big Jim back into the crowd. Across the street, shop owners and customers alike paused in their dealings to watch the drama unfold. Kate pulled at my shirt, wanting me to do something.

I yelled, "Now wait, y'all just quiet down," and held up my hand until everyone had either heard me or tired of shouting. "I don't know what's gotten into y'all, but I'll say it's a sad sight. Now let me and Kate get our boy inside. I'll tend to each of you in turn. But I expect I'll start with Widow Cash there, as she seems to be the only one with any sense at all."

I led the way up the stairs. Zach still clutched at my neck. Kate walked beside me, telling everyone whatever it was would be fine. She touched the dignified old lady who waited at the door on the elbow and said, "Come on now, Dorothea. I'll sit you in Jake's office."

The foyer filled to near capacity. Someone (I think it was Bobby, but some memories fade) knocked over what was left of the gallon of paint I'd used on the door, spilling dribbles of gray onto the floor. Zach climbed down off me and watched with growing amazement, no doubt thinking this was the very sort of thing he'd never be privy to if stuck in school. I settled them all as best I could and walked to my office. Kate stood just outside the door.

"What do you want me to do?" she asked.

"You come on with me. I've no idea what's going on, but I know enough that I'll need you."

I took the chair, Kate sat on the corner of the desk. Dorothea

Cash—Widow Cash since her husband, Hubert, met his reward in the summer of '04—sat erect and still in the vinyl seat across from us. A worn leather pocketbook sat on her lap. Her yellow dress clashed with the blue in her thinning hair. A thick string of pearls hung from her wrinkled neck.

I said, "Now, Widow Cash, what can I do for you today? Aside from your grocery shopping, of course, which I promise to tend to as soon as I get these people out of here."

"There won't be any shopping today, Jacob," she said. Her tone was clipped and to the point, with a hardness that raised my eyebrows.

"Why's that?" Kate asked.

The old woman looked at us with lips stuck in a pucker from years of sucking on the same cigarettes that had done in Hubert. She set her jaw, said, "I'm here to turn m'self in," and held out two fists that looked no bigger than plums. "Go on, Sheriff. Do your duty."

Kate's hand moved to her chin. She scrunched her eyebrows and turned her head to me.

"Well now, ma'am," I said, "before I go and cuff you, maybe you should tell me what it is you're turning yourself in for."

"Murder."

The hand that held Kate's chin dropped to her lap. "Dorothea, you couldn't so much as hurt a bug."

"Nonetheless," the widow said, "killin's what I did. I killed that boy. Hurt good old Andy too. And your poor brother, Kate." She leaned forward and put a hand to Kate's leg. Tears welled in her eyes. "I'm so sorry."

"Dorothea," I said, "we know who did that."

"Them boys mighta, but 'twas done in my name. 'Cause of my sin, as the paper said." Dorothea Cash's shoulders slumped. She reached for the pearls around her neck and felt them like worry stones. "My heart overflows with the stench of iniquity."

I rubbed the stubble on my jaw and felt my hand tremble against the skin, made a fist, and shook out my fingers. The tremble was still there. Tiredness, I supposed. And Taylor, whom I thought may well have been watching me even then to see if I'd call Alan Martin. I looked out the window at all those people in the foyer who'd been brought there by Trevor and his article. I saw no strangers.

Dorothea rubbed her pearls and looked at me. "I miss Hubert. Miss him terrible. I can drive, Jacob. Never do, but I *can*. And even if I didn't, it's only a short walk to market. But I like you chauffeuring me, because it's nice to have a man around. I didn't think it was a sin." She leaned forward, voice cracking. "I don't regard you in the carnal way, Jacob. I need you to know that. And I need you to know that too, Kate."

Kate's eyes bulged. I opened my mouth to speak, but all that came out was a long exhale that melted into a whistle halfway through. I thought of all those Monday trips to the market, of how Dorothea had always worn her best dresses and how much she said she appreciated me holding the door open for her and carrying her groceries inside. How I would often enjoy a glass of lemonade on her porch after. I never thought a thing of it—who would?—but now I found I couldn't look the Widow Cash in the eye.

"Well, I can't speak for Jake," Kate said, "but I'm fair certain you've nothing at all to worry about, Dorothea. Now why don't you go on home and rest awhile, okay?"

"You know where to find me," she said. "I throw myself on your mercy, Jacob. Just mind that's all I'll throw on you."

She left. Kate and I looked at one another with a mixture of veiled amusement and outright shock. Hollis tipped his hat to Dorothea and replaced her in the chair, saying how horrible he felt about Eric and Andy and Timmy because it was all his fault—his and Jenny's. To Hollis's reckoning, he'd not only transgressed but had enabled others to transgress as well, and that was even worse. The Good Book frowned upon a great many things, but on being a stumbling block most of all. Then it was Mayor Wallis, who confessed how awful he felt about that whole mess with Justus and then railed against Trevor, telling us he was going to wring his nephew's scrawny neck for writing that stupid article.

By then more people had trickled in, souls heavy with burdens real and imagined, all more than willing to confess their wrongdoings if it meant the devil would walk in Mattingly no more. I pleaded for them to leave, but the crowd held fast.

Kate volunteered to take over. I let her. When I left the office and strolled out back, Bobby Barnes was sitting in the vinyl chair that had become a confessional, blubbering on about how it was all his fault. I didn't know if Bobby blamed the town's troubles on his drinking or that time he'd peeked under Kate's dress in the second grade. I didn't much care.

I suppose you know why I got out of there and what I did next. There's no easy way to say it. I will say the call to Alan Martin didn't go as badly as I'd feared. There had been no sightings of Taylor Hathcock in town or elsewhere, and Alan thought keeping a steady rotation of troopers in the area no longer made sense. I agreed, and the little boy in me felt a weight lifted. The man in me kept wanting to push that weight down until it forced me to do something. The little boy won.

It's our desire to be left alone that causes evil to flourish in this world. I understood I was being a coward, but in many ways I'd always been such. Besides, shame has no weight against fear. And I was afraid. I was afraid because Taylor was watching and Taylor *knew*, and how either was possible was something I couldn't understand but believed with all my heart. And just as Phillip said, there was power in believing.

· 12 ·

The bear had first come to the wood when the earth was still rough and magic yet spilled over its brim. He had remained there since, as both guard and witness to a thin place in the world that marked the boundary between light and dark.

The Hollow had called to many beyond its borders in the bear's long years, ones who stood on their hind legs and dressed in fur they themselves could not grow. He'd always found the Two-Legs puzzling creatures, easily pitied were it not for a pride that convinced them to mock what their minds could not comprehend.

He beheld the coming of the Old Ones when they first crossed into this valley and those who came after—Two-Legs who called the valley home by felling the forest and scoring the earth. They tamed the wild land even as wildness raged in themselves, and called the bear's home accursed even as they drowned in their own foulness. They crafted a barrier to stand as warning where the Hollow bordered their lands, yet their twisted nature turned warning to invitation. The Hollow always called. The Two-Legs always answered. They came to the bear's wood seeking power and truth and found their own end.

The bear had watched them all with the same detachment he would employ when inspecting the crawlies that scurried along the barren ground. They were beneath him, unworthy of effort and attention. The Two-Leg that denned atop the ridge and claimed the Hollow as its own was no different. The bear tolerated that one as much as he had the others who'd come before and the many who would come yet.

Yet the bear's patience for the mate the Two-Leg had brought into the forest grew thin. That one had not been drawn. And now he studied them both with increasing interest. Because a new thing had come to the wood with them, and the bear knew not what it meant.

He had trailed the Two-Leg's mate since it left its den. He kept its scent close and moved among the trees with a silent grace that belied his massive weight. He watched it tug and tuck at the thin pieces of raiment that covered its nakedness.

Where the Two-Leg was going held much less interest than what it had brought along—something neither beast nor spirit, but Other. And while the bear could perceive that the Two-Leg knew only that the Hollow's eyes were upon it, he perceived the Other knew more.

It was only when they reached the field of stones that the bear understood where it meant to venture. All the Two-Legs drawn to the Hollow found the hidden place. He let them move into the center of the field before letting himself be made known. The bear pushed against the nearest tree, an oak that had sprouted and grown beyond his height until the dead soil had strangled its life. The tree gave way and exploded into the field, stopping the Two-Leg in its tracks. It spun toward him, paws held out in shock. The Other turned as well and watched as the bear moved into the field, facing them. He brought his snout up and sniffed, rising on his hind legs, at once engorging himself on the Two-Leg's fear and choking on the Other's indifference.

The frail creature shook, its eyes wide. The bear lowered itself onto its four paws and drew closer. He sniffed at the air and found only one scent, putrid with fear. The Two-Leg stumbled back, groveling and shaking its head, and then spoke its language: "I have no quarrel."

The bear moved closer as the hard earth sank against its paws. He rose up again and bellowed its call into the long, wide expanse of the Hollow, raging over the insolence of this tiny thing in front of him and its unworthiness to tread upon the Hollow's sacred places, wanting to water the brittle grass with the Two-Leg's blood. But then the Other stepped between them and froze the bear in place with a power not even the Hollow could summon. The bear snorted, filling the air with long streams of mist and snot that showered its prey. The Two-Leg cowered in a ball of bone and flesh upon the field, crying as though wounded. The bear looked deep into the Other's eyes. His mind came open with the sound of flapping wings and rushing water. The bear remembered. He remembered true.

He settled his front paws into the earth and lowered his head to the hard ground, feeling the Other's light upon him. He turned and made his way back through the field as the Two-Leg raised its head, speaking its words.

"I have no quarrel," it said, again and again, repeating them with a greater voice each time as though believing those empty words held power. The bear turned back as it neared the trees. The Two-Leg stood finally and tugged at its raiment, ignorant of the Other that remained at its side. Such was the curse of all lower life, the bear believed—they adorned themselves in fur they could not grow to prance and preen before all they could see, and yet they lay naked before all they could not.

· 13 ·

It was no mere bear that meant to devour Lucy Seekins. That, she knew well. No mere bear could outweigh her by a ton and wield a paw larger than her own head. No mere bear could have eyes like that. The monster of the Hollow drifted to the edge of the field as she spoke Taylor's incantation once more. When it paused, what flooded her was a fear more alive and deep than any Lucy had ever known. If the beast had a mind to finish what it had started, there was nothing she could do.

It reached the edge of the woods and turned a final time. One of its eyes was white, piercing, the other red and deep. Both seemed filled with a kind of wisdom Lucy could not comprehend. The red eye settled on her with a grip that stole her breath. The white one stared not at Lucy, but at a place just beside her. She rose and looked at that place, saw nothing.

"I have no quarrel," she whispered.

The bear regarded her. Its fur was a deep brown that soaked the sunlight that shone upon it. It lifted a snout that had gone gray with age and sniffed once more. When it turned to disappear into the trees, Lucy felt the very ground beneath her shake.

She placed her hands upon the dead grass, squeezing it through her fingers. For the first time, Lucy Seekins found she was thankful to be alive. It had been Johnny who'd told her to play dead if she ever found herself confronted by a bear. She'd laughed at the notion, telling Johnny the only wilderness she ever planned on seeing was whatever farmer's field the next party was in. Yet Johnny's wisdom had saved her, and in that moment Lucy loved him again.

She looked to the thick oaks over her shoulder. The path lay inside. Lucy had never been good with directions, yet she had quickly found that didn't matter in the Hollow. She thought she could leave Taylor's cabin and start out for the rusty gate or the river—could even wander through those thousands of acres of mountain land with her eyes closed—and still arrive at this field. It was as though her body were a compass and the grove her north, a positive tugging at her negative self. Now she felt that same pull again. She rose and turned into the trees, matching her steps with wary looks behind.

The grove called in a siren's song. Lucy came to the Hole.

It was wondrous, that floating halo of black so pure and serene it could only have been dug by gods. The pull on Lucy gave way. Her strength went with it, leaving her prostrate on the bare earth like a pilgrim in front of a shrine. She remained there, mouth agape, wondering how it was that she could be made so whole by such nothingness.

She rose when her strength returned and twice circled the Hole, watching it fade and reappear again. Lucy examined the small, gnarled bush and the red berries growing upon it, then walked to a section of the horseshoe-shaped wall that surrounded the grove like a womb. The vines covering it were thick and gray. Lucy reached for the nearest one and eased it to the side. She drew back when a shock of red peeked out, as though the limestone beneath bled. Her hands moved forward again despite her mind's pleas and pulled a section of the vines aside.

Seared into the face of the rock was the upper part of a handprint. Lucy pulled back more and found another, this one small, and yet another, larger one. She tore at the vines, reaching as high as she could, ripping at them as sweat gathered in her scraggly hair. Her chest heaved. Her fingers came back raw and bloodied.

Hours passed before she could pull no more. The three sides of the grove had been stripped bare of vines in a wavy pattern that more or less corresponded to Lucy's height, revealing hundreds of red handprints. Some bore the length and width of a man's hand, fingers splayed as if tearing into the rock itself. Others were thinner and smaller, bearing the gentle touch of a woman. Still others bore the tiny handmarks of a child.

It was a sight that struck no dread in her. There was no sudden wave of horror as when the bear had exploded through the trees, no urge to run. Lucy felt instead the strong call of familiarity, as though a thread had been tied through each of those souls and now through her own self, binding them together.

Like a family, she thought.

It was an understanding that consumed her. Lucy could do no more than fall into the soft pillow of gray dirt and be filled. She was thankful that Taylor found her later, thankful that he did not scold her for her tardiness or remind her the Hollow was no place for noisemakers. He only eased her into his arms and let her wails carry. He let her give voice to her joy.

· 14 ·

Mattingly's chapter of the Veterans of Foreign Wars occupied a one-story brick building on the outskirts of town. Aside from the occasional gatherings to plan parades and funerals and talk of old war stories (many of which were inflated by jars of Hollis's moonshine), the meeting hall sat empty and forgotten. But not that night. The smell of ancient cigars might linger like ghosts and the pine floors may have been bowed and dull, but the VFW was still the only place large enough to hold everyone who arrived with one singular purpose on their minds—to decide how best to drive the devil back to hell.

Kate didn't mind that Jake wanted to arrive early. Being there to welcome people inside, pat their arms and give them hugs and say how well they all looked, would go a long way toward easing simmering fears.

The gathering hall consisted of little more than a wide rectangle with a raised stage at one end. Joey and Frankie Munroe (who were not only upstanding members of the rescue squad, but just after their graduation had helped chase Saddam out of Kuwait) arrived early to set up neatly spaced rows of folding chairs. They filled the room and left just enough space down the middle and sides for movement. A lectern stood in the center of the stage, flanked by an American flag on one side and the Commonwealth's on the other. Three more metal chairs sat just behind and to the left. Big Jim Wallis occupied the first, as was his custom. Reverend Goggins sat in the middle (the preacher was not to speak that night; Big Jim asked him to just sit there and remind people God was on our side). The last belonged to Jake. Though the meeting was not scheduled to begin for another half hour, the hall already stood nearly filled. Farmers spoke with merchants as hill folk mixed with town folk, all producing a low hum that rang off the moldy white walls.

Kate took her place in the second seat of the second row and said hello to Hollis and Edith Devereaux, seated in front. She placed her notebook in the chair on the aisle—that would be Lucy's place, should she come. Zach took the seat on Kate's other side. More people filed in through the open double doors in front. They descended upon the room like ants, covering the chairs until the chairs were gone, then taking up the empty places in the back and on the sides. Kate said hello to as many as she could, one eye on them and the other on the entrance. Just as Joey and Frankie went to close the doors and call the meeting to order, dirty-clothed and short-haired Lucy Seekins walked in.

"Save my seat, honey," Kate told Zach. "I'll be right back."

Kate leaped—there could be no other word—and walked to the back as quickly as she could. She took hold of Lucy's shoulders and told her how well she looked, even if the girl did not look well at all. Lucy's eyes were swollen and red, as if she'd spent the better part of the day in mourning.

"Is everything okay?" Kate asked.

"Yes, ma'am." Lucy looked down and brushed the front of her clothes. She chuckled. "I know I don't look it, but I've never been better."

Kate said that was good, but those words came out sounding hollow and tinny. Someone who'd never been better wouldn't look like that.

"I saw Johnny Adkins and his folks a little bit ago. They're in the middle to the left. If there's not a spot, I saved you a seat up front with me and Zach."

Lucy's eyes scanned the crowd. "I think I'll just sit with you," she said. "If it's no trouble."

Kate smiled. "Not at all."

She closed her fingers around Lucy's hand and guided her down the aisle, aware that the people they passed were gaping at the strange haircut on the girl from Away. Kate found her seat taken by Bobby Barnes, who spoke to Hollis in frantic whispers as Zach pushed against his shoulders. Little could be heard above the crowd, but Kate could make out plenty of Bobby's begging, an equal amount of Hollis telling him no, and Zach saying as politely as he could that Bobby was gonna get out of his momma's chair one way or the other.

"C'mon, Hollis," Bobby said. "You cain't *do* this."

"I tole you, boy, I'm done. Git what you need at the Texaco."

"Timmy's closed up 'til he heals, Hollis. 'Sides, what he's got don't do me good like Jenny does."

"I'm *done*, Bobby," Hollis said. "Now get on afore Edith's ears decide to work."

"Bobby?" Kate asked. "Mind if I sneak in here with my boy?"

Bobby looked up and excused himself with a look of anger and ache. Kate took her place beside Zach and picked her notebook up from the chair on the end.

Lucy sat there. She leaned over and asked, "What were they arguing about?"

Kate pointed her chin at the couple in front of her. "That's Hollis Devereaux and his wife, Edith. They own a farm out on 664."

"And the other man?"

"Bobby Barnes."

Lucy turned, watching Bobby go. "What was he wanting?"

Kate didn't want to say, what with Lucy being so young and impressionable. Then again, what harm would there be in telling the girl what everyone in town already knew? Besides, Lucy was actually *talking*. And her shoes, Kate saw, weren't angled to the door.

"Bobby has his struggles," Kate said. "Always has. Hollis runs a still in the backwoods of his farm."

Lucy's posture stiffened. Her fingers drew in on the sides of her tan shorts, stretching them against her plump legs.

"You mean moonshine?"

Kate nodded and whispered, "Don't say anything, though. Edith doesn't know."

Mayor Wallis stood and walked to the microphone. Kate's eyes wandered to a family at the opposite end of the first row, close to the wall. Mother, father, son. Each wore the faded overalls common to hill folk, each either a size too big or small.

The boy—he couldn't be much more than Zach's age, Kate thought—turned his dirty face to her and smiled through a set of blackened teeth.

"Let's all rise," Big Jim said.

The room filled with the sounds of sliding seats and standing bodies. Hats were removed, hands placed over hearts. Faces turned to the flag. Kate looked down to see Lucy hadn't moved. Her eyes were still on Hollis, boring into him. Kate tapped the girl on the shoulder and motioned for her to stand.

Big Jim began the anthem. The crowd joined in. Kate's gaze cut from the stars and stripes to the small farm boy to her right, who was too thin for his clothes and too worn to offer much more than simple muttering. She heard the faint echo of ". . . and justice for all" and was struck by the irony of those words and the sight of that wanting child, whose life no doubt contained so many things but lacked so many more. There was justice for some, Kate thought, but there was little for hungry, dirty boys.

The crowd sat as Mayor Jim Wallis began his speech. Kate leaned over to Zach and asked, "You know that boy down there?"

Zach looked and nodded. "He's Harley Ruskin. He goes to school sometimes."

"Know where he lives?"

"No. Want me to find out?"

"Yes."

Kate tousled his hair and smiled. Church, Jake, and Timmy had always been her means to add names to the notebook, but Zach had often been her secret weapon when it came to the town's younger children. He knew just how to approach them and how to glean the necessary information about what they liked and where they lived. He enjoyed helping his momma with her names. In ways that both encouraged and saddened Kate Barnett, it was the strongest link she shared with her son.

She opened her notebook and leafed through the pages as Big Jim told the town how things were bad but they'd been worse before. Under Lucy's name, Kate wrote the date and *Harley Ruskin*.

"What are you doing? Why's my name there?"

Kate covered the page even as she knew whatever goodwill she and Lucy had built in the last minutes had left quicker than it'd come. She looked up. Lucy stared at her, wanting an answer. Kate could only tell her the truth.

"These are people I've helped," Kate said. "Your name's in there because I want to help you."

"Let me see," Lucy said.

"No. It's private, Lucy."

"My name's in there, let me see."

Kate drew her hand away. Lucy studied her own name and rifled the pages with her fingers.

"You've helped all these people?" she asked.

"Yes."

Big Jim ended by saying the sheriff was there to both talk and listen. Kate looked up at her husband. Jake's face bore the stubble of weeks without a razor, and his hat looked too big for his body. She'd never seen him like that, and she thought lack of sleep had little to do with it. Jake's eyes darted from one side of the room to the other, as though not curious to see who had come, but anxious to see who had not.

Jake rose when Big Jim motioned him to the lectern.

"Thank y'all for coming," he said. "Just wanted to give a rundown of what's happened and what's still going on, as everyone seems to have their own view of both. I hear Andy'll be okay. Timmy too. Eric Thayer's funeral was today. I did not kill

Charlie Givens. I need to make that plain." Jake swallowed and leaned back. The deep sigh he meant to keep to himself went through the microphone instead, filling the hall like a loud wind. "I sent the county police away this morning."

A sharp murmur rose from the crowd. Kate felt Lucy's eyes leave the notebook and settle on Jake. Kate stared at him as well. She wondered why her husband had kept that from her.

Jake held up a hand and said, "I sent them away because all they were doing was making everybody scared and nervous. Fact is, Taylor Hathcock's nowhere around here. He's gone. I think so, county police think so. He's not a town problem anymore. We need to get things back to how they were, and having them around here won't get that done."

A few in the crowd believed that right enough. Most felt otherwise. They left their chairs to voice their concerns in angry shouts. Big Jim and the reverend tried to settle things. They could not. Jake banged his fist on the lectern, told everyone to quiet down and give him his say, but they were frothing now, venting their fear. And just as Kate thought they were all barreling down a hill in a car without brakes, the VFW's doors exploded open and proved just that.

Kate's head turned. The room was silent but for the heavy footfalls of boots on the old pine floor. The man walking toward the front stood tall, chin up and chest out. He focused not on the eyes of those around him (many of which were either batting in disbelief or looking for the fastest way to the doors), but upon Jake. Jake shifted his weight and tugged at his shirt collar, trying to breathe. Kate reached for Zach's hand and shushed Lucy when she bent her head to say something. Mayor Wallis's face melted into deep reds and blues. Trevor Morgan sat frozen, too stunned to even write in his notebook. He could only watch as Justus stopped at the first row and eased the battered fedora he wore away from his eyes. He looked at Jake and smiled. It was all sharp teeth.

"Hello, son," he said.

· 15 ·

I heard Big Jim yell, "Arrest that man!" and turned just as he bolted from his chair with such force that it toppled backward and crashed, sending Preacher Goggins into a short but violent spasm. The mayor looked at Justus and then at me. "It's your sworn duty, Jake. You take him in."

My mind registered the fact that Kate had drawn Zach close. The rest of my thoughts were a jumbled mess of shock and dread. My head swooned in a way that was part tired, part hungry, and part scared. Mostly scared. Not because I thought Taylor was there (he wasn't, I'd made myself sure of that), but because of the man who had come in his stead.

My father stood there, facing me in front of the town. He crossed his thick arms in front of his chest, sinking the straps of his overalls into his shoulders. It had been seven years and hard living, but he looked every bit the man who'd left Mattingly and vowed to never return.

"Jake?" Big Jim asked. "You hear me?"

"Heard you, Jim," I managed.

It was all going too fast for me to process, like watching a movie stuck in fast forward. I forced my right arm behind my back. What I felt was not Bessie, but the top of my belt. Justus smiled again, baring a set of tiny, tobacco-stained teeth.

"Heard you too, Mayor," Justus said. His eyes cut to the mayor long enough to send Big Jim looking for his chair. "What say, Jake? You gonna come down here an' cuff me?"

He held his arms out, shook them, and raised two busy eyebrows. I held my ground.

"Dint think so," Justus said. He lowered his arms and shook his head, then gave me a weak wave as he turned to the gathered crowd. I saw a folded copy of the *Gazette* in his back pocket and cursed Trevor again. "Somethin' stinks in here," he boomed. "Smelt it all the way to the hills, I did. Worried me so much I come on down, make sure there's still a town."

The tendons in my neck stood out in long, sharp lines. I looked at Kate for help, but none was there. She was as scared and frozen in place as everyone else. So too was Zach, who stared at Justus with eyes so wide they almost seemed to be devouring him. In that moment there was nothing I wanted more than to know my son had not understood what Justus had called me. The fear on Zach's face said maybe that was true, and the relief I felt shamed me.

"Found buildin's," Justus continued. "Saw churches an' stores an' a piddly-lookin' no excuse for a newspaper." He sneered at Trevor, who sank even farther in his chair. Justus turned to me just long enough to say, "Saw a *sheriff's* office," then turned back around. "But I dint see no town. Thought for a second the Lord done scooped y'all up. Then I thought nosir, most y'all're more suited for Judgment than Rapture."

He looked at the mayor as he said that. Big Jim's face went from rosy to crimson.

"But then I saw ever'body cowerin' here like a rafter full of turkeys in a rainstorm, too senseless to keep from smotherin' yourselfs in your own fright. What could be, I thought to myself, that'd turn men to cowards? What'd be that you women would feel no indignity aside your despair? Have your mommas suckled you against trembling breasts that turned you *yella*?"

Chins fell to chests one by one. Hats and caps lowered. Palms pressed over lips. I tell you this, and I say it true: had I honor enough, I would have done the same. Justus's presence frightened me, yes. But it also shamed me. Because as broken and jagged as that old man's heart was, there was no doubt it still beat, and from the right places.

"But now I know." Justus reached into his back pocket and lifted the newspaper high, shaking it. "It's this, ain't it? This sorry tripe what ain't fit to use in my outhouse."

The pages crinkled under his rage. He shook them at Trevor. Trevor shook more. I don't mind saying I took some sense of satisfaction upon seeing that. Then I realized that if I'd have gotten Trevor to tremble such just before he'd left Saturday night, maybe we wouldn't have been in this mess and maybe Justus would have still been in Crawford's Gap where he belonged.

"You tell me how two men can come up in Mattingly an' kill," Justus said. "You tell me how one of 'em can light out in the wind and be gone. Tell me what sort of good folk there is that can look upon all that's been done and say it's *their own fault*. That *they deserved it*. I know an' love Andy Sommerville. I know an' love Timmy Griffith. An' I dint know that boy, but I know he's innocent just as I know innocent blood calls out for justice even as it soaks into the hard ground. Now I ask, who's gonna give him that justice? You, Hollis?"

Hollis didn't move.

"Bobby Barnes?"

A nod—small, but there.

Justus turned. "Jacob?"

I blinked. Words stuck in my throat. I was glad for that, because I didn't know what words they were.

"I ain't seen no po-leece round here," Justus said. "That mean you gonna step up, Sheriff?"

"Taylor Hathcock's gone," I managed. I said this into the microphone to make it sound louder. "County police agree with me."

Justus snickered. Even that was a boom. "Gone, he is? They been lookin' elsewhere too, I imagine?"

I didn't want to answer that. Justus only asked questions when he knew their answers. He knew the police had been looking for Taylor. Looking everywhere.

"You got all these po-leece lookin' everywhere else for a man, an' they ain't found 'm yet? Where's that tell you he is, Jake?" He didn't give me time to answer, but turned to the crowd instead and slapped the newspaper into an open palm. The sound was like fireworks. "He's *here*. In this town or in them hills, it don't matter. An' I say it's high time somebody does somethin'. Any man who feels a conscience to protect his fam'ly, you meet me tomorrow on the courthouse steps. Ain't no law in this town gonna bring him in. We'll make our own law."

Justus turned to face me one last time and went back the way he'd come, straight down the center of the meeting hall. He'd almost reached the doors when I called his name.

"I don't want no trouble," I said.

He stopped and turned. "That's the problem with you, boy. Don't matter how much a body don't want trouble, trouble still finds him. Finds us all."

Justus left, slamming the double doors and scattering Joey and Frankie in the process. The crowd drowned in its silence, thinking their own thoughts. What those thoughts were, I cannot say. I can only tell you mine. They said that Trevor Morgan had not reported the present as much as he'd divined the future. Because the devil hadn't walked in Mattingly on Saturday night. He'd waited to make his appearance on Monday evening.

Part IV

No Home for the Weary

· 1 ·

Taylor took in the whole story with as much interest as if he were listening to someone talk about the weather. He remained paitent, waiting for Lucy to get to the important part. She never did. Instead, she spoke of people Taylor neither cared for nor understood, jumping from what someone said to what another did, losing him in the process.

When the tale was blessedly over, she said, "I don't know who he was. I don't think anyone ever said his name. But he was scary. And he's coming after you."

Taylor propped his elbows on the table, rocking it toward him. He bent forward and folded his hands beneath his nose. "You find Kate?"

"Did you hear me?" Lucy asked. "They're coming after you, Taylor. Jake convinced the police to leave, but I'd rather have them after me than that man."

"That man ain't important," Taylor said. "What's important's *Kate*. You say Jake was there, and you said he's her beau. She had to be there too, lady."

Lucy said no. Then she said, "But I asked around about her. Kate's a good person, Taylor. Everybody says so. She's kind."

She reached across the table and took Taylor's hand. Her skin felt smooth, like a lamb's ear, and her eyes sparkled in the light from the candles she'd brought back from town. Taylor hadn't asked her to do that, and yet she had. That small act spoke more to him than Lucy Seekins could know.

"Kate's no such thing as kind," he said. He kept his hand still, not wanting to break her touch. "She's weaved a spell 'round that town. 'Round Jake. But make no mistake on what I say. I know the truth."

"She helps people," Lucy said. "Poor people. They say she has this notebook she carries with her all the time, and she keeps the names in there. How can someone like that kill a boy?"

"A notebook fulla names, you say?" Taylor smiled. "I envy you, Lucy Seekins." He squeezed Lucy's hand. "You've the world ahead. And though it may be a false world, it can shine fair. You bear no weight but for what's on your bones. There's other heaviness, and it's more burdensome. You get some years on, you'll see life's a hard going, and the load placed upon you may be of our own doing and it may not. Such is my story. Jake bears that weight as well. But Kate? By the evil in her heart, she bears the weight most of all."

Lucy nibbled at her bottom lip. "Kate wouldn't kill anyone."

"How's it you know that?" Taylor asked. "You've yet to chance upon her."

He kept Lucy's hand in his own and felt the sweat pouring from her fingers. He spotted the quick heartbeat beneath her blouse and noticed the way she suddenly couldn't look at him. There was little wisdom in Taylor Hathcock, but he was wily; no one could survive in the Hollow that long without wits. A part of him cried out that Lucy was lying and that she would be his end. Yet that voice was met by another, smaller one that pled for Taylor to no longer look for deceit in Lucy Seekins for fear of what would be found. That small voice won out. It was simply good enough that Lucy was there and had thought to bring candles. Love covers a multitude of sins. Loneliness does too.

"I carry no hate for Kate Griffith," Taylor said. "I did once. Now I know the harm she did me turned to blessing. You say she carries a book to record her goodness. I know why. Just as I know those names add more red than black to the account she owes. And I do not carry hate for Jake. Him, I mourn."

"Why?"

"'Cause Jake's a killer too."

"Taylor—"

"He is," Taylor said. "I bore witness to it myself. You say Jake looked scared up on that stage? That's why. Because he knows I still run free, and I know the truth of what he done. He's a man on the outside but a boy inward. He ails, lady. Kate too. Such is why this Holler means to have an end and why there's prints from the Hole. I've been called to Wake them both when the time comes. My love will set them free."

Lucy's eyes began to water. Taylor took a measure of pride that the beauty of his words had drawn such a reaction from her.

She said, "You told me you wouldn't hurt them."

"'Tis my destiny, lady."

"What did Kate do to you, Taylor?"

Taylor lowered his gaze, telling himself no, don't you dare. But the words were already over his lips, and in a whisper Lucy barely heard.

"She told me she loved me."

There was no more talk of Jake or Kate that night. Lucy took the bed of boughs by the fire, Taylor the cot. He decided he would let the candles burn that night. Sometimes Taylor saw things in the dark, horrible things that frightened him because he thought they came not from the Hollow but from his own heart.

He'd nearly settled into sleep when Lucy asked, "Why can't we just stay here together, Taylor? You and me and the grove. If this is all a dream, then nothing else matters."

"Because I'm Awake, Lucy Seekins," he said. "I'm Awake and in the dream both, and I am the only one. Knowing the truth yet bearing up under a lie is a burden you won't want to bear. This Holler wants me to right a wrong. If I do, maybe he'll free me to find what lies on the other side. My fight's fading, lady. I grow weary of this world."

The fire crackled. In the distance a coyote called.

"I'm not going back there," Lucy said. "There's nothing for me in that town."

"And what will people say has become of you?"

"I don't know. I don't care. No one will notice anyway."

Taylor didn't think that right. Someone would know the lady had come up missing. Someone might even have the presence of mind to think he had something to do with that. That notion struck Taylor as useful if the time came.

"As you wish it, Lucy Seekins," he said.

"What if you're wrong?" Lucy asked. "What if you're wrong about Kate and Jake? About everything?"

Taylor had thought of that often in his long years in the Hollow. He now thought of it again. Even the most devout had their doubts. The conclusion he reached this time was the same he'd reached in all the others.

"This here life can't be real. It hurts too much."

"But what if it is?"

The answer Taylor gave was the only one he could.

"Then I'm hellbound, lady."

· 2 ·

It was enough that most of the town believed me when I said Taylor was gone, or maybe it was because Justus was so convinced Taylor wasn't. Whichever the case, that Tuesday Big Jim Wallis decreed life in Mattingly should return to normal. Kate knew Zach wouldn't take this well (not only did normal mean a return to math and spelling, it meant facing up to Danny Blackwell), but she thought I'd be pleased. Normal, after all, was all I wanted. Yet I greeted the news that morning with a silent apathy. She guessed aloud that it was my nightmares, a wise enough conclusion given the way I'd tossed about in the dark. But I hadn't dreamed the night before. Taylor and my father had kept me awake in a way that my fear of Phillip never could.

Just as quiet was the ride to school. My mind was torn in half the whole way there, seeing all those children and knowing Taylor could be waiting to pluck any one of them away. Especially Zach, who sat mute and glum in the backseat. But there was nothing I could do about that. I'd sent Alan's men away and told the town Taylor Hathcock was long gone, and I could no more keep Zach home than I could tell everyone that Taylor was close, that he'd always been close, and now he had a smart one with him. Zach's only words when we dropped him at school were the "Love you" he offered when I let him out and the "Okay, Mommy" to Kate when she asked that he call her later.

Thankfully Kate's mind wasn't on my furrowed brow as

we drove the few blocks from the school. She had fallen into her notebook instead and remained there until we turned onto Main Street. My hand tightened around hers. She looked up to see a mass of men gathered at the courthouse steps, spilling out all the way to the sheriff's office. Fifty of them, maybe more. All riveted upon Justus, who stood at the top step pointing to a map taped to one of the wide stone columns. Several of them wore knapsacks. Many wore camouflage or military jackets. All of them wore guns.

Mayor Wallis saw us park and made his way over. Sweat had already turned his white dress shirt a dull gray beneath his suit jacket. The cigar in his mouth had been chewed to a mashed nub.

"You see that?" he asked. "I can't even get to my office. You do something about this, Sheriff. You send those men along. They're armed, Jake. *Armed*. This ain't no Wild West show, this is a proper town."

I looked out from beneath the brim of my hat and considered this, knew it was right. I also knew there was little I could do about it. Justus divided up the men and pointed to various spots on the map like a general giving orders. It was a bad sight made worse by the approach of Trevor Morgan's car, which slowed and then stopped where we stood.

He rolled down the window and smiled. "Morning, Uncle—Mayor. Jake." Then a smile and, "Hello there, Kate."

"Where you going, boy?" Big Jim asked. "Figured you'd be on that crowd like a wolf on fresh meat. Your readers need to know that man's impedin' the usual machinations of their town."

Trevor leaned out the window and looked back toward the courthouse. "Figure I have plenty of time for them." He looked at me and added, "Not like they'll be arrested or anything. Got an errand to run in Camden."

My head turned at that word. "What's in Camden?"

"Now, Sheriff, I'm the one who usually asks the questions. Chasing down a lead. All I'll say."

He offered his good-bye and drove off, waving his hand out the window. Kate watched Trevor go and turned back to the business at hand.

"Jake, the mayor's right," she said. "Can't you do something? Tell them to gather somewhere else maybe?"

"He means to do it here," I said. "Right here in front of everybody. Show the town he's not afraid. They see that, maybe they won't be afraid either." I stood there watching Justus. "Pretty smart, really."

"Smart?" Big Jim asked. "Now look here, Jake. I know that man's your daddy, but he's a wanted criminal charged with almost killing three men. I ain't gotta stand here while my own sheriff calls him smart. Listen." He pulled at my elbow to gain my attention, then drew back when I gave it. I might stand idle as Justus did my job for me, but I would not abide being manhandled. Every man has a line in him that won't be crossed. "You know I didn't approve of you being elected sheriff. How could I, given what Justus did? But you're here, and I've accepted it. Now I need you to decide if you're gonna do your job or not."

As it turned out, Justus made my decision for me. He parted the men like Moses through the Red Sea and made for the nearest truck, which was Bobby Barnes's old Dodge. Bobby followed as the others made for their own. The street erupted in a series of backfires and growling engines.

I turned to Kate and said, "Gonna patrol the north hills to Boone's Pond. I'll be back for lunch, if you have a mind to join me."

"Okay."

Bobby's truck pulled to the curb where we stood. He rolled down the window and leaned back as Justus leaned forward.

"We're bound for Riverwood," he said. "Gonna split up there and cover the ground west to Three Peaks. Lots of places to hole up around there."

I said nothing. Nor did Big Jim. He'd challenged Justus enough at the meeting. He had no stomach for more.

Kate said, "You shouldn't be doing this, Justus. You'll only stir the town."

"Stirrin's what this town needs, Katelyn." Justus turned to me. "You comin'?"

"Got work," I said.

Justus turned up his nose. Bobby offered a sad shake of his head. Do you know what that feels like, having the town drunk look on you with pity? It was one brief moment, but it was a look I knew I'd remember for the rest of my life. And yet that didn't stop me from going north as Bobby and my father drove south.

· 3 ·

Taylor had tried once to use the binoculars to peer in the direction of the rusty gate—this was some weeks after what happened along the riverbank, back when he considered every snapping twig and whispered breeze to be either a ghost or townspeople bent on justice—but what he saw was distorted and far away. Once, as an experiment, he'd taken them atop Indian Hill to look past the river bend to the cliffs beyond—as close as Taylor ever wanted to get again. The binoculars hadn't worked there either. It was only when he panned the lenses down toward town that the images shone clear and close, so that was where Taylor had trained them since. That was where he trained them now.

Kate was down there. Lucy hadn't seen her yet, but others had. And Kate had married Jake. That last bit of information was old to Taylor now, but it still carried a charge. He'd seen the group of men leave the center of town, but no truck or car matched what he thought Mattingly's sheriff would drive. There had been women on the street. Taylor believed Kate was surely among them, but he couldn't remember her face well enough to pick her out. The years had dulled his memory at the edges. Taylor had forgotten much, and what he recalled was little more than scraps of litter that blew across his mind in sporadic waves.

He had gone without a fire and breakfast that morning, leaving Lucy at peace. She'd done well the past days; sleep was what she needed now. Taylor knew the lady had much on her mind. As did he.

Because the Hole called to Lucy Seekins, and in a way it never had to him. Taylor had known that the moment her eyes beheld the grove. He'd known it more when she'd dared to go there without him the day before. And as he sat upon his log that morning (seeing the town, yes, but looking into his own heart more), Taylor thought of how anxious he'd been watching her go and how much that feeling had frightened him. He'd gone for Lucy later—just to see to her safety, he told himself, though he also told himself that was a lie—but the elation that had come upon finding her safely in the grove gave way to the shock at what she'd found.

The hands. Lucy had found the hands.

And not only that, the lady had also faced the bear. The evidence of that had been all over the field and plain enough for even a blind man to see. That she had and that she'd lived could only mean one thing.

Taylor heard her shuffles before her shadow fell upon him. Lucy sat at her place on the log. She'd exchanged the shorts and shirt she'd worn for jeans and a white camisole. They remained in silence for some time and watched the sun make its slow arc over the valley below. The mountains in the distance were a deep blue, like waves gathering to crash.

Lucy said, "I grew up in Washington, DC. That's about as far away from here as a place can be and still lie in the world. My friends and me used to stay up all night. Carrying on, partying, you know. Usually it was at my apartment, because Dad was always gone. When morning came we'd all go up to the roof and watch the sun come up over the office buildings and warehouses. It would start out orange, then turn red in all the smog."

Taylor considered this and said, "That sounds plain awful."

"I didn't used to think so. Just a couple days ago, there was nothing I wouldn't do to get back there. But now . . . yeah. It does seem awful, doesn't it?"

Taylor laid the binoculars on the log and turned to her. "We should have us a word, lady. About what you seen at the Hole. All else'll wait."

Lucy glanced down at her feet. The sun colored her cheeks like roses. Taylor looked away. "What were they?" she asked. "Those hands."

"The Hole was here before there was a Here," Taylor said. "We all got a middle, Lucy Seekins. World's no different. What lies in that grove is the world's middle. It's a holy place in need of a Keeper. Those handprints, they're a chronicle. That's the best I can say. Those walls are a record of the ones this Holler's called to itself. We answered, me and all those come before me, stretching on back generations, maybe thousands of years, and we wandered this wood and found that special place. It becomes ours to tend. The berries on that bush in the grove? That's why they're there. You mash them up and dip your hand in, and you put your mark upon the wall. My own hand's upon that wall along with all the rest. It means we're bound. We belong to this Holler and we cast all else aside. Never thought you'd find them. I never wanted to take you there, lady, but you needed proof of the things I speak. Now the Holler's spoke. It means to make you Keeper next."

Lucy looked at Taylor in a way he could not comprehend. He saw in her countenance joy and sadness, pain and elation.

"What do you mean?" she asked. "Are you leaving?"

"I don't know, lady. The dream's a mystery. I told you of the burden I keep. I believe to Wake would be a fair going, and I'd oblige someone to lay me down when the time comes. But I'm not going soon. There's too much work to do and too much for me to show you. After?" Taylor shrugged. "All I have will be yours then. But mind what I say—you'd leave all else behind, for this life and after. Those eyes you feel on this side of the rusty gate are those who've come to the grove before. Such is what I believe is true. Absent with the body and present with the Lord may be the rule down in the world, but not here. This Holler's a selfish lover, Lucy Seekins, and will not abide a divided heart. Once you give yourself over to it, here's where you stay. This will be your kingdom, but it will also be your cell."

Lucy's eyes went to the wild spaces around them. She looked to town. Taylor looked at her again and saw how comely she was. Her hair had gone without a brush for two days and was jagged by sleep and wind, but she was wondrous just the same.

"My mother died when I was born," she said. "My dad told me that I came out wrong. I think about that a lot, how I came into the world crooked. My dad used to call her Smiles. He calls me that too, because he says I smile like her. He says she always smiled. I guess that's true. That's what she's doing in all the pictures I've ever seen of her. But sometimes I think she's not smiling at all. Sometimes I think she's trying to tell me something, like when those pictures were taken she knew I'd see them and she wouldn't be here, and she wanted to tell me all the things she wanted me to know. Sometimes at night when the weather's turned bad, I think I hear her in the rain. But I can't make out what she's trying to say. It's like the pictures that way.

"My dad blames me for her dying. I can see it in him when he looks at me. I think that's why he's gone so much. I think he hates it that it wasn't up to him which one of us to keep, me or her. He'd have chosen her. I can't blame him. I never thought there was much hope for me."

"I won't hear that. There's hope, lady. Always." Taylor inched himself down the log. He took Lucy's hand and placed it to her chest, holding it there. "What do you feel?"

"My heartbeat."

"No, lady. I say that's hope. As long as you feel that life in you, there's hope still."

Tears welled in Lucy's eyes. She tried to pull them in and could not. Taylor put his hand to the place on her cheek the sunlight had warmed. She gripped his fingers and said, "All my life I wanted a family. What I got instead was a father who's about to send me away and a mother who couldn't bear to be in the same world as me."

"I'll be your fam'ly," Taylor said. "It'll be us. Us and this Holler, if it deems you worthy."

Lucy went to his arms. Taylor held her in the same way he imagined her father should have—tight, so she'd never leave. He let her cry and watched the Hollow's hard earth drink her tears like a desert drinks the rain.

"I want to be like you," she said. "I want to be here with you. I'll do anything."

Taylor smiled. There was no hiding it. "You want to be like me?"

Lucy nodded.

"To be what I am means doing as I've done, lady. Nothing more or less. But you have to choose to be here. All we are is what's left of the choices we made. This Holler's no different. You want to call it home and me your family, all it asks of you is what it asked of me—a sacrifice."

"I don't understand," Lucy said.

Taylor moved close. He put a hand to Lucy's knee. "What I'm saying, Lucy Seekins, is you gotta Wake somebody."

· 4 ·

It was Tuesday, and Tuesdays meant a patrol through the hill country past the Devereaux farm. That's what I called my drives when in the presence of Kate or Zach or any of the townspeople. Headin' out to patrol, I'd say, as though that were some monumental task fraught with peril. All I really did was stop by Hollis's and say hello, maybe have a glass of Edith's sweet tea, then drive seven miles or so on to Boone's Pond and see if the fish were biting. No better fishing in Mattingly than Boone's Pond.

So when I told Kate I was going to patrol, I was only doing the normal thing. That's what Big Jim wanted from all of us. And me heading north while Justus and his men headed south? No significance there at all. Such was what I told myself in the kindest, most convincing way possible. I'd do my job and my father would do his, which offered me little comfort. The rest? Well, I supposed the rest was up to God. That offered me little comfort as well.

I'd been raised to believe in the God of the New Testament, the God who became man and preached grace and forgiveness and died for my sins. It was a faith I never doubted until the day I met Phillip along the riverbank. Oh, I still went to church after. I still prayed and amened during Preacher Goggins's sermons. Still ate the wafer and drank the grape juice each month. Still believed. But it was never Jesus I saw when I closed my eyes and folded my hands. From then on, it was Jehovah. The Holy Judge.

The road wound past the BP and Hollis's farm, but I didn't stop for a glass of tea that day. Four miles on and three miles from Boone's Pond, I turned down a one-lane stretch of hardpan seldom traveled but for party-seeking teenagers. The road weaved through miles of hill country before ending in a sudden T.

It was only when I turned left for the mountains that I realized where I was heading, and it was only when the hardpan turned to a dark, packed clay and I made a left turn through a broken place in the oaks that I realized I could not turn back. And I remember thinking, *Why not? Why not this place?* Because the rusty gate had always called to me in much the same way that Phillip's grave called to Kate. The only difference was that my fear had made me run from my past, while Kate's had kept her there.

I sat for a long while, watching sunlight fall upon one side of the gate and gray fall upon the other. I reached for Bessie and stepped out to the iron piling on the left. It was taller than me and as thick as my own waist, fastened deep into the earth. I ran a tired hand along its flaking edge to the top and then over, where a series of ten horizontal bars ran a dozen feet or so to the piling on the right.

I don't know who built that gate or when. The general consensus among the old-timers was that the gate was there before the town, and to ponder more was to waste your time. It was as good an answer as any.

The gate couldn't keep anyone out, of course. All one had to do was step around either side and keep walking, right on to Indian Hill if they had a mind. But I don't think the gate's there to keep anyone out. I think it's a warning.

I bent and studied the hundreds of names that had been scratched into the iron over the years. The oldest had been carved into the middle crossbar, and those etchings lay so faded they appeared as ancient runes. Outward toward the edges were names I knew—Hollis's and Justus's close together, Trevor's and Bobby's lower, near the bottom of the left piling. I found Andy Sommerville's name and Timmy's as well, along with a frantic scrawl that spelled out *JIM*. I guess the mayor had not been so big the day he'd carved those three letters. He'd been too afraid to linger even long enough to add Wallis on the end.

There was no carving that spelled out Taylor Hathcock. I thought that meant little. My own name was missing, after all. And not only had I faced the gate, I'd walked on. Then I'd been a boy intent to prove himself a man. Now I stood there a man who understood he'd always be a boy.

I brought Bessie forward and ran her curved head along the gate's upper bar, watched as sunlight glinted off the blade. In a way it had been my daddy's tomahawk that had brought me there at seventeen, or at least the promise of her. Back then Bessie held a place of distinction on the mantle, flanked by a picture of her in my grandfather's hand against the backdrop of some Pacific island and a picture of her in Justus's hand in the middle of some Vietnamese jungle. There'd been a spot reserved there for me as well—holding her in the Iraqi sand, perhaps. But that had been Joey and Frankie's war, not mine. By then I'd seen enough blood.

Justus had already thought me weak. Staying behind while a war was on only cemented that idea. My momma got the cancer when I was ten, died when I was eleven. I always felt there was more of her and less of Justus in me, and a part of my heart went soft when she passed. Still, I couldn't bear knowing my father thought of me that way. Justus thought that way still when he handed Bessie to me the day he left for Crawford's Gap. I took her anyway. It was the closest he'd ever come to saying he loved me.

Daddy, he never shed a tear when Momma passed. I cried for months and cried more when he called me a boy and said that's all I'd ever be. That's why I went to the Hollow that day after school. I wanted to carve my name and show Justus I was a man. Then I decided mere carving wasn't enough, instead I'd walk those woods all the way to the top of Indian Hill. I'd see if the end of the world truly lay on the other side, and then I'd etch my name. Generations of boys would bear witness to that deed. JAKE BARNETT would be the name darkest and deepest in the gate.

I stepped into the Hollow that day with my chin high and my shoulders back, just the way Justus walked into the VFW. I returned shaken and bloody. And in between . . .

Forgive me. Such things are hard to tell. The scar on my arm? I got that scar along the riverbank that day. And just like the scar, that day was imprinted on me. I carried it and always would. Kate had asked me at the kitchen table what happened the day I walked into the Hollow. I could not answer her. But if I had, I would have said what happened was I found more than the end of the world atop Indian Hill, I found the river and I found Phillip. What happened was I found him just after

Kate played her trick and the white butterflies were there and there was blood on my clothes and I ran home knowing my life was over because what happened was Phillip died and I had killed him.

Years later townspeople would still gather on porches and at storefronts to speak of weather or crops, and if their meeting drifted from mere passing by to getting comfortable, their talk meandered to how Phillip McBride's body was found. They would puzzle over the strange phone call Sheriff John David Houser received three days into the search and a week before Phillip's death was declared a suicide. They would describe the masked voice on the other end that said Phillip's body lay along the riverbank in Happy Hollow. Some said that voice was Phillip's own, a reaching out from the grave. But that was not so. That voice was mine, and even as I'd spoken the words I'd felt the first head winds of a remorse that would grow to a gale as the years went on.

Standing at the rusty gate so many years later, I vowed Phillip would be a secret I took to the grave. No matter how that secret rotted my insides and no matter how he haunted my dreams. No matter, even, the threat to my town. I knew it was selfish. And yet I knew I would rather let Taylor Hathcock run unfettered than glimpse the disappointment in my family's eyes if they ever found the truth. Especially Kate's. For her to know what I did would not only bring her rage, it would make her doubt I'd ever loved her at all. Because Kate had always laid Phillip's death upon herself, but that debt was mine.

And Taylor knew that as well, and Taylor was close.

I stood at the gate for a long while before making the drive back to town. Had my mind been in the now, I would have no doubt seen that someone had been there, and recent. Taylor had erased the tracks made by Lucy's car, but I would have seen the evidence of the pine boughs he'd used. I would have followed that faint trail and found the black BMW they'd left hidden in the trees for the forest to swallow.

But I was not in the now. I was in the then, where I'd been all along.

· 5 ·

What Zach told the school secretary was that he'd forgotten his homework and needed to call his momma. Rachel Fleming saw through the lie at once (especially after spying what Zach had written on the piece of paper clutched in his hand), but she slid the phone to him anyway and decided the papers on the other side of the office really should be filed. Rachel smiled as Zach curled his hand around the receiver and waited for Kate to answer.

Kate never wanted any attention for the help she provided the needy. She took great pains to let God see in private what she thought people couldn't see in public. But there are few secrets in a small town, and Kate's was almost as universally known as why Hollis spent so much time in his backwoods. Yet no one spoke of what Kate did, simply because they knew why she did it. That included Rachel Fleming, whose name could be found in the middle of page 74 in Kate's notebook and who, some ten years prior, had woken one morning to find a box of clothes and three Barbie dolls on her crumbling front porch.

Zach told Kate that Harley Ruskin wasn't in school that day, but Harley's teacher (that would be Bobbi Jo Creech, whose name could be found halfway down page 52 of that very same shabby binder) had been more than happy to provide him with the necessary information. Kate wrote it all down in her notebook—estimated clothing size, toy preferences, and the Ruskins' address. She told Zach he was a good boy and that God would forgive his fib about the homework. Zach hoped both were true.

Most of Kate's business was transacted at the Family Dollar, which was located a block from the sheriff's office next to Wenger's Pharmacy. The Super Mart in Camden offered a larger selection of wares, and Kate would likely have gone there over the years had it not been for Elmer Cohron, the Dollar's owner. Like everyone, Elmer knew what Kate did with all those clothes and toys. Unlike everyone, he wasn't shy about letting Kate know in his own way. He rung everything she purchased for the poor at cost, then would always slide the receipt across the counter, offer Kate a sly wink, and say, "You're a good woman, Kate." Elmer held fast to tradition that morning. As did Kate, who held fast to a tradition of her own and drank Elmer's words as one dying of thirst.

· 6 ·

She was on her way back to the sheriff's office when Bobby Barnes's red Dodge turned up Main Street. Justus rode with him. Kate wasn't surprised the truck's bed was empty of their quarry. In her mind, if Jake said Taylor had fled, then fled he had. The rest of Justus's convoy trailed behind. They scattered for parking spaces along Main Street near the diner.

Kate had just decided to cross the street and avoid them when Justus raised his hand. He made his way over, stopping on the sidewalk before coming too close. A wide grin, which Kate translated as either arrogance or spite, crossed his face.

He pointed to the box in her arms and said, "That for my grandson?"

Kate shook her head. "You gave up your rights to a grandson when you left, Justus. You know that."

Justus's smile disappeared. He ran his tongue over his lips. "Ain't found'm yet. We'll regroup over dinner, then swing west to Hilltown. They'll likely spot an interloper."

"If there's an interloper to be found," Kate said. "Jake says he's gone, Justus."

"You believe him?"

"He's never lied to me."

Justus seemed to take that as truth, though he said, "Jake had a weight on him at that meetin'. He's worn, Katelyn. 'Twas plain."

"That had nothing to do with Taylor Hathcock."

"Then what's it to do with?"

"That's family business," Kate said, aware that she'd just stung him again. She waved at the trucks around them and the men walking into the diner. "And it's made worse by all that, if it matters to you. You being here just makes Jake's job harder. Can't you see that? Why don't you just go back to where you came from?"

"I'm settlin' accounts," Justus said. "Jake wants me gone, there's an easy way. All he's gotta do's bring me in. And afore you say else, I'll say it's been as easy for him to find me all these years as it is right now. Jacob always knew where I was, just as he knows where I am now."

"Turn your own self in, then," Kate said.

Justus shook his head. "Gotta be Jacob."

"Why?" she asked, and in a voice so loud that those near them paused in their coming and going to turn their heads. The box shook in Kate's arms. She was happy it was there, and not only because delivering it would count toward redemption. If her hands had been empty, Kate was sure they would ball into fists and wail upon Justus's barrel chest. She would do it, and she would bear the consequences. "Why can't you just leave us *alone?*"

"Jacob's soft, Katelyn. That's why. Because that man's still out there, I feel it in my bones, an' because my boy's no good man t'catch him."

"You've a nerve to speak of good men," Kate said. "Jake never raised a gun in anger. He's kind."

Justus boiled. "We Barnetts owned that farm for generations, girl. We worked it, sweat and bled in it, prayed over it, 'til Big Jim cast his eye there and seen dollar signs. I knew the black in his heart. He wanted that land hisself. To *develop* it. An' he knew about the note I took out when the crops failed. Miss two payments, that's enough for him to make the bank call the loan, knowin' I couldn't pay. That's when he sent those men out. They came on my land, Katelyn. *Jake's* land. *Zach's* land. *To take it.* You ask anyone in this town, they'll say I was justified in what I done. All I wanted was my own blood to stand with me, but he refused. You say Jacob is kind, I say his kindness is panic without teeth."

"Those men were just doing their jobs," Kate screamed, and now everyone stopped. "You could've killed them."

"If that was my aim. But it wasn't."

"But it was close enough. And what did all that cost you, Justus? You ran away when Jake begged you to stay and face what you did. You lost the farm anyway. You lost your freedom. You lost your *family.*"

"I ran because I had to," Justus said. His voice cracked. "John David Houser called and said he had a warrant his heart wouldn't allow him to serve. Said he was sworn by the law to do his duty as sheriff, but he was sworn by the man he was not to arrest a man for something he'd have done hisself. I knew his mind. He was tellin' me to go afore he got there. Jacob was the only one who said I was in the wrong then; Jacob should be the one to bring me in now. Because that's his place. He wears the badge, Katelyn. That's how it should be."

"No, Justus," Kate said. "How it should be is that you go. You go before it's too late."

Kate stepped around him. Her shoulders stooped under the weight in her arms. She turned when Justus called her name.

"Bernard Wilcox, husband of one, father of two. Harvey Lewis, divorced, father of three. Clancy Townsend, husband of two, father of four, grandfather of six."

"What?" Kate asked.

"Those are the men I shot that day. I expect no one remembers them now, just as you. But know well I remember them, Katelyn. I see their faces in my dreams and I speak their names when I wake, an' they'll follow me until I stand in judgment from man and God. I'm sorry for what I done. That's why I call. That's why I'm here. I'm tired of runnin'. I pray for grace but I'll abide by punishment, if that's what it takes for me to move on. Do you understand?"

Kate hefted the box and walked away. She said nothing, but she understood. Kate understood well.

· 7 ·

This time Lucy didn't tell Taylor where she was going, and there was no bear at the edge of the meadow to greet her. There were eyes, though, always those eyes. Watching her the way neighbors will when strangers move in down the street—keeping distance, waiting to see how things will go and if there will be trouble. Yet Lucy walked on unafraid and unbothered past the boulders that littered the dead ground and through the trees to the stone-lined path. To the grove and to the Hole.

She sat cross-legged and watched that perfect black sphere, her pupils swelling and her breaths low and soft. It was a terror and a wonder, and both held a beauty. Lucy had been obsessed with many things over her short life—boys, love, attention. A dead mother. But now she understood that the Hole was no obsession. It consumed her. No, it *completed* her. In a way she had never thought possible. She felt a wetness on her leg and looked to find drool staining her jeans. Lucy wiped her mouth, understanding the hunger she felt.

One day, what consumed Lucy would be hers alone. One day, her own mark would be put upon the wall.

Her world in town had been snatched away by her father and Johnny Adkins. Lucy had once mourned that loss, but no longer. Now she understood that life had been taken away because a better life was coming, and she wanted nothing more than to see that life flourish. To do that, she would have to kill. She would have to kill like Taylor killed that boy.

But was it killing?

Was it really?

Taylor didn't think it was. If anything, he thought what he did to Eric Thayer was the opposite of killing. Taylor said he'd given life to that boy, and if that was a sin it was okay because it let God forgive, and forgiving was what God did best. Lucy didn't know about all of that. She'd grown up placing her faith in Nothing rather than Something, and the books she'd left shredded and ripped on her living room floor didn't say much about a deity, except that there probably wasn't one. But when she beheld the Hole's solemn gaze, Lucy knew everything she'd believed and all that those dead old men wrote was wrong. So very wrong.

Yet not so wrong that the question of whether she was about to become a murderer mattered to Lucy in the least. That she would do such an act was not questioned. People did horrible things every day in the name of love. They lied and killed to belong. She would be no different.

In the end Lucy saw it best to believe whatever would make the going easier. She would Wake, then. Not kill. The only thing left was deciding who it would be. And that was where Lucy faltered.

Whom among the town did she love enough to set free? Was there one whom she believed should be spared from further years? Someone whose heart hurt even worse than her own? Lucy thought no. She had loved many people in many ways, but she found that love did not extend to mercy.

Her eyes fell from the Hole to the footprint in the dirt that Taylor had shown her. Left, he said, by a magical some *(thing?)* one who had breached the line between the real and the not. Lucy leaned over and traced the outline of the shoe with a small rock she found at her feet.

Would a *thing* wear a shoe? Would a spirit? No, of course not.

Only a person.

She faced the Hole again and turned the pebble over in her hand. Taylor had said the Hollow's few living things dared not approach the grove (Lucy took that as true, had seen the bear turn away herself), because it was holy and all else was soiled. And yet if one thing could breach that blackness, couldn't another? What if that Hole wasn't a hole at all? What if it was a *door*? And if that door swung open to this side of the world, could it not swing open to the side of another?

Yes, she thought. *Maybe.*

Maybe and let's see.

And with the same amount of thought Lucy had given when she'd told Taylor Hathcock to get into her car, she let the rock in her hand fly.

She reached to pull the pebble back, but it was too late. It sailed true, spanning the ten feet between her and the Hole in seconds. What came next was not the vengeful wrath of a bothered god nor the shattering of reality. The rock was simply there and then not. Lucy leaned forward, listening for perhaps the splash of the stone hitting water or a faint thud as it rolled and stopped. No sound came, but that changed nothing in Lucy's mind. The pebble had gone somewhere.

She decided the mystery in front of her would be hers alone. And if Lucy Seekins would not secure her place in the Hollow by waking someone she loved, she would do so by killing someone she hated. Really, what difference did it make in the end?

Lucy wiped the drip from the corner of her mouth and smiled.

· 8 ·

Standing once more at the rusty gate had rattled me. Seeing Justus and his men when I returned to town rattled me more. But walking into the office and finding what was on Kate's desk? That nearly did me in. Because that could mean only one thing, and with Taylor Hathcock still about, there was no way I was going to let Kate go anywhere alone.

I heard the faucet running in the bathroom and walked to the box. Inside were three pairs of jeans, four T-shirts, a handful of candy bars, and a small toy tractor.

A boy, then.

Kate and I were no different than most in Mattingly. Sheriffing didn't pay much and never had. We kept two months' pay in the bank for emergencies and a few twenties in an old coffee can in the kitchen cupboard. We got by. But even if Elmer Cohron had always sold to Kate at cost, I figured there were seventy dollars in that box. I couldn't help but ponder just how much money I'd handed to that notebook over the years. All spread out, of course, which made the sting more a dull hurt. Plenty for a new truck for her or a new motor for the Blazer or something extra for Zach under the tree come Christmas.

But to ask her to stop would be to deny Kate the hope of making amends, and I held that hope as precious even if I believed it impossible for myself. Phillip was dead. There would be no second chance for either of us. All we had was the penance of names scrawled in her binder and rocks stacked along a riverbank in my dreams. I had resigned myself to both, even forged a kind of peace with them. But then Taylor Hathcock had turned the life I lived when awake into something far more frightening than the life I lived when asleep, and he had done so with five simple words:

I know what you did.

"Jake."

I turned as Kate slipped her arms around me.

"Hey, you," she said. When she kissed me, my lips were pursed and cold. "How's your ride?"

"Fine." I tried to smile. "Saw Justus and the boys over at the diner. They decide to call it quits?"

"No. I ran into him a little while ago. He said they didn't find anything and were going to swing west this afternoon."

My face relaxed a bit, though not enough for Kate to see. Justus hadn't found Taylor. I knew I should see that as a bad thing for the town, but that was all set aside for the good thing it was for me. It was a horrible thing to think. And while I wanted to believe much of it was because I felt so tired and stretched inside, I knew it was not.

"I don't think they really want to find anyone," Kate said. "They just want an excuse to load their guns and hunt for something other than deer and bear. You know men, Jake." She flipped the brim of my hat up with a playful flick of her hand and smiled. "They always wanna play cowboy."

"What else did Justus say?" I asked.

Kate's grin held but flickered. "Not much. I had to get back." She motioned at the box. "Had my hands full."

"So I see. Who's that for?"

"A boy named Harley Ruskin."

"Don't believe I know any Ruskins," I said.

"I didn't either until the meeting. They were the family on the front row along the wall. Guess you didn't see them." She rummaged through the box on her desk, making sure everything was there and nothing had been left out. "Can't blame you, what with Justus and all. I got Zach to find out a few things for me and went down to the Dollar while you were gone. I'm gonna run it out there now."

"Where's he live?"

"North of 664," she said.

North. Justus and his men had searched south and west. I'd started up 664 on my morning drive but had swung east instead. That meant north had gone unsearched.

I know what you did, Jake. You tell Kate?

I scratched an itch on my lower lip that wasn't there. My fingers shook. It reminded me of how Bobby Barnes looked the day I'd come upon him in Hollis's woods.

"Why don't you wait a couple days, Kate."

Kate's brow ridged. She cocked her head to the side as though I'd started a joke in the middle. "Why?"

"I don't know. Everything's just so . . . bad. Right now."

"You got that right," she said, closing the box. "That's why I'm going. That boy needs some sunshine in his life, Jake. We all do. Giving him some will give me some too."

"I think you should just wait."

Kate reached for her notebook and looked at me. "What's wrong with you?"

"Nothing," I said. "I just think it's best if you stay close to town."

"Well, I think it's best if I go."

She stepped around me and gathered the box from her desk. The notebook went atop it. I blocked her path when she turned.

"How about I go with you?" I asked. "Everything's been so crazy that we haven't really spent any time together. Be nice, taking a ride."

Kate finished the smile she'd begun earlier, as though she'd taken that to be the rest of my joke. "Jake, you know I have to do this by myself. Always have. It's my burden and my pleasure. Besides, someone has to pick up Zach after school."

"We'll be back in time," I said. "Don't go today. Please, Kate."

The box tugged on Kate's arms. This load was heavy. All of them were, I supposed, regardless of how old she'd been when she lifted them or what they carried inside.

"I've been thinking about him," she said.

"Who?"

"Phillip."

I shifted my weight, holding my right elbow with my left hand. The room grew smaller, brighter, and the soft yellow of sunlight through the shades turned brilliant. I licked my lips, suddenly thirsty.

"I guess it was Eric Thayer," Kate said. "He was so young, Jake. Like Phillip was."

"Kate . . ."

She shook her head and wiped her eyes on her shoulder. "That's why I have to go, Jake. I have to help Harley because I didn't help Phillip. And I have to do it alone."

Kate raised her heels and kissed my cheek, then stepped aside. I searched for anything that would keep her there, any lie or excuse. But every step she took away from me was one step she may have been taking toward Taylor, and with such thinking, only the truth would do.

She'd just shifted the box to her hip to open the door when I said, "Taylor's not gone."

Kate looked at me. "What?"

"Taylor Hathcock isn't gone. He's here. Close to town."

"How do you know that?"

I gritted my teeth. The thirst had turned into a sharp pain in the back of my throat that I couldn't swallow. I couldn't look at her.

"Because he called me."

Kate sat the box down. "When did he call you? Did you tell Alan?"

I shook my head. "Called me Sunday night. You were asleep."

"What did he say?"

"That he was close. Always has been. Told me to pull the county police out of town."

"And you did?" Her tone was a blade that cut through me. "You did what he told you to do?"

"He knew you, Kate. He knew Zach."

"How can he know us?"

"I don't know," I said. "I think someone other than Charlie Givens was helping him. He said if I didn't call the police away, there'd be more trouble."

Kate screamed, "More *trouble*? What were you thinking, Jake? That man killed a *boy*. He hurt Andy and my *brother*."

She fell silent, her mind tumbling, and then her eyes bulged and her mouth fell open as she stumbled on yet another terrible truth.

"He called you Sunday night, and the next day you not only call off Alan's men, you stand in front of the whole town and say Taylor's gone? How could you do that, Jake? You lied to them." Another pause. "You lied to *me*."

And after this, after it all, I could only say, "I had to."

She picked up the box again and twisted it to her hip as she reached for the knob. "No, Jake, you didn't."

"Kate, you can't tell anyone. Please. For me."

She stopped but would not turn. Could not face me. "Don't burden me with your sins, Jake. My own are heavy enough. Justus said you were weak. Soft, he called it. He said that's why you have to be the one to bring him in and why you never will. I told him he was wrong on both counts. I guess I'm the one who was wrong."

And then she was gone.

· 9 ·

In a strange way, Kate supposed her anger was the only reason Harley Ruskin would get his blessing that day. Had she not been so mad at Jake, her mind would have centered on the fact she was driving into the hill country alone with a killer on the loose. A killer who knew her name.

The Ruskin home place was neither home nor place, but a leaning wooden structure sitting off a dirt road behind a set of thick pines. The steps leading from the rotting porch had long crumbled, leaving a gap between there and the ground small enough to manage but large enough to snap an ankle. A mongrel dog sought refuge there from the sun, its pink tongue lolling in the dirt. Kate thought it was either near sleep or death and did not dwell long on which. Her thoughts focused instead on her own sinking heart.

Evidently Pa Ruskin put little stock in lawn maintenance. A sea of dandelions stretched between where Kate hid and the front porch she meant to reach. There was no way to navigate around, no alternate route she could take. The weeds sprouted even in the gravel driveway, which was empty but for a rusted station wagon. The family vehicle, she supposed. And that was another, though less pressing problem.

The Ruskins were home.

The house windows were propped open with whatever had been handy—a wooden potstick, a broken branch from the oak just outside, a tennis shoe propped on its heel. What shingles remained on the roof huddled in small patches near the edges. To the side of the house, a sagging clothesline held four pairs of overalls in various sizes, one pair each of men's and boy's boxer shorts, and two enormous bras. Behind the house was a large garden. A barn stood in the backyard, which seemed in so much better shape than the house that Kate thought it would do the Ruskins well to make their home there instead.

She watched all of this from just inside the stand of pines along the road. Harley's box sat in front of her. She waited with a patience that was almost saintly, trusting the same God who had never forgiven her to offer the grace of a moment. Her hair was pulled into a ponytail, as it always was when she delivered her packages. Kate had always told Jake that wearing her hair that way made it easier for her to sneak and spy. That was close enough to the truth, but not all the way there. Kate wore her hair such because that had been the way she'd worn it the day she killed Phillip McBride.

The screen door opened. Kate sank farther into the trees as Harley Ruskin's father walked out. He paused where the steps should have been and turned back to say something (Kate thought it was either "Bye" or "Love you," she couldn't be sure) and stepped down into the yard. The dog did not move. Pa Ruskin went for the station wagon and tried the ignition four times before it caught. Kate held her breath at the thought of him taking a right out of the driveway and seeing the Blazer parked just down the road. She breathed when he turned left instead.

One down.

Ten minutes later another door screeched, this from the back of the house. The slow-moving image of Harley and his mother appeared around the side where the clothes hung. There was no telling why the boy had been allowed to stay home from school. He certainly didn't look sick, which left only the possibility of the Ruskins wanting to stay clear of the devil. Harley swung the clothes basket from his right hand, holding it high so it wouldn't touch the ground. He gestured with his left. His mother nodded. She placed a hand to his back and patted it in much the same way Kate would pat Zach. It was the touch of a mother to her child, a brief but not unnoticed transmittal of love. They plucked the clothes from the line, leaving the pins to dangle in the breeze, and left the basket there as they walked hand in hand toward the barn. Kate eyed them. She eyed the way to the Ruskins' front porch as well. And the dandelions. So many dandelions.

As soon as Harley and his momma disappeared inside the barn, Kate sprang from the trees. The box shifted in her arms with each footfall, threatening to throw her off balance. She raced across the front yard, grimacing as she trampled one yellow weed after another, fighting back the nausea building in her stomach. The dog lifted his head and offered a tired bark. Kate bounded over him and onto the porch, setting the box by the door. She spun and galloped back over the dandelions, forcing that welling sense of revulsion down until it lurched forward with more power than she could fight. Kate did not so much run back into the trees as dive. She kicked off her shoes as she landed. Sweat gathered on her brow. That sick feeling, a notion that she'd just been poisoned, swept over her. She leaned forward and vomited into the soft bed of pine needles.

Harley reappeared minutes later and gathered the hamper. His momma followed, carrying a basket of eggs. The smile on her face was a temporary cosmetic that smoothed out the dark lines and deep wrinkles of a hard life. The two of them disappeared behind the house. Kate heard another screech. Five minutes later Harley Ruskin walked past the front door.

He saw the box and stood there, not knowing what to make of it, then walked out onto the porch with his hands in his pockets. He toed the package with a bare foot and looked out over the yard, then back inside. He inquired of his dog and received no reply. Only then did Harley bend down and open his blessing.

The quiet day in Mattingly's hills was broken by a shout of joy that was part Christmas morning and part summer vacation. Harley leaped and bounded inside, not even thinking of taking the box with him. He pulled his momma through the door and showed her everything, the jeans and the shirts and the treats, even the plastic toy tractor that had found its way to the bottom of the box. Ma Ruskin's face held a mix of shame and wonder. She turned and gazed out to the scrabbling dirt road beyond.

It was a beautiful moment. It was magic and hope and love. And yet Kate showed no satisfaction for the joy she'd brought. There were only the wet eyes and trembling lips of someone weary of trying.

She left soon after, skirting past the Ruskins' home before Harley's pa could return. The drive back to town was quiet and hard. It was two o'clock when Kate reached the town limits. By then Harley's face had left her memory. What replaced it was Jake—Jake and his lies. But before Kate could tend to that, she had to finish what she'd begun.

She pulled through the open gate of Oak Lawn and left the Blazer idling atop the knoll. The day was quiet, bright. It was springtime, that season when life rises again. Kate took her notebook from the seat and walked the rows of headstones until she reached the spot where Phillip's body lay. She plucked the twigs and leaves that had fallen onto his marker, tossing them absently onto the grave beside (KENNETH WELCHER, that stone said, DEC 12, 1904 – JUN 22, 1967 A GOOD MAN GONE FROM A HARD WORLD). Kate had never known Kenneth, nor if he had been a good man, but the truth of that last part was plain. She sat in the grass and opened her book to the top of page 212.

"Harley Ruskin," she whispered. "He's a young boy, just about Zach's age. I went to his house today and left him a box. Clothes mostly, since I thought that's what he needed most. But I got him a toy and some candy too, because every child should have those." Kate sniffed. She looked at the headstone in front of her and wished the bones beneath could hear through the earth and rock between them. "It was just a joke, Phillip. That's all I meant it to be. I'm so sorry."

The tears came then, just as they had after all the other boxes delivered to all the other front porches. And just as she had all those other times, Kate prayed that somehow Phillip would hear her words and offer his forgiveness.

· 10 ·

The wooden target out back of the sheriff's office wasn't Zach's alone to use. The path leading to and from had been made by boots much larger than his, just as the deep gashes in the rings of the tree round had been made by one who threw Bessie with much more violence.

I stood at the head of that worn path now. My eyes blinked against exhaustion and strain as I stared at the target, giving it face after face.

There was Zach, who would be in school for another hour. With all that weighed on my mind, I still hoped my son had made his peace with Danny Blackwell that day. I hoped he would always make peace and always do the right thing so he would not grow up to lie to the woman and the town he loved.

Then came Kate, who had gone to the hills carrying both a box and my secret. I didn't know what she would do with the latter, but I knew she'd use the former to take another step along a road with no end.

There was Trevor Morgan, who had done more to harm Mattingly in the last days than any devil.

My father was next, the almost-murderer who had come down from the mountains and claimed my place as town protector, and who in many ways had haunted me more than Phillip McBride ever could.

There came Taylor, who knew what I had done to Phillip

in the Hollow the day Kate played her trick. The face I saw there was more a rendering and based solely upon Timmy Griffith's description, but it was Taylor enough. His picture settled into the contours of the wood. My fingers twitched at my right side, wanting to move. It could not. That image was not real, yet I was as afraid of it as I was everything else.

Taylor's likeness stretched out to the edges of the target and faded. I blinked, not understanding the image my mind conjured next. The skin on this face was gaunt and sallow. Dark, wide eyes stared out from beneath a black hat, cutting first right and then left, searching not for something to find but somewhere to hide. It was the face of a man stranded in a fate of his own making, caught by a rising tide upon slippery rocks.

My hand moved before that picture could change. I reached behind my back and drew the tomahawk forward, flipping the handle in the air and catching it behind my right shoulder in one smooth motion.

Bessie flew. Her arc held true, the blade cleaving the air between me and the target in mere seconds, striking the small space in the wood I saw as the drawn brows over my own eyes. The iron head lodged itself there to the hilt.

"Not bad."

I looked to the door. My right arm crossed my body, frozen in the throw's follow-through. Justus's body took up nearly all of the doorway. The only bits of light that leaked out from the office came through the tiny slits above his head and the spaces between his arms and sides.

"Reckoned I'd find you here," he said, and then he smiled in a way that told me he was both proud and disappointed that he'd guessed right.

I straightened and asked, "What are you doing here, Justus? Bobby Barnes get tired of chauffeuring you around?"

"No." He turned his body and eased into the grass. "Sent'm home. All of 'em. Start again tomorrow. Where's Katelyn?"

I walked to the target and pried Bessie from the wood. "Had an errand to run."

"And your boy?"

"School. State your aim."

I brought Bessie back up the path. Justus waited for me there.

"Come to make peace," he said.

"You want peace, go on back to the Gap. Leave us be."

Justus looked at Bessie. "Why? So I can leave you to play while a murderer goes free?"

"Taylor Hathcock's not your responsibility."

He thumped me in the chest, daring me to do something. "That's right, he's *yours*. I ain't runnin' off again. Did that once, look where it got me. Right back here. Fate or the Lord's will, Jacob, take your pick. You want me to go? Arrest me."

Justus held out hands so big I thought handcuffs would never get around them even if I tried. His shadow covered me.

"You know what you did goes beyond this town," I told him. "State and county want you, not me."

I wheeled and fired. The crack of blade meeting wood echoed off the walls. The corners of Justus's mouth rose and his eyes lit, but he said nothing. I walked to the target. "Why are you doing this? Why are you *here*? This town gave you a way out seven years ago. John David had the badge, but he never looked for you. Town wouldn't let him because they thought you were in the right, and I believe he felt the same, though he never said it. Even Big Jim let you go."

"Jim Wallis got what he wanted," Justus said. "I'm the only one that man's afraid of. He didn't get the farm or his strip mall, not yet, but he managed to chase me from Mattingly.

Town wouldn't let him chase another Barnett. That's why they gave you the badge, Jacob. An' they mean you to use it. To keep the peace, within this town and without it."

I pried Bessie from the wood and said, "Go find Alan Martin in Stanley. Turn yourself in to him, but don't come to me. I'm your *son*."

"*That's why I'm doin' it*," he roared.

I froze halfway to him. Justus stared at me, jowls straining and cheeks flushed, then he looked away. I believe he saw my fear and was ashamed. Whether that embarrassment was because of the way I'd reacted or because he'd made me react that way, I didn't know. But I knew that all men, no matter how tall and wide they get or how much gray sits atop their heads, are still boys inside.

"I look to heaven an' feel hell, boy," he said. "I'm plagued by those men I shot. It's the livin' that haunt me, not the dead. You too. You haunt me too.

"Your momma took my heart with her to the grave; I'd none left to raise you up with. Her passin' broke you just as much, an' I couldn't put you together again. You're weak on the inside, boy. I been waitin' up to the Gap for years, hopin' you'd come get me. I knew you never would. You spent your whole life sittin' down. But I knowed the day'd come when you'd have to stand up, and that time is now.

"Town needs you out there lookin' for Taylor Hathcock, not here pitchin' Bessie. They're grumblin', Jacob. I hear it. You bring me in, it shows them people you're a Barnett. It shows them you can *stand*. That's why I cain't turn m'self in and that's why it's gotta be you. You were the only one to speak agin' me when those bank men came. I shoulda listened to you then, but I dint know."

"Know what?"

Justus slipped his hands into his pockets and sighed. It was a small gesture, one I saw every day from a hundred different people and for a hundred different reasons. It was the sign of a man about to say there was no rain for his fields or a woman about to speak of a child who'd run off to the city with the wrong boy or girl. It was a precursor to talk of the mysteries of life and the balefulness of the world.

"Some choices you live with only once," he said. "Others you hang on to forever. Took me seven years to learn that lesson, but learn it I have. I'm tired, Jacob. This world's no home for the weary."

I stood there staring, not believing what I'd heard. All the people in the world, and it had been Justus who'd gotten a look into my own soul. Not Kate, not anyone else. Justus. And yet all I could do was walk the rest of the way up the path and say, "I'm busy."

Justus lowered his head and flashed a bitter smile. When he looked up, his face held the same stony expression I'd known all my life. It was the one my father had worn when he said my momma was dead. It was there again when I was fifteen and he'd dipped so far into Hollis's brew that he hit me. That was the day I wiped the blood from my lip (it was a cut just like the one Zach got, I remembered; that same jagged line from my mouth to my nose) and said I was going to finish school and leave Mattingly, leave the farm, but most of all, leave him.

That look had been there the day I returned from the Hollow with my arm torn and my jeans streaked with my own blood. After Justus wanted to know what had happened and I was too afraid to answer with the truth.

It had been there the day Sheriff Houser begged my father to run and I'd told him to stay, to face his failures in the way I'd never faced my own. And it had been there as Justus became a fugitive and I said he would be a stranger to his family.

"Goin' north t'morrow," he said. "After that we'll go house to house if we hafta. Got more men comin'. Preacher Goggins says he'll get every able body in church t'help. You won't find that man, Jake, we will. And then he'll 'fess. He'll 'fess to everythin'."

Justus turned to go. I gripped Bessie and fired at the target. This time the blade made a quarter turn too many. The head met the rounded hunk of oak and bounced harmlessly to the grass.

Justus looked back long enough to say, "Good thing about a tree? It don't kill you if you miss."

· 11 ·

Taylor knew where Lucy had gone as soon as she sat beside him. It was the smile on her face—a wide, contented grin Taylor could never coax from her but the Hole always managed to grow there. He put the binoculars down and looked at her.

"When we were driving up here the other night," Lucy said, "I had no idea where I was going. Some of those streets were ones I never even knew were there. I thought you knew them because you grew up in town. But that's not true, is it? You knew those streets because all you do is sit up here and look."

"You're a bright one, lady," he said.

"Why though? I mean, you can do anything. You don't need to work, you don't have any responsibilities. You're the freest person I've ever known, but you're chained to this old log."

"I'm seeking Her," Taylor said.

"Kate."

"That's right."

As if to underscore that point, Taylor lifted the binoculars again. The night was coming on and there was little to see, but that didn't matter. He had never let the thought that he was blind to what he saw get in the way of truth.

"You told me she said she loved you," Lucy said. "I need to know more."

"Why's that?"

"Because I do."

"She played a trick on me long back." He kept the spyglasses up, not wanting Lucy to see what might be written on his face. "She told me she loved me, but she played a trick instead. There was trouble with a boy because of it. Jake played his own part."

"What kind of trouble?"

Taylor winced from behind the lenses and said, "Blessing, I mean. There was blessing because of it."

"Who was the boy?"

Taylor shook his head. "My time down there was short. Dint know his name. Jake and Kate, now? I knew them. Everybody knew them."

"What kind of trick was it?" Lucy asked.

"A mean one," Taylor said. "Ain't no other kind. She told me she loved me and she tricked me for sport. Tricked the boy too. Tricked us both. Kate Griffith saw to his end, and Jake stood idle. But I saved that boy."

"What do you mean Kate saw to his end?" Lucy asked. "How'd you save the boy?"

Taylor shook his head. *A blessing*, he thought, *'twas a blessing*. He tried to convince himself that was so even as memories pulled him back to that day along the riverbank and the sight of the flint knife in his own hand and Jake Barnett rounding the bend. He took the binoculars away, tried to chase away that remembrance, and when he did he thought for a moment there were three people on the rotten log instead of two, there was him and there was Lucy and there was also another, a boy in short jeans and a hooded red sweatshirt, but Taylor's heart begged him to remember no more, and the three of them became two again.

"How've you spent your day, lady?" he asked. "You thought on what I told you?"

"Yes," she said. "I'll do it."

"What's he call himself? Or is it a her?"

"A him. His name's Hollis Devereaux."

Taylor nodded. He didn't know a Hollis Devereaux and thought he wouldn't. "Have you dealings with this man?"

"No," she said, "I know him, though. What he does. I promised myself I'd see to him if I ever got the chance."

"Do you love him enough to set him free?" Taylor asked.

"I'll set him free."

"Such promises are easy to make and hard to keep, Lucy Seekins. You'd do well to know that."

"This is my home now," Lucy said. "I'll do what I have to do to stay."

Taylor looked down over the town again, which was now dark but for tiny specks of light downtown.

"You cannot take my blade," he said. "It's precious to me and holds a power you can't wield. Gun's cleaned and loaded, though. Can you shoot?"

"A boy taught me how once," Lucy said. "His name is Johnny. Or was. He's gone now."

Taylor asked, "Are you sure you have this in you, lady?"

Lucy smiled. He saw it was not a pretty smile, more like a bobcat's just before it pounced.

"I've never been as sure of anything in my life, Taylor. He'll be in his woods. I know where they are. I'll find him. If it takes forever, I'll find him."

Taylor knew that was true. What he didn't know is if the lady beside him would succeed. It took love to Wake someone, but all he saw in Lucy Seekins was hate.

"Besides," Lucy said, "none of this is real anyway. Right?"

Taylor didn't answer. All he said was, "Tomorrow. It'll be tomorrow."

· 12 ·

Zach Barnett may have been only six and fuzzy on if there really were pots of gold at the ends of rainbows or where babies came from, but he knew when his parents were fighting. It wasn't so much that things got louder around the house, it was more they got quieter. That night the silence held such a presence that he felt it was a living thing.

The air itself carried a charge like lightning that could strike anywhere at any time. Zach felt one of those bolts when his daddy snapped at him for not wanting to take a bath. He caught one from his momma when he bucked at doing his homework. It was the heavy clink of ice in their glasses during an otherwise soundless supper and his vain attempts at conversation that were met with stares and grunts. Not even Zach's news that he'd sat with Danny Blackwell at lunch and turned half his peanut butter and banana sandwich into a peace offering raised so much as an eyebrow. He repeated it twice, but neither one of his parents heard him.

They didn't happen often, these fights. Zach was thankful

for that. His teachers at school had yet to instruct him in many things (pots of gold and how babies got in women's stomachs among them), but his classmates had taught Zach plenty about divorce. No fewer than three of the kids in his first-grade class had mommies and daddies who didn't love each other anymore, and all three shared the belief that seeing your folks fight was much like seeing a red sky in the morning—it meant bad weather was coming.

Zach didn't think his folks were headed down that road. They most always got along. They laughed at each other's jokes and held hands and kissed a lot, and sometimes the three of them would get into wrestling matches on the floor. Zach didn't know a lot, but he knew about fighting and fun. He figured that if you put those two together, that made love.

So that night Zach did what every child would do—he kept his head down and his mouth closed, and weathered the storm. He didn't ask to throw Bessie in the backyard and didn't complain when his momma said it was bedtime, and he found his grace in believing the next day would be better because tomorrow never had any hurt in it yet. When you're six, such things are easy to believe.

His momma still read him a bedtime story, and his daddy still ended the night by telling Zach he was proud of him and loved him. At least there was that. If his daddy had left that part out, Zach really would have started worrying about divorce.

Yet he couldn't fall asleep. It was everything that had happened in town. He understood this even if his parents had told him little. The kids at school had talked plenty about what had happened in town that week. After their peace had been made and the peanut butter and banana sandwich eaten, Danny Blackwell had told Zach it was a zombie that had hurt Andy, Timmy, and that boy named Eric. Knew it for a fact,

Danny said, "Because I sawed it on the TV and zombies eat *braiiins*." Zach didn't believe that for a minute (though he did pause to consider if there really was a brain-hungry zombie loose in Mattingly, Danny Blackwell would be the safest person in the whole town). He knew the one who had done those bad things had been just a man.

And yet to Zach, that notion was much scarier. He would have preferred the zombie. Because if it really had been just a man who had upended Zach's town, that meant his Uncle Timmy and Mr. Andy and that boy Eric hadn't been set upon by a monster, they'd been hurt—and killed, Zach knew that and didn't need Danny to tell him—by someone as normal as himself.

He knew about bad people. Reverend Goggins had told Zach how Adam and Eve were good until the devil talked Eve into eating that apple, after which Adam wanted his own bite. That's when everything went to pot, because that's when Adam and Eve looked down and saw they didn't have any clothes on. That's when sin started, the preacher said, and Zach always thought that must've been an awful thing to witness. He also figured he couldn't blame Adam and Eve for eating that apple. Experience had taught him people tend to want a lot of things, and the things they're not supposed to have especially. He had no doubt everyone's original parents had a rough go from then on. On those dark nights like the one he was mired in now, Zach would sometimes think about Adam trying to keep the weeds out of his crop and Eve hollering because it hurt so bad when those babies came out of her stomach and how they both must have spent a lot of time thinking on the good old days. But he bet they probably thought on that apple plenty too, and how good it tasted.

Yes, people were bad. They did mean things like hurt other

people and make mommas and daddies fight and pull on pretty girls' pigtails. They made you take the cap gun you kept hung from a peg on your bedroom wall and slip it under your pillow.

Zach knew that sometimes people died too, and sometimes that was because of bad people and sometimes not. He had two grandmas and one granddaddy in heaven. The other granddaddy—the one who'd once carried Bessie—had gone little mentioned in Zach Barnett's life, and whatever questions he'd posed had been met with silence on the part of his parents. That granddaddy had become a Secret, and Zach knew secrets happened whenever there was something bad to be hidden. But even if Zach was ignorant of the machinations of the world, he understood when one and one equaled two. He could come and go anywhere in town he wished and talk to anyone he had the notion to, but Zach's parents never let him near the phone when Mr. Justus started calling. And whenever the Barnett family was out to the Dairy Queen for supper or the carnival or church and Mr. Justus's name was mentioned, Zach's momma and daddy were always quick to shush and head on.

It was a surprising thing for Zach to hit on, even as young as he was—his folks had been trying to keep a secret so bad they'd given that secret away long before Mr. Justus called Zach's daddy "son."

Zach didn't know why he wasn't allowed to speak to Mr. Justus or what exactly Mr. Justus had done to get himself kicked out of the town, but he figured it had to be something bad. He'd heard his momma say once that Mr. Justus was headed for h-e-double hockey sticks when his time came. And that was the problem. Because Mr. Justus had to be a *real* bad man to end up there, had maybe even hated Jesus, and if that was true then it meant the bad in him was also in Zach's daddy and also in Zach himself.

That nugget of insight made him shudder beneath the covers.

But Zach thought his daddy was a good man, the best man. He was sheriff of the whole town, and everybody loved him. And he thought his momma was the best woman too. She helped people and had taught him to do the same, had even let him help her with her names. That was the second best thing in the world to Zach (throwing Bessie, of course, topped that list), and he'd grown to understand that real joy meant not getting from people but giving to them. That was the lesson his momma taught. "Doing for others who can't do for themselves is like digging for treasure, Zach," she'd often said. "It makes the bad inside feel better."

Zach thought on that and on all those good things he'd done with his momma and daddy, and he really did feel better. Yet there in the cool silence of the night, he also considered that his father had been acting different lately, like something was wrong. He'd tried to hide it, but Zach could see (and could hear as well, some of the screams those last nights had made it to his sleeping ears) that Jake Barnett was sick, and from more than just not sleeping.

He'd seen, too, that his momma's lesson about helping others was one she'd maybe forgotten. Getting those names and gathering up those boxes didn't make her smile so much anymore, and Zach couldn't understand why. It was like his momma was still trying to dig for treasure, but she was heaping all the dirt she dug up on top of herself.

Zach's last thought before closing his eyes was a prayer that he would open them to sunshine. He bolted upright not ten minutes later when he heard his father hollering and his mother saying it was okay. Zach saw a shadow cast on the white hallway wall. He wanted to call out, ask if that shadow was his mother or his father, but when he tried he could only produce a whisper. He reached for the cap gun under his pillow and pulled back the covers.

The shadow was still there, unmoving, almost as if it were waiting. For him. The muscles in Zach's face and arms tensed as he stepped around the toy town on the floor, wanting to say, Momma is that you, please tell me that's you and please tell me what's wrong with Daddy because I don't know what's happening to us and to everyone. He reached the open bedroom door. Zach's eyes followed the shadow to its source. The cap gun went limp in his hand.

His father had been dreaming. Zach understood this, and then he understood something else—the thing standing in front of him was what had brought that dream. The fear that fell over Zach wasn't from the way it looked or what it said, it was more a knowing that this was something he wasn't supposed to be seeing, that maybe no one was supposed to see.

And yet children hold their souls close and have not yet learned how to forget them, and so see it Zach Barnett did. Magic comes easy to children. It's only when they grow up that believing gets harder.

The boy Zach saw was not much older than himself and staring back at him. He wore a dirty pair of cut-off jeans and looked out from behind a broken pair of horn-rimmed glasses. The boy pulled back the hood of his sweatshirt and lifted his chin. Zach wanted to cry out. He would have if the boy's smile had not stilled him.

"Who are you?" he asked.

The boy brought a single finger to his lips.

Another secret, Zach thought. Something bad to hide.

He gave a promise that he would be quiet. But what Zach received wasn't a secret at all. It was the voice of heaven filling his mind.

Part V

Remember True

· 1 ·

I decided the next morning that the front door of the
sheriff's office really could use another coat of paint.
The outside first, as that was the side everyone saw. The
inside—the part only Kate and I had to look at—could be saved
for later. Looking back, I suppose there's not a little irony in
such thinking.

I'd put two coats on that door the week before. Friday,
that had been. I'd taken Kate up to the Lowe's in Stanley
(Kate had always been good at picking colors), and we'd held
hands the whole way there and back. She never asked about
my dreams and I never thought they were anything more
than guilt.

Yes, that had been Friday. The day before Eric Thayer had
died and Andy got burned and Timmy was beaten, before
Charlie Givens got scared into his grave and *I'm coming for
you, Jake, I'm coming for you all*, before the devil walked
in Mattingly and "I know what you did in the Holler that
day" and the town meeting and Justus. Back in a time when
all I had to worry about was keeping my fears hidden and

whether the gray on the door would look better in "squirrel" or "sterling."

But now it was Wednesday, and everything had changed.

Kate no longer spoke to me. We rode to the office that morning in silence, our only company the radio. I inched my hand onto the console, hoping she would place hers on top—by choice or force of habit, I didn't care—and lace her fingers into mine. She did nothing but stare out the window and keep her hand atop the notebook on her lap. She'd said nothing of her trip to the Ruskin boy's house.

The only words she'd offered me since I told her of Taylor had come after I woke screaming the night before. "It's going to be okay," she'd said. I was thankful to hear it, even if we'd both come to the point we didn't believe it anymore. Kate had wanted to know what I'd dreamed and said she'd dreamed as well—had fallen back to a warm spring day twenty years gone, when she took a boy's hand and led him behind the bleachers. She lay with me and said some ghosts never go away, and I knew that was true.

For me, I'd spent that night in front of a mound of rocks along the riverbank in Happy Hollow in a time I'd not yet lived. I stood with a man I knew to be Taylor Hathcock. Kate and Lucy Seekins were there too. And Phillip, standing in our midst with an upturned fist pointed to us all. There was fire and screaming, and there was an end.

I said nothing of this to my wife as we lay there in the stillness of the night. Kate fell back into her silence and found her sleep. I never did.

To make matters worse, that morning I found Kate's hush now extended to Zach. He'd gotten out of bed and refused to say so much as good morning to either of us. Kate and I both tried prodding some sort of conversation from him, but it was as if the times had rendered our son deaf and mute. And really, who could blame a child for being such? In many ways Kate and I had become the same. In their own way, everyone had.

We each went to our respective corners when we arrived at the office, Kate to her desk, me to mine. I watched her study her notebook through the window. Justus and his men were already out. To where and for how long was none of my concern. I was too tired. I leaned over the desk with my hand to my forehead and felt my eyes closing, thought this time maybe there was no going back, because Taylor was out there and Kate knew I'd let him go just as I'd let Justus go, and how in *the only way out is through, Jake, because I'm near and you're dead. Do you understand what I* jerked my head up and rubbed my eyes, blinking the dream away.

Kate looked at me through the window. I waved her off and decided to give Bessie a workout before tackling the door. Kate said nothing when I walked past her. I rested my hat upside down on the iron bench by the back door.

There were no faces on the target that morning, just an unsteady thumping of steel against wood and a worry that the shaking in my hands made Bessie miss just as often as she flew true. Twenty minutes later a layer of sweat had replaced the sound of Phillip telling me I could never go back again.

I'd just sunk Bessie into the target again when a voice said, "Easy there."

Kate was in the doorway when I turned. I thought she must have been the one who spoke, but she stepped aside so Trevor Morgan could walk through.

"Some people'd take that as a warning, Jake," he said. "You thinking of me when you threw her?"

I didn't say either way and moved down the dirt path,

smirking at the newspaperman's fancy suit. Fresh off the rack at the JC Penny, no doubt. "What are you doing here, Trevor? Ain't you got CNN to talk to?"

Trevor said, "I don't want no trouble," then smiled. "Wait, that's your line."

"Jake and I aren't having what you'd call a good morning, Trevor," Kate said. "You don't want to make it worse."

I freed Bessie, walked up the path, and spun, releasing her without looking. She landed square, the handle perpendicular to the ground. If I had nothing else right then, it was that Kate and Trevor had not witnessed another errant throw. I walked back and said, "State your business."

Trevor leaned against the wall. He looked first to Kate, then to me. "Came to make peace. What peace I can, anyway."

"That's two people in two days who've sought me out for that," I said. "Must be Christmas."

Trevor ignored that. "We both have our duties in this town, Jake. Yours is to protect it, by force if necessary. Mine is to protect it with truth. I had to run that story."

"The story, yes." I wedged Bessie free. "Not the tripe on the back page. I said stick to the facts. Telling everyone Taylor Hathcock's the devil wasn't a fact."

"That so?" Trevor asked. "Man blows into town leaving a trail of blood and destruction, then disappears into thin air? Leaves his partner to die out of fright? Sounds like the devil to me. What was I supposed to do, Jake?"

"Tell the truth," Kate said. "Let it speak on its own. There's a wide space between that and what you wrote, Trevor."

"Maybe." Trevor nodded. "Maybe you're right, Kate. But I got a feeling this isn't over. It's like an itch deep in my ear that I can't scratch. Been trying to figure it out. All I can come up with is that you're hiding something, Jake."

Kate looked at me. She kept her face stoic, but I could see the panic beneath. Panic and rage.

"Never really cared for you, Jake," Trevor said. "You Barnetts think you own this town, always have. That's bad enough. But you, Jake? You're worse. All you do is leech off the people who pay your salary. You treat this job like it's some kind of eternal vacation. I knew you'd lie down in all of this with Taylor Hathcock, but I didn't figure you'd hide. Sure, might be because your daddy's back in town. But there's something else, and I'm duty bound to find out what it is."

I passed them both, wheeled, and fired. Bessie flew, this time striking with such force that the three poles holding the target buckled. But the throw was off. I'd aimed for the center and hit the lower right edge instead, a good foot and a half from where I'd meant, and I thought of what Justus had said about a hunk of tree not striking back.

"Do what you gotta," I said, and I made my way down the path again.

Trevor grinned. "I am. Been doing a little digging. County police might not have found anything on Taylor yet, but I have."

I stopped. "What'd you find?"

"Not a what, a who. Taylor's aunt. She doesn't live in Camden anymore. Took off for West Virginia fifteen years ago. Not the sort of person who'd leave a forwarding address, if you understand me."

Kate reached out and took hold of Trevor's arm, a small act that only intensified the smile on his face. "How did you find her?"

"I might run a hick newspaper full of stories about crop futures and 4-H meetings, Kate, but I know what I'm doing. The other day when you two and Uncle Jimmy were gawking at Justus and wondering what in the world you were going to do, I was on my way to the Camden post office. Postmaster there's been handling the mail for fifty-odd years. Figured he could steer me in the right direction. Mailman always knows everybody's business, doesn't he?" Trevor pulled a piece of paper from his pocket and waved it in my direction. "Name's Charlene Patterson. Lives in Parker. Just over the mountains a piece, I believe."

"Why not give that to Alan Martin?" I asked. "Or call this lady yourself? Why are you doing this for me?"

"I'm not doing this for you, Jake. I'm doing it for Kate."

Trevor kept the paper out. When I didn't move, he dropped it into my hat.

"Thank you, Trevor," Kate said.

"My pleasure."

I thought Trevor was going to add a little extra something on the end, something along the lines of *Anytime, Kate, you ever need something, you just let me know.* But before he could, the front door flew open with such force that the handle crashed into the wall behind. The three of us looked into the foyer through the open back door. A loud voice called for help.

Kate was the first through. The stranger was a short, portly man in a wrinkled suit that hung from a pair of rounded shoulders. He stood just inside the doorway, hands shaking at his sides. His bloodshot eyes flitted about the room.

He looked at Trevor and asked, "You the sheriff?"

"I am," I said, stepping around Trevor. "What's the problem?"

"My daughter's gone missing." The man twisted his neck and blew out a series of short gasps that sounded like muffled cries. "Something's happened. You have to come."

Kate's hand went to her mouth.

Trevor asked, "What's your name, sir?"

"Seekins," the man said. "My name is Clay Seekins. My daughter is missing."

· 2 ·

What little of the room Kate saw appeared as disjointed patterns of overturned furniture and sparkling glass, like something seen in a kaleidoscope. Faraway voices surrounded her. The lower half of Jake's faded jeans crossed the upper portion of her vision, there for a moment and gone. Remnants of the pictures that once graced the mantel lay at her feet. Jagged shards of glass shimmered in sunlight filtered through the living room window. And there was something else, something with words, wedged into the carpet. Kate reached down to pick it up and pinched a shattered bit of glass instead. It pierced the tip of her finger, drawing blood.

Another pair of legs, thicker and shorter than her husband's, moved from north to south along the periphery of Kate's downward gaze. She remembered those pants belonged to Clay Seekins and this was his house, this was Lucy's house and Lucy was gone. Clay said something—Kate couldn't make out what it was, but it had been loud enough to pierce the fog that had rolled in around her. He moved away as another pair of suited legs arrived, these not moving past but holding still. Trevor, Kate thought, those pants belong to Trevor, he'd come to the office wearing a suit in case the networks called but that had yet to happen. Mattingly's ills had reached only as far as Stanley and Camden. The world was full enough of bloodshed and hate; the death of a single boy didn't seem to matter.

She heard her name called. It was nothing more than dim

static, like holding a conch shell to your ear. Kate heard her name again. She felt hands upon her shoulders. She looked up to see Trevor's lips moving.

"What?" she asked.

"You're bleeding," Trevor said. He took her hand and held it up. A drop of crimson fell from Kate's fingertip to her palm. Trevor reached for the handkerchief in his breast pocket and wrapped it around the wound. "There. You okay?"

Kate wondered why Trevor was there and then remembered he'd followed Jake. Jake had told him to stay on the porch, but Trevor had rushed inside when Kate screamed. She remembered seeing him and Jake and Lucy's daddy and all that . . . that *destruction*.

And then, the fog.

Trevor held Kate's bloody hand, his fingers caressing hers. She pulled away, unsure if the revulsion she felt was from what she knew had happened in the living room or if it was the wounded look of rejection on Trevor's face. She unwrapped the handkerchief and handed it back.

"I knew there was more," Trevor said. "Hathcock hasn't gone anywhere. He's still here. He *took her*."

Old floorboards creaked above their heads. Kate looked to the ceiling and wondered when Lucy's father and Jake had left. Trevor said it again—"He *took her*"—and Kate understood it was not so much for her benefit as his own. He'd left just enough room for her to contradict him, but she couldn't. Trevor was right. And Kate knew it wouldn't be long until the same newspaperman who'd found Taylor Hathcock's long-lost Aunt Charlene would find that her husband had been lying to them all.

Clay Seekins walked down the steps. Jake trailed behind. Lucy's daddy looked as though he wanted to panic but his body wouldn't allow it. His suit jacket was gone, revealing a long curve of sweat that angled down from his chest. They reached the landing and made their way into the living room, where Kate and Trevor waited.

"There's no sign of her," Clay said. "I came home and found it like this, Sheriff, just like this. I called for her, but she wasn't here."

Kate didn't think it was possible for anyone to talk himself out of a dream (if so, she believed Jake would have done that long ago), but Lucy's father was trying to do just that. "I've been away on business. Didn't know what happened until I got back. I heard about that man and how he got away. He's got her, doesn't he? Sheriff? That man's got my little girl."

"We don't know that, sir," Jake said.

Trevor chuckled and shook his head. "Are you serious?"

Jake looked at him. "Thought I told you to stay on the porch."

"I got a right to be here, Sheriff. Unless this is a crime scene, of course." Trevor grinned, realizing he'd just set a rather nice trap. "You calling this a crime scene, Jake?"

Jake said, "No."

Kate's eyes bulged and caught fire. "Jake, you can't honestly stand there and tell us this isn't anything other than what we all know it is."

Jake moved farther inside the room and took off his hat, rolled it in his hands. Bessie bulged from the small of his back.

"Something's off, Kate," he said.

"Something's *off*?" Clay asked. He crossed the room to where I stood. "My daughter has been *taken*. Who knows how long?"

"Wait," Trevor said. "When did you leave town, Mr. Seekins?"

"Saturday," he said, "if that's any of your business."

"Sat . . ." was all Trevor got out, though Kate could guess

what he thought. Saturday had been four days ago, when Taylor and Charlie came to town. Taylor must have gotten Lucy while Jake was bringing Charlie in, maybe before Jake had even gotten to the Texaco.

Kate looked at the writing on the carpet and said, "Lucy was still here on Saturday. Sunday and Monday too. She sat with me at the meeting."

Trevor asked, "That true, Jake?"

"I remember seeing a girl sitting with Kate, yes."

Trevor took out his notebook and pen. His hand struggled to keep time with his thoughts. Kate didn't think Trevor would have to worry about deciphering what he scribbled when he got back to the office. This was a story that would write itself. She only hoped the town would believe Jake had simply been wrong about Taylor being gone and not that he'd lied.

Jake moved into the kitchen and toed a pile of smashed mason jars. "You've occasion to find yourself up on 664 very often, Mr. Seekins?"

The man bristled. "What's that have to do with anything?"

Jake shrugged and toed the pile more, turned to the open cabinet doors beneath the sink. "Man with a habit's apt to keep that habit a secret. Most folk who visit Hollis Devereaux keep their jars hidden until they turn them back in. Hollis, he offers a discount if you do. Kind of funny that someone'd come in here and take your girl, but not before rooting around in the one place where you keep your empties and taking the time to smash 'em."

Kate made her way to Jake. She remembered something Lucy had said Sunday afternoon, about the world being broken and the pieces not fitting. About her and her father getting into an argument. Lucy getting even.

"She cut her hair," Kate said.

"It's still on the bathroom floor upstairs," Jake told her. Then, quieter, "You should have told me that girl's troubles, Kate."

She whispered back, "You should have told me some things too, Jake. She's *gone*. It doesn't matter what happened with her and her father, she wouldn't run off. I was *helping* her. You kept that man near town and didn't do a thing about it, and now everyone's going to know."

"What are we going to do, Sheriff?" Clay asked. "You have to find her. That killer took my daughter."

"I don't think that's what happened." Jake pointed at what was left of the mason jars first, then to the destruction in the living room. "This doesn't look like a struggle to me. Looks more like a lashing out."

"You're saying Taylor Hathcock didn't have a hand in this?" Trevor asked. He looked up from his notebook, pen poised on the paper, ready to write either way. "That it, Jake?"

Kate looked into her husband's eyes. They'd spent a lifetime together and had called themselves blessed because of it, thankful they had found warmth next to each other in a cold world. But he had lied to her. There was no way around that, nor was there any way Kate could help but wonder what else Jake had lied about. She knew what Trevor would write if Jake answered no. She knew how the town would react. And yet none of this mattered. All Kate wanted at that moment was to see a glimpse of the Jake Barnett that had been hers before the nightmares and before Taylor, before she felt the world had left her and moved on.

Jake kept his hat in his hands. His jaws clenched and loosed into a look of surrender. "No, Trevor. I can't say Taylor Hathcock wasn't involved."

Trevor smiled. When he said, "Thanks, Sheriff," he was already halfway out the door, leaving Lucy's father with Kate.

· 3 ·

He couldn't hold his silence until the next day's paper. Trevor told everyone he met between the Kingman house and the *Gazette* what had happened. More importantly, he told them what it meant. He told the lunch crowd at the diner and the loafers on the courthouse steps. He told Justus and his men, who'd just gotten back from another fruitless search in the hills. He told his uncle, the mayor.

And by the time Lucy left with Taylor's shotgun for the rusty gate and the Devereaux farm, nearly everyone in town had reached a common accord.

Jake Barnett was no longer fit to serve as sheriff of Mattingly.

· 4 ·

Hollis Devereaux had remained close to the farm since Mattingly began its slow unraveling. The town meeting had been enough for Edith, who said she'd never witnessed such Christ-less behavior from people who supposed themselves washed in the blood. And poor Jake, she'd added, that good man had to stand there and be turned to a boy again by his no-count daddy. Shameful is what it was. So Edith had said on the drive home that night, and so Hollis had agreed. It *was* shameful, and in more ways than one.

They'd kept up with the news, of course. The newspaper box at the end of the Devereauxs' lane was dutifully filled every morning, and though Trevor Morgan had failed to match the impact of Sunday's editorial, it had not been for lack of trying. Hollis read Edith the day's misery each morning from the front porch, about how the Hathcock boy was still running around somewhere above ground and the Givens boy was still dead below it, how people were stocking up on everything from food to bullets. How Justus's roving posse was inciting more fear than comfort. Each morning Edith would wave a tired hand and proclaim she could stand no more. She begged Hollis to stay away from town. That suited him just fine. There was more than enough on the farm to worry about.

He did not share his wife's opinion that Justus Barnett was, in her words, "no-count." Many in Mattingly had never forgotten how Mayor Wallis had tried to take the Barnett homeplace (for the good of the town, Big Jim always said, though everyone but Trevor Morgan knew it was really for the good of Jim Wallis's own pockets). As such, Justus had become a loveable rogue over the years—a countrified Robin Hood who'd stood up to the powers that be.

It was Hollis who'd run groceries and moonshine up to Crawford's Gap every so often, and it had been Hollis who had given Jake's cell phone number to Justus along with a pre-paid cell phone he'd bought in Camden, all in the hope that father and son could reconcile. But the bonds of friendship the Barnetts and Devereauxs had shared through the generations could only stretch so far. Hollis had no interest in joining Justus in the search for Taylor. He knew how that search would end if Justus should turn Taylor up. Evil had come to Mattingly, but repaying evil with its own kind would solve nothing.

Besides, Hollis didn't think Taylor was blameworthy at all. Yes, Hathcock had killed that boy. And he'd put dear old Andy Sommerville near the grave and had given Timmy Griffith the whupping of his life. But charging Taylor Hathcock for that would be like charging a strike of lightning for arson. Everyone in town knew the devil was behind it all, just as Trevor had said. Lucifer himself had been loosed.

And it was all because of Hollis. Because of Jenny.

He'd known all along judgment would come. That the money Jenny provided was the only thing keeping Hollis and Edith afloat didn't matter. Hollis had chosen sin over faith, and that was his undoing.

By that Wednesday night, Jenny had been almost completely stripped. The boiler fire had been snuffed, the copper pots and piping dismantled. Hollis had considered selling the scrap (there was money in copper, not moonshine money but money all the same) and then thought no, the Lord wouldn't approve. He would instead haul Jenny to a corner of the north field the next morning and bury her there. It would be a solemn ceremony, but perhaps a redemptive one.

He was collecting the remnants by lantern light when he heard the first twig snap. Hollis looked in that direction and saw nothing but the night. He stood silent for a moment, listening. His shotgun lay propped against a tall stump by the flickering light. There was a time when such a sound would send Hollis grabbing for that scatter-gun, but not that night. It was likely nothing but a skunk or a possum. And anyway, Hollis was no longer afraid of the lawmen or their hellycopters. He'd already been caught.

He'd resumed his work when another snap echoed from among the trees, this one closer and loud enough to quiet the crickets. Movement came from beyond the arc of his light. Hollis straightened as a figure broke into the clearing. The lantern was too weak for him to make out who it was.

"Who's it?" he asked.

The figure said nothing and took a step close enough for Hollis to see the barrel pointed at his chest. Hollis looked to where his own shotgun rested—too far. He spoke in a voice that sounded much older than his seventy-eight years. "You mind steppin' a little closer, fella? I'd like to see who aims to end me."

The figure obliged, inching itself into the pale circle of light and then holding steady. Hollis could think of nothing more to say. He didn't know whom he'd expected—Bobby Barnes, maybe, there to beg for one more jar of peach because manhunting was such thirsty work, or maybe that fella in the suit who'd come by earlier—but it certainly wasn't the girl who stood in front of him. Her jeans were muddy, her shirt crumpled. Wild hate burned in her eyes. Tears stained her cheeks.

"What you doin' out here, little girl?" Hollis asked. He pointed to the shotgun. "An' with that, of all things?"

Her lips trembled against emotion and the weight of the iron in her hands. She said, "I have to wake you up."

Hollis looked at the gun against the stump. He was not surprised to find it had moved no closer. He looked back to the girl and said, "I expect you've done that. I'm many things, but at the moment sleepy ain't among 'em."

He took a small step forward and froze when the girl racked the shotgun's slide. She raised the barrel from Hollis's chest to his head.

"Don't you move," she said. "You peddle poison, Hollis Devereaux. You peddle poison that ruins lives."

A pain wormed its way down Hollis's left arm to his fingers, rendering him dizzy. He motioned to the pile of metal beyond them and said, "I tore her down. I ain't doin' that no more."

"You can't undo what's been done. You throw all that away, I'm still here. My dad's still here. *You're* still here." She shook her head. "What's been done always comes back to haunt. You brought all of this on us, and I'm going to end it. I'm going to end it and find my peace."

Hollis knew that was true—he had brought it upon them. He didn't know this girl or who among his many customers (some of which came all the way from Stanley) was her daddy, but he knew it was true. He thought of the money handed to him over the years and how it had fixed the truck and the tractor and put a new roof on the barn and kept the lights on when the sun scorched the fields. He thought of Edith sitting up in bed, waiting for him to lie down and tell her the day was over but another would come, and it would be fair because they would face it together. And then the girl's hand went to the trigger and Hollis thought if this was to be his judgment, then that would be fair as well. He would be set free in the place of his own sin and raised up in glory.

· 5 ·

"I love you, son, and I'm proud of you."

Zach stared at me. My smile was thin but there, peeking out from behind stubble that grew grayer by the day. I would hold that smile forever if that's what it took to show him nothing was wrong.

He didn't add his part. There came no "Love you and proud too" from my son, no hint that he was about to say anything. Only that stare. It was as if Zach looked at me as he always had but was seeing me for the first time. I leaned in toward him. My stomach growled.

"You hungry, Daddy?"

"Nope," I said. "Just supper settling."

"You dint eat nothing."

That was true enough. Supper that night had been prepared by three teenagers tasked with the night shift at the Dairy

Queen. After spending most of the day helping Clay Seekins clean up the mess Lucy (or, I had to admit, Taylor) made of his house, Kate wasn't much interested in cooking. Nor was I much interested in asking her to do so. The gulf between us had widened considerably in that time. Kate was still convinced Taylor Hathcock had struck again. So, too, was Lucy's father, who was also convinced that throwing away a single shard of glass was tantamount to destroying evidence. I'd tried telling both of them that the only thing Lucy had been a victim of was her own teenage hormones, but my words sounded false. For Clay, believing his daughter had been kidnapped was better than believing some part of her had simply buckled. And as far as Kate was concerned, there was no longer much I could say that she would believe.

Most of the town held that same sentiment by then. Trevor would have another story for the next day's *Gazette*, but it would be one everyone already knew. Mayor Wallis's Cadillac had raced up the Seekins's lane not thirty minutes after Trevor left, followed closely by Bobby Barnes and Justus in Bobby's red Dodge and Preacher Goggins. I'd turned them all away. Crime scene, I'd told them. It was all I could do.

"Daddy?" Zach said. "I said you dint eat nothing."

"Had half a burger."

"But then you got up and went to the bathroom." He lowered his voice. "I heard you pukin'. You sick, Daddy?"

I patted his knee and tried smiling again. "I think maybe. But not the flu or anything bad."

"Heartsick," he said.

"What?"

"You're sick in your heart. Momma too. She's been in your bedroom all night lookin' at her book."

"Where'd you come up with that word?" I asked.

"The angel told me. He said you and Mommy got bad things in your hearts that you won't let out."

"And what angel is this?"

"The one I saw comin' outta your room last night," he said.

I chuckled and patted his knee again. "You saw an angel in the bedroom?"

"'Course not. He was in the hall. I'm not scared anymore, Daddy. You shouldn't be scared either."

"Must be nice," I said, "having angels and seeing them. What'd he look like?"

"He had a costume on."

"Like Superman?"

Zach pursed his lips. He moved his arms from under the covers and crossed them. "I'm bein' for real, Daddy. He's protectin' us."

"Well, good then. I imagine we could all use some protecting right now." I leaned down and kissed the top of his head. "You get some sleep. That angel comes back, you tell him to stay close."

"He said he's always close. That's why I'm not scared."

I nodded and stood, thinking how wonderful that would be. I was about to tell Zach I was proud of him and loved him again but didn't. The threat of his silence was larger than the hope he'd keep his part in our nightly ritual. I realized then just how important those words had become over the years. Not only for my son, but for me. Standing there in his room, I couldn't remember ever wanting to hear "Love you and proud too" more.

"Daddy?"

"Yeah?" I asked.

Zach's eyes were nearly shut. His words sounded spoken through a thick curtain. "You're gonna go back. You have to."

"Back to where?"

"Where it got started."

"Okay, son. Get some sleep now."

I walked from the room and glanced at the light switch and smiled. Hanging on the peg beside it were Zach's cowboy hat, plastic badge, and holster. Poking up from the latter was the plastic handle of his cap gun.

That night I lay awake beside Kate and wished for angels.

· 6 ·

Lucy had been gone too long. It was a slow walk from the gate and Taylor didn't know how far into town she had to go, but it was still too long.

He wondered if the bear would come to bring news of where she was, as it often did when Charlie visited. Taylor thought no. The bear had gone missing since meeting Lucy at the grove. Retreated, perhaps, into the deepest parts of the Hollow, where an ancient sign warning WARE—NO FARTHER led to places even Taylor refused to tread. He was sure the bear would remain there until the end. Taylor knew this but did not know how, just as he knew the end was drawing close.

He should have gone with her, should have at least waited at the gate until Lucy returned. Not to help (that would be cheating, and while Taylor considered himself to be a great many things, he'd never been a double-dealer like Kate), but to be there for support. Yet there was no way Taylor could approach the rusty gate again, not with men looking for him in every place but where he was. And Lucy had insisted she leave the cabin alone.

And so there was only this. Only the waiting.

Taylor picked his book up from the log and brought it to

his nose. He inhaled age and water. The riverbank, he remembered. That's where he'd found it. After Kate had played her
trick and Taylor had found the boy and Jake had run screaming
over Indian Hill. The boy was gone by then

(No not gone he was Awake that boy was AWAKE)

and there was nothing Taylor could do but watch the butterflies. He sniffed the book again and remembered there had
been so many butterflies. White ones. He remembered thinking they were feeding on the boy's bloody places until he'd
gotten closer and seen they weren't. It was almost as if they
were protecting the boy, sheltering him from the Hollow's
grasp.

Setting him free.

Waking him.

Taylor had remained in the Hollow since that day, had
trekked its every corner but for where the sign read WARE—
NO FARTHER. And in all that time and all that going, he had
seen brown butterflies and black ones and ones mixed with
both, but he had never seen another white one.

He remembered thinking that men from town would
come. He knew Jake would confess nothing, but he didn't
think that would matter. Something would lead the men to
the riverbank. They would find the boy and they would find
Taylor and they would call him guilty and take him away.

"I was acquitted," he said to the night. But those words
plucked at that in-between place connecting Taylor's heart to his
mind, telling him that he was wrong, that not only was he guilty,
he was also damned, and in a brief but terrifying moment the
sepia lenses through which he viewed his yesterday fell away. He
saw the cliffs above the riverbank and the roiling waters below.
Taylor remembered reaching behind himself as the boy reached
out, remembered the boy tumbling backward, and there in the

shadow of the rotten log with the deep night pressing around him, Taylor Hathcock heard four whispered words:

I'm coming for you.

He spun, reaching for the flint knife beside him, and called the spirit forward. But by then Taylor's memory had stopped, and the veil between worlds lowered once more.

A clacking noise from among the trees turned Taylor to the cabin. The sound grew closer. But it was not a spirit that breasted the small rise ahead. It was Lucy.

She tripped when she saw him and cried out, stopping her fall with the shotgun she held as a cane. Taylor ran. The shotgun skittered across the hard soil. Lucy dug her fingernails into Taylor's back, pulling him to herself, and held on with what strength she had left.

"It's done now," Taylor whispered. He laid his hand to the back of her shorn hair. Each wave of tears sank Lucy deeper into his arms. It was as though all that held her together was her hurt, and as that pain was expelled, so too was her will. "I know it's a terrible sense. I won't say it gets better. Nothing noble's easy. Such is the dream we live, lady."

Lucy's head shook against his chest. She clenched her hands into fists and struck Taylor there twice, then held him again. Taylor walked her to the cabin and took her inside. Lucy slumped at the table just as she had those four long nights ago.

He brought water and took her hand as he crossed to the opposite chair. Lucy did not drink. Her body trembled beneath a cold Taylor could not feel and the flame in the hearth could not chase.

Taylor squeezed her hand and whispered, "Tell me how it was for you, Lucy Seekins. It'll ease your affliction if you open your heart to me."

Lucy opened her mouth to speak. What came out was too soft for Taylor to hear.

"What's that?" he asked.

"I couldn't."

Taylor released her hand. "What you couldn't?"

"I couldn't wake him up. I tried, Taylor. I wanted to more than anything. I told him I was going to do it and he just stood there waiting like he wanted me to but I *couldn't*." The crying grew until the power behind the wails robbed Lucy of breath. She reached for Taylor's hand. He was too shocked to offer it. "Please say something," she said. "Please don't be mad."

Taylor said nothing. His hand moved across the table and stroked her fingers but he said nothing, and then he watched as Lucy's hope gave way.

Lucy stood and moved to the cot. Taylor watched as she turned to him. Her shoulders convulsed beneath the weight of her tears as she lifted her shirt over her head. She let it dangle in her hand before dropping it to the soiled floor. She reached for the top of her shorts and let them fall. Her small-clothes came next. Lucy fumbled with them as her body shook, turning the act into an awkward act of seduction. Firelight licked along her curves, making the paunch of her stomach glow.

"You can have me," she said, and Taylor heard in that voice a want and a need and something he could only think was love. "I'll let you do anything you want, just please don't make me leave."

A bright heat rushed through Taylor. His lungs drew in deep, savoring breaths as that primal Other inside him was made drunk on her weakness. He went to her. Lucy did not shrink back but reached out, meaning to pull Taylor to the bed. Taylor took her wrists instead and kept her standing. He removed his black T-shirt and drew it over Lucy's head, guiding her arms through the sleeves. He closed his eyes as he pulled the shirt down until it reached her knees.

"There will be none of that, lady," he whispered. "I will not defile you, this night or another."

He sat Lucy at the edge of the cot and kissed the wetness from her cheeks. Taylor's breath smelled dank and rotten, yet to Lucy there was nothing but the tenderness of his lips.

"I can stay?" she asked.

"Your home's here." He let go of Lucy's hand and reached behind her for the mandolin against the wall. "I never knew what this was for. The cabin, the spyglasses, the log, all them I knew. Not this. But now I think I do. I've heard you hum often, Lucy Seekins. Your voice is fair." Taylor strummed the strings, not knowing how they worked. The sound he produced was stilted and garbled. "My grandpappy, he liked the banjo. He tried to learn me, but I never picked up on it. He always liked to play this old mountain church song. Drove me near crazy as I remember it, but those words stuck. I believe they were a herald of the life I'd find here."

He strummed again, moving his fingers up and down the neck. Trying to remember the tune. Trying to remember things that once were.

"Sing with me, lady," he said. "It'll be our song."

Lucy sniffed. "I don't know the words."

"I'll learn you."

Taylor's fingers worked. He sang the first verse and the chorus, trying to lilt his voice to hold the notes, and then began again—

"Sadly we sing and with tremulous breath, As we stand by the mystical stream, In the valley and by the dark river of death, And yet 'tis no more than a dream. Only a dream, only a dream, Of glory beyond the dark stream, How peaceful the slumber, how happy the waking, Where death is only a dream."

Taylor sang that first verse and chorus over, not remembering more. Lucy joined him. The notes from the old mandolin were rough and their voices rougher, but it was music just the same. They remained at the edge of the cot as the light between them beat back a building darkness. And for a few hours since time immemorial, song filled the Hollow.

· 7 ·

You're dead, Jake. There's nothing you can do about it. Can't you see that?

I aim the stone in my arms at Phillip's sneakers. He lifts his feet as I place the rock there and sets them back down, thanking me for the footrest.

"You're going to kill me," I say. "You're going to kill me because I killed you."

Did you? Who really killed me, Jake?

"You can't blame Kate. Kate was just a girl. Please just leave us alone."

You were just a boy, *Phillip says.* I was just a boy. Does that matter? I'm not going to leave you alone, Jake. Do you know why? Because heaven isn't without the past.

"What do you know of heaven?" I ask. "You say you're coming back, and Kate and I are dead when you do. You're more demon than angel."

I lift the next stone and try to cover Phillip's feet again. If I can just get his feet—if I can pin him there—maybe the rest will be easier. But as I set the rock down, Phillip's sneaker shoots out. He punts the stone like a football, and in a brief moment the motion eases the hood of his sweatshirt back just enough for me to see the scar on his neck. The rock gathers momentum as it topples down the pile, bouncing twice along the bank until it splashes into the river. And my first thought (if you can even call those sleepy rambles "thoughts") is I'll pick up the stone that's appeared at my feet and start over. But there is no new stone when I bend down, there is only the pile upon which Phillip and I stand.

Lift one of those, *he says,* you'll collapse the pile. Do you want to do that, Jake? Remember the cut you got when you fell in your dream? It followed you when you woke. What do you think will follow you if you're crushed by all these rocks?

"I want to go back," I tell him.

There is no back, Jake. There is no back, and heaven's not without the past. They didn't teach me that in Sunday school, but it's true. God wipes our tears, but not our memories. Our yesterdays remain. The bad ones especially.

He stands before me, blocking out the sun, and I am too tired to shrink back.

Seems strange, doesn't it? But remember, our tears are gone on the other side. Wiped clean by the very hand of love. Memories haunt you on your side of the veil, Jake, but on mine there is only their beauty. On my side, you see every life is magic. You see you were led even as you thought you wandered, and there was a light even in your darkness. And sometimes you are even given the grace to come back. To set things right.

"I don't understand," I tell him.

That's why I'm coming, Jake. To make you understand. *Phillip lifts an upturned fist.* To settle accounts and give you this.

"I don't want it," I say. "I just want you to go. I just want to rest."

Then you have to remember true. It's the only way. You're hanging on too tight, Jake. Time to let go. You have to tell Kate what you did.

"No," I scream. "I won't."

Is she a good woman, Jake?

"Yes. Kate's changed. She isn't the girl—"

—who killed me? *he finishes.* Do you know how it felt for me that day, Jake? Do you know how many days I passed Kate in the hallways between classes and watched her? How many lunch periods I spent longing to sit at her table, even the seat next to hers? Do you know how many nights I spent alone in a bare bed, feeling the sting of my father's fists and listening to the scrapes of mice in dark corners? I found my peace only when I closed my eyes and thought of Kate's face. But what could I do, Jake? Share my heart with her? Do you remember what everyone called me?

I did.

You say she's a good woman despite what she did? *Phillip asks.* Are you then a good man despite what you did? Are you not all equal, Jake? Kate suffers. You suffer. Taylor suffers. That's why I bring you here. That's why I'm coming for you all.

"How do you know Taylor?" I ask. "How does he know what I did?"

Soon, *Phillip promises.* Soon, if you all remember true. Look around you, Jake. What do you see?

Phillip lowers his hand and raises his head up and around. I follow his gaze. Yellows and oranges fall from the sky like water spilled onto a painter's palette. The broken woods around us glow an almost golden color. The air is stale but for a warm, sweet breeze. To me, it seems that everything around us, every sharp rock and gnarled branch, has been placed exactly as it should. And I

understand this was how the riverbank looked that day, and I
remember what I'd thought as I made my way to Indian Hill:
    The Hollow is ugly. The Hollow is beautiful.
    Do you know what the old ones call it? *Phillip asks.* That
time between sun and moon, when the world is neither bright
nor dim?
    I do. And when I speak, I feel a power attached to that word
and a kind of magic—"Eventide."
    Yes, *Phillip says, and though the hood is drawn over his face,*
I feel a smile on his lips.
    It lasts only moments when you care to see it. But there
are other eyes, Jake, and those eyes see hard. They see the
beauty that infuses every life, and how that beauty is twisted
to ugliness. They see children singing and hands clasped in
prayer and a babe's first steps, and they see old ones despairing
and fists clenched and death before its time.
    Do you know why I died, Jake? Why Kate keeps her note-
book? Do you wonder how it can be that some like you cling
to your When and others deny theirs so much that they fash-
ion their remorse into virtue? Because to those great watching
eyes, the world is always neither bright nor dim. Because there
is darkness in man and also a light, and by their mingling the
world lies at eventide.
    Phillip holds his fist out again. I see his fingers moving, struggling
to hold in what wants to come out.
    The door comes first, *he says.* The preacher will find the
door, and then the town. That's when you must choose to be
the man you are or the boy you were.
    "What door?" I ask.
    The father comes next. Then the book. The book will be
last, Jake. That will be the beginning of your end. That will
be what brings you back here.

"I'm never coming back here."

I feel another smile from beneath Phillip's hood, and then, He laughs at what we say we'll never do.

"Who?"

HE. *Phillip raises his fist for the last time.* You will all remember true, Jake. Then I'll come. I'll come for you all, and I'll have an end.

He steps to me, fist outstretched, and I run. I make for Indian Hill and the rusty gate beyond. I scream that I want nothing, that I will never come back to the river's edge, but Phillip calls back that I will. It is eventide, he says. *And though it is not bright, it is also not yet dark.*

· 8 ·

Kate struggled in a blackness so thick it suffocated. Lucy called, but there was no way to tell from which direction. In that black, left was right and behind was ahead and right side up was upside down. Kate only knew Lucy was fading. The echo told her that. It was dim and frightened and so far away that her name reached her in two syllables.

KA . . . te.

Kate tried to call out, but the black flooded her open mouth like oil. She gagged, coughing out clouds of white flickers that looked like butterflies.

She woke lying on her left side, knees drawn into a fetal position. The first rays of sun leaked through the open window. Robins and sparrows called out in song. The clock on her bedside table read 6:27. Kate slid back the small switch on the side, silencing the alarm before it could go off. She thought of Lucy. She thought of seeing her on the street in front of the sheriff's office sheared and bedraggled and how she said it had been a fight with her dad.

Getting even, she'd said—*Do you ever think there's a better place, not like heaven but maybe? Do you ever feel like everything's broken and the pieces won't fit together again?*

And there was something else as well, something Kate had found the day before in Lucy's living room that she'd not mentioned to Jake or Clay Seekins or Trevor, something in the carpet with *Safe and Effective!* written in purple on the front. A part of Kate had known even then that Lucy had run away. She'd sat with Kate and Zach at the meeting, not with Johnny Adkins and his parents. The only reason boyfriend and girlfriend would avoid each other at a time like that was if they were boyfriend and girlfriend no more.

And yet Kate had lied and said otherwise. She'd put all the blame on Jake and said nothing to the contrary when Trevor took the leap of connecting Lucy to Taylor. She'd kept still even when she knew Trevor would write a story that would end both her husband's career and their life in Mattingly. Lying there in the midst of another almost perfect morning in what was once an almost perfect life, Kate realized she had harmed her marriage more than any lie Jake could tell. She had sacrificed his reputation for fear of what Lucy's disappearance truly meant—that Kate had not done enough, and now another child was gone because of her.

In Kate's mind life was a scale upon which all stood. People were born in the middle and spent their lives drifting to one side or the other—teetering as their faith and love grew, tottering when they gave in to sin and hate. Kate's own scale had tottered the day she played her trick on Phillip, and there it had stuck. It did not move when Sheriff Houser got that anonymous call and Phillip's body was found, nor even when

Phillip's death was ruled a suicide. Kate knew she'd taken Phillip McBride's life even before he could take it himself, as did all of those who'd peered and laughed from the bleachers that day. And though those same classmates greeted Kate each day with genuine love—and though she'd begged for and received God's forgiveness every day since—still Kate had not felt that scale evened. Only the penance of serving children like Phillip would shift that balance. Kate had known all along it would take more than one notebook to gain freedom from her past. Now she knew there wouldn't be enough want in the world for her to be free of both Phillip and Lucy.

She felt Jake's hand touch her hip and turned. His face appeared drawn and thin in the morning light. Thick stubble filled in the shallow craters where cheeks had once been. The drawn skin over his stomach rose and fell against pajama pants that barely covered his hips. She and Zach had given those pants to Jake the Christmas before—blue ones with white pin-stripes and *World's Greatest Dad* stenciled on the right thigh. They'd been so tight that the drawstring had disappeared into the waistband, but he had refused to let Kate return them. Now a full three inches of that drawstring had been dug out and knotted just to keep the pants from falling to his ankles.

"Jake?"

His eyes were on the ceiling.

"You've been here all night?" She felt a sudden hope. It was a small one, but in light of her dream and *KA . . . te* and Lucy saying the world didn't fit anymore and the town about to discover that their sheriff had failed them all, even a small hope was reason enough to carry on. "You didn't dream?"

Jake nodded. Kate didn't understand if that meant *Yes, I didn't dream* or *Yes, I did.* He turned his head to her.

"I dreamed," he said.

"I'm sorry. I didn't hear you."

"I didn't scream," he said. "It wasn't that kind of dream this time. Because I gave up, I think. I was too tired, so I stopped and just listened. I think that's what he's wanted me to do from the start. He says he's coming, Kate, and I think he really is. He's coming for us all."

"Who?" Kate moved closer. Jake's breath smelled like drying moss, and a horrible notion came to her—*My husband is dying from the inside out.* "Who's in your dreams?"

"Phillip McBride."

"Phillip?" she asked. The name came out cracked and unnatural, as though Kate believed its mention could summon forth the demon that slept under all those names in her notebook and all those trips to the Family Dollar. Jake's face blurred behind the tears that formed in her eyes. "Why are you dreaming of Phillip, Jake? What do you mean he's coming for us?"

The telephone rang. Jake reached for it before the noise woke Zach. Kate took his hand and held it. The ringing continued.

"No," she said. "Don't answer it, talk to me. Why are you dreaming of Phillip?"

The answering machine picked up—Zach's voice saying thanks for calling the Barnetts but we're out now and if you want to leave a message go right on ahead. A beep sounded next, followed by the breathless voice of Reggie Goggins.

"Jake?" he said. "Jake, you there? You gotta get down to the sheriff's office. Trevor's got a story about you, and someone's done something. I'm not gonna be able to keep the people away, and I don't want them to see it. Jake?"

Kate reached over me and grabbed for the phone. "Reggie, what's wrong?"

"Kate?" he asked. "Listen to me. You gotta get down to the office right now, before anyone sees."

"Why? What's happened?"

"I don't know what Jake did or didn't do, but I don't want things to get worse. You have to come up and clean off that door before the stores open, Kate. I'm gonna go try, but there's nothing here at the church."

"Clean what up, Reggie? We can't come now. Zach isn't even up and—"

"*Right now,*" the preacher said.

He hung up. Kate placed the phone back into the cradle.

"What's wrong?" Jake asked.

"I don't know. He said something happened at the sheriff's office and we have to get down there. Something about the door."

To Kate's amazement, her husband's skin found a paler shade of white.

· 9 ·

Lucy woke when she reached for Taylor and found nothing but knotty clumps of soiled mattress. The cabin was empty. Breakfast waited on the table—more stew and another cup of tea from the smell, both of which were fine—and the fire in the hearth was more ember than flame.

She put a hand to her head, meaning to brush the hair from her eyes, but felt only skin and stubble. Lucy carried no remorse for what she had done in front of her bathroom mirror those nights before. The looks she'd gotten from those in town—Kate's and Zach's, everyone's at the meeting, even Hollis Devereaux's—never once swayed her to think that taking those scissors to her hair was anything but right. But sitting there on Taylor's bed, Lucy found she had gained her freedom from one prison only to find herself in another. If the night before was any indication, all she'd succeeded in doing was making herself uglier.

She found Taylor at his overlook. Lucy thought it a wonder he hadn't worn two half-moons into that rotten log, given how much time he sat there. She wanted to believe that wasn't always the case, that Taylor spent so much time there now simply because winter had turned to spring and the valley lay in blossom. But a part of her knew that wasn't true. In her mind Lucy could see Taylor huddled there against the falling snow and the bitter January wind, his binoculars in one hand and his book in the other. And if there was madness in that thought, it was tempered by Lucy's next—that of herself huddled against that same snow and wind, though seated at the Hole rather than upon the log.

Taylor's book was there that morning, but not the binoculars. His back slumped as Lucy sat.

"Fair morning," he said.

She looked out toward the valley. A jagged line of rising sun eased its way southward, marching for the bends and dips that made up the hill country below. Mattingly lay nestled among patches of forest and square fields that stretched on forever.

"It is fair," Lucy said. The perfect word.

She said no more, fearing where things would lead. They would have to speak of her failure the night before. No consequences had been discussed before she'd left to cross the rusty gate, but Lucy was smart enough to know some sort of payment would be required. The longer they sat in silence, the longer she could pretend nothing had changed. Yet as the minutes ticked on and the sun crept up the mountainside, Lucy came to see Taylor's silence as proof things had not only changed, but there was no fixing them. It was the same sort of unease she felt when her father left on his trips. Taylor had spoken of a coming end. Lucy didn't know what he'd meant, but she thought whatever it was could only be made worse if she equated the man beside her with the man who had abandoned her.

"I'm sorry," she said. Lucy didn't look at Taylor as she said those words. If she had, she would have seen the way his elbows drew in to his sides and the way his legs crossed. She would have seen his quick breaths. "I meant to kill—*wake*—that man. I know that doesn't count for much. It doesn't for me. I guess I just don't believe like you do, Taylor, at least not yet. That shotgun was pointed right at him, but the second my finger went to the trigger, something stopped me. I don't know what it was. All I know is when I was looking at him before, I saw the man who ruined my life. But when I looked at him down that barrel, all I saw was a tired old man."

The Hollow stood still and silent around them. Taylor cleared his throat but said nothing. Lucy felt both of the things she held most dear slipping away.

"And I'm sorry for the other thing I did," she said. "I didn't know what else to do, so I just did what I've always done. I thought it would make you let me stay. I've been waiting and hoping for one thing all my life, Taylor. Eighteen years of shooting stars and pennies found heads-up on the street, all those times I'd closed my eyes to blow out birthday candles and waited in line to sit on Santa's lap. Those nights when I'd hear my mom's voice in the rain and pray to a God I knew wasn't there. All that wishing, all just to be loved so hard that I'd know what it felt like to belong somewhere. And after all that hurt and praying, I finally got to a place where everything I'd ever wanted could be mine for just one little squeeze of my finger. And I couldn't even do that. Maybe you said no because you're older and you think I'm just a kid, but I'm not. I'm eighteen now. I'm an adult living out here in the wilderness and running from bears and whatever else lives here, and I'm no girl. I'd rather be with a man now. I've been with too many boys."

Lucy felt as though she was navigating a thin wire over a deep canyon. In such cases the best thing was to keep moving forward. As long as she talked, Taylor couldn't.

"It's okay that you said no," she said. "I knew you were mad." And there was one last option, this so terrible only because it was so likely. "Or maybe you just think I'm too fat and ugly and don't have any hair."

There was nothing more she could say, no further defense she could offer. Lucy could only endure the silence now. She could sit still and quiet upon that log for however long Taylor allowed it and face whatever came next with the same hard resolve he summoned to face his every day, and she would hide the tears that spilled from her eyes.

Taylor did not look at her. When he spoke, his voice was as quiet as a breeze. "It's a hard thing, waking a man. I believed you could, but mayhap that burden lies with me alone. If so, then I welcome it. I'd drown in that pain afore I'd have you dip your toes in it. You say it hurt, lady, looking down that barrel? I say there's a worse hurt that comes after. That's the dream. The dream wants to keep everyone here. Wants to feed on us. I'm the only one strong enough to save the slumbering. I shouldn't have asked you to help."

"But that can't be right, Taylor," Lucy said. "What you say works fine up here, but it doesn't make sense down there. You say people don't die and that only you can wake them up, but you've been up here alone for so long you've forgotten that people *leave*. Dying or waking, people do it every day. People like my mom and Charlie. So how can you be the one making it happen?"

Taylor offered no reply. For a long moment, Lucy considered just how fragile his notions were. She believed Taylor was occupied with much the same. And yet even if that seemed to trouble him greatly, Lucy was unbothered. People believed all sorts of things. That there was a God or there were many or none, that there was a heaven and a hell or a great yawning empty. Why not believe the world was a dream? Why not put your faith in whatever made your living easier? She and Taylor were still together. Still in their fairy tale. All else didn't matter.

Lucy reached across the log and took his hand. "I love you, Taylor."

Taylor nodded, that was all, but Lucy saw his eyes grow soft and moist. That was well enough. She would rather hear silence from people than words they did not feel. Lucy had heard such words often enough.

· 10 ·

I saw the crowd first and knew they hadn't gathered that morning to seek pardon. This time they'd come to hear me beg my own.

Their heads turned at the Blazer's approach. Zach said nothing from the backseat. Kate was silent as well. She reached for my hand when she saw the mob at the steps, one so large that it spilled out onto Main Street.

We parked at the curb. Bobby Barnes, Justus, and Mayor Wallis stood facing the door at the top of the steps. Their collective girth made it impossible for me to see what they were looking at. The crowd fell silent as we got out and stepped onto the sidewalk. Reverend Goggins picked his way through the people.

"I'm sorry, Jake," he said. "I tried. I ran back here after calling you, wanting to find a bucket or a sponge or . . . or anything. But Trevor saw it. He was putting out his papers. Wasn't anything I could do."

My eyes scanned the people around me, most of whom I'd known all my life. They were men and women I sat with in church and greeted on the streets each day. People who had shared the comings of children and the passings of loved ones, livelihoods gained and lost, presents and futures heavy with hope and anguish. None of them were what anyone would call great. Mattingly was a small town of small folk who only wanted to live quietly. It was peace they wanted, no less than I did, and a desire to hide from the shadows that crept over the world. That very desire was why I'd agreed to become sheriff, but it was not until that morning I realized that to my town—to my friends—it lay upon me to keep those shadows away.

"It's all right, Reggie," I said. I looked over the preacher's shoulder and up the stairs. Bobby faced me now. Justus and Big Jim still did not. "What's going on? Someone try to break in?"

The reverend said, "No."

Justus and the mayor parted to either side of the entrance. When they turned, Kate uttered a moan. One word had been spray-painted across the door in bold, wide letters:

COWARD

"What's that mean?" Zach stood on his toes, stretching his skinny neck as far as it was able. His mind gathered in the letters and his mouth tried to sound out the consonants and vowels. "What's that mean, Daddy?"

Only Bobby spoke. He waved a folded newspaper at Zach

and said, "Means your daddy's bore false witness, boy, which is bad enough. But he lied 'cause he was a'scared, and that's worse. Maybe you should go back up Hollis's way again, Jake. Get you sum'more of Jenny's courage."

The crowd gasped. Zach's face fell into a deep shade of crimson. He stormed through the people before Kate or I could stop him.

"You take that back," he screamed. "My daddy's scared of *nothin'*."

Kate ran after him. Zach charged up the steps. Justus stood unmoved, watching. Mayor Wallis moved forward to catch him, but the boy was too quick. Zach slipped beneath Big Jim's arms and slammed into Bobby, and when he realized the town drunk was taller than Danny Blackwell and wouldn't be moved, Zach clamped his mouth upon the first patch of soft skin he could find.

Bobby howled. A smile crossed Justus's face. Kate reached the top step and grabbed hold of Zach, wrenching him away as he kicked at Bobby's legs.

"My daddy's *brave*," he screamed. "My daddy's the bravest man in the *world*."

Kate opened the door and carried Zach inside. The mob's eyes shifted back to me. Several people closest took a small step back, believing my calm countenance a precursor for fury, the way the air stills before a storm.

But there was no anger in me. There was no anything.

I had feared two things in life—that Kate would discover what I did to Phillip, and that the town would discover everything they believed of me was a lie. What rendered me numb at the sight of that door wasn't that the second of those fears had now come to pass, but that I didn't need to hide anymore. Everything in my world was either coming to rest or falling to pieces, and in that I found a freedom that not even the judging eyes of my friends could steal away.

"Well now," Justus said. "Reckon that Barnett spunk skipped a generation."

A few chuckled. Bobby Barnes tried but could only manage a rough smile through his clenched teeth. He rubbed the inside of his elbow where Zach had bit him. I stepped past the reverend and walked up the stairs. Bobby and Mayor Wallis made room. Justus did not. He held his hands out, framing the door like a game show model displaying what I'd won for all my hard work.

I turned to face the people. "Who did this?"

Bobby spoke: "Maybe it was Taylor Hathcock."

"If 'twas," Justus said, "then it's proof the devil ain't ignorant."

The crowd found no amusement in this.

Mayor Wallis stepped forward and snatched the newspaper from Bobby's hand. He held it up to me and said, "Could've been anybody, Jake."

The headline was just as large as the one Trevor had used Sunday, only now instead of TWO DEAD, ONE SOUGHT IN GAS STATION ROBBERY, there was a slightly smaller copy of the word on the door. Below that was SHERIFF'S KNOWL-EDGE OF CRIMINAL'S WHEREABOUTS QUESTIONED AS LOCAL GIRL GOES MISSING. Beside it was a picture of Lucy. She was smiling.

Big Jim said, "Jake, I need it straight. You know where Hathcock is?"

I looked at the paper

(COWARD)

and then to the mayor. Everyone's eyes on me, waiting for my answer. When I said I didn't know where Taylor was, I believed that true. And yet a part of me said it was simply another lie.

Big Jim studied me and offered a small nod. He shoved the newspaper back into Bobby's chest without looking. "Wish I could believe you, Jake. We've had our differences, everybody knows that, but I always thought you a good man." He turned to the crowd. "Town's lost confidence in you, though. A girl's gone missing, and I have it on Trevor's word that her daddy and Kate both think Taylor Hathcock had something to do with it. I'm calling an emergency vote of the town council tonight on whether to keep you as sheriff or not. You're expected to be there."

Justus stared at the ground. I can remember many times when my father had looked disappointed in me, but that was the first time he'd ever looked ashamed.

No one in the crowd moved. The day would start soon. More people would come from the neighborhoods and hills to buy their groceries or shop at the Dollar or gather for breakfast at the diner. All of them would have Lucy on their mind. Lucy and me.

I opened the door and reached inside for the brush and can of paint I'd left on the floor. I pried the top away and stirred the brush inside as Bessie pressed against my back. She'd never felt so heavy there, like a millstone. I began covering the COWARD in thick, broad strokes.

No one offered to help.

· 11 ·

It took two coats of paint.

The merchants left to open their businesses and the others to tend to their errands. Many of the shop owners decided that was a fine time to sweep their sidewalks. They worked their eyes as much as their brooms. Bobby Barnes drifted to the courthouse to rally the day's posse. Only Justus remained. He stood in the center of the steps with his hands shoved into the pockets of his overalls. A part of me wanted to ask him to take those hands out. I thought there might be spray paint on them.

"You stay behind to make sure I painted this right?" I asked.

Justus shook his head. "What'd you know about Hathcock, Jacob?"

"I don't know where he is."

"Ain't what I asked."

I tossed the brush into the empty can. "Doesn't matter. Big Jim's calling his meeting. I'll be done. Job never suited me anyway. This town only wanted me for my last name, not my first."

"What you mean it don't matter?" Justus asked. He took a step up and breathed in deep, held it like it was about to explode. "What happened to you? You shame me, boy. I brought you up best I could. Weren't a perfect daddy, maybe not even a good one, but I raised you t'be a man. A man woulda chased Hathcock to the moon if that's what it took. He'd be out there right now lookin' for that little girl, not colorin' over his sins with a brush. A man'd be doin' what's *right*."

"You've no place to tell me what's right," I said.

Justus took his hands from his pockets (they were clean; I didn't know whether that made me feel better or worse) and placed them side by side in front of himself.

"You're true on that," he said. "We's standin' right here, Jacob. Don't you see I'm tryin' t'help you? Take me on inside, I've no fear. I'm ready to stand in judgment for the wrong I did. It's you who ain't."

The shopkeepers gave up their ruse of sweeping. Their brooms now hung limply from their hands. Down the sidewalk, Bobby Barnes and the rest of the men stared. Justus clenched his fists when I moved my hand, but I only adjusted my hat. I turned to the door and walked inside, leaving him on the steps.

Kate stood by the window rubbing the smooth skin on her throat. She held a tissue in her hand. "Alan Martin called. He got a copy of the paper somehow. Said he's coming down to talk to you. I sent Zach out back to calm down. He was on the sofa when you came in for the paint. I didn't . . ." She rubbed her throat again—her way of trying to keep in what meant to get out. "I didn't want him to see you have to do that."

I nodded. "Thanks."

"What did Justus say?"

"Wanted to know what happened to turn me yellow."

"You're not a coward, Jake. No one believes that."

"Fifty people on the sidewalk and somebody with a half-empty can of spray paint would say different."

Kate's chin trembled. She took a step toward me and stopped. It was as if she wanted to move closer but had to stay away. "I'm so sorry, Jake. It's all my fault. I know Lucy ran away. She was having problems with her daddy, and Johnny Adkins broke up with her. I think Clay found out what they were doing and Lucy said she was getting even and it was my *book*, Jake, it was my stupid *book*. I wrote her name down and now I've lost her like Phillip's lost."

"No," I said. "That's not true, Katie."

"It is, Jake. All I've ever wanted to do is leave him behind, Jake, but he won't let me. And now you're dreaming of him. He's haunting me, and he's hurting you because of it. Please forgive me."

And though there was nothing to pardon, I said I would.

I would pardon Kate anything. Forgiveness is an easy thing to offer when it's all you've ever wanted to receive.

"I'm gonna go in my office," I said. "Pack some things up."

"What do you mean?"

"Big Jim's having a meeting tonight. Town's lost faith in me. They're going to call a vote, Kate. I won't give that man a chance to fire me. I'm quitting."

Kate's voice cracked, "Jake, no. You can't let that happen because of me."

I shook my head. "It's not you. I'm tired, and I just want to put an end to it all. We'll stay until we can sell the house, then go someplace else. Stanley maybe, or Camden. Make a fresh start."

"Jake, this is *home*."

"Not anymore. I'm tired, Kate. I'm tired of trying to be someone I'm not, and I'm tired of trying to fit in with a town that'll always compare me to my father. I'm tired of coming up short, and I just want to start over again."

I went to my office and pulled Bessie from my belt. She went atop a desk that held nothing more than a lamp, a telephone, and two scuff marks in the left corner where I'd rested the heels of my boots every afternoon. I placed my boots there now. I figured that was all I could do.

A fresh start. That's what I'd said. I'd never dreamed of leaving Mattingly, but now it made perfect sense. Maybe everything from the nightmares to Taylor to Justus to Trevor's articles to the COWARD on the door wasn't so much God punishing me for my sins as it was God trying to get my attention. Trying to help me.

Telling me to move on.

Maybe that's what Phillip meant when he'd said I was hanging on too tight. That I had to let go.

I heard the sounds of boots on the foyer's floor and looked up to see the top half of Zach's cowboy hat coming toward the office. He sat in the vinyl chair across from me and leaned back, shooting his heels to the corner of the desk.

"Hey, bud," I said.

"Hey, Daddy."

His face was vacant, though his black eye leaked tears. A thin runner of drying snot ran from his left nostril to his ear.

"You okay?" I asked.

"That Bobby Barnes is a mean snake of a liar."

"Bobby's just doing what Bobby does. It'll be okay." I took my heels down and placed my hat next to Bessie. My hand went to my chin. "Gonna have to get you to school, I guess."

"I don't wanna go today," he said. "I just wanna go home."

"Can't yet. Got some stuff to do, and somebody's coming to see me."

Zach lowered his feet and studied his hands. "You paint that lie off the door, Daddy?"

"Didn't get it off, but I covered it."

"But you'll fix it, right?"

"What do you mean?"

Zach leaned forward, knocking his hat askance as he did. He took it off and placed it next to mine. "Don't matter if you painted over it," he said. "It's still there. An' what if it rains and washes that new paint off?"

"What you think I should do, then?" I asked.

He shrugged. "Reckon you gotta get a new door, Daddy."

I looked at him and smiled in that way parents often do— that slight upturn of the mouth that's part amusement at the simple way their children see the world and part longing to see that same way. Those grins don't often last long before they're swallowed by a sigh. Mine lingered, though. And then it hardened.

Zach leaned forward and cupped his hand to his chin, mirroring me. His hat lay atop the desk next to mine, and his eyes matched the tired, puffy look of my own. It was as if he had become a key that unlocked a room of mirrors inside me, and everywhere I turned I saw myself truly. There were no sunken cheeks in that reflection, no silvering stubble or waning waistline. What I saw instead was the boy I once was and still remained—a youngling caught in the widening shadow of a Barnett name that for generations had been carried by men whose word was a bond and whose honor was unquestioned. Until the day I killed Phillip, I had carried that name well. Afterward I saw it as no less a mark than the one God put upon Cain.

Justus said he'd raised me a man, but that wasn't true. He'd raised me to believe a man never stumbled. He never failed, never hurt, and if he did it meant he was something less. And now, looking at Zach, I realized I was teaching my own son something far worse—that it was better to run from the past than to face it.

I rose from my chair and reached for the plastic bag hanging from the bookcase. Zach moved back as I laid it across the desk. I undressed in front of my son, let him see every bone and crevice in my wasting body, and took the uniform from the wire hanger. I dressed slow, putting the shirt on first and the pants last. The silver BARNETT name tag glittered. I put my boots on and stood, holding my pants up with a hand. Zach watched as I tightened the belt as much as I could. Still, the clothes swallowed me.

"What'cha doing, Daddy?"

I reached for Bessie and tucked her into the small of my

back. The extra bulge did what the belt could not. I thought my pants would hold.

"Gonna go get a new door," I told him.

Zach followed me out. Kate looked up from her desk and said something I didn't hear. I was too busy thinking about the door and Phillip.

How he'd said the door comes first, and the father comes next.

· 12 ·

What Kate asked was, "Jake, what are you doing?"

She wanted to ask more (*Why are you wearing that uniform?* came to mind first, *Exactly how much weight have you lost?* a close second), but he had already crossed the foyer to the door.

Zach trailed close behind. His cowboy hat bobbed on his head, and there was a smile where tears had been.

"Daddy's gonna get a new door," he said. "You comin', Momma?"

"What?" she asked.

Jake paused at the entryway and turned. The space between them covered nearly fifty feet, yet Kate saw a fire in his eyes she hadn't seen since their schooling days.

"You should stay here, Zach," he said. "I don't know how this'll go."

"*No*sir," he said. "I'm comin' too."

Jake nodded. He looked at Kate. "Might need you, Kate. You always had a way of calming folk down."

She rose from her desk, leaving her open notebook behind. Jake took the steps down and turned a sharp right for the court-house. Dozens of men had gathered there each morning that week to look for Taylor Hathcock. On that day it looked like hundreds. Kate knew why. Most of those men were fathers, and many had young daughters at home.

Justus stood at the top step. He pointed to the big relief map of the town and surrounding wilderness. Bobby Barnes stood beside him, nodding like a proper underling. His strides were long and purposeful. Kate broke into a jog. Zach ran with her. He laughed.

"Jake," Kate said, "slow down. What are you doing?"

"My job."

He didn't break his stride. Justus looked up and saw their approach. The pause he gave was too brief for the crowd to notice, though the catch in his next words was enough to turn Bobby's head. A county police car worked its way up Main Street and parked in front of the sheriff's office. Alan Martin got out and walked inside.

Kate said, "Jake, Alan's here."

"He can wait."

"Jake. *Jake.*" She reached out to grab him and missed, then took hold of him on her second try. Jake turned but didn't stop. "I don't know what you have in mind, but I don't think this is the right time for it. Let's wait until Justus sends them out to wherever they're going, okay? Let's just go back."

"There's no back, Kate," he said. "Only way out's through."

They pushed through the crowd. Kate lifted Zach into her arms, fearful that he'd be trampled or lost. Justus stopped barking his orders. Jake took the stairs one by one as Bessie's handle tapped the back of his leg. Kate remained below, conscious that both she and her son now stood between a crowd of angry men and the man the crowd blamed for why they were there.

Mayor Wallis and Trevor stepped out of the courthouse. Big Jim asked, "What's this, Jake?"

Bobby smirked. "Well, cain't you see, Mayor? Must be Halloweentime." He looked at Jake and said, "That there's a nice-lookin' costume, little boy. Ain't got no treat for you, though, seein' as how I'm involved in man work. Don't you go play no trick on me, now."

Justus studied Jake's uniform and pressed his lips into a fine line. When he spoke, his voice was soft. It may even have held a bit of wonder. "State your aim, Jacob. Say it well, for all to hear."

"Justus Barnett, I'm placing you under arrest for the shooting of Bernard Wilcox, Harvey Lewis, and Clancy Townsend."

Kate's jaw went slack, as did Big Jim's. Trevor took a step away.

Bobby said, "Now what's this, Jake? You ain't got no right doin' this. You ain't even gonna be sheriff no more."

"I'm sheriff for now," Jake told him. Then, to Justus: "Ain't gonna read you your rights, because I don't know them all. Don't have my cuffs either. But I expect you to come along with no trouble. Don't make me raise my hand, because I don't know if I can."

A low grumble rose from the men, coming onto Kate like a wave. Zach clutched her neck. What she did next was not out of her own fear, but the fear she felt in her son. She whipped around before the crowd could come forward and planted her feet firm.

"Dare anyone take a step," she said. "Dare you all, and I will remind you there is another Barnett here, and she can rage as fierce as any man."

The rumble ceased. Jake took hold of Justus's wrist. Bobby reached to break the hold. Jake brought his free hand behind his back and pulled Bessie, flipping the handle in the air. Cold steel settled against Bobby's neck. He drew his arm away.

"Mind your manners, Bobby Barnes," Jake said. "And know your place."

A grin lay on Justus's mouth. Upon Kate's as well. Bobby had been bested by two Barnetts that morning.

Justus said, "Best you best step away, son. Ol' Bessie's been a bit bucksome of late, an' Jake looks a might shaky this morn'. He's apt to slip and give you a shave that's more than whisker."

Kate looked and saw Justus was right. The fire in Jake's eyes burned hot enough to reach his fingers. Bessie shook in his hand. Yet she knew her husband well despite what secrets he carried, and she knew what Jake felt was neither anger nor fear. It was hurt. Whatever of Justus's strength and rightness never made it into Jake's genes, they were still of the same blood. And yet Jake's father had just called Bobby Barnes "son."

Bobby nodded. Whatever words he had a mind to say stopped where Bessie's blade met him. He backed away slowly.

Jake led Justus from the steps. The men parted before them. Only Mayor Wallis and Trevor followed. The rest were held at bay by their own shock and Kate's backward glances. She and Zach went ahead and opened the front door of the sheriff's office, mindful of the still-wet paint.

Alan Martin was on the sofa when they walked in. He stood when he saw Justus.

"Jake?" he asked.

"Be right with you, Alan."

He led Justus past his office and down the hallway.

Kate put Zach down and said, "You keep the mayor and Trevor company, Zach. We'll be right back."

"I wanna come," he said. "I wanna talk to'm. What'd he do, Mommy?"

Kate said, "He just got tired, honey. Like we all do. Now go."

Zach shuffled away and asked Big Jim, Trevor, and Alan if they'd like a cup of water. Kate followed Justus and Jake to the cell. Jake pulled the door free and moved aside. Justus hesitated. To Kate, that pause was neither a denial of what was happening nor a refusal to accept it. It was more the kind of stop that comes when you find a place of rest at the end of a long walk.

He stepped inside. Jake closed the door so slowly that the locks barely clacked. Justus stepped forward and grasped the bars with his hands.

"I'm sorry," Jake said.

Justus nodded.

"I'll be back. Have to talk to the police about what Trevor wrote."

"Talk to him like you talked to me," Justus said. "Straight and true."

Kate watched as Jake moved down the hall and called for Alan, who followed him into the office. She wanted to check on Zach but didn't want to leave Justus. Seeing him in that cell made him look worn. Worn and small.

"I'm sorry too," she said. "You should have just stayed away, Justus."

"No," he said. "It's like you told the boy. I'm tired, Katelyn. Town needed me. My town. Reckon it'll be yours and Jake's to keep now, and the boy's once he's grown."

Kate thought of what Jake had said about leaving.

"Never got to know the boy," Justus said. "Zach. I know it's my own fault, Katelyn, and keepin' me from him was just as much my doin' as yours. But I want you to know that that misery's laid heavier on me than the men I shot. That boy's my blood. You raise him up to be a good man."

Kate gritted her teeth and swallowed. She would not let

Justus see her cry. She would stand tall and face him with her chin up. She would be a Barnett.

The office door opened. Alan and Jake walked down the hallway to the cell.

"This is Alan Martin of the county police," Jake said. "He's gonna take you in."

Jake took the key from his pocket and turned the lock. Big Jim and Trevor said nothing as Jake led Justus through the foyer. Moving shadows fell through the windows and onto the floor, evidence of the crowd that had gathered outside.

"You sure about this Seekins girl, Jake?" Alan asked.

"I am. Kate knew the girl. She'll vouch that she was having problems at home."

"He's right," Kate said. She looked at Trevor. It was plain that he didn't believe her. It was plainer that Kate didn't care. "I was trying to help her, but it wasn't enough."

"And you have no information on Taylor's whereabouts?" Alan asked Jake. "Because if you do and you're not telling me, Jake, it's aiding and abetting."

"I don't know where he is, Alan." And before Trevor could speak up, he added, "I'm gonna chase down a lead, though. It's a small one. I'll let you know."

"Okay. I'll take Justus in and start a missing person's report on the Seekins girl."

They left then, Alan and Justus first, Jake trailing them. Justus passed his eyes over Kate. He smiled and settled on Zach. "Good-bye, boy. You have lion's blood in you. Don't forget that."

They put him in the backseat of Alan's car with much of the downtown in attendance. The only one smiling was Justus. Alan pulled away, leaving Kate at the window. She watched her husband tug at a uniform he thought had always been too big for him.

· 13 ·

Had Taylor been looking through his binoculars just then, he would have wondered who the old man in the back of that county police car was and why that man was grinning so hard. He would have also seen another man wearing what looked like someone else's clothes watch that police car go. He would have seen that man step inside the sheriff's office on Main Street just long enough to say good-bye before climbing into a rusting Chevy Blazer and driving out of town toward the western mountains. But those magic spyglasses weren't to Taylor's eyes. They were beside him on the log instead. And though he was indeed gazing down over the town, all he saw was his own lonely self.

He thought of the footprints and how he'd found them Friday night on one of his rare trips to the grove. How he'd followed them all the way to the rusty gate. It was Taylor's obsession with Kate that had made him believe those prints would lead to town and to her. That was why he'd convinced Charlie to take him to Mattingly in the first place.

But then everything changed. Charlie was gone, for one. Where exactly Charlie had gone was a question Taylor had tried to ignore until Lucy had spoken of it earlier.

Dying or waking, people do it every day. People like my mom and Charlie. So how can you be doing it?

Taylor had no answer for that because Lucy had been right. He'd been in the Hollow so long that the workings of the world below had slipped him by. Of course people left. He'd known that himself once upon a time, had he not? What did that mean, then?

He sat with his book in his lap and the tip of his pencil hovering, wanting answers but finding none. Taylor never wrote down how it was that people could Wake without him in their presence. He only scrawled at the bottom of a page that was written on and erased and written on again hundreds of times over the course of twenty years:

All's still a dreem.

Yes. Because Taylor's book said so and that was his Bible, and when the Word clashes with the world, the Word must always win out.

Yet not even this contradiction was enough to sway Taylor's mind from the higher things he pondered.

Lucy had saved him from a fate that would have mirrored Charlie's own, and in the course of their days since, Taylor had come to think he'd saved her as well. He'd shown her as much of the truth as he dared. He had told her of the dream and taken her to the Hole. Taylor thought that well enough. Maybe even too much, given the depths of Lucy's pining to redden her hand upon the grove's wall. There were wonders in the Hollow more powerful—more holy—but Taylor had believed exposing Lucy to those would imperil her. If the lady had been consumed by the sight of a mere puddle, what would the sight of an ocean bring?

So he was content to keep the farther reaches of his kingdom a secret, knowing it was for Lucy's own good. To show her more would mean Taylor opening his heart, and the gate at that entrance was just as rusted and unused as the one that guarded the Hollow.

And yet that had now changed as well, and for one simple reason.

Lucy loved him.

Taylor Hathcock did not know how old he was. Time, like death, was a notion that slipped away in the Hollow. He only knew that in the long days stretching behind him, no one had ever voiced those words. Not his pa or his ma, not his grandpappy. Nor even his aunt, who had taken him in not out of tenderness but duty and, as far as Taylor knew, had never bothered to raise a call when he disappeared. But now he was loved, and Taylor had never known how much he'd craved those words until he heard them. The prospect of sharing his life with someone—of sharing everything— struck him silent.

Taylor stopped at that thought—sharing everything. That was it, wasn't it? That was why those prints had led to Lucy Seekins instead of Kate Griffith. That was why Lucy had said maybe Taylor wasn't supposed to find the one who'd risen from the grove, but the one who'd risen was supposed to find him. Taylor had thought that notion wrong at first. Now he felt it right. That's why the Hollow had drawn the lady to him. Because Lucy would love Taylor and Taylor would love her back, but he would have to share everything with her first. He would have to take her to the riverbank. That was where his aid would come, to make an end at the beginning.

He turned, meaning to perhaps say those words back for the first time, but found himself alone. Taylor turned and found the camp empty but for a few piles of junk and the shrill sound of the breeze through the aluminum chimes hanging from the cabin. Lucy was gone, cast out by a silence she'd taken as judgment. Taylor called her name in a loud, anguished cry that was as close to prayer as he'd ever managed. And when Lucy appeared from the door of the cabin, he felt the rusted gate upon his heart swing open.

He went to her, mindful that his steps had quickened to a run. Lucy's look was one of shock and confusion that melted away when he held her tight to his chest. Taylor put a hand to the back of Lucy's head and stroked hair that looked like the dark fronds of a flowerless plant. He put his lips there. She smelled of pine and earth and wind.

"You're the only one that's ever known me as a good man, Lucy Seekins," he said. "If at the end of our path you'd still have my heart, it'll be yours."

He felt Lucy's arms wrap his waist, as though she were cradling a newborn. The Hollow stilled. There was only them, and there was only now.

Taylor released her and said, "Gather supplies. Food and water. And bring my scatter-gun, but mind it's still loaded."

Lucy gazed up at him with eyes like two black diamonds, and Taylor loved them. "Where are we going?" she asked.

"Far beyond the grove," he said. "To where the river and the dream begins. If you would love me, lady, you would love not just some of me, but all."

· 14 ·

Parker, West Virginia, wasn't really a town at all, at least not in the way Mattingly was a town. There was no square or clock tower, no blocks of clean streets that led to places of trade. It was instead a wasted space that looked ready to fall off the world's edge. What buildings I passed were only ramshackle collections of fading wood and brick behind sidewalks overrun by wire grass.

The lone school was a cinder-blocked rectangle with *Parker Elementary* wood-burned into the sign out front. A Baptist church with a similar sign (this one reading a simple *Jesus Saves*) stood just down the road. Its white spire reached into the sky like a beacon summoning the lost. Beside that stood the Parker post office. I stopped there and spoke with the postman, a thin, frail old man with yellowing teeth and stale breath. He directed me eight miles on to a dilapidated trailer park named Jollyview, which seemed to me as ironic as calling a dead and mountainous land Happy Hollow.

I parked behind a blue Ford wagon and made my way up a path of river rock to the small, shaky porch of Charlene Patterson's single-wide. A television blared inside. I heard the shrill yap of a dog. I knocked three times and turned to the narrow street that connected the fifty or so homes to the main road out front. A boy Zach's age ran from the door of the trailer across the way, clothed only in a soiled pair of underwear. A woman's voice called out, demanding his return. The boy screamed back an obscenity. A mother carrying a baby walked past oblivious to the scene, as if such sights were common. The babe in her arms sucked at a bottle filled with what looked like soda. Music blared from an open window farther down. Far away, someone screamed. I took this all in as I waited for Taylor's aunt to decide whether or not to answer the door, and the word that came to my mind was the one Phillip had used to explain where the world lies.

"Eventide," I whispered.

I turned when the door cracked open. The woman on the other side of the broken screen wore brown pants and a white T-shirt, hanging from a body that was all bones. Her sunken eyes stared out from beneath hair the color of dried glue.

She raised a cigarette to her mouth and exhaled a long stream of smoke through her nose. "Who're you?"

"Sheriff Jake Barnett, ma'am, of Mattingly, Virginia. Would you be Charlene Patterson?"

The dog barked again. Two small paws rose up from the bottom of the door, revealing the scraggly face of a malnourished Pomeranian. Inside, a TV preacher yelled.

"Only if I got no choice." She inhaled deep through her

mouth, then blew out through a pair of wide nostrils. "Mattingly, you say?"

"Yes'm. Need to talk to you about Taylor Hathcock."

She nodded. "Which is it? You find'm, or you find what's left of'm?"

"Neither," I said. "But I am looking."

"He ain't here," Charlene said.

"Thought as much, but I was wondering if I could come inside and sit a spell, ask you some questions. It's been a long ride."

Charlene waved her cigarette. I thought that gesture was meant for me to go, but the sagging door opened. The dog, no higher than my knee but twice my size in its own mind, leaped forward.

Charlene screamed, "Mitzi, git back here, you mangy beast," and kicked the dog with her foot, sending the animal deep into the home. "Confounded stray's what she is. Fed her once an' she never left."

I removed my hat and stepped inside. The dim living room was bare but for an easy chair, a crumbling sofa, and the blaring television. A layer of yellow nicotine stained the walls. Two framed pictures graced the space above the sofa. The first was of an angel standing over two frightened children as they crossed a buckling bridge at night. In the other, two ball-capped boys with hands stuffed into overalls stood in deep conversation along a dirt road. A caption in the middle read, *You been farming long?*

"Sit if you want," Charlene said. "Got nothin' to offer but instant coffee in dirty water."

"I'm fine." I settled myself at the edge of the sofa and pulled up my sagging pants, wishing I hadn't left Bessie in the truck. "Sorry to bother you, ma'am, and to bear you bad news. I'm afraid Taylor's killed a boy."

Charlene sat in the chair and smoked. The preacher on the television expounded upon how the richness that God promises extends to the pocketbook as well as the soul. It was a sentiment I thought believed easily enough by a man in a thousand-dollar suit. Not so much by a poverty-stricken old woman in Parker, West Virginia.

I spoke up: "We had fingerprints, but they turned up nothing. The only way we know it was Taylor was because his partner confessed. Man by the name of Charlie Givens."

"Don't know'm," Charlene said.

"I was more interested in why Taylor doesn't seem to exist, at least according to the Commonwealth. And for reasons more personal than you understand, I need to know his past."

"Ain't much t'say," Charlene told me. She snuffed out her cigarette and traded it for a fresh one she pulled from a pack by her chair. "Other'n Taylor's no-count. Guess you good Mattingly folk done found that out, though. His pa's a drunk what killed hisself thirty year ago. Misstook the barrel of a gun for a smoke, or so they say. Me, I know better. Sometimes a body gets tired of livin'. S'pose you seen summa that, Sheriff, you bein' a lawman. That tired can get so bad you'd rather see hellfire than another day of the same ole. Taylor's got that same blood, I always knowed it. Somethin' in that boy broke off. It was bound to happen and cain't blame his pa for it. As I judge things, what broke in that boy got bent in the womb.

"His ma was my sister, and as I am, I can say she was a harlot outright. What time she didn't spend in the Camden bars was spent at the abortion mill up Stanley way, lettin' doctor men reap what life the no-counts she fell in with sowed. Taylor grew up and fell away." She took a long drag and blew out slowly. "His ma fell in with a drugger when he's sixteen. Man wanted her for his own use but had no use for Taylor.

Since he was givin' her the poison she needed, that choice was simple in his momma's mind. She dropped Taylor at my door an' left. I never saw her again."

She paused to flick her ashes into a small bowl. The TV preacher said the reason we all weren't happy was because we didn't believe enough.

"I'm sorry, ma'am," I said.

The woman either didn't hear me or chose not to. "Brought'm up best I could, but he's lost by then. World put Taylor 'neath its boot. I sorrowed over'm until I learnt under a heel's where he belonged. Truth is, I always knew there'd be blood if that boy was set loose. He'd disappear to the woods for long stretches and come home only t'eat. Schoolin' did him no good. Got kicked out one after another."

"And you don't know where he is now?" I asked.

She shook her head. "Thought he's dead."

I nodded. A dead end. I'd expected as much (and despite finding the mettle to arrest Justus, I'd hoped for as much too), but at least I could go back to town and tell Kate and Trevor that I'd tried. I reached into my back pocket for a small notebook and pen.

"I appreciate your time, Ms. Patterson. You think of anything else, you give me a call."

I ripped the page and handed it to her. Charlene didn't say if she would or wouldn't, she only showed me the door.

· 15 ·

Lucy suffered no illusion that she'd seen the whole of Happy Hollow in the past five days. Still, she could not believe how far that land stretched. They'd walked for hours, and

Taylor said there were hours to go. As big a world as the space between the cabin, the grove, and the gate seemed, it was only a sliver of that great and dying wood. Lucy felt a sense of wonder and of being swallowed alive. Thick, gray branches hid much of what was to be seen. The hills and dips were endless, all carpeted with dry leaves that covered jutting roots like laid traps. Several times she heard the distant sound of rushing water seeking the path of least resistance. Lucy thought that would be a difficult task in such a place as this. In the Hollow, resistance seemed the rule.

Taylor led the way, the shotgun resting in the crook of his arm and his flint knife ready. He had walked beside her while the sun stood rising and bright, even held her hand as they traveled. But he had gone on ahead as midday came and the first shadows of afternoon fell. Not much, only a step or two, but enough for Lucy to think he was nervous of having her near.

"How much farther?" she asked.

"Yon," is what he said.

It was a distance Lucy didn't know how to measure. "I can carry the gun for a while. I don't know why you brought that anyway. Haven't seen the bear at all. Or anything, for that matter."

"Believe I'll hang on to it," Taylor said. "Where we're going, lady, one can never be too restrained."

"And where are we going?"

Taylor stopped along a path that Lucy believed existed more in his mind than in the dense woods around them. He turned and hefted the shotgun to his shoulder.

"No one's ever told me they loved me, Lucy Seekins, nor have those words ever moved over my lips. Yet I do love you, and I say it true. You say I'm a good man, and so I am. But you cannot rightly love me, because you adore what you do not know."

"I don't understand," Lucy said.

"You will. At the end of this path lies my beginning." He moved a hand behind his back and brought out his book. "Where this was given me."

"Is it far?" she asked. "I want to see the Hole again."

"Where we go counts more than the Hole, lady. Does your treasure lie in red upon the walls of the grove, or does it lie in me?"

He turned and walked on. Lucy followed, drawing herself farther into the Hollow's waning light. She remained close and did not turn back, conscious that she had not answered his question.

· 16 ·

There was one last stop before returning home, one I wasn't aware I was making until I'd geared the Blazer into park in the south lot of the Stanley hospital. I walked into the patient entrance and tipped my hat to the elderly woman at the desk, then took the elevator to Andy Sommerville's third-story room. I was near his door when my phone rang. I reached for it and stepped aside. The number wasn't one I recognized.

"Sheriff, this is Charlene Patterson."

"Ms. Patterson. Everything okay?"

"Well as can be." She coughed. The sound was thick with phlegm. "I remembered somethin' after you left. About Taylor."

"What's that?"

"His schoolin'. Told you he bounced around an' never could stay in one for long. He always had a rage in him. They put him in Camden and Stanley both. I forgot they put'm in Mattingly for a spell too."

Something that felt like a bubble formed deep in my stomach.

"He was at Mattingly?" I asked. "What year?"

Charlene fell quiet. "Ninety, I s'pose it was. Taylor started in the fall, then quit. They were gonna put'm out and I begged them not. It was his last chance, you see. We wrangled until they let him come back. Springtime that was, if I recollect right. Went two weeks, then one morning he left and never came back."

That bubble burst with a pop I could swear was audible. Whatever emotion that filled it—I couldn't tell exactly, but there seemed equal parts worry, despair, and panic—leaked out in sweat.

Ninety, she'd said.

"Are you sure that was the year?" I asked. "I graduated in '90, and I don't remember him."

"Why would you?" she asked. "Boy like that, only there three weeks?"

I found myself standing in front of Andy's door. He looked at me from the bed and waved.

"You didn't report him missing?" I asked.

Her voice was cold—"He's a man then, an' I was tired. I couldn't wrangle him no more, Sheriff."

I supposed that was true enough. I thought it also true that Charlene Patterson had never seen Taylor as her blood at all. He'd been more a stray like Mitzi, one she would feed only when it barked and kick away when it barked too much.

"They called, a'course," Charlene said. "Principal first, then the sheriff. Wantin' to know if somethin' happened to'm. Don't know why they bothered since no one ever bothered before. I told both of 'em Taylor'd just had enough. They said there's been some trouble and had to check."

Some trouble, she'd said, and at those two words all feeling left my body. It couldn't have been Taylor, I thought. And yet in that same thought I knew it could have been. It could have been anyone. Phillip was the only one people remembered.

It explained how Taylor knew me. Most of all, it explained how he knew Kate.

Andy will tell you we visited that day. He'll say I sat in the chair at his bedside and asked him questions that he answered as best he could. He'll also say I acted mighty strange the whole time. I guess that's true. Fact is, I don't remember any of it. Not a word. I suppose it's just the same as when I'd passed him that last Saturday morning and forgot to wave. My mind had been full of Justus that day on the road, but there in Andy's bed it was full of 1990 and Mattingly High School. Nineteen ninety in the spring, and that warm Friday afternoon when Kate had played her trick and I had gone to prove myself a man.

· 17 ·

There wasn't much sense sending Zach to school, not after what had happened. In a moment of near jest, Kate thought the truant officer would be calling if her son missed another day. Her concerns weren't allayed when she remembered the responsibility of keeping Mattingly's children in class rested on her husband's shoulders. Given the way Jake had acted that morning, Kate half expected Bessie's blade to lie at her own neck, followed by a warning to get Zach to school or else.

Jake hadn't called since leaving for West Virginia. Nor

did Kate call him. There wouldn't be much to say other than Mattingly had been all but set afire by Justus's arrest. Bobby Barnes proclaimed the whole thing a charade to cover up whatever other sins Jake had buried. He'd left soon after to make a pass through the hills beyond Crawford's Gap, but with fewer men than Justus would have mustered. Trevor Morgan had disappeared as well, though Kate didn't know whether it was to begin the next day's front-pager or to prepare for the meeting that night. Alan Martin called to say Justus had been processed. Bringing in a wanted fugitive was surely a pretty feather in the state investigator's hat, but Alan seemed to take no pleasure in it.

Any one of these developments (the last especially) would normally warrant a reaching out, but Kate kept the phone on her desk. She wouldn't bother Jake with information she knew he had run away from, and instead let Reverend Goggins drive her and Zach home.

As the day wore on and afternoon turned to evening, Kate found herself checking the lane from the living room window at regular intervals. It didn't help that Zach's behavior had gone oddly calm. Kate had resigned much of the afternoon to comforting her son, but that comfort could only come if Zach was upset. He had asked nothing of Justus's arrest or why his daddy had donned his uniform or where he had gone in it. Nor did he ask Kate to sit in the living room chair and rock awhile, as he usually requested when troubled. It was as though Zach had found a resignation in everything that had happened or a reason for peace. Kate didn't know which it was. She only wished she could share it.

Jake made the turn up the lane near suppertime, just as she made another pass by the window. Kate went to call Zach from his bedroom, then swallowed the words when she saw how fast the Blazer approached. Something

(No, she thought, *not something but something else, not one thing but one thing more, because we're all on a ride that never stops but just keeps going faster)*
had happened. She opened the door as Jake got out.

"What's wrong?" she asked.

Jake came up the sidewalk nearly running, hat blowing back in the wind. He caught it with the hand that wasn't holding Bessie.

"Yearbook," he said.

"What?"

He took the porch steps two at a time, switched the hat to his full hand, and reached for Kate's arm. Jake's touch was soft, and she felt the tremble in his hand. Whatever hardness had been in him on the courthouse steps was gone now. She followed him inside.

"Our senior yearbook," he said. "Do you still have it?"

"I don't know. Why?"

"I talked to Taylor's aunt. He went to the high school. Same year we graduated."

Kate felt a sudden cold that tingled the skin on her arms. "What? How can that be?"

"He wasn't there long. A week or so in the fall and then again in the spring, but I'm hoping it was long enough to get his picture taken." Jake placed both his hat and Bessie on the television stand and rubbed his head. "Taylor knew things, Kate. He knew *me.* And I'm supposed to know him, or at least I think I am. I need that picture."

Kate couldn't feel herself moving, nor could she hear herself when she said, "Our closet maybe."

He guided her to their bedroom. Kate went to her hands and knees inside the closet, breathing in the thick dust that had settled onto the wood floor. She pushed aside boxes filled with things long forgotten, hoping the yearbook wasn't among them, hoping Jake was wrong. Her eyes settled on a box in the back corner. Written in black marker on the side was *Kate's Things*.

"Help me," she said.

Those words were meant as a prayer; Jake took them as a request. He bent down and pulled out the box. Kate removed the top. Gathered in a neat pile inside were a paper-clipped stack of movie stubs and pictures of her and her friends, and a senior superlative certificate that proclaimed Kate Griffith as the most popular girl in school. There was nothing in that box dated beyond the day Phillip died. It was as though Kate's life had stopped that Friday afternoon, and since then she'd been trying to start time again.

Beneath all of this was the yearbook.

Jake set the rest aside and flipped through the pages, past names and faces they knew still. The freshman class first, then the sophomores and juniors. Kate bargained with the God she'd always loved but knew could never love her back, telling Him that He could have anything, anything at all, if Taylor's picture was not there.

She scooted from inside the closet to beside Jake as he turned the page to the senior class. Kate's eyes fell upon Jake's picture, taken with how young he looked—a boy in a man's suit. The page turned. There was her own face, body turned in profile and eyes ahead, flashing a smile that still charmed so many. Kate backed away as Jake turned the page, somehow knowing (knowing all along) what she would find there. Hers was the last picture and the last of the Gs. What came next would be *H* and Hathcock.

Kate heard the squeak of Zach's bed and his feet hitting the floor. Jake fell still. She reached for his knee.

"I found him," he said.

Kate reached for the yearbook and gently took it from his hands. She cradled it in her arms and then brought the page to her eyes. She saw the name listed second on the left side. She saw Taylor's face. The long, stringy hair and the tattered Molly Hatchet T-shirt. The eyes filled with anger and an inability to do anything about it. Kate's face turned the color of candlewax as her world shattered into a thousand tiny prisms in front of her eyes. It was not Jake's fault, everything that had happened. Not even Taylor's. It was hers. It was Kate's alone.

"You know him," Jake said. "Don't you?"

Kate nodded, barely keeping down the bile that rose from her stomach. The yearbook fell onto her crossed legs. "He was the other one I tricked. The one with Phillip. No one ever knew what happened to him. He's come back, Jake. He's come back because of me. Eric Thayer died because of *me*."

There came a knock at the door, followed by another. Hard, with a sense of urgency on the end.

Zach called, "Momma, Daddy, Devereauxs are here."

Jake winced, but Kate said it was okay, she was okay. It was, as far as she could remember, the biggest lie she'd ever told. Jake left and walked down the hallway to the living room. Kate remained on the floor just long enough to turn to the next page in the yearbook. To see Phillip's face. She followed, then, keeping the yearbook to her chest. Jake had just opened the front door as Kate entered the room.

"Hollis," he said. "Edith. What brings y'all out?"

Hollis took off his cap and held it in his hands. "Jake. Sorry to trespass on your evenin' like this. Had t'come, though. Weren't no two ways about it." He nodded past my shoulder and added, "Evenin', Kate."

Kate clutched the yearbook tight. Her cheeks felt hot, but they were not moist. At least, she thought, not yet.

"Hollis," she said. "Hello, Edith."

"Came out soon as I could," Hollis said. "Woulda been sooner, but I been up all night an' workin' all day. Edith, she cain't see the paper enough t'read it. It sat in the box 'til just a bit ago. That's why we come."

Jake said, "Well, if it's for support, I thank you, Hollis. But me and Kate have something to talk over, and—"

Hollis drew in his eyebrows. "No, Jake. Ain't that. It's the girl. The one that's come missin'. Well, she ain't. Missin', I mean. I seen her last night."

· 18 ·

Taylor's cabin lay some eight miles northeast of the rusty gate. The river lay three miles to the gate's northwest, and the grove where Lucy's treasure lay stood ten miles due north. Draw a line connecting those four points, and what you have is the shape of a rough diamond. At its center stood a waterfall that emptied into the wide stream Taylor and Lucy now crossed. Taylor knew this waterfall well. It was where he'd huddled in fear the night Phillip was killed.

He was aware that part of the wood (as well as whatever may dwell in it) had not seen a man in twenty years and a woman in perhaps forever. That alone made Taylor mindful to keep the shotgun cocked and Lucy from wandering. Not that the latter would pose a problem. She had inched so close to him in the last mile that they were nearly conjoined. His left arm was drawn straight and down in front of her, like a shield.

"You feel it, don't you?" he asked.

Lucy said nothing, but gave him a short nod.

Taylor led on, his silence a calm sea that hid churning waters beneath. He'd carried the memory of what had happened over Indian Hill in broad strokes, with the details left as irrelevant. He'd remembered the boy, but only from afar. Not because Taylor had moved on, but because of what he feared by looking too close.

They came to a small gully lined with smooth limestone sides. A thick layer of decaying bones lay upon the bare floor below. Lucy pulled Taylor closer.

"Don't be roused," he said. "Critter bones is all. They fall in there and can't find escape. All those boys you bedded, girl, the momma you think's gone and the daddy who cast you off, they's all like those dead bones yonder, caught in a place of no leaving."

Evening fell. They traveled on until they looked up to a mound of earth rising from the Hollow's floor too perfect to have been formed by time and chance. Its sides were equal slopes of gently curving soil that rose to a thick copse of evergreens. Tall, browning grass grew along the sides. Taylor figured if there were any doubts left in Lucy that the Hollow was a living thing, the sight of that place would sear them closed. It was as though that great forest was a scarred old woman, and this was the place from which it took her sour milk.

"Indian Hill," Taylor said. He looked at it with a longing that had awe at the top and dread at the bottom. "What lies beyond is the river, the cliffs, and the whole of me. For good or ill, Lucy Seekins, is for your heart to reckon."

They took the hill hand in hand and reached the top as the sun fell over the mountains beyond. Taylor watched Lucy as what lay on the other side stole the little breath that remained in her. The river stretched out below them, sinking its way south and east through a gap the eons had carved through the cliffs. Water glittered in the soft rays of eventide like untold millions of churning diamonds that sparked and faded and sparked again. Rocks and deadfall lay strewn along the banks, marking the boundary of waterway and forest.

"We could live here forever," she said. "Couldn't we?"

Taylor nodded and looked out, far past the river bend to the cliffs. What he saw there struck him with horror. He squeezed Lucy's hand.

"Taylor?" she asked. "What's wrong?"

"There's no place for that. That shouldn't *be*."

"What shouldn't?"

"There."

It did no good. Taylor could see Lucy peering out past the river beyond the hill and into the untrodden forest on either side, but there was too much there. Too much wonderful.

"Don't you see, lady?" Taylor asked. *"I didn't do that."*

He pointed to where the fading light shone brightest, far down the riverbank along the steep cliffs, where a mound of heavy stones lay piled high to toppling.

· 19 ·

I stood there as Hollis's words washed over me, trying to understand what he was saying, wanting to know what it meant.

Kate stepped forward and placed the open yearbook on a small table by the television. "What, Hollis? You saw Lucy last night?"

"Yes'm," Hollis said.

"Where?"

He shifted his weight and looked at Edith, who had gotten her mind lost somewhere between the porch and the living room. She had done so with increasing regularity over the years, first in short moments and then in longer ones. Hollis told me once that he believed the place his wife went was a world of fuzzy edges and faint echoes just next door to our own. It pained him to see his wife fading away like that, though for that one particular time I believe Hollis took Edith's going as a blessing. It meant she wouldn't hear what he had to tell. And yet I wondered then just how much Edith Devereaux had known about her husband's illegal activities over the years. I wondered how many of her fading spells were biological and how many were simply a blind eye turned to what she didn't want to see. We all had secrets we kept and lies we told, and often the greatest among them were the ones we kept from and told to ourselves.

Hollis looked at me and said, "On the back forty. Been cleanin' up there. Devil's done found his way here, Jake, as you well know. And as you may not, 'twas me who blazed the path he took."

I didn't see the sense in arguing that point. If that week had taught me anything, it was there was blame enough to go around.

"And Lucy was there?" Kate asked.

Hollis nodded. "Come up on me like a ghost, Kate. Thought she was Bobby at first." Edith made a move to the sofa. Hollis guided her there before adding, "She pulled on me, Jake."

I chortled and felt a pang of guilt when I saw Kate's serious look. But it was the only reaction that fit the picture in my mind of Lucy Seekins holding a gun.

"She pulled on you?" I asked.

"I'll swear to it. Brought up a scatter-gun bigger'n her own self, leveled it right here." Hollis pointed to his chest. "Said . . ."

"What, Hollis?" Kate asked. "What'd she say to you?"

Hollis's eyes found his feet. He looked like a felon receiving his sentence. I thought of Justus and how he would look like that soon.

"Told me I peddled poison and ruint lives, an' that I cain't undo what's been done because it comes back to haunt. That true, you reckon?" When he looked up, there was a pleading for comfort in his eyes. "Tell me it ain't, Jake."

But I could do no such thing. There could be no comforting Hollis Devereaux, at least not with the truth. Because the truth was that some things in life couldn't be undone, and those were the shadows that followed you forever.

"Did she say anything else, Hollis?" Kate asked. "Did she look hurt or hungry?"

"Don't rightly know, sorry t'say. I was more concerned with what that shotgun looked like than her. She was gonna run me through, Kate. She said I'd brought all this on us, and truer words were never spoken."

Kate said, "That's not what she meant, Hollis. She was speaking of her and her daddy, not the town. You have occasion to entertain Clay Seekins on your . . . back forty? Heavy-ish man, wears a suit?"

Hollis thought and then nodded. "Don't know all the names of those I entertain, I'm afraid to say. But yes'm, I know a man in a suit. I didn't know it was that girl at first, even after I saw her picture in the paper. She done shaved her head or somethin'. Looked like she come down with the mange. And she was talkin' funny too. Said she had to wake me up."

My ears perked at that.

"What is it, Jake?" Kate asked.

I looked at Hollis. "She said that? It was those words?"

"Yessir."

"Timmy said Taylor told him those same words. Asked Timmy if he was awake."

Kate's hand went to her mouth. All the lies Trevor had spewed with his pen, one had turned to truth. Taylor had Lucy.

"Was she alone, Hollis?" I asked. "You didn't see anyone else skulking about?"

"Dint see no one. One person get the drop on me in my own wood? I reckon maybe. But two?" Hollis shook his head.

"But how can that be?" Kate asked me. "If she was alone, why didn't she run to town? Why didn't she run to me?"

I thought I knew, but decided to keep silent on it until I was sure. Telling Kate the girl she'd so wanted to save had taken up with the one she'd lost so long ago would only break her heart all over again. And yet as awful as it sounded, it also sounded right.

My mind thought back to what Taylor had told me Sunday night.

But I got tricks too. Charlie weren't the only one helping me. Got me a smart one.

I know what you did to that boy in the Holler that day, Jake.

I see far.

I always been close.

Close.

My knees buckled. Kate reached for me. There was little strain on her part; I couldn't weigh more than a hundred and fifty pounds. All dreams and no meals made Jake Barnett a sickly boy.

"What, Jake?" she asked.

"I know where they are," I said. "Taylor and Lucy both. They're in the Holler."

The weight of those words settled into Kate's face first, then Hollis's. Only Edith remained unperturbed. Such places as Happy Hollow didn't exist in her sideways world. She looked up and smiled as Zach came into the room. He bent over the yearbook on the table and a dawning came over me then, like putting the last piece of a puzzle in place and finally seeing what picture it made. The door had come first. Then the father. Now the book. All that was left was the choice, and I found that choice easily made.

"I'm calling Alan."

Kate said, "No, Jake. There's no time. We can be there in half an hour."

"We?" I asked. "You're going nowhere near the Holler, Kate, and neither am I. Alan can get some men up there—"

"No, Daddy," Zach said.

"I'm going," Kate told me. "This is because of me, Jake. Lucy's with him."

"You have to stay here with Zach."

"No, Daddy," Zach said again. He had his eyes to the yearbook and gave the Devereauxs only a passing glance. "You hafta go. Mommy too. He told me so. Mr. Hollis and Miss Edith can take care of me."

"Son," I said, "we're not going anywhere."

"You hafta, Daddy. Don't be scared."

I looked to Kate. "I'm not doing this."

"Then I'm doing it alone," she said.

She went to Zach and covered his face and neck with kisses. He stood strong and let her cry, then pressed his head against my vanishing waist.

"Don't be scared," he whispered.

Kate stood at the door, aware that her courage would flee if she didn't leave soon. I took my hat and told Zach, "We won't be long now. You mind Hollis and Edith."

Zach wiped his cheek. He reached for Bessie and handed her to me. "He said you'd need this."

Zach and Hollis stood at the door, watching as we left. Our son held his head high, but that only betrayed the tremble in his chin. Kate took a long look at him. She waved in a way that made me feel it was a kind of good-bye.

As I pulled from the lane onto the road, I could not look back for the same reason. I was afraid looking back and seeing Zach at the door would mean I wouldn't come back or Kate wouldn't. All those songs and stories say you should always say good-bye and I love you before going anywhere. Because you never know. You might get in a wreck or have a heart attack, or just down the road's when that aneurism you didn't know you had finally decides to pop like a squashed bug. But I wanted to lie to myself just one more time. I wanted to believe where Kate and I were going was no more dangerous than taking a drive down into town. I wanted to believe it was all going to be fine even if I knew it wasn't.

To me, life was a wheel that starts turning at birth. Slow and rocking at first, faster as we get on. Always moving from a start that gets dimmer to an end that comes nearer. And at that end? I think there's just a single door that opens to either eternal bliss or punishing torment. I could avoid that end no more than anyone else who'd ever breathed life into their lungs. One day I, too, would have to turn that knob. But how I got to that door and what was waiting on the other side? That was up to me. God knew, but He let me choose. Life might be a straight shot from yesterday through today and on to tomorrow, but that wheel spun by, coming back to a place it had already been. And that was where we all chose our fate— there along that slow grind.

I knew someone would die that night. Me or Kate or Taylor or Lucy. Someone. But when Zach told me he'd seen Phillip, I understood that I didn't have a choice but to go. My life had stuck like a bad needle on a record because I'd always had it in my head that I could go back and undo what I'd done. Part of that was true. I could go back; I often did. But none of us can write a new beginning to our story. All we can do is start a new end.

That alone was what took me back to the Hollow. That alone was what kept me from turning back even as I met Kate's stare and knew her eyes looked not at me but at a time long gone. I trusted that hope for a new end to carry us even as I felt that wheel spin around and back. Back to the day Phillip McBride died in body, and Kate, Taylor, and I died in spirit.

Part VI

Settling Accounts

· 1 ·

I t is May 25, 1990, and there is a sweetness in the air like fresh
life. The mountains stand so clear and close they seem to have
uprooted themselves and taken a ten-mile step nearer to town.
The sun is bright and hot—close, Kate remembers. Yes, closer even
than the mountains. She shields her eyes against that glare and
looks out beyond the crowded football field to those blue peaks,
thinking this is how the future looks. Clear. Clear and bright.

It's Field Day, the day after final exams and mere days until
graduation, and the faculty of Mattingly High School has thrown
up its collective hands and surrendered to summer's call. Three
hundred teenagers spread out along the track and football field,
some sunning themselves in the home and visitors' bleachers,
others seeking shelter beneath the peeling scoreboard or entertain-
ing themselves at the booths and refreshment stands the Student
Government Association has erected at the fifty-yard line. What
teachers who have bothered to attend are huddled in metal folding
chairs in the far end zone, sharing summer plans and how glad
they are to have survived another year.

Kate is holding court in the visitors' bleachers, gossiping with

BILLY COFFEY

the crowd around her about who has done what to whom and when and for how long. There is talk of prospects and plans. A few of her friends have been accepted to the university, a few more to smaller colleges nearer and farther from town. Most, however, will remain in Mattingly. They will find work in the shops along Main Street, marrying and having children. Kate wants both of these worlds. She will stay in Mattingly and try the community college in Stanley and see what happens.

She hears Jake before she sees him, down on the field in the middle of a crowd at the bottle toss. Two baseballs rest in his left hand, one sits in his right. Jake draws his arm back and forward in a blur, and in the next instant Kate hears the echoing smack of bottles tumbling and people cheering. Everyone cheers but one. Trevor Morgan stands in the midst of his fellow students with his hands in his pockets.

Kate watches Jake and remembers that day in second grade when he saved her honor at Bobby Barnes's expense. She remembers the card she made for him five years later, when Jake's mother took ill and passed on. Their lives have crossed many times since, as all lives cross in a small town. And though Kate knows neither when nor how, she believes their lives are destined to cross once more, and this time their hearts will entwine.

The bleachers are full. There are good friends and friends Kate knows only in passing, all of whom have found themselves drawn here to rest and remember. To be with one another, if perhaps for the last time. Chatter dies slowly. Laughter calms and wilts. It's as though each of them is looking down upon more than a football field, they are looking down upon the most important parts of their young lives. And Kate believes these people—these friends—have each come to the end of the same long thought: this is a beginning, and this is an end. For Kate Griffith, it means the end of being the popular one, the pretty one, the leader and the trendsetter. There will be no fawning over her at the community college, no one vying for her attention. She will be a face, nothing more.

She looks down over the field and sees two boys, each apart from one another and everyone else. One sits cross-legged in the grass, his pimply face and spectacled eyes deep in a book. The other stands leaning against the goal post. His long hair blows in the breeze and his hands are shoved into a pair of filthy jeans. Kate knows one of them—Phillip McBride is his name, Phil the Fairy to both his classmates and, in hushed whispers, most of the faculty—but she does not know the other. Nor does she care. Because the mountains now seem to have retreated and the sun has grown dark and distant, and Kate does not need to know either of those two boys to hate them. To her they've become warnings of what her own future holds. She will be forgotten. Ignored. Kate has ascended to teenaged greatness (at least by Mattingly's standards) without even trying, but now that she has it she finds it hard to give away. In that moment, too, too hard.

She speaks up then, and the place from where those words come is neither a soul full of malice nor the cold heart of a bully, it is only from a frightened girl who wants to hang on to the little she has. And for all the times Kate has looked back on this moment to what she did, this is the first time she remembers why.

She only wants to keep mattering.

"Let's play a trick," she says.

Heads turn around her. Frowns lift. And just as in all those times in all those years before, every one of Kate Griffith's adorers says amen.

She slips down the bleachers. Kate goes to Phillip first, as he is closest. Kate turns to look back at the bleachers (even now she hears pockets of sniggers) and feels her ponytail whip against the side of her neck and the sun against her tight jeans. She skirts the football field toward Phillip, whose nose is still in his book. His eyes wander up when the first edges of Kate's shadow touches his knee. Kate sees Phillip's chest tighten when he realizes it's her. He blinks twice, and Kate knows she made him do that. She relishes that power. She grips it and holds tight and vows to never let it go.

"Hey there, Phillip," she says. "What'cha reading?"

His tongue slips from his mouth and over his lips, wetting them. "Shakespeare," he tells her.

"Well, now's not the time for homework, silly."

"I know," Phillip says. His voice comes out shrill and high, like a chipmunk's. "I like it. It's pretty."

"Read me some."

Phillip grins—This is happening, Kate believes he's thinking, this is really happening—and settles upon a page. He clears his throat and pushes his glasses toward his nose.

"'Take, O take those lips away, That so sweetly were forsworn, And those eyes, the break of day, Lights that do not mislead the morn: But my kisses bring again, Bring again—Seals of love, but seal'd in vain, Seal'd in vain!'"

Kate brings a hand to her mouth. Phillip looks upon the smile she hides with a kind of awe.

"That's pretty, Phillip," she says. "I don't know what any of that means, but it sounds fair."

"I didn't write it," he says.

"You've crushed on me for a long time, haven't you?" Kate asks. Phillip's mouth falls open, making her laugh again.

"It's okay," she says. "I've crushed on you too. Never could tell you that. You know how people here are. But we'll be graduating soon, Phillip. You live in the hills, I live here in town. We might not ever see each other again. So I was thinking now's the time to do all those things we've never been able."

She sees Phillip knows this is true—that in fact he may have been thinking that very thing over the past weeks. Yet fear pinches his lips closed.

"Phillip," she says, "do you want to kiss me?"

He does not speak but his eyes say, Yes, yes, and yes please, and his head manages a nod.

"Come on," Kate says. "Let's go somewhere private."

She leads Phillip away, back toward the bleachers where fifty heads have turned in the opposite direction. The two of them step onto the track and to the other side. Phillip stops. There is a moment of panic when Kate fears he knows something is wrong, that a pretty her would never want to kiss an ugly him. She turns around, meaning to tell Phillip to hurry, Field Day's almost over and this will be his only chance and doesn't he want this moment just as badly as she?

But there is no need for such falsehood. Phillip has only bent to the soft grass and plucked a handful of flowers. He holds them up, offering them, and Kate can barely contain her laughter because they're not flowers at all, they're

("Dandelions," she said.

Jake took his eyes off the dark road that led to the mountains and asked, "What'd you say?"

Kate only muttered, "That's why I hate them now, because they remind me of me," and she fell silent again.)

Kate takes the weeds and thanks him. Phillip reaches out and takes her hand. His fingers are slippery and his breaths come out heavy. He says, "If you let go, I'll float into the sun."

Afternoon light bathes the backside of the bleachers. Phillip looks up to see legs but no eyes. There is chatter and laughter and the metallic ring of feet upon stairs, and Kate thinks if she doesn't hurry someone will falter, someone will squeal, someone always does. Sweat covers Phillip's face. He pushes his glasses up.

"I have to go make sure no one sees," Kate says. "You wouldn't want to be the one to spoil my honor, would you, Phillip?"

"No, not ever."

"Good. You wait here. Close your eyes. It'll be better that way. But don't peek. If you peek, I'll know and you won't get a kiss. Okay?"

"Okay," Phillip says.

"Good. Close them now. Shut them tight. I'll be right back."

His glasses slip down. Phillip lets them hang. Kate smiles as she walks away, sure he will wait. For her, Phillip McBride would wait forever. She waits until his eyes are closed and runs, tossing the dandelions as far beneath the bleachers as she can.

· 2 ·

"I'm looking toward the Holler on that day."

Taylor looked from the fire he'd built to Lucy. An orange glow colored her face, and though the night was warm and the flames burned hot, she huddled close. The rocks laid by hands that were not his own towered over them. Those stones frightened Taylor. They frightened him more than anything had in his life.

"I'm only a child, lady, no older'n you, but I've wandered this Holler often. Fashioned my flint knife in this wood just the week before. This land begins toward the hill lands in Mattingly and ends in the hill lands of Camden, as you may know. Where it ends is where I lived with my aunt. Charlene's her name. She says the devil lives in this wood, and I think to myself mayhap he does or doesn't, but it don't matter because the devil's more a friend to me than anyone else. It draws me, this Holler. As the Hole draws you now.

"So there I stand on that warm day, walled in by boys and girls who are my age in body but only children to me in mind. I don't know them and they don't know me and we all agree that way is best. I don't like Mattingly. It stinks of corn and cows. I'm just a ghost there. I come to school and no one speaks to Taylor, no one sees Taylor, no one knows Taylor. So I stand against those poles that day while everybody's playin'. I feel this flint knife in my pocket and look out over the mountains to where this Holler lies. I count my minutes until I'm free of that school and can run here.

"That's when I sense her coming. Sashaying her way through that bright green football grass. And though my eyes are still on that wide patch of dead trees midway up the mountains, I know it's Kate Griffith who walks my way. She don't know of me but I know of her, and I know of Jake. Them two see the school as I come to see this Holler, and by that I mean as their own. She's grinning as she nears, like she sees my own heart set to fluttering. I always thought Kate is fair. Her eyes are like evening, and I feel if I stroll there, I will stroll forever.

"She helloes and asks my name, but my tongue's too knotted to speak. She chuckles (like birdsong, that titter is) and says it don't matter if I talk or not. She says she's watched me all day. I doubt that in my head—a ghost is all I am, and even those who see ghosts see them as there for a blink and then there no more—but my heart says, No, Taylor, don't you go thinking that right yet, you just let me feel some for a while.

"Then she says, 'Would you like to kiss me?' and I near crumble at her feet.

"She takes my hand and leads me longways past the teachers and the kids, back to where the bleachers sit. We're close there, and she turns and hushes me.

"'Be quiet and close your eyes,' she whispers, and then she says it's unmanly to kiss a girl otherwise.

"There's a voice in me that speaks then, telling me to never mind what she says, that something's wrong about a girl as pretty as that kissin' a boy whose name she don't even know. But another voice, this one louder, hushes that speech with a fire that shuts my eyes tight. I mean to have Kate's lips, my heart says.

"She leads me stumbling behind the bleachers. There's talkin' everywhere, people laughing, having a grand old time. And then it's like the world hushes.

"Kate stops me and whispers, 'Come here.'

"I lean in and meet her mouth, and there's a softness that steals my breath and weakens my knees. But I know it's only for a moment, that feeling. It don't matter a whit how good anything is, all things fade. But to *see* her! To hold that picture in my mind. I think that would last me forever. So I open my eyes."

Taylor stopped there. Lucy's gaze fixed to his. He shuddered despite the heat of the fire.

"What?" she asked. "What happened, Taylor?"

He said, "I open my eyes, and it's not Kate's lips upon mine. 'Tis a boy's."

· 3 ·

Kate sensed the thick night as Jake stopped the Blazer. They both climbed out. Jake stood at the rusty gate, tracing the names scratched into the iron with his fingers. His lips moved, but Kate couldn't hear if he was speaking to her or himself. The noise was too great. Not in the woods (even then there was only silence, as if both sides of the gate were caught in an inhale and waiting to breathe out), but in her own mind. It was the sharp sound of—

· 4 ·

—*Laughter! Rolling down from behind the bleachers like a waterfall, spilling onto Kate like cool rain on a hot day, joyous bursting, cackling voices of friends and friends in passing, howling and teary and jubilant, faces turned and pointed to the boys—the two poor HILL BOYS—locked in an amorous kiss.*

Kate wails with glee, drowning herself in the hilarity. The dirty boy—Kate will not know his name is Taylor until twenty years later—has already opened his eyes. He steps back in a grimace and swipes at his mouth, which only makes them laugh more. Phil the Fairy jumps when the laughter starts, his eyes wide at the sight of where his lips had rested. There is no shock to him, no horror, and upon seeing him as such, Kate feels the first fringes of a fog that will damper her life from this moment on. Phillip McBride looks as one who has woken from a dream he knew was too good to be true.

They run, each of them. Phillip one way and the dirty boy the other, pushed by the mocking at their backs through the exits on either side of the football field.

Aside from Kate and those on the bleachers, no one sees them leave. It's just as well; no one had ever noticed them before, and only Phillip would be remembered after because only Phillip died.

Kate holds her hands aloft, reaching for the sound of acceptance—of glorious worship—and drinks until she's full. She laughs (oh, how she laughs!), yet even as she does, Kate remembers the look on Phillip's face, and even now there is a dark knowing in her mind that something more has happened here, something far worse than she could have ever intended, and that her laughter will end in tears.

· 5 ·

"I tore off," Taylor said.

Lucy's hand had slipped into his sometime during the telling. It was an act that stood in contrast to the hate on her face. Taylor hoped the girl's rage would stay on Kate and not veer to him. The story was near its end, and though Taylor was still sure what had happened after he ran from the football field that day was true—was *good*—he remembered he had not woken Charlie or Lucy's momma and yet they were gone still.

"I have my Aunt Charlene's car—she lets me have it on schoolin' days and hoofs it to her own job down at the laundrymat in Camden—and I go's fast as I can. But no matter how much gas I give that old Ford, I cain't outrun the memory of that boy's kiss. I'm past the Mattingly line and I can still hear them cackling at me, saying 'Stupid redneck' and calling me a boy lover. And I see Kate too. Oh yes, I see her well, and I know that memory of her I feared would slip my mind will now be there always.

"Charlene, she's got beer in the fridge. She sips and swallows and then cusses my ma for the drugs she takes. I drink until the heat I feel from Kate turns cold, and then I go to the only place that gives me comfort. It's this Holler that takes me. I'm not laughed at here, and I'm not made sport of. Here, I'm a king.

"I walk on 'til the sun's low on the mountaintops. Hours, I reckon it was, up from the lowlands to these cliffs right above us. That's when I hear a sound of mourning that buckles me. I been in this wood many a'time afore then. Seen things. Heard things. But I never saw or heard no sound like that. I turn to run off, but that sound gets closer, callin'-me like. I reach to my pocket for my stone knife. There's a stand of rock up there and a small path for game, and when that noise comes around those rocks, I see it's the boy.

"It's the *boy*. The one Kate *tricked* me with. He starts sayin' he's lost, that he cain't go home wailing to his folks and so he parked his truck and now he's lost, but I know it's deceit. He followed me. I know that more than I've ever known anything. How else would we both've gotten to this same place at this same time?

"I tole him to get goin', but he didn't. He's wailing and walking to me, saying to me, 'I'm lost, I don't want to be lost,' and then he reaches out his arms to give me a hug, aiming to *touch* me, and in my head I see Kate and I hear that cackle rising louder, calling me hillbilly and boy lover, and then . . ."

Taylor reached into his back pocket. He felt the flint knife there but drew out his old book instead. His eyes grow wide at something he'd never considered before. "'Twas not out of love, lady. Not at all. I hated him."

· 6 ·

I turned from the Hollow and faced Kate. Her shoulders were hunched and she held her arms folded across her chest, as though holding herself against a cold only she could feel. Her eyes were fully on me. She had left whatever place her mind had visited on our way to the gate, and the long trip back had left her looking tired and worn. My heart broke for her.

We were bound together, Kate and I. Not simply by love

or duty to our son, but because of Phillip. Because of what had happened on a day that to most of the billions of people in this sad world came and went no different from any other, filled with the same trifles to endure and worries to dwell upon. That day had been long forgotten to them, and yet for Kate and me it came to define not just the lives we would live from then forward but the people we would become. Standing there watching the moonlight glint off the tears pooling in her eyes, I knew she had suffered more. Kate was loved and accepted by our town. Yet she was still held responsible for Phillip's death in everyone's eyes but my own, no matter how many boxes she delivered to the doorsteps of Mattingly's poor.

Yes, she had suffered more. I understood that. But I also understood I had borne more. Kate had carried regret all those years, a mourning for what she'd done. I carried a remorse for what I hadn't, and that burden is heavy and hard to lay down. But there at the rusty gate with the peak of Indian Hill looming far, I knew that was what I had to do. And I prayed that if I couldn't find the courage to lay that weight down, I could at least find the strength to loosen my grip.

I turned away and set my hands upon the gate. My words were soft and slow.

"I saw Phillip after he ran off that day. I saw him here. And then I killed him."

I couldn't face her. Nor could I look ahead to all those miles of dead trees soaked in a moon that only made everything frighten me more. I could only be silent now and steel myself against whatever might come.

What came was a soft and broken voice carried by the breeze: "What did you say?"

"I saw him here," I said. "I didn't know anything of what had happened. I saw everybody up in the bleachers for Field

Day and I remember hearing them laughing, but I didn't know what it was about. I was down on the field, showing off. Being the man. I had eyes for you then, Kate. I've loved you ever since I can remember. Couldn't believe it when we started dating. I thought you were just too pretty and too good for me. I still think that."

I heard Kate's feet shuffle. The way she spoke my name shamed me. It reminded me of the way I'd spoken Phillip's name when he first entered my dreams. It was a plea. I could only face the gate and shake my head.

"I decided that morning I'd come up here after school was out," I said. "It wasn't so much I was graduating as I was getting ready to turn eighteen. You leave off school and get that age, people start calling you a man. I didn't feel much like a man, though. Momma was long passed, and it was just me and Justus. Hard, living under that shadow. He always wanted to make me into him, and I always wanted it. But it wasn't in me, Kate. My heart was too soft to let me be a hard man. That made me weak. In his eyes, and my own.

"Never put much stock in coming up here and scrawling my name, but I decided to do it anyway. I figured it would be the kind of thing Justus would approve of. And I guess I thought I'd have at least that to lean on—I could say I came here to the gate, just like all those men in all those years. I know it sounds stupid, but it felt like doing that would make me part of something. Like I belonged.

"So when Field Day was over, I climbed in the truck and drove here. Parked right there where the Blazer is. And let me tell you, Kate, I felt then what I feel right now. This place births a fear in you like none other. I just sat there behind the wheel, half of me saying go ahead and get it over with, the other half telling me to turn tail and run before whatever hell lives here gets hungry. It was Justus's face that settled things. He was all I saw, and that's why I got out.

"All I had was my old Buck knife. Justus still had Bessie then, and whether he'd pass her on to me was still a subject of question." I touched the steel at the small of my back, reminding myself that that issue, at least, had been settled. "My hand was shaking like you wouldn't believe when I took that knife out. Every boy's heard stories of the Holler. You hear them growing up. The good ones'll put a fright in you, but none of them match being here. You can feel it. It's like a blade dangling over your head, getting ready to drop.

"I don't know what made me look up. Maybe it was my fear looking out or maybe I heard something back in the trees. I saw Indian Hill up there. It was day still, but it was closing in on . . ." I paused. "Eventide. I could see the pines atop it, the only green things for miles. And I got this idea then, crazy as it was—*nobody's probably set foot on that hill in all of history.* I still think maybe that was true. Who'd go all that way up there through this wood? Who'd have that kind of guts? No one. Not even my daddy had gone past the gate.

"I lit out before I could talk myself out of it. Turned my back probably a hundred times in the first hundred steps, just to make sure the gate was still here and I hadn't been swallowed up. My heart beat so hard I could feel it in my throat. But I kept walking. All the way to the hill. All the way, Kate."

I turned. It was just for a moment and just to see where Kate was. She'd taken two steps closer and was holding herself tighter. I looked back to the gate. To the hill.

"Made it up there just as the sun was going down. I saw no devils and heard no ghosts. There was just an empty quiet. And you know what? It's beautiful up on that hill, at least as beautiful as anything in the Holler can be. It's dead land out there, but it's untouched. There's a magic to it. The river's on the other side. It comes down through some cliffs and winds on down. To town eventually, I guess.

"And I thought, *Coming this way wasn't so bad. If I hoof it down to the river, I'll be back before night.*

"If I'd do anything over in my life, Kate, it'd be that. It doesn't seem right that a life can turn on one choice, but it can. I walked down the other side and came to the river. Followed it around the bend to where the cliffs lay. I thought I'd pushed my luck far enough and started to turn back when I saw something lying on the bank just a-ways ahead. I didn't know what it was, but I knew it wasn't driftwood and I knew it didn't belong. There were butterflies all around it. White ones. They'd light on whatever it was and flit away, circle around and land again. I got closer and saw it was a boy—it was Phillip. His glasses were lying near, all broken. His body was broken worse. His blood was all over the rocks. The butterflies were feeding on it." I shook my head. "It was like bees to honey."

Kate began to cry. I wanted to go to her but didn't. I'd started this tale, and I meant to have its end.

"I didn't know what to do, seeing him that way. I looked up and guessed he must've tumbled from the cliffs, but I couldn't understand how he'd gotten up there and so deep in the Holler. That drop, it had to be thirty feet at least. Phillip's lying there and his arms and legs are at these angles that aren't possible, and I'm shaking as I stare at him and I feel eyes on me, like something's watching. And then all of a sudden he reaches out for me. He's trying to talk but he can't because he's so banged up. He's just wiggling his fingers like, and he's making these noises like a hurt animal and I just screamed. I screamed, Kate, and then I ran. I turned and took three steps and stumbled on the rocks. Landed on my arm"—I pointed to my scar—"right here. Then I got up and ran harder than I've ever run in my life. Back over the hill and on through the Holler and I don't care what devils I see or what ghosts reach up for me from the dirt, all I want to do is run. All the way back to the gate and my truck. I'm shaking so bad and crying so hard when I get there, I can't even turn the engine over. Once I do, I'm gone. I flew, Kate. Wonder I didn't run off the road."

Far away, Kate spoke. "You didn't tell anyone?"

I shook my head. "Meant to a thousand times. Justus asked about the gash on my arm. I couldn't tell him the truth. I knew he'd ask why I didn't bring Phillip out or why I didn't go straight to Sheriff Houser, anything other than run away and leave that boy to die. And then I got to thinking maybe Phillip hadn't been in that bad of shape, maybe it was the Holler playing tricks or maybe Phillip was playing a trick himself. Maybe he'd just picked himself up after I ran off and walked back home with a big laugh. That's what I told myself—that if I told Justus and he'd got the sheriff out there and Phillip was nowhere to be seen, it would be worse. I figured I'd keep quiet and wait. Just one day, just to make sure. But that was my shame talking.

"Saturday morning came and went. There was no word. Then Justus came home from town that evening and gathered Bessie and a light, asking me if I knew a boy named Phillip McBride. I told Justus I didn't really, Phillip was just a kid at school and everybody called him Phil the Fairy. Justus told me the boy was gone. They'd found his daddy's truck along a switchback in the hill country, and Sheriff Houser believed he'd either gotten himself lost in the woods or been taken by a sex pervert. It was too late for me then. If I 'fessed to what I saw, Justus and the sheriff both would've condemned me as a murderer. And that was true, what I deserved.

"I was in hell for another day, trying to find a way to go. I called Sheriff Houser Monday before school and hid my voice. He found Phillip that afternoon. Went into the Holler alone. No one dared go with him, not even Justus. Sheriff Houser said it was his duty. I thought about that often when they said I was the new sheriff. I think about it still.

"By then, what'd happened at school got out. So did the stuff about how Phillip's daddy always beat on him and his momma. They figured Phillip was upset and didn't feel like he could go home, so he got out of that truck and started walking. I knew you'd take all that blame, Kate. Even when they called it suicide, I knew you'd put Phillip's death on yourself."

Kate's words were a knife that sank deep—"*You never told me otherwise!*" she screamed. "Even when we started dating, Jake? Even when we were *married*? All these years, *and you never told me?*"

"I loved you," I said. I turned so she could see my face, and though I spoke with a desperation that neared anger, I kept my voice even. "I love you still. All I ever wanted was for you to think of me as a good man, Kate. What Justus thinks and Trevor and Bobby Barnes and the mayor, what the whole town thinks, doesn't matter. What matters is you and Zach."

I gripped my head, aiming to jerk the words out that my tongue couldn't carry.

"The burden I've carried, Kate. All that weight on me. I know the load you carry. I won't say mine is heavier, only that it's different. All a man has is his honor. It's the one thing that's his and the world can't take, and the only way you lose it is if you give it away. But once you do it's like you're walking around naked and cold, and you can have the love of God and the help of Jesus, but you live in hell just the same. I wish you could understand that, Kate. With all my heart, I do. But you can't. You can't know why I never told you, I can only hope you'll try and understand."

Kate took a step to me. The smooth skin where her jaws met bulged, and her eyes were two hard coals. All I had just confessed had been met with everything I'd always feared—Kate's love crumbled beneath her tears, spilled away, and I would never have it again.

"Don't you dare think only a man is saddled with honor, Jake Barnett," she said, "and don't you dare tell me only a man can suffer at its passing."

"I just wanted you to love me. I just wanted to protect what we have."

She shook her head. "What we have, Jake? What do we have? Everything we've built together is a lie."

"Don't say that, Kate," I said. "Please don't. Please just try to understand."

Kate offered no such consolation, nor did I deserve one. She only stood there, looking not into my eyes—I didn't think Kate could, and I didn't blame her—but at a spot over my right shoulder. Her eyes widened.

She reached for my arm and asked, "What's that?"

I turned back to the gate. Far beyond, a single white light burst from among the pines atop Indian Hill. It held steady and did not move, pressing back against the night like a beacon.

Phillip McBride had vowed to me that he would return for an end once we all had remembered true. Standing there staring at that speck of brightness, I knew I'd done just that. No less than I knew Kate had on our long ride to the Hollow. No less, perhaps, than Taylor Hathcock, who lay waiting for me somewhere in the endless miles of wilderness on the other side of the gate. And at the very moment Big Jim Wallis declared his emergency meeting to order (and put it on record that I was too cowardly to appear), I understood an end had come.

I stepped alongside Kate and took her hand. She allowed it.

· 7 ·

"That's Lucy," Kate said. "That has to be Lucy, Jake."

She stared at the faraway light (a pinprick from the distance between the hill and the gate, and yet that pinprick shone brighter than the moon) and gripped Jake with both hands. Kate moved only when she felt his hand feeling for Bessie. His face had drained of all color. He looked like one of the Hollow's ghosts.

"We should go back," Jake said. "Let me call Alan. Call everybody. Get some men up here."

Kate stepped away toward the gate and said, "No, Jake. Lucy's up there *now*. Go or stay or do whatever you want, but I'm going up there."

"There's worse things in the Holler than Taylor Hathcock, Kate. It isn't safe."

"I don't care about me and I don't care about you, I care about what I did to him, Jake. I care about what I drove that man to do. I care about *Lucy*. She's in trouble, and you'd know that if you'd spent your life doing anything other than hiding behind your lies."

Kate regretted those words as soon as she said them, though not enough to apologize. Jake's confession still stung. Yet the pain on his face hiding behind a pair of sunken eyes and graying stubble, the way his uniform hung from a pair of wiry shoulders, the thickening of his words as though spoken through a curtain of weariness, those things stung her even more. She could almost excuse Jake for running from Phillip that day. He was only a scared boy, after all. That Jake had made the phone call to Sheriff Houser didn't excuse his silence, but wasn't it something? Kate wanted to believe yes. She wanted to believe it if only because she had sought to prove one thing since that day behind the bleachers—people didn't have to remain what they were. They could change. They could become better. And wasn't she? Wasn't Jake?

And there was one last point, one Kate refused to let surface while Jake had told his story but one that shoved its way forward now: it wouldn't have mattered if Jake Barnett had brought the world upon the Hollow to save Phillip that day. To Kate, the one unchangeable fact was that Phillip McBride would have never pulled his daddy's truck over and taken a walk that ended in his death if she'd not driven him to do so. The truth would have changed nothing. Kate would still have carried the weight of what she'd done in a notebook full of good deeds the same way her husband carried the weight of what he would never become in Bessie. They would hold those things so close that even the smallest movement would be a reminder that neither of them could ever have the peace that comes from a conscience free of regret. Jake may have let Phillip die, but Kate would always believe she killed him.

"Come on," Jake said. "Stay close to me. Holler's not a place to be in daylight. I expect it'll be worse now."

Kate took Jake's hand. And though she understood they were no longer one, they stepped beyond the gate together.

Eyes upon her, so many eyes. Crawling over Kate's skin like ants. The dark closed in and those eyes watched and she knew it was death, it was all death.

She whispered, "The moon's gone," and in the silence of that great wood, her words sounded like a shout.

Jake looked up. The canopy of trees blocked the sky. He pointed to the top of the hill and said, "We've light enough. Quiet now. Mind your steps, and don't let go of me. The way's tangled."

They crept as quiet as they could through the brambles. Kate winced as thorns bit into her skin and kept Indian Hill in her sights. There was only that light shining out of the Hollow's dark throat, and when they finally crested the hill, that light came from everywhere and nowhere. It shined upon the pine needles like tiny suns and made the rocks at her feet glow in yellows and oranges. Even the gray dirt that covered the Hollow looked golden.

"Lucy?" Kate called. She shielded her eyes and waited for an answer. None came. "Where's it coming from, Jake? I can't see where to go."

Her eyes skated ahead to the right, where something tickled a low-hanging branch. Jake reached for Bessie and put Kate behind him.

"Lucy?" she called.

Kate's hand tightened upon Jake's even before her mind could accept what she saw. The world melted away and left only that small, childlike voice that lives in the heart of every person and tells us to turn back, to go no farther, because what lies behind may be grief but ahead lie all the monsters that have haunted all our dreams.

What came walking toward them from the trees was not Lucy Seekins. It was a dead boy.

· 8 ·

"What's that?"

Lucy flinched as Taylor's face, vacant and still through his remembering, now came alive in an expression of shock. He shoved the book back into his pocket and spun, reaching for the shotgun he'd leaned against a fallen log behind the fire. Lucy backed away, her eyes searching for trouble that for now only her railing heart could feel. Taylor swung the barrel wide across the river and steadied it upon a dark, far-off spot beyond the bend.

She put herself behind him and asked, "What is it? What are you pointing at?"

"*THAT.*"

Nothing. Lucy saw nothing but black sky and a moon that wanted to shine but barely could. There was the wide ribbon of river water wending its way around the bend and the deep woods that stretched on forever and that was all.

"Taylor, I don't see any—"

"Atop the hill," he screamed. "The witchlight."

Taylor circled the fire. Lucy caught the hem of his shirt and kept him close. Her eyes strained through the darkness and caught the gentle gray curve of Indian Hill rising from the forest, as lifeless as the world around them.

(No, she thought, not lifeless. There's something here, something close and watching, and there's something else close and watching too, and those two things are both different and the same.)

She said, "Taylor, I don't see anything."

Taylor pointed the gun—"*There.*"

Lucy pulled at his shoulder. He gave way only slightly and didn't turn his face to her.

"Taylor, there's nothing there. There's nothing on the hill, okay? You're just upset, but you have to stop because you're scaring me."

And that was true. Lucy had been scared ever since they'd arrived at that spot along the riverbank. Ever since Taylor had seen a wall of rocks he'd said couldn't be there and had fallen into his story. It was the strange sort of fear one feels upon reaching the end of a wide and lovely road to find the place you've been traveling to all this while is hell instead of heaven. Lucy's mind reeled as she saw the ugly patchwork of her life for the first time.

She saw the mother who had died and the father who might as well be dead. She saw Johnny Adkins and the long line of boys behind him, and how she'd taken their wide eyes and slobbering mouths as love. She saw herself naked in front of Taylor and the way he'd slipped his shirt over her bare shoulders, preserving what little of her decency she'd yet to give away. She saw the Hole in the grove and the red hands upon the rocks and Taylor speaking of a dream in which all were marooned and from which all must wake. Lucy saw all of these things and knew they were all her, they were all stitched together by a single thin thread that now began to fray at the horrible thought that Taylor's dream was like the light he saw shining from Indian Hill. Both existed in a fractured place in his mind that long ago had been bent by Kate Griffith behind the bleachers of the Mattingly High football field and then broken on the cliffs above them.

"Taylor?" she asked. "What did you do to that boy? The one Kate tricked. What do you mean it wasn't out of love?"

The trees to their left exploded before Taylor could answer. Lucy screamed as the Hollow gave way and parted in the presence of the bear she'd met near the grove. It moved on to the riverbank with a slow grace and stopped just beyond the firelight. The bear's white eye focused on Lucy. The red one went to Taylor. It was a grotesque sight that nearly made her scream again.

Taylor lowered the shotgun and propped it back against the log behind the fire. He approached the beast but kept his distance, careful not to step beyond the light. They faced each other in silence.

"He speaks of a coming," Taylor said.

Lucy shrank backward toward the fire, trying to escape the bear's look. "What's coming?"

Taylor turned to her. There was a smile on his face, a wide grin that offered Lucy little of the hope she craved. That grin was old and tired and looked like madness.

"My aid comes," he said. "My aid and my salvation."

The bear grunted. Its enormous black head swung from Taylor to the hill and back.

"How can a bear know that?" Lucy asked.

Taylor smiled again. "Have you learned nothing from me, Lucy Seekins? You think your precious grove would have a Keeper, but not this Holler? That's no more bear than I."

· 9 ·

He was as he'd always been in my dreams—the same frayed shorts and dirty sweatshirt, the same hood pulled tight over his head—but this was no dream and there was no waking up. Kate's grip on me went slack as Phillip neared. I felt her moving away and wanted to tell Kate to run, that Phillip McBride had drawn us there to have his revenge and Taylor was Phillip's trick so run, run far and hard to the gate but mind the rocks because they leave a terrible scar. My hand fell away from

Bessie. Phillip stopped between two pines that overlooked the expanse of the Hollow behind Indian Hill and stood there. The light from him shone out. He wore no smile.

Tears streamed from Kate's face. Her body shook as she stepped farther from me to him. "Phillip?" she asked. "Is that you?"

"Stop," I said, and when Kate didn't, I reached out and made her. "It's a trap, Kate. We have to get out of here. We have to go right now."

Kate shook my hand away. "Is that really you, Phillip? Please tell me that's you. Please say something."

Phillip only stared.

"Kate," I said.

"Phillip . . ." She moved away, closer to him, and in her eyes I saw all the things she'd wished to say if only she could see Phillip again. All the hurt and sorrow she'd endured. All the people she'd helped in his name and all the tears that had watered his grave. "Phillip? Phillip, I'm so sorr—"

Phillip's arm shot out to Kate. His hand was the same hard fist I'd seen in all my broken sleep, fingers tight and turned up to the black sky. Kate screamed and stumbled back. I drew Bessie. The handle stuck between my belt and the folds of my uniform. I panicked, pulling at my back and waist as Phillip reached his fist to Kate and Kate begged no, she never meant to hurt him, please don't. Fear flooded my every sense, drowning me and driving me mad as I finally freed the tomahawk and held it by the head rather than the handle. All I could do was throw Bessie like that, like the baseball I threw against those stacked bottles on that bright spring day when Kate played her trick. Yet what came next was not the cheering of a crowd but another scream from deep inside Kate, one that sounded of terror and rage and hurt—

"No, Jake, *NO*."

The blade careened at an awkward angle toward Phillip's chest. His eyes remained on Kate. He turned to me just as Bessie sailed through him as through air. The tomahawk bounced off the tree behind him and landed in the dirt. Phillip's arm moved my way, offering me what he'd offered Kate. From a faraway place I heard him say, *This is yours, Jake, this is what I've come to give you*, and I knew that whatever hell lay in Phillip's hand was the hell I deserved.

Kate said, "Phillip," and he turned back to her. She crept closer to him. "Phillip, please."

"Kate, get *back*," I said. "He brought us here. He told me he was coming back and we were dead, Kate. Please listen to me. We have to leave right *now*."

"No, no, that can't be right." She kept moving, shaking her head. "Do you watch, Phillip? Do you see us still? We were just kids. We were just stupid kids and we didn't know. I was afraid. So much sin happens when we're afraid. We've changed now, Phillip. I have a book. There are names in there and I help them because of *you*. I've tried so hard, Phillip. Please just tell me what I can do."

Phillip turned to face the river below. That simple motion said all that was needed. Nothing. There was nothing Kate could do, and I knew deep down she had always known that was so.

He raised his arm again, pointing beyond the hill where we stood. I moved to Kate and put a hand to her shoulder, telling her to stay. I stepped into Phillip's light and followed his finger down to the river.

Far off beyond the bend, a fire flamed. Its light played upon a mound of rocks I knew well.

"He's down there, isn't he?" I asked him. "Taylor? You've brought us to him."

Kate moved beside us. "Taylor's there? Is Lucy with him?"

Phillip nodded yes.

"Is she safe?"

This time there came no bow of Phillip's head, and in that silence much was said. None of us was safe now. None but him and Taylor.

"Do you want me to go down there, Phillip?" Kate asked. "Is that what I can do? Go down there for you? For Taylor and Lucy?"

Yes.

Phillip walked on then, down the hill to the Hollow below. Kate moved to follow him.

"No," I said. "Please don't. Those rocks down there, where they are. I *built* them, Kate. I built them in my *dreams*. I don't know how that's possible, but it's the truth. I'm not lying anymore. Someone will die down there, and it can't be you."

"Time for talking's done, Jake. Like you said, there's no going back."

"Think of Zach."

"Zach was the one who said we have to go," she said. "Going back will only put Lucy in more danger. I can't lose her, Jake. I'd rather lose myself."

"You don't understand, Kate. I stacked those rocks because I was trying to bury Phillip, but I couldn't. I couldn't *bury* him."

She looked at me and said, "Maybe that's why he's here, Jake. Because I've never been able to bury him either."

Kate moved away toward Phillip's light. I watched her go. And though every part of me screamed to run, I gathered Bessie and followed.

· 10 ·

The bear swung its wide head to Taylor. The light upon the hill began to move. Slowly at first and barely perceived, then faster. Coming to the river. To them.

"What comes?" Taylor asked. "Tell, friend."

But the bear would not. It turned its giant paws in the soft mud and moved off, back into the trees from where it had come. The light was near now, off the slope of the hill and onto the flatland, moving at a rate Taylor found impossible. He judged it would reach the bend in minutes at that speed. Salvation, the bear had said. That was what neared. And yet if Taylor's deliverance did indeed approach, why was his heart not overflowing with joy? Why was he even now fighting to swallow the whimper in his voice so Lucy would not hear it?

"Taylor?" Lucy whispered. "Taylor, I'm scared. I don't understand what's happening. Nothing's coming, Taylor. It's nothing at all."

That light, gathering like a rising sun. Lucy looked on. Taylor shielded his eyes as brightness broke over the bend and wondered how it was that she could be so blind. And yet he believed that even if Lucy could not see the light, she could see and hear the ones who came with it. She shrank back when she heard the sound of her own name called out.

"Kate," Lucy said. "Taylor, it's Kate and Jake. You have to do something."

But Taylor couldn't. Because while he was sure Lucy only saw two vaguely, he saw three clear. He saw Kate, he saw Jake, and he saw his salvation. Taylor shook his head no and no again even as his heart shouted yes. It shouted yes and it shouted that all had been for naught and all had been a lie, because no one dreams once they're Awake. Such is what he'd told

Lucy. No one dreams once they're awake, and why would you? That's why no one comes back.

If someone did, it meant the world wasn't a dream at all.

· 11 ·

Beyond the bend stood the fire and the rise of stones I feared had been laid as the marker for our graves. Kate's eyes strained ahead. Phillip walked in front of us. His strides quickened and then slowed when we lagged beyond the arc of his light. The river churned.

Two people huddled at the fire against the rocks. One stood tall and strong, the other shorter and scared. Kate lurched forward and called out, "*Lucy.*"

Phillip led us on, faster now, and I could not understand why. Kate and I were caught. He was leading us to Taylor, and Taylor was his trick, and yet the man standing against the fire ahead looked frightened and confused.

Lucy moved from her spot—not closer to us, but to Taylor.

"Lucy, it's me," Kate called. "It's Kate, Lucy. Come this way. It's all going to be all right now."

But I knew it wasn't. Taylor hadn't moved since we'd rounded the bend. Now he did. He ran behind the fire and dropped to a knee, reaching for something. Phillip turned to me, and I saw in his eyes a single word I could make no sense of. That word was *hurry.*

Taylor fumbled with whatever was in his hands, dividing his attention between the task at hand and us. When he straightened, my eyes caught a flicker of firelight against a long, muted barrel.

"Gun," I screamed.

Kate called out for me and then called louder. I couldn't hear her.

Nearly fifteen miles away in the crowded hall of the VFW, Big Jim Wallis was announcing to the town the official result of his emergency meeting with the council. The vote was unanimous, five to none. And at the very moment he deemed me dismissed as Mattingly's sheriff on the grounds that I had run from trouble, I ran toward it.

· 12 ·

Lucy saw Jake closing hard. Taylor turned to her and asked, "Do you trust me? Tell me, lady. Speak if you're sure."

Lucy said yes, but the quiver in her voice said she was no longer sure at all. Doubt had crept in as soon as she saw Kate and Jake round the bend. It swelled when she heard Kate call her name and saw Taylor kneel to the log behind the fire. And now that doubt erupted as Taylor raised the shotgun to her chest.

Lucy screamed and brought her hands to her face, sure Taylor meant to Wake her just as he'd woken Eric Thayer and as she'd failed to do with Hollis. She tumbled backward into the wall of rocks. The barrel of the shotgun followed her.

:::

"That's far enough, Jake," Taylor told me. "Step inside this ring, what happens is on you."

I skidded against the riverbank's soil and stopped just outside the fire's light. Taylor kept the gun on Lucy and turned. His eyes caught the small movement I made behind my back.

Taylor shook his head and smiled, daring me. I moved my hand away but held my ground. Standing there in the dark with the river churning beside him, I wanted nothing more than to be dreaming again. All the horror in all those nightmares could not match what I saw in the person on the other end of that barrel. Taylor Hathcock looked not like a man at all but a boy grown old on a diet of poison.

I saw Phillip's light spilling over my shoulder and heard Kate approach. She stopped when I stretched out my hand. Phillip passed through the gap between us and entered the wide ring of the fire's glow. Taylor wavered and shrank back, swinging the shotgun from Lucy to Phillip.

Phillip continued on, unconcerned. He walked through the center of the flames and stopped mere inches from the barrel.

"Fly from me, demon," Taylor cried. "I've no quarrel with you."

Lucy cowered against the rocks, her body shaking at the sight of Taylor shuffling away. She looked from him to me to Kate, then back to Taylor. It was that scatter-gun I should have been paying attention to—how the barrel wavered and how the finger upon the trigger shook, ready to fire. But Taylor's shotgun was the furthest thing from my mind. It was Lucy Seekins I watched and her face I read. I don't think she saw Phillip at all.

Kate eased from my side and skirted the edge of the fire to the rocks. Taylor's eyes followed her. Phillip moved, setting his body between them. In one slow motion, he raised an upturned fist to Taylor's eyes, and I understood that if Kate and I were in a trap, Taylor had been snared as well.

Faced with too many threats, Taylor seemed unsure where to steer the gun next. He settled on my head. He raised the stock to his cheek and stepped around Phillip's fist, moving me back. The barrel moved to Kate and Lucy and to Phillip again. Taylor stopped only when he reached a position between the fire and the rocks where he could watch us all.

"What hell have you conjured, Jake?" he asked. "Is this your play?"

Kate moved closer to Lucy, who huddled farther into the stones. Lucy's head shook no. I heard her whisper, "This isn't real, this isn'treal, thisisn'treal."

"It's no conjuring," I said. "Phillip's drawn us."

"No," Taylor said. "*NO*. Not him. You deceive me, Jake. He is my *aid*."

⋮⋮

Taylor's finger sat at the trigger, and he did not see Jake's hand draw back. His eyes were on the boy—not at his glow (witchlight was what he'd told Lucy, and witchlight it was, Taylor had seen plenty of that both in the Hollow and in his dreams) but at his feet. At the boy's shoes. He lowered the shotgun and peered at the footprints left in the riverbank's soft mud. Ones Taylor remembered well.

The shotgun trembled in Taylor's hands. He spoke with a reasonableness that sounded just short of insanity—calm at first, louder in the middle, and at the end a shout that echoed off the cliffs above: "You cain't be my salvation. You cain't be here, boy. I Woke you up. You came at me with your arms wide and I Woke you up, I Woke you up and *YOU CAIN'T COME BACK*."

The boy eased his arm to his head. When he opened his hand, there was only the brilliant skin of his palm. He drew back the hood of his sweatshirt and lifted his chin. Light poured forth from the wide gash where his throat had once

• 360 •

been. Taylor's knees buckled. Kate and Jake shielded their eyes. Lucy looked on into the night as though darkness surrounded them.

Taylor let the shotgun drop to his side. He reached into his back pocket with his free hand and drew out the same flint knife he'd carried into the Holler that day long ago. He looked at Lucy, his eyes filling with a terror that stopped her. It was a look Taylor never expected to share with his true love. It was hope lost.

:::

"Stop it," Lucy screamed. "Stop it stop it stop it. There's no one there. Can't you see there's no one there and why don't you just go and leave us alone?"

Kate came to her slowly and crouched by the rocks. From the corner of her eye, Lucy saw Kate's hand rise to stroke the jagged ends of her hair. She didn't feel Kate's touch. Lucy could feel nothing at that moment other than the slow unwinding of her life.

:::

"You did it," I said. I looked from Phillip to Taylor, to the knife in his hand. "You killed him. You cut his throat."

Taylor shook his head. "That weren't what happened, Jake."

Phillip looked at me and then to the crags above. And was there the faint start of a smile upon his lips?

"You were both up there, on the cliffs. Is that right? They found his daddy's truck on that switchback. Sheriff Houser said you must've took a walk and got lost. What were you doing here, Taylor? Were you running away too? Both of you, to here. Somehow in all this land, you reached the same spot. And then you murdered him."

Taylor said, "I . . . *Woke* . . . him."

"That's how you saw me," I said. "You were watching the whole time. Phillip was bashed to pieces when I found him. That gouge on his neck, it'd just look like he'd hit another rock when he jumped. No one ever thought otherwise because no one ever thought anyone else'd be in this Holler." I looked to Phillip. "You never spoke in my dreams. I heard you in my head. Because you couldn't talk. You traded worlds and came back, but you couldn't talk."

A smile. That's what I saw upon Phillip's face. And when he once more raised his fist slow to Taylor's eyes, I saw in that smile not a threat to take but a want to give.

Taylor raised the gun.

"No," I said. "Taylor, listen to me. He doesn't want to hurt you. Neither do I. Let's just go. We'll take Lucy and we'll go. We'll end all of this."

"There will be an end, Jake. That end comes here."

Taylor put his back to the mound I had built, steadying himself. Phillip stepped forward, breaking the rough circle we'd all formed, and looked down when he reached the log Taylor had bent to before. I saw trouble on Phillip's face. I saw the same pleading he had shown before Taylor rose up behind that fire with a gun in his hands. Yet while then that look had been, *Hurry*, it now said, *Do something, Jake.*

I have often wondered how things would have gone if I had done something else. Despite what Kate and Taylor and I always thought, it was choice rather than fate that governed our lives. It was choice, not Phillip, that had brought us to the riverbank. It was a frightened girl choosing long ago to play a trick on two innocent boys, and those boys choosing to be led away by her. It was a child who'd lived in his father's shadow until wilting, choosing to go to the rusty gate to prove himself a man. It was Phillip choosing to wander through the woods rather than go home, and it was Taylor choosing to give in to his rage. In her own way, Lucy was the same. The only difference between her and us was that she had chained herself to a dead mother while we had chained ourselves to a dead boy. Now we were all there, four poor souls who could no longer carry the burden of knowing all that lay before us would always be colored by all that lay behind. God in His mercy had allowed us to settle our accounts and put an end to our struggles. And Taylor meant to put an end to those things as well.

Taylor looked from Phillip to Kate. The gun swung there. "You ruined me."

Phillip looked at me, pleading. My hand moved slow, an inch at a time.

"I'm sorry," Kate said. "I'm so sorry, Taylor."

Lucy rose from her crouch. She took two steps before Taylor stopped her. "Go, lady," he said. "Back to where we started. Holler's yours now, and all that's in it. I'll keep them here. They won't follow."

My hand, closer.

Lucy took Taylor's words like a punch. "No, Taylor, I'm not leaving you."

"Go now," he said. Tears welled in his eyes. "I'd not have you see what comes."

"Don't go, Lucy," Kate said. "It's going to be okay now. We'll take you home."

Lucy wheeled and screamed, "This is home. Don't you understand that? I'm never going back there."

My hand shook against fear and fatigue. I thought of the

tree stump behind the sheriff's office and how Justus said trees don't kill you if you—

"Stay if you want," Taylor said. "Only step away from Kate. Jake's right. It ends here."

Kate shrank against the stones and called my name. Phillip raised his fist to Taylor a final time. Waving it. Begging.

Taylor moved his finger from the guard.

Kate screamed at the trigger's pull.

Bessie flew.

· 13 ·

You hear stories of time slowing in the midst of something gone terribly wrong. It was true with me that night along the riverbank. But at first it was more like time skipped, that there was a moment when Bessie sat tucked at my back and another when her blade cleaved the air. Taylor raised on Kate and I saw his finger squeeze on the trigger, and I ask you this: What man would not do as I then did? What woman? That's what I've told myself. I tell myself that I saved my wife, even if I really didn't save Kate at all.

Because just as Bessie closed the distance between Taylor and me, that trigger pulled. And what followed was not an explosion of buckshot, but the dry click of an unloaded gun.

And then time slowed. Kate's mouth stuck in a scream. Her hand covered her face as her body slumped against the rocks. I froze in my follow-through as that click came and I knew I'd let Bessie go and there was no pulling her back. I knew it even as I heard the wet, heavy thud of the blade entering Taylor's chest just inside his left shoulder and a sound like *Hawp!* as the air was forced from his lungs. The shotgun clattered onto the riverbank. Taylor's head jerked back. He fell as though pushed by a hard wind.

Time lurched forward again when Lucy screamed.

She was too late to catch him. Taylor landed in the shadow of the rocks and did not move. Lucy knelt over him. Her fingers trembled over Bessie's buried head. Blood flowed from the wound in Taylor's chest like a hidden spring.

"No," she wailed, just that word again and again, like some mantra that would undo what had been done. "NOTHISISN'TREAL."

Taylor reached for the tomahawk and grasped it by the haft, wrenching it from his body. He coughed a spray of red into Lucy's face. She gasped and tried to wipe it away, but the blood mixed with her tears and streaked her face. Lucy's hands went from Taylor's chest to his head, hoping that touch would be enough to anchor him to the world. Phillip watched. Light still shone from within him, yet it only made the despair on his face clearer and deeper. Kate rose from her place against the rocks and stumbled toward Lucy.

Taylor's eyes were wide with surprise and pain. He reached for Lucy and said, "Run now, lady. We'll have our day."

"No," she cried, "I'm not leaving you, I'm—"

Kate placed her hands on Lucy's shoulders, trying to ease her away. Lucy twisted and shot a fist upward, missing Kate's face but connecting with the side of her head. I caught Kate as she wheeled backward.

Phillip moved beside Kate as I went to Lucy. She reared up again, this time reaching for Bessie, but I kicked the tomahawk aside and took hold of her. "If you want him to live, you'll get aside."

She moved, placing Taylor's head in her lap. She stroked his matted hair and watered his cheeks with her tears.

I took off my uniform shirt and pressed it against Taylor's wound. He cried out. I looked around for help. My eyes met Phillip's. He pointed to the log behind the fire, where a small pile of shotgun shells lay.

"Why?" I asked him. "Why'd you make me do that?"

Taylor coughed again. After came a gurgle and, "Should've been done long ago, Jake. Don't pay no mind."

To Lucy I said, "He won't last long if we don't get him out of here."

Lucy stroked Taylor's cheeks, grounding him, keeping him there.

Kate moved from her place beside Phillip and went to Lucy. Her words were gentle, like coaxing a lost child in from the dark. "Come on, Lucy. We have to get him help. We have to get you help too."

Lucy's hands settled at her thighs. I saw that as invitation enough. I took off my belt and cinched it round Taylor's chest, pressing my shirt to his wound. I took his arms and pulled him up. Taylor cried out again as I tried to hoist him over my shoulders. Kate left Lucy to help.

"No," I said. "Tend to the girl. I have to do this myself."

Phillip looked at me and raised his fist as my knees buckled under Taylor's weight. A crunching sound came from my back. Still, I straightened.

Kate went back to Lucy. This time the girl did not protest. She stood hunched over, as though sheltering a dying ember.

I felt Taylor's wheezing against my shoulder. The riverbank stretched out before us. Far in the distance stood Indian Hill. It was miles that way to the gate. Miles and uphill.

I turned to Phillip. "Is there another way?"

Phillip's eyes went to Lucy. He nodded yes but slowly, as though wanting to say the long way was best.

"Show me."

He led us on through the trees. I carried Taylor as Kate fell in behind me. Lucy was last upon the riverbank. None of us saw her reach down for what my fear and weariness had left behind.

· 14 ·

To Lucy the way was through utter darkness, and though she perceived Jake as leading, she could not understand how he knew the way. Taylor lay draped over Jake's shoulders. His breaths were labored, and his blood soaked Jake's neck and chest. Lucy wrapped Taylor's ponytail around her hand. She sang in a soft voice the song they'd shared upon Taylor's bed, of how death is only a dream of glory beyond a dark stream. Kate draped an arm over her. If that arm lowered itself just a bit more to where Jake's tomahawk lay waiting, Lucy would shrug her off.

Lucy felt a pain she could not measure, though one tinged with a kind of sweetness. In the shards of her broken heart, she now knew Taylor in a way the sharing of their bodies could never promise. Love cannot be called true unless two people know the pains of one another as well as the joys. Lucy had suffered much in life, but Taylor had suffered to the point where all was lost and living gave way to mere survival. Now at the end, that was a hurt Lucy knew well.

She also knew they meant to take her back to town. Lucy would return to her father, and even if Taylor survived, she would never see him again. He would be sent away, as would she—if not to prison for trying to kill Hollis, then to Glendale or Lipscomb or some other private school where her father could stay away from her and keep an eye on her at the same time.

And their Hollow, their lovely Hollow. Gone too, and forever.

:::

The faint peak of Indian Hill disappeared, swallowed by a forest so thick and pressing that it stole my breath. For too long the dark land beyond the rusty gate had fed upon Taylor's anger and regret, trading his memories for madness. Now that source was fading, and the Hollow began to rouse and fight. Phillip's light pushed against a darkness that pushed back. The eyes were on us all. Whispers from amongst the trees called out in wailing, mournful tones. I faltered beneath Taylor's dying weight, the cords of my neck straining, willing my tired body to find one more step and then another. Other than a series of shallow moans each time I stumbled, Taylor remained silent upon my back. I implored him to speak, to hear Lucy's song. To stay awake. Kate took her hand from Lucy's shoulder and laid it at Taylor's back.

I asked, "How far?"

Phillip turned and brought up three fingers. Whether miles or hours, I did not know.

:::

Lucy, thinking that question had been aimed at her, said, "I don't know. I've never been this way."

Twisted saplings gave way to their tall and ancient kin farther on, which then thinned to a small meadow. Lucy's mind was still on Taylor when Jake stumbled to his right, bumping her. She reached to steady Taylor and felt her hips brush against something hard. A stone. There just to Kate's right was another, this larger, its gray face faintly glowing in the moonlight. Four more lay just ahead. To her left the trees rose again, towering and thick like a wall, and that cinder of hope in Lucy Seekins now flickered once more.

She broke away and rushed for the forest. Kate's voice called out into the night—"Lucy, where are you going?"—but the words only pushed Lucy harder. Toward the trees and the path beyond. Toward what she prayed was home.

:::

Kate ran after her. Phillip followed close, leaving Taylor and me alone in the field. My lungs burned and heaved too much to call for them. My shoulders and back were a mass of knots and pulled muscles. I watched as Phillip's light faded in the dense trees, unsure what to do. Taylor answered for me, using the precious little air he had left.

"Fly, Jake, for my sake and the sake of our loves. That way leads only to death."

· 15 ·

It was only by Phillip's light that Kate could weave around the trees. She called for Lucy again as the ground went soft beneath her shoes. Kate looked down and saw that the forest floor had become a path.

Lucy disappeared ahead. Kate's legs ached from the long run. Her face stung with tiny red scratches from the branches that had poked her. Phillip ran ahead, pushing her, barely keeping her in his light. Kate followed him and stopped in horror.

There in the grove the moonlight shone down upon the cliffs like falling water, making the red hands upon the walls shimmer. But it was the Hole that held Kate, that perfect sphere of tarry black that hung in the air and contradicted everything she thought could never be.

And Lucy stood not ten feet away from it, staring into its face.

Phillip motioned for Kate to follow and stopped her well away from Lucy's reach. Kate understood why. He was afraid of what Lucy would do to the woman who had ruined the man she loved. The hair on Kate's arms stiffened as she neared the Hole. She willed herself not to look and found that will crumbling. Kate turned to the Hole, and beyond that thin shroud she felt every nightmare she had ever dreamed and every monster she'd ever imagined.

"Lucy," she whispered, "you have to come with me now. I have to get you away from here."

Lucy only stared. Her eyes were two giant ovals. "I'm not going anywhere," she said.

"Taylor needs help. If we don't get him back to town, he won't make it."

Phillip took a step past Kate, closer to the Hole.

Lucy's voice came from a place that sounded far away: "Doesn't matter. I know that now."

"It matters," Kate said. "Everything matters. Come with me, Lucy. Please? We'll go back to Jake and Taylor. I want to help you, but you have to trust me."

"But I don't, Kate," she said. "I don't trust you. Taylor told me what you did. You say you want to help me, but do you really? Is it me you want, or do you just want my name to write down in a book you use to tell yourself what a good person you are? Do you see all those people when you help them, or do you see Taylor and that boy? And do you see the good you did after, or do you only see that the thousand good things you do won't ever make up for the one bad thing you did?"

Kate's lips trembled. She said, "That's not true," but the murmur of her heart and the look Phillip offered told her it was.

"It is true," Lucy said. She reached out a finger and traced the edges of the circle in front of them. "You shouldn't burden yourself with that, Kate. Do you know why? Because Taylor says none of this is real. He says it's all a dream."

"It is real, Lucy."

"Is it? Tell me something, Kate. Is there someone beside you right now?"

"Yes," Kate said. "His name is Phillip McBride."

And though Kate knew Lucy could not see, Phillip held an upturned fist to her.

Lucy nodded as though she'd known that answer before it was given. "To me, there's no one but us here. What kind of *real* is this if there's a dead boy here that only you can see, Kate? Or if there's a hole in the world that has no business existing? Taylor's right. But he's wrong too. It can't be the same for him as it is for you or me." She looked from the Hole and took hold of Kate's shoulders, squeezing them as her eyes grew wide, as though she'd just stumbled upon the answer to every riddle that had marked her sad life. "Don't you see, Kate? *We can't all be having the same dream.* It's just me. No one's dreaming but me."

Kate moved her hands to catch Lucy's elbows. Lucy was faster. She stepped away and pulled Bessie from under her shirt. The blade gleamed with Taylor's blood. Phillip watched in helpless dread, pushing his fist closer.

"I want to feel warm covers over me and the breeze on my face," Lucy said. "I want to see a morning that promises a new day. I want to see my mommy and hear her say she loves me. I want to wake up, Kate. I'm tired of dreaming."

She turned and ran. Kate screamed for Lucy to stop, please, God, stop. Phillip raced ahead and reached the mouth of the Hole just as Lucy let Bessie fall. He turned with his hands outstretched and a look of despair upon his face.

Lucy jumped. Her arms were wide, embracing her end.

· 16 ·

Taylor and I reached the grove just as Lucy jumped toward that *(Tear*, I thought, *that's what it is, like the world's just wallpaper and this is what lies under it all)* black circle. I saw Lucy reaching for Phillip and Phillip ready to catch her. And when their hands met, I saw Lucy pass through him like a memory. Phillip closed his eyes as the Hole erased Lucy a piece at a time—her arms first, then her head and torso, and last the toes of her sneakers. He drew his arms across his chest slowly, as though pondering what almost was.

Phillip had always watched us. That week he had walked with us as well, hidden but for those small moments when he nearly reached out and grasped us. Whispering Kate's name as she spoke with Lucy outside the Sheriff's office. Whispering *I'm coming for you* to Taylor as he waited for Lucy to return from Hollis Devereaux's farm. Robbing me of sleep and strength. Waiting until we all remembered true. Lucy Seekins had played no part on that clear spring day in 1990, but Phillip had watched her that week as well. I believe he saw much of his old life in her. He knew that pain of wanting to love and never being loved. And I believe even now that Phillip will close his eyes and breathe in the pine and earth that was on

Lucy's skin as she passed through him. Because heaven is not without the past.

I heard Taylor's pained moan in my ears. The weight upon my shoulders doubled as he pressed in on the back of my neck. His blood and my sweat made it impossible to keep him centered. Kate fell to her knees and sat motionless at the mouth of the Hole. It was as though Lucy had taken the air around us as a souvenir of the world she left behind.

Taylor said, "Take me there, Jake."

"I can't. If I do, I'll never get you back up."

"Take me there."

I struggled down the remainder of the path and laid Taylor at the Hole, then knelt to Kate. I eased her head onto my shoulder.

"Where did she go, Jake?" she asked.

I couldn't answer. The two of us stared ahead, me trying to make sense of the insensible, Kate praying that what could go in there could somehow find its way back. Whispers descended from the trees like leaves rustled by a strong wind. Phillip stood in our midst, shielding us with a light that waned to no more than an arm's length. He pointed to the woods and then to Taylor, whose eyes were vacant and shone as glass. Blood soaked through the shirt over his wound. Phillip did not speak, yet I understood. We could not tarry.

"Leave me lay, Jake," Taylor said. "This wood has bound me. Let me rest, and let the eyes upon us be my judgment."

I squatted down. Pain seared my side. And though every part of my careworn body longed to let Taylor lie there, I said, "I'm not letting another person die in this Holler."

I pulled him partway up before the muscles in my arms seized. I cursed as Taylor fell back to the ground. Kate moved behind him and lifted his shoulders.

"No," I said.

"Let me help, Jake," she said. "You can't do this on your own."

Phillip reached out his fist.

"I have to," I told her, told him. "Taylor is my burden. I have to do this. Me."

It was with an anger that I couldn't do it that I lifted Taylor to my shoulders. I made the bloody shirt over his chest a pillow against my neck, then rose on two quivering legs. The whispers grew. Tendrils of dim fog wove among the trees on the hillock above.

"How far?" I asked Phillip.

He spread his arms wide.

Kate looked down and reached for Bessie. She said, "Let me help you, Jake. Please. We won't make it."

"Stay in front of me," I said. "If you're in front, I'll be okay. Just keep in Phillip's light."

We moved back up the path and away from the grove. The eyes crowded in. Whispers became chattering. As we crossed into the trees, Kate turned to look at the Hole a final time.

We came to the field and crossed back into the deep woods. My body cried for the rest it had been denied for weeks as my boots struggled to find footing beneath Taylor's mass. Twice I stumbled, nearly pitching my load. Phillip kept his eyes ahead and around, marking what we could not see. His light waned.

Kate placed her hand over her ears. "Laughing, Jake," she said. "I hear laughing."

She shook her head, trying to force that noise away.

Phillip's light pulsed as he fought against what lived in that darkness. He looked at me often, plying me forward with his fist. The fog gathered into sexless bodies that stared out at me. I saw faces of those who'd taunted and hated me—Bobby Barnes and Trevor Morgan. Justus. Andy Sommerville asking why I never waved the day I'd passed the BP. Eric Thayer standing with Taylor's knife still in his chest.

My eyes went to the small patches of dead earth in front of me. One step at a time, one foot in front of another. Phillip moved on as we huddled in the fringes of his light. My struggle was with my own body and the body draped over me. Phillip's was with the powers and principalities that encircled us all.

We came to the waterfall when Taylor said, "I feel this Holler, Jake. It comes for us."

My foot caught the root of a dead maple, sending me sprawling. Taylor landed and called out in an agony that the Hollow tasted like sugar. Phillip and Kate turned back. In my exhaustion I saw the trees bend to swallow us. Hands that were neither beast nor illusion reached out and drew back, taunting.

I lay on my back in the midst of hell and found I could do no more. Kate fell to her knees at my side, crying. She took Taylor's hand and my own, linking us together. Phillip McBride stood over the three people who had killed him. He had drawn us for an end. That end was now.

Lying there on that hard earth, Phillip finally broke me. I had been stripped bare by all those years of worry and dread and all those sleepless nights of running away from what I only ran to again. I'd lived in fear since the day Phillip died. Lived, even, as a coward. And yet as the Hollow's eyes closed in around us, I saw that it may have been fear that had made me run from the riverbank that day, but pride was what had kept me running since. Pride, not fear, was what had plunged my life into darkness. Pride, not fear, had kept me from unburdening Kate of her guilt. Pride, not fear, was what convinced me to do as Taylor had said and call Alan Martin's men away.

Pride, pride all. One that said I had sinned alone and so must bear the suffering for it alone. No less than Kate, who had given joy to hundreds of children but who had never given joy to herself. No less than even Taylor, who had hidden both himself and his guilt since that day upon the cliffs in a place of no hope. We were all trying to survive our weariness alone.

Phillip looked down to me and raised a fist as the truth of why he had returned shone as brightly to me as he had appeared atop Indian Hill. And in that moment, I understood. I understood everything.

We were not dead because Phillip had come back. Phillip had come back because we were dead.

"Help me," I told him. "We can't save ourselves."

The light in Phillip returned with a smile that shuddered the Hollow. He raised his arm high into that black sky as the shadows closed in. And when he opened his hand, there came a sea of white and the sound of ten thousand wings.

· 17 ·

The butterflies shot as lights into the Hollow's night, angling out into all directions, filling every black space. A cry rose from the heart of that cursed wood louder and more pained than any Taylor had offered, and from a wound far deeper. The lights buzzed and hummed in a song that hurt my ears with their beauty. They swirled into a sphere that gathered around us. The air inside that bright dome turned from poison to sweetness, filling our lungs with life beyond any living Kate and I had ever known. Of all the things from that night, all those wonders and terrors, that is what I remember most. Ask Kate and she will say the same—from there to the gate, we breathed heaven.

And yet Taylor's wound still bled and his breaths still faded. I rose to lift him. He shook me away.

"Too late for me, Jake," he said.

"No," Kate said "We're almost there. You just hang on."

She eased her arm behind Taylor's head and bent, kissing him on the forehead. And whether he was too tired from our journey or too enraptured at finally feeling the touch of Kate's lips, Taylor did not protest when we lifted him from the ground. We carried him, Kate and I, she at one side and me at the other, sharing our burden. Phillip led us as that dome of lights swirled, making noonday in the midst of the howling darkness just beyond. Even now I cannot explain how that felt, knowing perfect protection surrounded me even as we walked through the valley of the shadow of death. Often I long to feel that same assurance again. Often I believe that assurance is ours to have if we only believe.

The tips of Taylor's worn boots skidded across the ground. Kate and I labored on, but with new strength.

"She loved me," Taylor said. I felt a trickle of blood down my arm. "Spoke those very words. I spoke them back but did not know what they meant. Now she's gone. She's gone and there is a hole in me not of your making, Jake. It pains more than your blade. Is that love I feel?"

Kate was the one who answered. "It is," she said. "That's exactly what it is."

Ahead the light danced upon the faint outline of angles and curves too precise to have sprouted from the Hollow's dead ground.

"The gate's near," I told him.

Taylor coughed, spraying red mist into the air. "Am I a good man, Jake? Speak true, I beg."

"There's none good, there's only grace and hard trying. Such is the truth, Taylor, and for us all."

I felt Kate's fingers lace into mine across Taylor's back.

"Is there no forgiveness, then?" he asked. "Is there no mercy for me?"

Phillip turned to me. Each hard, shuffling step I took for the gate brought a new image—the red angels on the BP's floor, the wounds on Timmy's head. Phillip tumbling from the cliffs as Taylor pushed him, his throat too mangled to even scream. Phillip reaching out a bloody hand to beg for help as I ran. Kate walking across the football field with her ponytail swaying, fetching one boy and then another.

"There is mercy," I said. "And there is forgiveness even for you. And after comes a long walk, but the going is fair."

Taylor whispered, "Sorry, I'm sorry," and I wanted to believe that wasn't an apology to me or Kate or even Phillip, but an offering up of sins long harbored and finally let go. But I suppose such secrets are known only between a man and his Maker, and are hidden from all others on this side of heaven.

"We're almost there, Taylor," Kate said. "You hear me? You just hang on."

We reached the gate as one. Phillip remained behind the bars as Taylor's lungs filled a final time. His body shuddered against our shoulders as a long, mournful cry fell over the Hollow. Taylor Hathcock breathed out his spirit as we crossed beyond the dark mountains he'd called home for all those years, and though Kate and I could carry him no more, we did not want to let him go. When we laid his body down in soft grass, it was like laying a sick child down to rest.

"Let's go home," I said. "I never want to see this place again."

Kate stepped to me and took my hand. Phillip remained on the other side of the gate. She looked at him and knew his mind.

"He's not coming," she said. "We'll go home and so will he, but for now those are different places."

Phillip smiled. Kate left my side and crossed back into the Hollow. She stood facing him, her eyes red and tired. There were no words. I knew words felt as empty to Kate then as the names written in her book. She held out her arms against the swirling lights around them, and Phillip met her with an embrace she felt not with her body but with her heart. Phillip healed my wife with that hug. He'd come for Kate and freed her from the bonds she'd long placed on herself. It was forgiveness he offered, and a plea for Kate to go on with her life. To live. To love. Standing there watching her, I felt a newness and a joy that had long departed.

Kate released him and returned to my side. Phillip turned and walked into the Hollow. To the grove, I guessed. On to home. He paused among the trees and looked back to me. Phillip said nothing, but there were words enough in his gaze. It was that same forgiveness and that same plea to move on, but it was also a knowing of what lay in my heart. I did not feel Kate's joy, nor had my own chains been loosed. I was still dead and Phillip knew it. He knew it, and he said it would be yet awhile longer.

He raised a hand and smiled, then turned away. Phillip McBride had looked upon us with mourning atop Indian Hill. Now he looked upon us as friends well met and not long parted. We would gather again on some far-off day—Phillip, Kate, Taylor, and I. We would meet along the banks of a greater river and stand in a brighter light, and we would rejoice. I did not doubt it would be so. Life is a wheel, after all.

The Beginning

The service was brief and without song beneath a clear sky, exactly a week after Reverend Goggins preached of life's burdens and the faith to overcome them. The words had come easy to him in the pulpit that day, as soft words often did in hard times. Yet the preacher struggled as he stood over the pine box that held Taylor's body. He spoke of how Mattingly's devil had been only a man, and how that man had suffered as all who believed themselves flesh and bone and water and nothing more. He prayed for the wisdom to set aside yesterday and embrace tomorrow.

Zach, Justus, and I put our hats on at the preacher's amen. He asked if any of us needed a word and took his leave when we all answered no. It was peace rather than counsel that had brought us there that day. Peace and a new beginning.

Kate's eyes met mine. I offered a nod and smiled as much as a funeral would allow. She placed her notebook under her arm and took Zach's hand in her own. They set out for the knoll just ahead, leaving me with Justus. His eyes were to the casket.

"Good of the town to do this," he said. "Must've been a hard coming to."

I nodded. "Was the preacher who did the convincing. Taylor's aunt refused the body. So did Camden. Her I could almost see, but I've no idea how a town can deny a man rest in their ground. Reggie said it was the Christian thing to do."

"Ain't always easy," Justus said, "abidin' by the Lord."

"No, sir, it sure ain't."

We stood there silent. Justus stared at the pine box as I tilted my head toward my family. Zach swung Kate's hand forward and back in giant arcs as they weeded through the gravestones. Few things matter more in the world than keeping family close. I vowed that from then on the Barnetts would never roam far from one another.

"What happened out there, Jake?" Justus asked. "In the Holler. What was there?"

I'd vowed I would tell him everything, and I did. I spoke of Phillip and Taylor and Lucy, of the Hollow and the Hole. I spoke of my dreams. Justus took it all in with an impassiveness that looked near boredom and altered his expression only once (it was an upward twitch of his left eyebrow upon learning that Bessie had fallen, however briefly, into Lucy Seekins's hands).

Otherwise his face remained blank and pointed to the blue mountains rising in front of us. It was a sight I imagine Justus Barnett never expected to see again after being hauled away in the back of Alan Martin's car. Nor had he expected Alan himself to plead with the judge to grant him bail. Yet what had shocked Justus most of all—and what brought a warmth to his cheeks even after such a sorrowful tale as mine—was that bail being raised by the townfolk. Pocket change and crumpled dollar bills for the most part, all delivered by Big Jim Wallis's own hand. My father told me it was grace, no less than that. Grace perhaps meant to bring him inside the gates of Oak Lawn with his son that bright Sabbath morning, to hear my words and see my face and know that both were true.

"Sheriff Houser tole me afore he passed you was the one made that call," he said.

"What call?"

"One sayin' Phillip McBride was layin' in the Holler."

I felt the blood leave my face. "How'd he know that?"

"Said a shirtsleeve weren't enough to hide a voice he'd known near eighteen years. But 'twas more'n that. He said was the way you acted after. How you'd cross the street whenever you saw him comin', how you'd keep your head low in church like you was hidin' from the Lord. I didn't believe him at first. 'No way,' I tole him, 'not my boy.' But in my heart I knew he was right, Jacob. I seen those things m'self."

I didn't know how to react. Humiliation seemed the most appropriate, though in many ways anger felt right too. "Why didn't you say anything to me?"

"Shame, I reckon," he said. "Not just mine, knowin' what you did. Your shame too. Ain't a person alive don't carry disgrace." He lifted his chin to Zach, who traveled with Kate among the gravestones. "Even the boy'll carry that someday. People say you can let it go or put it down. You heard the preacher's prayer awhile ago, petitioning the Lord for wisdom to do just that. I don't think the Lord'll allow such. That memory, it stains you. All you can do is learn to carry it well. That's what I hoped for you, Jacob. Because our yesterdays stick."

"Heaven's not without the past," I said.

"What's 'at?"

"Nothing. Something Phillip said."

Justus nodded, knowing that expression rang true for his own life. "Your grandpappy used to tell stories of the Holler. He hunted near that black wood often enough and put his name on the gate like us all. He heard things, he said. Saw things. Reckon summa those tales weren't so tall." He shook his head at Taylor's coffin. "Can't imagine dwellin' there like that boy did."

"I think whatever dark lay in the Holler was light compared

to the dark already in him." I reached into my back pocket and drew out Taylor's book (*Phillip's book*, I thought). "Found this on him. Taylor must've been carrying it around for years. I've been going through it," I said. "Toward the back. There's one page he never touched with his scrawls. I figure that one was special to him."

Justus licked a forefinger and turned the brittle pages, each covered with so many scribbles and erasures it was impossible to make out much. He stopped at the clean page he found. I watched my father's lips move in silence over the poem. Justus read it once, then again. The third time, he read the first stanza aloud:

"'Take this kiss upon the brow! And, in parting from you now, Thus much let me avow—You are not wrong, who deem That my days have been a dream; Yet if hope has flown away In a night, or in a day, In a vision, or in none, Is it therefore less gone? All that we see or seem Is but a dream within a dream.'" He closed the book and handed it back to me. "I'm afraid fancy words never spoke much to me, Jacob."

I looked out across the cemetery. Kate and Zach were half-way up the knoll. She let go of his hand long enough to bend to the grass.

"Kate said fella named Poe wrote that," I said. "She remembers because she had to do a report on him back in school. I figure killing Phillip left a stain on Taylor the way you said memories stain us all. That regret must've eat into his heart like a cancer. Guess he found that poem and his mind lit on a way to turn his sin to virtue. I think even before that day behind the bleachers, Taylor's world was like a picture hanging tilted on a wall. After he killed Phillip, that picture tilted more. Instead of trying to square the corners, he just tilted himself to match it."

"And the boy?" Justus asked. "Phillip. Come back to what? Set things aright?"

I nodded.

Justus looked out over the mountains. He said, "Grace, then," recalling his own.

"Grace," I agreed. "But it's a grace I mourn all the same. I knew nothing of Phillip other than his name and what we called him, but the light I saw in him told me his soul pointed heavenward when Taylor released it. Can you imagine what it felt to trade heaven for earth, even for a moment? To return to what hell lives past the rusty gate?"

I remembered how the Hollow pressed in as we made our way back. How those woods came alive and grew hungry and how Phillip's light had faded as he fought.

"It was grace truly, and we were the heirs of it. And it was love. God's love, yes, but Phillip's as well. He must have loved us, Justus, for the thing he did. To the heirs of grace, grace is free. But what does grace cost the giver?"

Silence fell as we each pondered that question. Kate and Zach reached the top of the hill. She bent down to Phillip's grave and laid her notebook there. On top, she placed a bouquet of dandelions.

"Katelyn said you made plans to leave," Justus said. "Hollis tole me town voted unanimous to let you go on sheriffin'."

A long pause, then, "I brought Taylor back, everyone saw Lucy Seekins wasn't with him. All I could say was that she's missing, and I suppose that's near enough the truth. Her daddy's gone. Some trip somewhere, he said. I think a part of him knows he'll never see his daughter again." I tilted my head to the knoll. "Kate believes the girl will come back one day. I believe she may be right. I don't think what Lucy Seekins fell into was a hole at all. I think it's a door to someplace. Maybe everyplace. Explains a lot of what tends to happen around here. I figure if something can fall in there, something else can fall out. Maybe something worse than the Holler that's around it. Town needs as many Barnetts as it can hold, and a Barnett sheriff especially."

Justus's stone face cracked at those words. What came was a smile. One in need of much practice, but a smile all the same.

"What about you?" I asked. "What will you do?"

"What I must," he said. "Stand in front of an earthly judge and plead my guilt, just as you did in front of a heavenly one. Mayhap I'll find that same grace, if God wills it." Justus put his hand to the scruff on his face. "For now, I should like to go meet my grandson proper, if you and Kate abide it."

"That'd be just the thing."

I walked on, meaning to lead my father past Taylor's body to the knoll where my family waited. Justus remained where we were.

"Jacob?"

I turned to him.

"I love you, son, and I'm proud of you."

I saw my father's face and I saw myself, and in the dwindling space between us a small white butterfly passed.

"Love you and proud too, Daddy," I said.

We walked together to my wife and son beneath an empty sky that touched the floor of heaven. And there among the dead, I returned to the living.

Reading Group Guide

1. The core of this novel deals with the ways Taylor Hathcock and Jake and Kate Barnett live with the sins of their shared past. Taylor has managed to survive the twenty years after Phillip McBride's death by twisting a rationalization (however flimsy that rationalization is) around it. Kate has spent that time trying to atone for her part in Phillip's death, attempting to balance that one horrible act with hundreds of loving ones for the town's poor. For Jake, Phillip's death is something he tries to keep buried even though it has come to define not only his past, but also his present and future. Given that we are all saddled in some way with having to live with past failures, which of these three characters would you say best describes the manner by which you cope with the past?

2. Phillip tells Jake that heaven is not without the past, hinting that in some way our memories of this world, both good and bad, are preserved in the next. Do you agree with this notion? If so, how would you reconcile the belief of many that heaven contains no remorse? If not, what do you think would be lost when our memories are wiped away?

3. Taylor warns Jake that if Jake doesn't call the state police away, his sins will be made known not only to the town, but to Kate and Zach as well. Conversely, Taylor says if Jake will simply leave him alone, the secret of what Jake

did to Phillip will continue to be Jake's alone. "They'll fester on your insides," Taylor says, "but you'll live on the outside. Ain't that what matters to you in the end?" The answer to that is, of course, yes—Jake has clung to that very belief ever since high school. Given his character, do you think Jake would have continued to hide his past if the nightmares had never begun and Taylor had stayed in the Hollow? Do you think Kate would have continued gathering names for her notebook? How do you think this would have affected their marriage as the years went on?

4. My favorite passage to write in *The Devil Walks in Mattingly* was Zach ruminating on Adam and Eve eating the apple, how he bet they both spent much time afterward pondering "the good old days." Yet Zach also believes that Adam and Eve thought about how good that apple tasted many times as well. What do you think Zach meant by this? How does this notion of pleasure play into the sins we commit?

5. In Jake's final dream, he promises he'll never return to the Hollow. Phillip replies by saying that God "laughs at what we say we'll never do." What do you think that means?

6. Lucy Seekins is perhaps the most tragic character in the book. She chose to leap into the Hole to find her dead mother rather than face a world where she believed no one would love her. What do you think Lucy found on the other side?

7. Jake, Taylor, and Lucy share a similarity in that all three grew up with fathers who were either absent or abusive. What weight, if any, would you place on that as a factor in the sort of people they became? Is it a reason, or an excuse?

8. In your opinion, who really killed Phillip McBride?

Acknowledgments

I t's difficult to know where to start giving thanks for a book like this; so many have done so much. I'll begin with my wife and children, all of whom have learned over the years that Do Not Interrupt also means It's Okay To Sneak Into The Office And Lay Your Head On My Shoulder. I love you all, and I couldn't do any of this without you.

My thanks to Kathy Richards, who keeps a pen-and-paper guy like me functioning in a world of keyboards. To my agent, Rachelle Gardner, who always seems to know just when to call.

I have the pleasure of working with the finest publishing people in the world. Amanda Bostic, Daisy Hutton, LB Norton, Becky Monds, Katy Bond, Laura Dickerson, and Ruthie Dean have shown a continual faith in me that I could never repay. It's a blessing to call you friends.

And to you, Mr. or Ms. Reader, thank you for picking up this book. I'm hoping the Grandersons have found their peace, at least what peace this life allows. Then again, one never knows what's waiting on ahead. The road is long, is it not? Long and full of magic.

About the Author

Photograph by Joanne Coffey

Billy Coffey's critically acclaimed books combine rural Southern charm with a vision far beyond the ordinary. He is a regular contributor to several publications, where he writes about faith and life. Billy lives with his wife and two children in Virginia's Blue Ridge Mountains. Visit him at www.billycoffey.com.